Books by B. ʼ

Visit BVLarson.com for more information.

Rogue World

(Undying Mercenaries Series #7)
by
B. V. Larson

Undying Mercenaries Series:
Steel World
Dust World
Tech World
Machine World
Death World
Home World
Rogue World

ISBN-13: 978-1520888903
BISAC: Fiction / Science Fiction / Military

"Great empires are not maintained by timidity."
– Tacitus, 101 AD

-1-

We all live on balls of dirt, essentially. Rocky planets that form around relatively stable stars in a tight orbital band—a zone where liquid water can form on the surface.

That's what we all have in common, all the beings living on one island in the sky or another. Once you've visited enough new worlds and gotten to know a few of them, it seems like one man's alien is another man's local inhabitant. I think most humans who've traveled among the stars can't help but question their place in this vast cosmos of ours when they finally return home again.

Gazing out into the evening sky from my parents' back porch in Waycross, Georgia Sector had left my mind full of such big thoughts. The first stars were popping into life in the heavens, and they made me think.

That was unusual for me, as I normally spent my time between deployments drinking, working on farm buildings that were almost falling down, and trying to get lucky with the ladies in Waycross.

But tonight felt different somehow—and it was better. After I'd teleported my daughter Etta and my momma back home from Dust World, I'd realized I'd gathered my family together in one spot for the first time.

For a while, the togetherness was sheer bliss. Even Della, Etta's mother, came by now and then to check on her little girl. I wouldn't exactly call that "motherly instinct," as Della never had been the nesting type. Della had good survival instincts, but socially she was pretty disconnected for a human being.

Della's behavior had always seemed downright weird to my mom, and she'd taken it upon herself to provide all the care and attention that Etta needed.

The only problem was that Etta didn't really *want* much affection. She was the daughter of a wild woman from Dust World and me. I didn't know which one of us was responsible for any particular genetic aspect of Etta's personality, or if it was just due to a rough upbringing on Dust World, but it hardly mattered. The long and the short of it was that since coming to Earth, Etta had spent most of her time running around in the swampy forest out back of my shack.

"James?" Momma asked me one muggy evening in April. "How are we going to get her into a regular school next year?"

"Uh…" I said, giving my skull a scratch. "I'm not sure that it would be wise to even attempt such a thing. We might be liable for damage to public property—and injuries, maybe. We might have to home-school."

Momma turned pale at the thought, but she didn't argue, she just sighed. She knew I was right.

I felt kind of bad for her. Etta had a room painted pink in the main house, a pile of self-dressing dolls with nanite clothing, and enough pretty dresses to impress a Sunday school teacher. But she ignored all that stuff.

"What's she doing out there in that bog today?" Momma asked me.

"Well…" I answered reluctantly. "I think she's adding to her bone collection."

Etta had a fascination with bones. She found them everywhere, often digging them up with a stick or other improvised tool. It was kind of an unusual hobby for a nine year old girl.

"She'll be a great mind someday, son," Momma said, putting up a brave front. "At least, that's what I keep telling myself. She'll be an archeologist or something."

"Maybe she takes after her grandpa like that—on Della's side, I mean. He's the most respected scientist on Dust World."

"The Investigator?" she asked, suppressing a shudder. "Yes, I met him a few times when I was staying out there. A ghastly man."

I figured it wouldn't help at all to admit I agreed with her. One time, the Investigator dissected me after Della had killed me. I'll never forget the smell and look of my own death laid bare on a slab.

"Just seems like we have so little time to enjoy moments like this," Momma said. "And when we do have time, they never quite turn out like we'd hoped. Well, I'm going in to make dinner now. Etta will come home hungry at dusk—she always does."

Something in her tone made me frown and look at her. "You aren't regretting living with us, are you Momma?" I asked. "You don't seem happy."

She looked surprised. There was a sadness in her eyes, but I didn't understand it. I'd brought home her granddaughter—and sure, the child was a little odd—but one would think a granny could look past that.

"No, no," she said. "I'm very happy to have both of you here. More than you know, James."

She went inside then, and I stared after her in confusion.

My dad came out to talk to me a moment later. He looked as long in the face as a bloodhound. That's when I began to realize something was seriously wrong.

"Let me guess," I asked him as he pressed a cold squeeze-bottle of beer into my hand. "It's about immigration. You broke your contract and they're giving you hell about it."

He nodded slightly. "That's part of it, actually," he said.

"Those damned chair-monkeys!" I growled. "It didn't cost them squat to transport Momma to Earth, but they're still trying to charge you for the trip back, aren't they?"

"Sort of," he admitted. "Your mother signed an emigration pledge, remember? They charged her very little to go out to

Dust World, as long as she agreed she'd never come back. You brought her back, James."

"So it's my fault? Should I steal another teleport suit and air-mail her back out to the stars?"

"Please don't," he chuckled quietly. "Just forget about it. We'll pay the fines and make do. We don't want to burden you with our troubles—in fact, I promised your mother I wouldn't say a thing."

I stared at him for a second. "Well then, you lied, didn't you? I get it already, and I'm willing to help. I've been paying rent here, and I'll double it."

He perked up a little. "That's very generous of you, son."

"But that won't be enough, will it?" I asked him suspiciously. "What's really wrong? Are the hogs threatening to put you guys in jail for coming back to Earth?"

"No... but our Hegemony Coverage has lapsed."

"What? Your healthcare? You can still pay cash, right?"

He shrugged. "Let's just drop it."

I drained my beer as we watched the sun go down. Just about the time I began to get worried, and the first wave of skeeters took a shot at my bare arms, Etta showed up.

She was just a shadow at first, slinking around behind my shack. She came toward the house when I hollered about suppertime. My dad took one look at her and exploded in laughter.

"Etta?" he asked incredulously. "Have you covered yourself in mud?"

"Yes," she said. "The insects here bite."

"That's right," I told her, "but you can't come into the house looking like a swamp-monster. Get the hose around on the side of the house and spray off—not onto the windows either."

We got her cleaned up, and we praised her latest bone specimens.

"Is that a dog's skull?" my dad asked in mild disgust.

"No..." she said. "I think it's called a fox."

I eyed her thoughtfully. "That's a rare animal in these woods. You sure you didn't help this fox along to becoming a pile of bones?"

4

She straightened up and looked indignant. "That wouldn't be the same thing at all. Just look here, at the wear on this jaw. It's been cured in the bog for years."

We inspected it, and we both had to admit, she'd found an honest-to-God skeleton.

"What are you going to do with this one?" my father asked.

"I was thinking of reconstructing him—posing him, maybe."

"Yeah..." he said.

Etta was like Della in that she didn't understand the natural squeamishness of Earth people. She didn't seem to know that her grandpa was unsure about her hobby. She was so fascinated by her collection, she probably couldn't grasp why anyone would be upset about it.

Throwing a towel around her wet clothes, I led her into the house.

We ate dinner, and everything seemed fine to me. Sure, Mom was a little quiet, and my dad was thoughtful, but they'd told me things were all right, so I didn't let their mood bother me.

It wasn't until the next morning that things took a bad turn.

A small hand touched my shoulder waking me up at dawn, and that hand gave me a shake.

This might not seem odd to you, but it was to me. No one got all the way into my shack without waking me up—at least, not too many people did. Claver had managed it, but he'd done so using a teleport suit. Della had snuck in, too, but I'd caught her before she could lay a hand on me.

As a man who'd spent more than a decade getting killed and revived again among the stars, I'd developed a keen sense for danger. Even when I slept, I never really let my guard down. A part of my brain was always on the alert.

Immediately upon contact, I bounced off the couch with a combat knife glittering in my hand.

"Hush," Etta said. "It's me."

Squinting and bleary-eyed, I lowered the knife. "I told you before, girl, you can't just go sneaking up on me like that. It's not healthy for you—or anyone else."

5

She wasn't listening, as usual. She was at the window, peering out of a tiny crack in the faded curtains.

"What's going on?" I asked.

"There're men at the house. I slipped out my window and came to get you—was I wrong? Should I have fought them myself?"

"What in the living Hell are you…?" I asked, coming to lean beside her and peer out.

Etta was right. A white air car had landed in our driveway. Air cars were expensive. We didn't get them often out here in Waycross. My family's tram was worth maybe one percent of the value of a shiny new air car.

"I didn't even hear them land," I said.

"You have to run," she said, looking at me seriously. "I'll guide you. I have several shelters in the woods nearby. We'll wait for them to leave."

"You're assuming they've come for me."

She shrugged. "Don't they always come for you?"

Etta had a point there, they usually did. I was the only one in the family that had repeatedly irked the law—although I had a sneaking suspicion that Etta might take that distinction away from me by the time she grew up.

"That emblem," I said, pointing at the blue-green stylized emblem of Earth that was stamped on the air car door. "That means they're some kind of hog. Local, District—maybe even Sector level."

"What do they want?"

I sighed, threw on a shirt and stashed my knife in my back pocket. "I guess it's time I found out."

Walking down the short path between my place and my parent's house, I tried to calm down. There was no reason to assume that these hogs meant my family harm.

But I'd had so many bad run-ins with officials like these it was impossible not to feel a simmering sense of rage. As I walked, I repeatedly told myself I wasn't going to kill anyone—not today. It became almost a chant in my mind.

What I saw when I got close erased my promises. I sprang forward, eyes blazing.

6

My mom was on a gurney. It was a powered model, and it hovered about two feet off the ground as a single blue-suited attendant walked beside it.

My mom looked sicker than I'd ever seen her. She had her eyes open, but they were squinting in the morning sunlight as if it pained her.

"Get your hands off my ma, you hog!" I shouted.

Startled, the attendant craned his neck around and his eyes bugged out.

I had my combat knife out, and it was whirring with power. Twin serrated edges worked in opposite directions, ready to chew through meat and bone like warm butter.

"Who the hell are you?" the man asked.

He didn't pull a weapon, or even run. He just stared at me in complete shock. He looked so startled, in fact, I didn't bother to kill him.

"Momma?" I asked. "Are you okay?"

"Calm down, James," she said. "They're just bringing me home."

Her voice was weak and raspy. I didn't like it. Not one bit.

"What'd you do to her?" I demanded from the blue-shirt medic.

He had one of those clipboard-type computers, and it was filming me.

"I'm streaming all of this," he said nervously. "Any assault will be—"

"Will be too damned late for you," I finished for him. "Now, answer me."

He licked his lips and eyed my knife. I switched it off and lowered it, but still held the handle in a white-knuckled grip.

Before he answered, he dared to glance toward his air car, which I now realized was outfitted to carry gurneys like the one my mom was on. He did a double-take when he looked that way, though.

Etta was there, stationed between the attendant and the car. There was no escape for him. She was small, but she had a knife of her own. It wasn't powered, but it looked wickedly sharp in the pink light of dawn.

"This is crazy," the attendant said. "I'm reporting all of this. You people are crazy. All I'm doing is returning this patient. We picked her up last night on an emergency call. Today, the hospital in Albany released her. That's all I know."

I looked at my mom. "Is that right, Momma?"

"Yes, you big oaf. You're getting far too carried away. Get me into the house."

She apologized to the attendant, and we got her off the gurney and into the house. The man with the air car lit out of our driveway like all the bats of Hell were chasing him. That was just fine by me.

"I can't stay mad at you," she said. "It would be wrong. I should blame myself—I should have told you."

"What's going on? Are you sick?"

"Yes, she is," my father said from the porch.

He looked old, and sad, just like my mom. They were both about sixty now, and nothing shows a person's age like the morning light.

We all went inside, and I helped my dad make breakfast. As we prepared our morning meal, my parents began to explain.

"Your mother contracted something nasty back on Dust World," my dad said. "A poison, maybe. Or possibly a nanite infection left behind by the squids who used to plague that planet."

"Why didn't you say anything?"

"Could you have done anything about it?" Momma asked.

"I don't know... maybe."

"Would it have made you happier to know I was sick?"

I didn't answer, because the answer was obvious.

"Well," my dad said, "Whatever it is, it's killing her slowly."

"I have good days and bad days," Momma said. "Sometimes, I have to go into Albany for a complete blood transfusion."

That sounded stupidly expensive to me, and it was.

"The hogs can cure *anything*," I told my parents. "There's hardly a disease out there that we haven't conquered. Hell, they could grow you a new body if they really wanted to."

My mom shrugged. "I guess that's so, James. But everything has a price. Nothing's free—not really."

I was in a bad mood after breakfast. I paced and muttered. They watched me worriedly. I was glad Etta had gone out again to play in the swamp. She didn't need to see her daddy brooding.

"Now son," my dad said warily. "Don't you go off and do something crazy, you hear me?"

"That notion never crossed my mind," I assured him.

I even summoned up a smile to go along with that lie, but I could tell he wasn't buying it.

He knew me too damned well.

Later that day, I contacted the Sector Office of Hegemony Care. My mom needed something better than out-patient visits. Whatever she had, it was clearly getting worse. There was supposed to be a procedure for fixing people who came down with alien pathogens, and I meant to find out how it could be done.

If my mom had been a legionnaire, there wouldn't have been a problem at all. They were cleared for such things by default. It was expected that soldiers traveling to the stars might pick up any number of illnesses. Worst case, they could just recycle us.

But my mom had been listed as an emigrated colonist. She wasn't even supposed to be here on Earth. The fact that she *was* here didn't seem to trouble anyone in Hegemony Care's bureaucracy at all.

After my channel was accepted and allowed to connect, I was surprised to see the screen on my tapper stayed dark. I'd expected it to light up with a face, even if it was one of those too-perfect virtual agents.

But instead, it was audio-only, like something from a century back. After waiting around on hold through a dozen AI voices that didn't help at all, I got a human to come on the line. That was a miracle all by itself, but even then the story was far from over. Getting anything useful out of a government-type was always difficult.

"I'm very sorry sir," the prim-sounding rep said, "but your mother has a half-share account."

"What the hell does that mean?"

"It means she must wait," he said.

"How long?" I demanded.

"My screen is giving me an estimate of 3.7 years. But I must caution you, these estimates are usually optimistic."

"Four years? She'll be dead by then!"

"I'm sorry sir, but care in this category is rationed for non-essential citizens."

I could feel myself losing it. The sensation of a complete breakdown and possibly violent fit was right there, already past my guts and half-way up my throat to my brain. I fought it back with difficulty. If there was one thing I knew about bureaucrats, it was that yelling at them rarely helped.

"Okay…" I said, making a herculean effort to sound normal. "I want to buy up my parents' medical to a full-share."

"I'm sorry sir, there aren't enough credits in their accounts to—"

"*I've* got credits! I'm buying up their account myself."

The line fell quiet for a while. I heard clicking, more quiet, then finally the agent came back on the line. It felt weird to be dealing with someone with voice-only tech. That sort of thing was antiquated in civvie life. You only ran into it when you talked to the government.

"I'm sorry sir," the man said, "but the enrollment period for that action has passed for this calendar year. We can't change the nature of any service plan again until December."

It was July 8th. At this point, my face was getting hot, and I could feel it contorting uncontrollably.

"Okay," I said, "forget about the insurance. I'll just pay for the treatment myself—with cash."

"That size of transaction using credit coins would be illegal in your Sector—"

"I don't mean *literal* cash! I'll transfer the money, bank-to-bank."

Silence reigned again, and I heard more clicking. The guy wasn't even bothering to tell me when he was going to ignore me for a while. He just stopped talking whenever he felt like it.

"You're offering to pay the entire sum?" he asked after a time.

"That's what I said, dammit!"

More tapping.

"The charge will be nearly two million Hegemony credits. That's just an estimate, mind you. The real rate could rise depending on a wide variety of circumstances."

That made me gulp. I didn't have that much.

"That's more than my family paid for all five of my years in high school!" I complained.

"Considerably more, I imagine. The trouble is that once you go outside the boundaries of your subsidized Hegemony Care package, you run into commercial pricing—which is significantly inflated."

"All right," I said, closing my eyes and rubbing my face. "I don't care, I can get a few extra credits with loans—that'd be okay with you assholes, wouldn't it?"

"Of course it would, sir," he said brightly. "In fact, we're offering a special this month on long-term payment plans."

"Right… Let's do it."

The line went quiet again, and after a while he began to read some kind of speech to me.

"The Hegemony Care Act of 2121 requires me to inform you of certain realities," he began. "Sometimes, when people are in this unfortunate situation, they make emotional decisions they regret later. In short, our data core AI is advising against your actions today."

I frowned. "What's that mean?"

"Well sir…" he said hesitantly. "I'm obliged to inform you that your mother's life expectancy isn't guaranteed to improve in this case, even if the procedure is successful."

"I understand all that, but I'm authorizing the payment on the chance that it will."

"Very well, then! You've been informed of the situation, and you've waived your rights. We're all set. Report for processing at your nearest Hegemony Wellness Center within twenty-four hours of this call's termination. Failure to do so will result in a recalculation of the prices currently listed on your tapper."

"Report for processing?" I asked. "You mean me or my mom?"

"You, of course. You're the one taking on the financial burden. We can't perform this transaction online. You'll have to go down to the Wellness Center and present your case in person."

My frown had been returning, and now it grew even deeper. I'd just begun to believe this part of the nightmare was over, but something in what he'd so offhandedly said had set off an alarm inside my thick skull.

"What're you talking about now? Make *what* case?"

"The case for this scheduling change, obviously. You have to understand your payment terms aren't the only consideration involved. Other citizens of greater stature are already in the priority queue."

"So what?" I demanded, unable to keep my cool any longer. My voice had finally risen into a shout. "If my mom had a full-share account she'd be getting the treatment right now!"

"That's not what I'm talking about, sir. There are only so many of these procedures to go around. The total number has been allotted for this year. To put your mother onto the list, someone else will have to be removed. That decision has to be made by the panel governing the Hegemony-Care Wellness Center."

My eyes were squinched closed by this time. He was telling me that I was offering up two million credits as a bribe to the government, and if they decided to take it, my mom would live because they'd let someone else's mom die.

How had Hegemony Care turned into this? Such grim life or death choices, endless government regulations and accountancy… I felt sick in my guts.

The fight went out of me as I thought about the reality of pushing some other non-essential citizen over the cliff in favor of my mom.

"Sir?" asked the prim man on the other end of the line. "Is there anything else?"

"Yeah," I said. "Cancel the whole damned thing."

He began talking again, but I hung up.

I was just going to have to find another way.

-3-

That evening, I tucked Etta into her bed with some old story about a boy magician and waited until my parents were asleep. Then I walked down our country lane toward Waycross. It was only a few miles, and the humid air did me good.

The fireflies were out in force as it was dusk in early June. They glowed and dimmed rhythmically in the woods beside the puff-crete strip of road just like they'd done for a thousand years or more.

Walking in the cool darkness helped me think. A bit of solitude, and some country quiet—it was good for the soul.

My destination was a local bar with a single pool table and a regular crowd of perhaps ten. I knew them all pretty well, even though I only ventured into town once every week or two. I needed some beer, and I didn't want to drink alone tonight.

My little communion with nature didn't last long. I'd only made it a mile or so down the road toward town when a car appeared behind me.

I tensed up, because the approach wasn't a normal one. The local folk out here drove cheap, rattling trams with old-fashioned tires. Hovering models and outright air cars were quite rare.

This vehicle was too damned quiet. Trams whirred and chugged. This thing, whatever it was, glided over the puff-crete like a ghost.

On impulse, I stuck out my thumb and walked backwards, waving for the driver's attention as the vehicle approached.

This gave me two advantages: One, if the car turned out to be trouble, I would at least be facing in the right direction when it reached me. Two, if they were friendly, they might give me a first-class ride.

The vehicle slowed, and I forced a grin. The headlights played over me, blinding me. Were they checking me out, or sizing me up? I couldn't be sure, so I kept grinning like a fool.

"Get in the car, McGill," a voice called out.

A head on a scrawny neck had poked out the window. I was greatly disappointed as I recognized the snotty voice that was speaking.

It was none other than Primus Winslade.

I lowered my hand and retracted my thumb. Walking up to the hatch, I looked him over. He sneered back.

Winslade was a ferret of a man. He was Imperator Turov's butt-boy, and he seemed to enjoy the role.

"I was hoping it was Galina herself," I said.

"Do not call her that, Adjunct."

It bugged Winslade that I'd managed to be intimate with Turov on any number of occasions, certainly more often than he had despite the fact he'd followed her around like a puppy most of his adult life.

"I don't accept rides from strangers," I said, and I turned around and kept walking.

Winslade rolled after me, his engine revving in annoyance.

"Get in this car, that's an order!" he shouted.

"I'm a Legionnaire on furlough, not a hog," I told him. "Unless you're activating me and willing to pay, that is."

Legionnaires worked differently than the regular Hegemony military. While we were on active duty, we were paid handsomely. That was only right, as we tended to get killed a lot. But when we were languishing between contracts on Earth, we were paid a rather thin wage. In order to make me follow orders like a soldier, a hog had to, in effect, activate my contract.

I was a bit surprised that Winslade didn't fume at me. He chuckled knowingly instead.

"Having some money troubles then, are we?" he asked. "Perhaps I can help with that."

Just about anyone who's known me for long will tell you I'm slow on the uptake at times. Don't get me wrong, in combat I have fine reflexes. But when an unexpected social situation arose, I just seemed to have trouble figuring out what was happening right off.

But my mind went "click" when Winslade let out that sly chuckle of his.

The whole situation seemed fishy. Not six hours after I'd found out about my mom's condition, Winslade had arrived and tracked me down. I needed money for my mom, and he just happened to show up in my neck of the woods and mention money in a snide way.

Now, all that could be nine kinds of coincidence—but unfortunately, I don't believe in coincidences.

I stopped walking and turned around toward Winslade, whose face was lit up by the green instruments inside his cockpit.

My grin expanded on my face, and I gave him a thoughtful nod.

"I'll take that ride after all, Primus."

His ferret-like eyes narrowed for a second. Maybe, just maybe, he could sense the change in my thinking. Before, my grin had been friendly and unassuming. Now, however, it had taken on a predatory cast.

The difference was subtle, but it was undeniable all the same.

-4-

The hatch on Winslade's vehicle popped open, and I climbed inside. He gripped the wheel, and the air car suddenly vaulted into the sky with a stomach-lurching thrum of sheer power.

"This is Turov's baby, isn't it?" I asked.

"You should know it rather intimately."

He was right, of course. I'd taken liberties on a few occasions with Galina right here on these supple, tank-grown leather seats. In fact, the interior of the vehicle had me remembering sweet visions of revelry. I sure was wishing she'd been the one to come out and pick me up instead of sending her repulsive minion.

"Ah, come on," I told him. "Don't be sour about another man's conquests. After all, I happen to know you nailed her yourself, in that very driver's seat."

He looked startled. "What are you talking about?" he snapped.

"Don't you remember? She told me all about it one time when we were having an afterglow drink together. The story was so vivid, it's almost like I was there myself, peeping from the backseat."

Winslade's face pinched up into a sour expression. "You're mistaken, McGill. You're drunk, aren't you?"

"What? Not a drop, I swear—but wait, you're right. It wasn't *you* Galina was talking about. It was another fella—sorry."

Winslade was positively pissed off now. That had been the goal of my bullshit story, after all.

"You must stop calling her Galina, or I'll drop you out of this air car from a mile up."

I gave him a booming laugh. It made him cringe a little.

"I'd like to see you try to shove me out the hatch. Where the hell are we going, anyway?"

"Nowhere. I came down to talk—in private. The car has been outfitted with a signal blocker."

I glanced at my tapper, and I saw he was right. It was blinking, and there was no repeater available for it to connect with.

"So, talk," I said.

"Here's the deal," he began. "Drusus will summon you shortly to Central. You will go there, as you must. But you will refuse the mission he has for you. Under no circumstances will you accept his offer for a special operation."

"Why not?" I asked. "I need money—as you seem to know."

"Yes, and you will be taken care of. You'll have all the money you need and then some. You'll be able to pay for your mother's treatment and buy a car like this one with what's left over, if you want to."

I knew what was up at that point. He'd flat out admitted he knew about my sick momma before I'd told him a thing.

Winslade had made a crucial error. When a man got between me and my fortune or my girl, that was one thing. But to set up a situation where he could determine whether my own momma lived or died? Well sir, that was a bridge too far in my book.

"Well?" Winslade demanded. "What do you say? Have my words penetrated that Cro-Magnon skull of yours, or should I repeat them more slowly?"

He glanced over at me when I still didn't answer. He read my expression, and he knew he was in trouble.

19

It's my eyes. People tell me that sometimes I have the eyes of the dead. It's a legionnaire thing. The look of a primitive animal ready to commit murder. That look comes over a legion man when he's beyond angry. It usually appeared in the middle of deadly action, and it signified there were no longer any higher-level brain functions to get between a man and his hands. That way there was nothing to slow a man down when it was go-time.

Winslade managed to tighten his grip on the steering wheel and spin it over hard to the left. We went into a spiraling dive. Warning lights flashed and alarms beeped all over the cab.

My big hands caught him by the throat, despite the fact he managed to bite my left thumb. Soon, that same thumb was plunged two inches deep into the flesh of his throat.

He didn't even have time to suffocate. I'd wrecked his larynx and broken up the cartilage of his windpipe, but strangulation takes too long in my book. I closed off his carotids and the blood stopped pumping to his brain.

Seconds later, he was out. Unfortunately, we were too damned close to the ground by then.

On impulse, I reached out and killed the car's engine. Some flashers were still going off irritatingly, but I ignored all that.

It was too dark to see the trees below as they rushed up to meet us, but I could smell the pines when I popped open the cupola by tugging on the emergency loops.

We were still falling, spinning, and the night sky outside was full of cold, glittering stars. In the distance, I thought I could pick out the glow of Atlanta's streetlights on the horizon.

Damn, it was as fine a night to die as I'd ever seen. It was pretty country, and my only regret I could later recall was that my drastic action might start a forest fire. I hoped the recent rains would prevent the trees from lighting up.

There was no point in even trying to survive the crash, so I unbuckled my belt and enjoyed the ride to the finish. I might even have whooped and hollered as we slammed down in a fiery mess somewhere in the Blue Ridge Mountains—but I don't remember that part. I only remember the *intention* to do some whooping.

By killing the air car's power, I'd switched off whatever blocking system the vehicle had used to keep my tapper from connecting earlier. As my last conscious act, I pressed the emergency transmit button on my tapper. That caused a burst of packets to connect to the local network on the ground, and thereby update my mental state in the Data Core up at Central.

Then, a few seconds later, I was dead once more.

* * *

Reviving was nothing new to me. I'd done it more times than I could count.

I like to think every death I'd suffered had been for a good cause—even if I knew that wasn't true. My death in the air car crash I would forever account as a good one.

Consequently, when I came out of the oven—or the flesh-printer, or whatever the hell these alien contraptions really were—I was in an excellent mood.

Those that were assembled to witness my rebirth, however, weren't in such fine spirits.

"McGill, you *fuck!*" Turov hissed into my ear. "Play dumb, or I'll destroy you!"

I couldn't see her yet, and that was a damned shame. Galina Turov was a nightmare of a woman. She was about twenty years old physically, but at least twice that in the mind. She'd been revived young, and she'd liked it and kept the look. The result was kind of like having a prom queen with a vicious temper and a conniving attitude ordering people around.

In short, she was just the kind of woman I found myself spending too much time with as the years went by.

Fortunately for both her and me, her request was one I was practically born and bred to perform.

"What happened?" I asked. "Did that fool Winslade blow up the air car?"

Big hands grabbed my arms and pulled me off the gurney. I stood, but weakly. My freshly regrown legs weren't quite ready to hold my weight yet. I swayed, leaning even more than I needed to against the orderlies that propped me up.

21

"McGill?" another voice asked.

This time, I could see the blurry shape of the speaker. It was Equestrian Drusus, a smaller man with a regal bearing.

Not so long ago, he'd briefly been placed in charge of all Earth's defenses during the war with the Cephalopod Kingdom. Politics and jealousy had not thwarted his authority, and now he was one step above Turov in rank.

Squinting and rubbing at my eyes determinedly, I managed to see the three gold sunbursts on Drusus' shoulders.

Standing at his side with her arms crossed under her perky bosom, stood an angry-looking Galina Turov. She had only two sunbursts on her epaulets, and that's why she wanted me to say nothing about what Winslade had offered back in that ill-fated air car.

"Ah," I said, peering at her. "There you are. I seem to have a hangover this morning."

"It's midday," Turov snapped.

I looked around at the two of them. "You left me dead for a while, huh? Why's that?"

"We were weighing our options," Turov said.

"That's not exactly true," Drusus said. "We had to investigate the cause of the crash before we revived each of you separately."

"What'd the report say?" I asked in a conversational tone.

They narrowed their eyes at me. You have to understand that I had a certain reputation—well-deserved—of being a troublemaker.

"It was inconclusive," Turov said. "*You* tell us what happened."

"Well…" I said thoughtfully, formulating my lie.

Clearly, Turov didn't want me talking about how I was being offered a bribe to refuse Drusus' mission—whatever it was about. Many men in my position would have told the truth anyway—but that just wasn't my way. I tended to hold the truth in a vaunted position in my mind, as if it was some kind of lofty goal, a regal thing beyond the ken of mortal man.

Instead, I smiled at them. "Winslade said something about coming down to pick me up and bring me to Central," I said. "I don't know why. Why don't you revive him and ask about it?"

"We'll do that in good time," Drusus said. "But you must excuse me, McGill. I'm having trouble believing that this violent event was an accident. How exactly did you end up burnt to ash in a Georgia forest?"

"Well, I do live down there," I said. "And I already told you why I was in the air car. The only mystery to me is why it crashed. Is there any sign it was shot down?"

"None."

"Hmm… Pilot error, then?"

Turov relaxed and uncrossed her arms. She didn't exactly smile at me, but her face had softened. I was bullshitting, and that made her happy.

Drusus, on the other hand, had a suspicious look on his face. He'd never been an easy man to fool.

"McGill, I am capable of remembering recent events. You and Winslade have a particularly rocky history."

"What? You mean about killing each other and so forth? That's old news. It's beneath any Legion Varus man to hold a grudge like that."

"Just so… Very well then."

He turned to the bio adjunct running the revival machine. "Revive Winslade. Contact me when the task is done."

He walked out then, and I watched him go with a slack expression.

Turov came to stand nonchalantly nearby.

"I know you blew up my air car, you *dick*," she whispered harshly.

I glanced down at her in feigned surprise. She glared back.

"That's simply untrue, Imperator. I was aboard, I admit that. But as God is my witness, Winslade was driving. I think you should talk to him about it."

"Are you claiming you don't remember anything from that flight?"

"No, not really. I remember getting aboard, and I remember taking off. But once we were up there, my mind is a blank. Next thing I knew, I was popping out of the oven here at Central."

She licked her lips thoughtfully. "It could actually be true that you don't remember. Winslade might have used the blocker aboard my car…"

"Why, Imperator!" I exclaimed. "I'm surprised. Did you know those devices are illegal?"

"Shut up. Let me think. If Winslade was using the blocker, you would have no idea why the crash happened… but it still stands to reason that you caused it!"

"But why would I do that?" I asked her with the most innocent, blank, dumb-ass look I could muster.

She sighed, and I could tell right then she believed me. The fine art of lying was all about playing your part to hilt. You couldn't do it halfway. You had to be absolutely firm in your determination to obscure the truth. Any hesitancy, reluctance, or even a sense of amusement would give a man away every time.

"Dammit," she said. "If Winslade's mind is a blank, I'll never know which of you two assholes destroyed my air car."

"Well, if it's any consolation, I'm mighty sorry about that fine vehicle of yours, sir."

"That isn't any comfort at all," she said, and she stalked away to the exit.

I found some clothes and followed her out into the endless, echoing hallways of the giant pyramid-shaped building we called Central. Feeling pretty good, I whistled an old tune as I walked.

Turov noticed me following her and caught me staring at her butt. That was something of a hobby of mine with any attractive woman, but in Turov's case it was a real treat.

She had a body that belied her rank and her personality. What's more, I was intimately familiar with every detail of it.

"I'm taking this elevator, Adjunct," she said in an unfriendly tone. "And you're not coming with me."

"No sir," I said.

She stepped aboard the elevator and opened her mouth to tell it where she wanted to go, but I interrupted her.

"I think I'll just head up to Drusus' office instead," I said.

Her hand snapped out, catching the elevator door and pushing it back. It had just about closed in my face.

"What?" she snapped.

"Well, when Winslade picked me up on the road back in Waycross, he said something about a mission Drusus wanted me to go on. I thought I would just head on up there to his floor and—"

"You will do no such thing!" she hissed, coming out of the elevator and glaring up at me.

"Uh... What do you suggest then, sir?"

She sighed, her small shoulders moved up and down in an exaggerated shrug. "All right. Come with me. Keep quiet until we get to my office."

It was a nice quiet ride up there. She kept her promise not to talk, and I did the same. It really wasn't a challenge for me.

Turov, on the other hand, seemed to be squirming with questions. She wanted to know how much I knew—and how much Winslade had told me before he went splat at my side.

I could have told her, of course, but I wasn't in an informational mood. If there was one thing I'd learned from my fellow schemers in life, it was that keeping quiet often paid big dividends.

"All right," she said when I reached her office. "You can stop this farce."

"Uh… which one?"

"I mean stop pretending you don't know what's going on. You're playing me, and I don't appreciate it."

In my mind, I was the one being played. That's why I'd killed Winslade. He was a snake under the best circumstance, mind you, and deserved a good killing just on principle any day of the week. But in this case, he'd tipped his hand. Turov knew I was in financial trouble—that much was clear. What I suspected was much darker.

I suspected she and Winslade had helped engineer my circumstances. I didn't think they'd made my momma sick, but they might have leaned on some government types to make sure her required treatment was out of my financial reach.

"Okay," I said after a brief delay. "I'll stop pretending."

She squinted at me suspiciously. "That's it?"

"Yup."

She nodded. "Okay, play it that way. You're going to be summoned to Drusus. He will offer you a mission that will take you off-world. You will refuse that mission, on the basis that your mother is sick and needs your care."

It was my turn to give her a suspicious stare.

"What do you know about my momma?"

"Nothing," she said, "and I want to know even less. What I do want is for you to stay on Earth. For this simple act, your mother will receive the care she needs. Is that understood?"

"Are you threatening my mother's life, Imperator?" I asked, with just a hint of danger in my voice.

She turned away from me before answering and retreated behind her desk. I knew that was because I had a certain reputation for violent outbursts. Mind you, the recipients of these outbursts were always highly deserving of their fates.

"That's why you killed Winslade, isn't it?" she asked me.

"What? I don't know. I died too, remember?"

"That doesn't absolve you of anything. I know you, McGill. You'd happily destroy yourself to avenge a slight from another."

I shrugged, unable to deny her words.

"All right… It doesn't matter. The car was insured. I'll suffer with the deductible and the increased rates… but it doesn't matter. What I'm willing to offer you is what you really need. Your mother will get her treatment. All you have to do is refuse to accept Drusus' mission."

"Well now," I said, "it might not be as simple as all that. What if he orders me to take the mission? He can do that, you know."

She shook her head. "He won't. He wants a true volunteer."

With a sudden motion, I lifted my hands and slammed them together, making a booming clap. Turov jumped visibly, and her hand flew to the butt of her pistol.

"Well then!" I said loudly. "We're all good here. Thanks for filling me in, Imperator."

She licked her lips nervously and eyed my sidearm as if making sure it was still in its holster. Slowly, she slid her hand away from her weapon and gave me a flickering smile.

"Go visit Drusus now," she said. "Don't hint that you know about the mission. Don't mention anything we've talked about here."

I nodded reassuringly and stepped out of her office. Her eyes followed me warily. *Damn*, did everyone think I was some kind of murderous psychopath?

In the elevator on the way up to Drusus' office, I worked on my tapper. It had been quietly recording my conversation with Turov, and I wanted to make sure it had caught all the incriminating details. My final clap, in fact, had served to stop the recording.

The sound was crisp and clear on the playback. I smiled, knowing I had a chip to bargain with at last.

Drusus was in his office, and he barely looked up when I got past his staffers into his inner chambers.

As was customary, I waited at attention in front of his desk. At last, making a wry face, he looked up from his work and faced me.

"Adjunct James McGill…" he said. "You're a hard man to gauge, do you know that?"

"That's what people tell me, sir," I said. "Keeps my enemies guessing and my friends nervous."

He chuckled and shook his head. "I have to admit, after this latest stunt I almost changed my mind about meeting with you today."

"Stunt sir? You mean the accident?"

"Yes… Another deadly accident involving you and Winslade… What are the odds?"

"Um… it was a damnably unusual wreck, I would argue. I suspect Winslade's driving first, and Turov's poor schedule of maintenance second. Air cars aren't like trams, you know. You have to do more than just pour in a can of oil now and then."

Drusus nodded sourly. "I thought you'd say something like that. Tell me, McGill, is Turov still breathing downstairs in her office?"

"Of course she is, sir! What are you suggesting?"

"Never mind. Here's the deal: I need you. I hate to admit it, but I need a man who gets things done no matter what stands in his way."

"In that case, I'm that man."

"Right… but don't you even want to hear what the mission is?"

"Not particularly. But I do want you to hear something."

I played the recording for him, implicating Turov and Winslade in a conspiracy. I figured that if I didn't even know what Drusus' mission was about, my case would be even stronger. I'd look like an innocent party—no mean feat for a man of my stature.

Drusus listened and his face darkened as the recording finished. He rubbed at his face. Instead of flying into a rage and ordering Turov to be arrested, however, he looked worried.

"I thank you for bringing that to my attention, McGill. I'd like to ask for a favor."

"What's that, sir?"

"Destroy that recording. It will only cause us greater trouble—in fact, it may already be too late."

My face went slack in incomprehension. "I don't get it, sir."

"No... I don't either, not entirely. Let's just say that Turov has connections. Everyone knows that, but over the last couple of years since the Cephalopod attack, I've become increasingly alarmed at her resiliency."

"Uhh... I'm not sure what you're talking about, Equestrian."

"Have you ever wondered why she wasn't permed for her treasonous behavior during the Cephalopod War?"

"I just figured she weaseled out of it somehow."

"It was more than that. Some people high up in our government—those who serve on the Ruling Council of Hegemony itself—they're behind her."

"I see. That would explain a lot."

Drusus got up from his desk and paced behind it. While he did that, I pretended to dutifully erase the recording of Turov's voice. What I really did was change the name of the file and encrypt it. A man could never have too many aces up his sleeve, to my way of thinking.

"I know you had a close relationship with Nagata in the past," Drusus continued. "He was the man who sat in this very chair I'm in now."

I looked at the chair in question doubtfully. Nagata's office hadn't even been on this floor.

Drusus caught my expression and shook his head. "I meant that figuratively, not literally. I'm a three-star officer with similar duties. I'm one of the few obstacles in-between Turov and her personal goals. That didn't work out too well for Nagata, did it?"

"No, sir. He got his ass permed."

"Exactly. I don't intend to suffer the same fate. What I want to know is if you'll stand with me on this."

I looked at him in mild surprise. People tended to order me around, or ask me to do things that were questionable in nature. But they rarely asked me to take a loyal stand.

"Well…" I said, "I've always liked and respected you, sir. Even after you left the legion and moved up to work here at Hog-Central."

"That's very considerate," he said, and I couldn't tell if he was being sarcastic or not. "But I'm asking for your support in a personal way. Are you a man I can count on if things go badly around here—again?"

"My first loyalty is to Earth, then my family, then Legion Varus, in that order," I said seriously. "After that, though, I'm willing to call you a friend and stick my neck out to help if I can."

"That's the most I can hope for, I guess. Thanks for the honest answer."

He pushed a small box across his desk toward me. I eyed the box, frowning. I didn't open it right away.

"You sure you want to do this, sir?" I asked him.

He met my eyes and nodded.

I thought about bringing up my mom about then—but I didn't. It just seemed wrong to ask him for a political favor right now. He was talking about serious legion business. Nothing about our discussion was private or personal. It was all appropriate—if unusual and outside of normal channels.

After looking at the box he'd scooted in my direction for a second, I scooped it up and opened it. A moment later I took out the twin silver bars of a centurion.

I'd been promoted, just like that.

Somehow, I figured the promotion was only going to get me into deeper trouble. But I plucked the bars out of the box anyway and touched them to my lapels. They quickly consumed my Adjunct's insignia, embedded themselves into the fabric and stuck there. It was as if they'd been there my whole life.

-6-

Drusus never did tell me exactly what he wanted me to do for him. The precise nature of this "mission" I was supposed to go on wasn't even described.

He did tell me, however, to report to the labs deep under the bedrock of Central in the morning, equipped for hazardous duty.

I left his office worrying about my mom. If this activity ended up perming me—always a possibility when the word "special" was attached to any mission—there was no way she would survive to see Christmas. The thought of Etta and my dad spending a lonely Christmas together briefly crossed my mind. Then I got back to problem-solving.

As a man with a long history in the Legions, I wasn't completely without resources. I took it upon myself to contact certain people who might be able to help, or at least to steer me in the right direction.

The first one to respond was Della. That was probably because we had a kid together, and she might have assumed it involved Etta. It was nice to know she cared in her own way.

"What's wrong, James?" she asked, her face swimming into existence on my tapper.

"Nothing," I said. "At least, not with me or Etta."

"What's the problem then—wait, you're not calling for a date, are you? That ship has sailed, as you Earthers like to say."

31

"No, no. Nothing like that. I'm calling about my momma. She's sick."

"Really...? Yes... now that I think about it, I think I knew that."

I frowned at her. "Why?"

"Because I've seen the look. A grayness to the face. A bloodless look. Does she bleed at night—inside?"

"Yeah," I said, amazed. "How'd you know that?"

She composed her thoughts, and her eyes took on an unfocused look. "Some of our people used to get like that back home on Dust World. But the last of them died off when I was a child."

I narrowed my eyes. "Not you though? Not Natasha, or Etta?"

"It generally strikes the aged. But we have so few of them on my home planet."

I knew all too well why there weren't any old folks on Dust World. Life there was just too harsh. Oh, there were a few old-timers around, like her father the Investigator. But one could argue he was far from a typical person.

"So what is it? What do you think is wrong with her?"

"Nanites," she said. "They're everywhere, you know. In the dust, in the water, even in the cells of the plants and animals we eat. We developed them many decades ago, and the first colonies were wild. They escaped, some of them. Now, they infest and feast on any host they can find."

An involuntary shudder threatened to sweep through me, but I quelled the urge. You haven't seen death until you watch a grown man consumed alive by a swarm of nanites. It was like watching a dead thing decompose before your eyes—only, the victim was very much alive.

"Nanites..." I said. "They're inside her? That's fixable. I can just set up an EMP wand and zap her with it."

Della looked thoughtful, she nodded, but with an unconvinced air.

"Maybe," she said, "but the internal damage is probably already done. Scarring of organs. Tiny leaks caused by laceration from their metal bodies—microscopic wounds that won't heal. She's probably going to die, James."

32

"Why didn't you say something about it, then?" I asked loudly.

She shrugged. "I didn't think of it until now. Until I thought about how she looks, and where she's been living."

The situation was astounding to me. Earth was sending out colonists to Dust World every week, and I didn't know if anyone knew about that particular danger. Possibly, Hegemony knew full well and just didn't care. The strong would survive, and the weak would be left to their inevitable fate.

"I'm sorry, James," she said. "On Dust World there's no cure, but you can try your EMP idea. In my experience, a person either heals over their scars, or they can't and they die."

Heaving a sigh, I said goodbye and closed the channel. I contacted my dad and gave him a rosy version of what Della had told me. He headed off eagerly to the hardware store to build an EMP device. It really wasn't a hard contraption to construct when you were only trying to disrupt something the size of a nanite.

Next, I contacted a bio named Anne Grant. We'd had a thing going years back, but I hadn't talked to her in a long time. She came online warily.

"James?" she said. "Just so you know, I'm married now. I've left the legions, and I—"

"Hey," I said. "It's okay. This isn't some kind of midnight booty-call. But it's nice to see your face and hear your voice just the same."

She gave me a cautious, flickering smile.

"Listen," I said, "I've got a problem."

I described my momma's situation in detail, and she listened in concern.

"Nanites?" she asked, marveling. "I remember them—so strange. We still can't make them reproduce themselves independently, you know. Only the Dust Worlders have managed that trick."

"Yeah, that's great. Do you think anyone can help her?"

She thought about it, then shook her head. "I'm sorry James. You could use a cellular regrow agent, to speed healing after you've killed the nanites, but their tiny metal corpses will still be in her system. They'll clog her organs and arteries, like sand in gears."

"Then you think she needs a regrow, huh?" I asked. "That's what you're saying."

Anne looked at me sharply. "Where'd you get that idea? She's a civilian, James. The data core isn't even tracking her body, much less her mind."

"Yeah…" I said, my thoughts moving down new paths. "Well, thanks for the professional info, Anne. It's been real nice talking to you."

She smiled. "You too. I hope everything works out—oh, and James?"

"Hmm?"

"I'm not really married."

I smiled. "Yeah, I know. Takes more than an amateur to pull off a lie on old James McGill."

She laughed. "I should have known better than to try."

We got off, and I was left thinking. There wasn't much time. If I knew my higher-up officers, they were likely to send me off to get permed on one mission or another until they got it right.

Accordingly, I contacted my dad again. He had Etta with him, and they were at the local drone-repair shop, picking up parts to build their EMP wand.

"While you're at it, Dad," I told him. "Run that wand over yourself and Etta."

"Do you really think—right. I'll do it. Repeatedly."

"Good. And Dad? Do you think you could bring Momma up here to Newark? To the Mustering Hall?"

"The what—why?"

"So she can take a look at the legion recruitment center. I know she's always been interested in the place. I want her to see it while she can still get around."

He stared at me through my tapper as if I'd gone insane.

"James…" he said slowly, "I beginning to think you've gotten one of your strange ideas."

"Not at all," I assured him. "I just remembered they've got morning tours at the Mustering Hall, and I wanted to show her around."

"Uh… okay," he said, squinting at me in suspicion. He knew something was up, but he didn't want to blow a chance at helping Mom by asking too much about it. He'd learned a few things by raising a son like me.

"Bring Etta along, too," I said, "and be here by morning."

"What? Morning? We'll have to drive all night."

"Yeah… better get started."

He nodded, giving me a bewildered but intense look.

"All right. We'll be there."

Before he disconnected, I saw through his tapper he was moving fast. He trotted toward the exit at the automated store. He had an armload of stuff and a long night ahead of him.

I'd given him hope. I knew that, and I prayed it wasn't a mistake.

Maybe I could do something to help, and maybe I couldn't. It was hard to tell until I got into the thick of it.

Checking the time, I saw it was just about nine pm. Doing a quick person-search on my previous call, I located Anne. She was only about twenty miles away in a suburb. Shrugging, I decided it wasn't too far. A man might as well go for the gusto when faced with a future full of deadly unknowns.

I rented an auto-cab and fed it the address with a swipe on my tapper. It whisked me away and I sat back to enjoy the city lights.

Anne was surprised to see me at her door—but not *too* surprised. She knew me pretty damned well. Her talk of not having a husband—well, to a man like me, that was just about as clear an invitation as a woman could provide.

After a little bit of quiet talking at the door, she let me inside. The rest of the evening, as they say, was preordained.

I woke up the next day a tiny bit later than I meant to. It was at least a half-hour past dawn, and I had a hell of a line-up of activities.

After jumping out of bed, I rushed to the shower. Moving as fast as a late soldier can, I cleaned-up, dressed-up and raced to the Mustering Hall.

Warm water splashed over me in the shower as I worked my tapper like a pro. I sent a message on to Drusus indicating I'd been momentarily detained, with full apologies and lots of "sirs" written in there to cushion the blow.

Speaking of which, Anne had snuck into the stall behind me and wrapped her small hand around my chest. She put her head against my back even as I finished my message and fired it off.

"Begging for more time, is that it?" she asked, smiling. "I know what that means, James."

"Huh?"

"Don't play coy with me. I saw you telling your officers you'll be late. You didn't even ask me if I could make a morning of it."

"Oh…" I said, feeling a small twinge of concern.

I'm a man who tends to overschedule himself under the best of circumstances, but this morning's punch list was getting unmanageable. I was supposed to report to Central, meet my parents for their tour and satisfy Anne one more time—all at once!

Thoughtfully, I looked down at her sweet face. She was quickly drifting to the top of the list. I'd always had sort of a nurse-and-patient thing going for her. She'd presided over more of my revivals than anyone else I knew. That made a man feel close to a girl, believe it or not.

Sucking in a deep breath and chuckling, so it didn't turn into a sigh, I grabbed her and went into motion. She was taken by surprise, but she soon melted.

"You haven't changed a bit," she said when she got her mouth free of mine for a moment.

I didn't say anything. I had to make this good, and quick-like. It was pressure, but I didn't mind that. I had fun anyway, even if I was distracted.

Anne seemed bemused by what she took as an urgent passionate need on my part.

"You weren't like this last night," she said. "Are you okay, James?" she asked, cupping my face in her hands.

We were up close, wet, and about as intimate as two people could be right then.

I smiled. "I'm fine—but today I'm headed somewhere sketchy. I might not come back."

Her face fell. "A mission? Another deadly mission? Why don't you quit today? I'd like to spend the day with you instead of reading later on that you were permed."

For just a second, I considered her offer. But I had to reject it.

"The legions are a way of life for me now," I told her. "Love it, hate it—it's my existence. I never get old, and I never seem to get enough."

She sighed, hugged me, and let me go. I watched her dress in slow-motion.

"I'm telling the truth about this mission," I said. "I'm not just shining you on for another girl—not this time."

Anne nodded without turning back to face me. "I know. That burst of passion this morning—that convinced me. That seemed like a man who knows he's about to die—again."

"Yeah... Well, I'll see you as soon as I can, okay?"

I gave her a kiss, but she never answered me. I left her place, and once I was out in the hallway, I began to race down the corridors of her apartment complex at a dead run.

Twenty minutes later I was dropped off at the Mustering Hall. My parents were there, looking nervous. My mom was holding onto my dad's arm. Was she getting weak again already? She'd had a transfusion just a day or so ago... The condition seemed to be getting worse.

"Where's Etta?" I asked.

"She didn't want to come," my mom said. "She found some new pile of mud and sticks way south of our house. She can't talk about anything else."

"Okay... well, come on, we've got to move."

They hobbled after me, and I noticed neither one of them was moving as fast as they used to. How damned old were they now? Maybe I wasn't even sure. Dying and coming back all the time made it so I could hardly keep track of my own age, much less theirs.

"Here," I said, as we reached the door.

It was a smart door that I hadn't laid eyes on for a few years. It had a handprint-reader on the door and a stained screen above it.

I had my dad apply his hand first—the door rejected him immediately.

Part of the legion recruiting process began right here. If you tested out as substandard in any obvious way, the door wouldn't even let you inside to be humiliated by further testing.

I'd expected nothing else, but I still had him try three times. Each time, the door refused to open. There was one good thing about coming late, there was no line. We took our time.

I walked my momma up to the door next, and she rolled her eyes at me when I repeatedly applied her hand to the door. At last, after she'd been rejected over and over again, she objected.

"James, if you're trying to make me feel better, you're failing miserably. I know I'm a broken down old woman. I don't need some government AI to confirm it!"

"I know, Momma," I said. "I'm sorry. One more time."

38

After a final rejection. I applied my tapper to the door—not my hand. The door went green and popped open.

On the other side was an irritated-looking hog. I knew him, fortunately. He was none other than Tech Specialist Ville, the same man who'd steered me down to Varus on the lower deck of the Hall years ago.

He must have died in the recent squid invasion, however, because he looked a mite younger than he had when I'd last seen him. He had no paunch, and his hair was all present and accounted for.

He squinted at me in shock.

"McGill?" he asked. "*The* James McGill?"

I smiled. "That's me, Specialist Ville."

He chuckled and shook his head. "What the hell are you doing here—and who do you have with you?"

"I'm so sorry to bother you," I said, "but my folks have never been down here before. They kind of wanted to see how the process worked."

He shook his head slowly. "They give tours, but that's only on weekends. You should bring your folks back then, Centurion."

"Yeah... but they're only here for a day. Can you help me out?"

He stared at me then looked around for any officers that may have been lurking around. There weren't any.

"I'm not supposed to. The recruitment system is live. Recruits are trying out right now—and the crop is thin, let me tell you."

"It always is," I said sympathetically. "Well? Just for a few minutes?"

The tech specialist sighed, and he turned his back on us. He was a man after my own heart. If he didn't see it, it had never happened.

But I wasn't quite done pestering him yet. "Hey," I said, poking him in the back. "How about letting the machine drop their imprints—you know, the data disks that look like a credit coin?"

"What the hell are you going to do with those?"

"Nothing," I said. "I'll return them in a few minutes. But you can't get the full effect if you don't have a disk to start tests and all."

Shaking his head, he tapped a few buttons and a rattling sound rang out in the pan near the door. I scooped up the coin-like data disks and led my parents quickly away.

"This is something, James!" my mother said. "I didn't know you had this surprise tour waiting for us."

"Uh-huh. It's my big surprise. I'm going away for a short time, and I wanted to show you something before I leave."

"Away?" she asked in disappointment. "You're not going on deployment again, are you? What about Etta?"

"That girl can look after herself."

"She sure as hell can," my father muttered.

"James, why are we walking so fast?" my momma demanded. "I'm feeling faint."

Instead of slowing down, I reached down and looped my arm under hers. I half-lifted her off the ground and hurried her along.

I think my dad had an inkling of what was really going on. He lifted her other arm, and between the two of us, the old lady's feet hardly touched the floor.

"This isn't the recruitment lines," she complained.

"Yeah, I know. Now listen, when everything breaks, you guys head through that door right there, you hear? Get back to your tram and head home. Don't call me—don't call anyone."

They stared at me in shock. My father nodded grimly, but my mom's jaw sagged open. She'd been treated to any number of my shenanigans back when I was a kid, but she didn't fully realize that I'd become a professional disruptor of peace as an adult.

My dad was white-faced, but he was game. He didn't know what my plan was, but he understood the stakes well enough.

I took the two tiny silver disks and put them into his hand, closing his fingers into a fist on top of them.

"Don't lose these. Not for anything. Let them cut off fingers and toes first."

He nodded again, looking a little sick.

I left them there—standing at the emergency exit. They looked so old and bewildered. It gave me a pang. At what point had they become the ones I had to care for, instead of the other way around? I didn't know exactly when it had happened, but I didn't like the feeling at all.

In order not to alarm them anymore than I had to, I walked away at a brisk, but less than desperate pace. The second I could, I ducked down the escalators toward the legion booths in the basement.

I was surprised to see that the Varus booth wasn't there anymore. That meant they had to have been moved upstairs. Could that have been due to my influence?

Nah, I told myself. It was never good for a man to grow a swelled head. The legion had proven itself over the years, that's all. We were no longer shunned—we were still infamous, yes, and nothing like respectable—but people had decided we had value after all.

"Hey, Varus!" shouted a tough-looking noncom from Legion Solstice. "You lost?"

I flipped him the bird without a glance and headed for the bathrooms. Once inside, I entered the first stall and locked the door. There was no one in the place, fortunately.

I made the mistake of glancing at my tapper then—I'd been avoiding that all morning. There had to be fifteen red-message lines on there. I was over an hour late for Central, after all.

Fumbling in my urgency, I dug a plasma grenade out of my pocket. Then I took my combat knife off my belt and engaged in a little bit of field-surgery on the device.

The bathroom door banged open while I worked. Someone stalked into the room.

"Hey, Varus," he said. "You shitting yourself in there? I've got a few friends outside. We want to talk to you."

"Just a minute," I called to him, gritting my teeth as I worked on my grenade.

Officially, I wasn't supposed to have explosives on me in the Mustering Hall. As an active-duty legionnaire, a loaded pistol and a combat knife were acceptable—but not a grenade. Fortunately, I'd never been a fan of persnickety regulations.

"You're not getting out of this so easily," the man said. "We're gonna have that talk, hot shot."

"Yep, we sure are," I said in an agreeable tone.

Muttering, he left.

I finished my work, dropped the grenade into the toilet, and flushed it right down. Right then, I wished I hadn't locked the stall door. I flipped the tab up quickly and nervously. Then I headed for the door. There wasn't going to be much time left.

Stepping outside, I saw three men waiting for me. They were all Solstice. They saw my rank, and they looked surprised. I was a Centurion now.

The days of rough-and-tumble enlisted rivalry between the legions were mostly in the past for me. At the officer level, things became political. You screwed each other over with budgets, mission-assignments and promotions—not your fists.

"Why didn't you say you were an officer?" my original harasser complained.

"I don't recall you asking, Veteran."

Shaking his head, he waved, and the three of them began to slink away. They'd been more than ready to start something with a Varus man on his own—but messing with an officer would've resulted in more than a day in the stockade.

"Wait a second," I said, reaching out a hand and hooking him by the back of his collar.

He wheeled around, snarling, but I pointed back into the bathroom with a friendly expression.

"You want to have some fun? Off the record, just man-to-man?"

He looked at me warily. "One-on-one?"

"That's right—unless that's too scary for a Solstice Veteran. I hear you still pee your sleeping bags at night, and I wouldn't want to scare you any further."

He showed his teeth, which were stained and filthy. He flexed his knuckles, and he nodded at me. He was a big boy—not as tall as I was, but broader of shoulder.

"Step right in there," I said. "I'll follow a minute later so it doesn't look funny."

"You're on, Varus!"

42

He stalked into the bathroom alone, as his friends had all moved on by now. I did a U-turn and hurried for the escalators. There couldn't be but a few seconds—

Crump! It was a weird sound, one I knew all too well. A plasma grenade had gone off and weaponized the restroom.

Plasma grenades were odd weapons. They grabbed up whatever was around them, changed their form, and blew everything outward as shrapnel. Even water turned into a thousand tiny needles, liquid transformed into solids and blasted in every direction at once.

Alarms went off all over the Hall. People froze and looked around in shock. Terrorism, a squid attack, some kind of horrible error in the maintenance AI—who knew what had gone wrong? Someone triggered the evacuation script, and the doors flew open.

People trotted by me for the exits, but I didn't hurry. I walked with Varus pride.

When I stepped outside, I squinted up at the sun and summoned an autocab.

Then I looked at my tapper and swore. There were twice as many messages as before. It was a good thing I'd silenced all the tones, buzzers and ringers. The damned thing would have made it hard to concentrate if I'd been listening to all that.

"Damn," I said aloud. "They must really want me on this mission."

-8-

The cab took me straight to Central. But before I could make it to the elevators, a group of stern-looking hogs encircled me.

"Uh... what's up, fellas?" I asked.

"You're under arrest," barked the most disagreeable looking individual. "We're to escort you down to the lower lab complex."

"That's mighty friendly of you guys," I said. "It just so happens that's where I'm headed."

He snorted. "Don't even think of taking any detours, McGill."

"Wouldn't dream of it. No way I can get lost with you guys crowding around. And to think, people say hogs have no sense of hospitality!"

They fell silent on the long elevator ride into the lower bowels of Central. When we arrived at last, we passed through some pretty serious security. I was relieved of every weapon I had on me.

"This way, Centurion," said a fine, tall girl with a pretty face and bony arms. She looked like a runway model to me—not your typical government type.

I followed her with gusto, but my high spirits soon faded. Drusus, Graves and Winslade were waiting for me in the dark labs ahead.

"What's the drill today, sirs?" I asked in a hearty tone.

"McGill…" Graves said seriously, "what have I told you about having respect for other people's time?"

"I do believe you've admonished me to show more respect on any number of occasions, sir—in fact, let me congratulate you on your promotion to the high rank of primus. It was greatly overdue."

Graves stared at me in an unfriendly fashion. "We're discussing kicking you off this project, McGill."

"I'd say that was a shame, I'm sure—if I knew what the project involved."

"He's hopeless," Winslade said. "Exactly as I told you. Unless you overrule me, Drusus, I'm kicking him out of the entire legion."

"On what grounds?" Drusus asked.

Winslade sputtered and pointed at me. "Can't you see, sir? Nearly three hours late! Reports of criminal activity fill his morning!"

"Criminal activity?" I gasped. "What? Since when is it against the law to bed a retired legionnaire?"

They all glanced at me.

"And who might that be, McGill?" Graves asked.

I smiled. I had them curious now. "You remember that bio who quit after the invasion?"

"Oh please," Winslade scoffed, "don't tell me it's Anne Grant."

"Well, how about that? Somebody remembers Miss Grant by name! Is there perhaps a bit of latent interest there?"

"Yes, I remember her—a very sensible girl by appearances. I'm surprised her judgment hasn't improved."

"He's just distracting you, Primus," Graves said.

That was a shocker. I hadn't expected Graves to out me so off-handedly.

"McGill," Graves continued. "Do you realize there's a recruiter from Mustering Hall who's just come out of a revival machine upstairs? He's demanding that you be arrested."

"Uh… he wouldn't happen to be from Legion Solstice, would he?"

"Thanks for verifying your involvement," Graves said.

45

"Now hold on," I said. "If he's complaining along formal channels, it's just sour grapes, sir. That Solstice man had it coming—it was just a little joke, anyway."

"A joke? Thousands of credits in damage, a ruined day of recruitment—you think that's funny?"

"Well…"

Graves turned away from me to face Drusus. "Equestrian, I hate to say it, but I concur with Primus Winslade. McGill should be off the mission roster. Hell, he should probably be removed from this service entirely."

Drusus hadn't said much for the last several minutes. He'd just been staring at each of us, listening. Now, he looked both thoughtful and sour at the same time.

"McGill is uniquely qualified for this highly hazardous duty. It's my decision, and I'm standing with my previous choice. McGill goes. Get him suited up."

"Sir," I said, "I'm proud to be your man. I'll make Legion Varus proud again."

To their credit, no one grumbled openly. Winslade looked like someone had kicked his cat however. His teeth were clenched, and his eyes were slits.

"May I be excused, sir?" he asked Drusus. "I've got duties to attend to."

Drusus nodded. "Graves will provide the briefing and oversee the insertion. Good luck, gentlemen."

Drusus left us, and I suspiciously watched Winslade scamper off a moment later. It didn't take a genius to know he was running off to report the situation to Turov. If Drusus had noticed, he apparently didn't care.

Soon, there was no one in the lab other than Graves, a bunch of techs, and yours truly. I was given a suit—and it looked familiar, sort of.

"Is that a teleport suit, Primus?" I asked Graves.

"Modified for human usage, yes."

The costume was a metallic black mesh with a durable insulated interior. It was kind of like a spacer's service uniform, or maybe a high-tech diving suit. There was a power-pack, however, and a digital gauge on the front.

The original teleport suits had been built by the Cephalopods with some stolen Empire tech thrown in. This suit looked like it was built to hold a man instead of a squid. The old ones had been huge and floppy, but in comparison this model looked like it would be a tight fit for a man my size.

"So... where am I going?" I asked. "And what kind of team do I have going with me?"

"You're flying solo," Graves said. "This is the only working suit we have at the moment."

"Why's that?"

"The original suits didn't hold up to extensive testing, and they apparently required maintenance that we didn't understand. They began self-destructing shortly after your teams' involvement during the invasion."

"Huh..." I said. "That's weird."

He narrowed his eyes in my direction. I could tell that he suspected I knew something about these suits that I wasn't sharing.

The fact was, the original suits had required usage of the Galactic Key to function. I'd hacked their security system, in essence, to get them to work. Trying to use them without understanding that step had probably resulted in the "accidents" he was describing.

My face was a total blank, and I barely looked curious as I rubbed at the fabric of the new model.

"Who's been testing this one out?" I asked him.

"Several hogs. They were scared at first, but we managed to do small jumps repeatedly, without an incident. Cannibalizing parts of the squid-made suits and designing components of our own, we've managed to construct a unit that can reliably fly distances of up to one hundred meters without error."

I stared at him. "One hundred meters? Like—about the length of this lab?"

"Precisely."

"So... where am I supposed to be going?"

"That's classified. Follow me."

Troubled, I did as he asked. We left the bustling techs behind and retreated to a small office off the main lab chamber.

47

"Primus?" I asked him. "Are you kidding me? You're expecting me to jump off-world, aren't you? This suit is a jury-rigged mess, I can tell just by looking at it."

"That might be true," he admitted. "It's experimental at best."

"Why don't we just have the squids cook us up an improved model?" I asked him.

His face pinched up in a frown. "You remember that fusion bomb you set off on Throne World—their capital?"

"Of course. It was my finest hour."

"Yeah, well… where do you think they manufactured their teleport suits?"

I squinted at him for a second. "Oh…" I said. "I get it. There aren't any more teleport suits coming from the squids. That's a crying shame. But I still don't get why I'm being sent off to test it in such a fired-up hurry."

"Because we have an emergency. The Mogwa are coming back—they've crossed the border into Province 921 and they'll arrive here soon."

My eyes bugged out at this news. "You mean the Nairbs, right?" I asked.

"No, the actual Mogwa. The Galactics are coming themselves this time. Battle Fleet 921, or at least a contingent of that force, has been ordered to return to our province and put down what is seen as a local rebellion."

"A rebellion? I haven't seen anything about that on the net vids."

"That's because *we're* the rebels—as far as the Mogwa are concerned."'

I blinked at him in confusion. "When did we declare independence from the Empire?"

"In their view, that happened when we fought a war with the Cephalopods and won. Now that the squid worlds are under our control, we're a danger to the Mogwa. We're in violation of a list of Galactic Laws."

"Right…" I said thoughtfully.

The only reason the Empire had survived for thousands of years was their strict maintenance of the status quo. Individual member civilizations weren't supposed to grow, research new tech, or even fight serious wars against one another. By keeping thousands of species frozen in development, the Empire had been able to keep us from challenging their power or otherwise disrupting what worked well for the elite races at the top.

"If they think we're a danger," I said, "well... there's only one cure for that."

"Exactly. Extinction of the rogue species. We can't confirm that's their plan, but we have to assume it's a possibility."

"Okay... but I still don't get what my part is in all this."

Graves poked at the suit. It rustled and the metallic links clinked audibly. "You're the only man we have that has successfully teleported to remote locations alone and survived. That's why Drusus is putting this on you, despite everyone's misgivings."

"Uh-huh," I said, not bothering to argue with him about it.

"Now," he said, "I want you to try to absorb the critical nature of this mission, McGill. I want you to be on your best behavior. You're not going out there to slaughter anyone— you're going out there as a spy, not a fighter. Your onboard body-cams will do most of the work. All you have to do is take a look around and get back here with whatever you can find out in five minutes."

"Five minutes?"

"Yes. This suit model has several improvements. One is that it holds enough of a charge to power two jumps. You'll fly out there, and after five minutes you'll teleport back."

"What if I can't do it? What if I'm captured or killed in that amount of time?"

He poked at the suit's digital readouts. "That's all taken care of. The suit is on a timer. You'll be pulled back here after five minutes, dead or alive."

"Hmm..." I said without enthusiasm, but after a moment, I grinned. "Well... okay then. I'll do it."

"Of course you will!" Graves snorted. "I'm not asking for volunteers. I'm ordering you to suit up and fly as soon as the techs have the suit ready."

"Uh... just one more thing, Primus? Where am I going, exactly?"

He looked at me in surprise. "I thought that would be obvious. We've spotted the approaching battle fleet, as I said. You're going to pop out there and take a look at their ships, hopefully learning of their intentions. Don't let them see you or detect you—that's an order."

I followed him back to the labs doubtfully. "That's a hard one, sir," I said. "Your people are in control of where I end up. If they miss, and I end up in the middle of the bridge on the flagship, I think somebody might just notice me."

"Let the techs handle that part. You've got no choice, anyway. None of us do."

I stopped following and lowered my voice as we came into view of the launchpad. Techs were swarming the suit, charging it up.

"Sir," I whispered, "I'm beginning to question the wisdom of this entire venture. I mean, if the Mogwa are already pissed and view humanity as a possible threat, won't this push them over the edge?"

He looked at me seriously. "You could be right. Hell, I don't know the answer to that. But the Ruling Council of Earth has made the call. You and I are just soldiers, caught up in following orders from the top. It's my opinion that they already know the Mogwa are coming here to remove us, and they're trying to get confirmation."

"But what good will that do?"

"Earth is building a new fleet. It's last-ditch, but we have to do something. If it comes right down to it, the Ruling Council is going to ambush the battle fleet the second it shows up. But they want confirmation from you, first."

The magnitude of the situation was beginning to sink into my thick skull about then. Don't get me wrong, I'm not a man who's easily spooked. But this was *big*. Real big.

They suited me up, taught me how to operate the digital controls, and hooked me up to some wires.

Then, they all backed up like I was wearing a suicide vest. I didn't blame them, because I was, sort of.

The timer on the suit started up by itself a few seconds later. That was rude, in my opinion. I thought a man ought to be able to at least flip a switch before he consigned himself to death.

But then, maybe I was old-fashioned.

The world shifted around me. It blurred and wavered. I was losing coherency as a singular mass. Soon, I knew, I'd turn into a smoky semblance of myself and port out.

It occurred to me as I began to fade from existence, that Turov and Winslade might have been right. What if they knew it was a stupid idea to piss off the Mogwa like this? What if they had some inside knowledge on what the Mogwa were planning, and what the mission orders were for the battle fleet?

It was a disturbing thought, but it was too late to act on it now. The last thing I saw before the world blurred completely was Graves. He was giving me a lazy salute.

I would have saluted back, but I was already insubstantial. A moment later, I ceased to exist on my fine green homeworld of Earth.

Already, I missed the feel of her under my feet.

-9-

The next moment I was aware of was all wrong.

I'd expected to appear inside an alien ship. My immediate plans for such a case were still in my mind, in fact. They were vague, but I believe the simplest plans work best.

First off, I'd hide. That was critical. I was supposed to appear aboard the Mogwa ship in a hold of some kind, which would've made stealth easier. From there, I was to learn what I could and teleport out again. How much intel I could gather in five minutes was a big question mark to me, but I hadn't planned this boondoggle in the first place...

Unfortunately, when my awareness returned, I wasn't on a Mogwa ship. I wasn't even in a teleport suit. I was somewhere else that was depressingly familiar.

"What's his Apgar score?"

"He's an eight-point-five. We're not going to get better than that."

"He's breathing. Pull the oxygen. Get his lungs working."

I was surrounded by bio people, orderlies and techs. A strange smell assaulted me. It was organic, wet—even *hot* in the nostrils. It was a smell like thick urine, maybe. I knew it all too well, it was the smell of my own rebirth.

"McGill, can you hear me?" Graves asked.

My mouth worked, but no words came out. I choked instead and coughed up a load of fluid from deep within my newly formed lungs.

"McGill, damn you, there's no time. I order you to report!"

"He can't even talk yet, Primus," the bio said.

She seemed defensive about me, but I felt gauntleted hands grasp my shoulders and haul me up onto my feet. I pitched forward and almost fell on my face.

Graves was standing in the way. My weak fingers grasped his uniform.

I couldn't see yet. The world was a blur. I felt like I was underwater during a rainstorm.

Something hard and cold touched my temple. I knew it was the muzzle of a pistol.

"Graves?" I managed to croak out.

The cold touch of the gun left my head.

"You can talk? Good. We have questions."

"Here," said the bio. "Here are some clothes, McGill."

"He won't be needing those where he's going," Graves said.

I took the clothes with floppy fingers anyway and stumbled out of the revival chamber. I started to get into the pants before a hard shove nearly knocked the clothing from my jittery hands. Graves marched me down the hallway, buck naked—my legs functioning better with each step.

"Sir?" I managed to ask. "Is there some kind of a problem?"

"Yes McGill," he said angrily. "The trouble is we sent a moron up into space to perform a spying mission. Somehow, he never came back."

"I didn't? How long has it been?"

He stopped and looked at me. I could see him well enough now to make out his craggy features. His eyes—they were the color of steel and even less forgiving.

"You screwed up," he said. "I don't know how, but you did it. The Mogwa have sent a transmission from the battle fleet on a deep-link call to Earth. They said a spy was apprehended after causing considerable damage to their ship."

"Yeah...?" I asked. "Was there a description of this madman?"

"No. All humans look the same to them. But they did run a DNA check and flags were tripped. You were supposed to have been permed many years ago, remember?"

"Oh yeah…" I said. "Good times!"

"Right… Well, now we're setting you up for another execution. It will be verified digitally and carefully choreographed. We're transmitting this to the Mogwa ship as evidence that we've done the job they ordered us to do years back."

While he talked, I struggled to get my wet, rubbery limbs into the uniform still clutched in my hands. I always had more trouble than most people did with smart-clothes. Each new uniform started off sized for your typical human. At two meters in height, it always seemed to take a few minutes for a fresh suit to believe it really had to stretch itself out to the limit.

"That's a damned good idea, sir," I said.

"I thought you'd like it."

Graves hustled me up the hallway to a door at the end. I could tell I was still inside Central, and the stale cold air of the hallway told me I was probably underground on one of the countless lab levels.

What happened next made me feel a little bad, but really, I argued internally, Graves had brought it upon himself. Honestly, you just can't tell a man like myself that you're going to execute him and expect him to stand around waiting for it to happen.

If his had been a standard execution, mind you, I wouldn't have cared much. But it was the permanent part of the equation I didn't like. I wasn't overly-attached to one carpet of human skin or another. If I died, well, so be it.

But no one likes the idea of ceasing to exist without at least being given a fighting chance. At that point, regulations, orders and the like all became moot to me.

I reflected as I tripped him up that Veteran Harris would have known better than to let his guard down around me. He would have expected a fight. Harris had tried to kill me personally a lot more times, after all, than Graves had.

Graves pitched forward with a grunt, and I landed a knee on his spine to keep him down. I reflected how unusual of a

54

situation this was. I'd never tangled with Graves like this before. It felt wrong to me, somehow. I regretted each hammer-blow I landed on the back of his thick skull.

Graves, however, wasn't a lightweight. Long after a man should have given up, he surprised me. He managed to twist his pistol around and fire a shot over his bloody shoulder.

Damn! That stung! I'd been burned in the throat.

I was seriously impressed. What a fine shot he'd managed to make, given the circumstances. He'd nailed me in a vital region even with his face planted on a steel deck and more hard punches on his braincase than most drunks get in a weekend. None of it had taken him out, or spoiled his aim.

Another man might have called it luck, but not me. I like to give credit where credit is due.

I rolled off him and lay back against a cold, puff-crete wall. My lungs were burning, and I heard a raspy, gargling sound. It was me, trying to draw a breath and failing.

I knew I was a goner even before Graves climbed painfully back to his feet. His face, and the back of his scalp were a mess. Between desperate breaths, he pointed his pistol at me.

With my right index finger, I swizzled up a load of blood from my larynx. I couldn't talk or breathe, but I had a little time left before I passed out.

I traced out letters on the steel floor. They were smeared, dark—almost black. Lots of people think blood is red, but really, it's almost black when you get a lot of it all at once and it starts to dry.

Graves watched me spelling. He didn't fire, and that was a good thing. Maybe he was curious, or maybe he thought it was only right that a defeated man be allowed to write his own epitaph—as long as he kept it short, mind you.

What I wrote made him frown.

"I remember?" he asked. "You remember *what*, McGill?"

But that was it for me. I sagged over and slumped, eyes staring.

I've died any number of times, and I can assure you that's what was happening to me right then.

-10-

It was a man named Claver who'd taught me the trick of getting pissed-off people to revive you. He'd said he kept coming back to life, despite all odds, by teasing his killers with a hint of information and leaving them wanting more.

It was like show-business, in a way. If your audience wanted a repeat performance, why, by damn, they'd come back later on and pay to see it again.

Coming out of the revival machine this time around, I was a bit more concerned. Was this all a waste of time?

"He seems groggy, and his numbers are off," the bio said.

"I don't care," said a familiar, gravelly voice. "As long as he can talk, I'm taking him out of here."

"Suit yourself."

Graves again? Great.

"Sir?" asked another voice, one that was depressingly familiar. "Let me get him moving for you. There will be no more funny business this time around."

"Suit yourself, Harris. But don't kill him until I give the order."

"I wouldn't dream of it, Primus!"

They soon had me off the table and staggering out the door.

The two men half-dragged me down the hallway. I let my feet flop and twist. Why not? This sorry version of James McGill might as well enjoy every moment he had left.

My eyes cleared before I reached the offices. They thrust another uniform at me, and I struggled to get into it.

Both men had pistols in their hands. They weren't taking any more chances with me.

"Is this to be another public execution, sir?" I asked Graves. "The last one went off the rails."

"No," he said. "We're done with that. We uploaded my suit-cam files to the Mogwa, proving you'd been killed. Hopefully, that will make them happy—but I doubt it."

"Well then..." I said. "Why did you get me started with breathing again?"

"You may not remember, but the last version of James McGill indicated he remembered what happened on the Mogwa ship. I don't know how that could be true, but we can't take any chances. We need intel."

"Ah, I get it," I said. "I'm supposed to tell you—"

"Excuse me, Primus," Harris interrupted, "but this is classic horseshit! McGill doesn't know his ass from a hole in the ground. He's just going to make up some crap to delay his next killing, and we're wasting time."

Graves looked at him. "I'm distinctly aware of that possibility, Harris. But this is an unusual situation. On the off-chance he knows something, I've been ordered to—"

Right about then, the situation took a radical turn. I know I didn't see it coming—even though it was apparently my idea.

A figure appeared behind Graves and Harris.

I was sitting on the floor in front of them, minding my own business. The room flickered, but I don't think they noticed. They weren't as attuned to teleportation effects, not having taken as many jaunts into the blue as I had.

What gained my full attention, however, was the figure himself. He was undeniably familiar and menacing.

Tall, suited in a costume of dark mesh, I found him an imposing figure. No wonder people were leery when I came near.

The figure was none other than James McGill. He was some other copy of James McGill from the past, of course. Probably the one who'd ported out into deep space and caused some kind of serious interplanetary ruckus with his actions.

Quick as a cat, he shot both Harris and Graves. They only had time to follow my shocked gaze and look around behind them before they caught a quick ride through the revival machine.

"Damn," I said. "That was nice shooting, James the former."

"Thank you—you're too kind, James the latter," said the other.

He stepped forward warily and crouched in front of me. I could tell he had a healthy respect for himself, as it were. It made me feel a puff of pride. Even unarmed and sitting on a steel deck, I was enough to make another armed version of myself worry.

"The question now," the intruder said, "is what are we going to do about me and you?"

"This is a whole new area of Galactic Law we're breaking right now," I agreed.

"Yes it is," he agreed.

I thought about it for a few seconds, eyeing my older self. He wasn't in good shape. He looked burned, somehow.

After about ten seconds, I came to a clear conclusion.

"You should probably just shoot me and report in," I said. "They'll want the cam feed that your suit recorded, that's for certain. I'm just a copy who knows nothing useful."

He nodded. "I was thinking along those lines," he admitted. "But it's a bit more complicated than that."

"Tell me," I said, "and talk fast."

He began talking, and I began listening. The longer we talked, the more concerned I became.

The situation *was* complicated.

A team of hogs showed up and began hammering on the door just as we were finishing up our little talk. I reached for Graves' fallen gun, but my copy shook his head.

"No," he said. "No sense in us both getting killed—again."

"Okay… You going out in a blaze of glory?"

"That's the plan. I'm screwed anyway. I *did* mention the radiation, didn't I?"

He had. One side of his face, in fact, was slagged and peeling. Both his eyes still worked, but one of them didn't have a full eyelid to close over it anymore. He figured he'd already gotten enough rads to kill a gorilla, and it was just a matter of time.

The older James threw open the door roughly, making it bang against the wall.

I don't know quite what the hog security team was expecting to see, but I'm pretty sure that the other me wasn't even on the list of possibilities.

James loomed large, pistol raised, and he shot the first hog in the face. A second head popped into view, and he shot that too.

The rest of them scrambled to the sides and clawed out their weapons. Stupid hogs. They should have had their weapons in their hands before they hammered on the door.

The situation was unfair, really. James McGill was fully in the fight, more than willing to die just for the cussedness of it. But the hogs still valued their own skins. It's hard to fight a skilled man who doesn't care if he lives or dies—ask anyone who's done it.

Before it was over, five hogs lay dead in the hallway. That was damned good killing. The total body count was seven, including Harris and Graves.

Damned fine.

When the other James was down and out at last, they came in for me. I was still sitting on the floor, but I was clapping now.

"Did you see that?" I asked a hog veteran. "He was hurt to begin with, too!"

The veteran put his pistol into my face. I didn't flinch, but I did look him in the eye.

"That was a copy of you, wasn't it, McGill?" he asked, his sides heaving.

"I think you might be right."

They hustled me to my feet, and I walked out with my head held high. They watched me like I was some kind of wild animal. I suppose that was only natural. Under the proper circumstances, I was capable of some pretty awful behavior.

The next stage of my day was the best of all. I got to preside over the rebirth of Harris and Graves.

When they came back to life, coughing and sputtering, I clapped them on the back like old friends.

"You missed it, Harris," I said. "That was some fine shooting. Best I've ever done. Seven dead, and all of it done with one bad eye."

"Fuck you, McGill," he managed to croak out.

Despite my welcoming attitude, they were both madder than puffed toads.

-11-

If anything, Graves had an even worse attitude than Harris once he was breathing again. He reached for the nearest available weapon with trembling fingers.

"Let's not start all that again, Primus," I said.

"Don't listen to this crazy ape, sir!" Harris called out. "Put him down, quick-like!"

"You killed me, McGill... " Graves snarled at me. "You son of a bitch—I'm your superior officer!"

"Yes sir, that's all quite true—and yet at the same time it isn't so. I, the person standing here before you, am innocent of that heinous crime. On behalf of that other psychotically disturbed and guilty version of myself, I must apologize profusely—and if it helps console you, your sacrifice wasn't made in vain, sir."

"What are you blathering about?" he asked, narrowing his eyes to suspicious slits.

"Just what I said, sir. This new version of McGill you see before you has it all. I'm in perfect condition, unlike the one that died in a glorious battle with a squad of hogs. I'm also in possession of several key facts that you, and all of Earth, need to know."

"That shit again?" Harris demanded angrily. "The last time you said that, your copy came in and shot us!"

"That will *not* happen again Veteran Harris," I insisted.

61

I quickly filled Graves in on recent events while he dressed and cinched up his uniform, peering at me with skepticism the whole while. Both he and Harris seemed to be in sour moods, but I didn't think the situation warranted it.

"So," Graves said, "one version of you came back here hours late and injured."

"That's right, I came back. Mission accomplished!"

"Hardly," Graves complained. "You haven't even told me what that other version of McGill told you."

"That's the critical part," I admitted. "But I need to get your agreement first that we are square. These hogs here are holding me under false arrest. This version of McGill hasn't done a damned thing."

"We don't need anything from McGill," Harris said. "His suit recorders will tell us everything."

One of the hogs, the one who was hanging onto my left arm, spoke up at that. "We can't do that veteran. We already tried. The teleport suit was damaged and all data was lost."

Graves looked at me with bitter suspicion. I shrugged in response.

"We could torture it out of him," Harris suggested.

"No…" Graves said, considering the idea. "He would just lie to us, and it would waste a lot of time."

He sighed at last in irritation. "All right, McGill. What do you want for your report?"

"Nothing special. All I need is my rank restored and all my crimes—known and unknown—forgiven."

"That's way too big of an 'ask'."

"Yeah…" I said, not bothering to argue. "How about this then? Just forget whatever I did for the last six hours or so? The whole mission."

Graves rolled his head back. "All right. But no holding back. Tell me what you know."

"It went like this, Primus—" I began, but Harris objected again.

"Primus," he said. "Don't tell me you're falling for this! He's just going to make up some wild story. He doesn't know shit from crab cakes about any Mogwa ship!"

I was beginning to get tired of Harris and his bad attitude. He'd never enjoyed anything more than seeing me executed, but it seemed like he was pushing his luck today. I made a mental note to help him change his mind if I got the chance.

Graves waved for Harris to be quiet.

"I agree to your terms, McGill," he said. "But only because we don't have much time. Now, for the love of God, tell me what the hell you did out there."

At this point I gave a cold look to the two hogs holding onto my arms. At a nod from Graves, they reluctantly released me. I struck an easy, thoughtful pose while Graves and Harris shivered and wobbled, dressing themselves with rubbery fingers.

"This is second-hand, sir," I began, clearing my throat, "but it's the best we're going to get at this point. James—that other version of me with the mean-streak—he popped out there to intercept Battle Fleet 921, which, as I understand it, is in the vicinity of Spica right now."

"That's correct. Go on."

"The problem was one of accuracy, sir," I said. "Apparently, the techs did a good job of matching velocity and momentum, but they put that other James McGill right up against the hull of the ship, rather than teleporting him inside the ship itself."

"Hmmm..." Graves said taking notes and recording me with his tapper. "The techs will be interested to hear that."

"As the Mogwa fleet was in a warp bubble at the time... well, you know there's a lot of deadly radiation inside those bubbles. James got burned, despite the shielding in his suit."

"Makes sense, go on."

"He got inside the ship somehow," I said, "but it took more than five minutes to do so."

Graves stared at me for a second. "Okay, but there's a snag... How is it he didn't just ride it out and get automatically teleported home?"

"Good question," I said.

"Damned straight it is!" Harris barked. His eyebrows were beetled together in a harsh frown.

63

"Fortunately," I continued unperturbed, "I've got a good answer. The hard landing on the ship's hull damaged the auto-return circuitry. James was forced to break in."

"Already off-script..." Graves muttered, making more notes.

I thought about calling foul on that one. What else could that poor McGill do? He could either float around out there and fry, or he could break into the ship. Didn't seem like much of a choice to me.

"Anyway, as I understand it he got aboard, took some vids, then teleported back."

They both looked at me with questioning expressions. "That's it?"

"Yes, but, that's not what makes this an urgent matter. We need to talk to Drusus because we've got this incursion by the Galactics all wrong."

Graves stepped close to me, and he stared up into my face.

"This isn't the time for extra bullshit, McGill. If you value your planet, you'll tell the truth."

"I am in full agreement, Primus! Seriously, this is a big deal. Take me to see Drusus, if you please!"

He heaved a sigh. Harris peered at me over his shoulder.

"He's full of it, sir. I've seen it many times. He looks dumb—and he *is* about as dumb as a rock—but he's got some kind of animal scheme going on inside his head anyway."

"I thank you for your support, Veteran," I said.

"Let's go," Graves said resignedly.

I followed Graves, and Harris followed me. I heard the man behind me muttering all the way to the elevators. When we reached Drusus' offices at last, we weren't kept waiting.

We walked in together. I hadn't been given my weapons back yet, either. I found that significant. They didn't trust me—not that I could blame them.

"James McGill..." Drusus said. "It seems I can't pass a day in peace around here without hearing your name."

"These aren't peaceful times, Equestrian," I said.

He walked around his desk to meet me. "What can I do for you?"

"I think I can help you," I said, and I quickly outlined the day's events. I left out most of the killing—Graves had covered for me on that as part of our deal.

"Yes," he said, "I do understand you've had a busy afternoon. Now, give me your report and make it quick."

"It's about the Mogwa, sir," I said. "They aren't coming here to erase Earth. They're coming here to trim down our empire."

"*Our* empire?"

"We gained three hundred worlds, more or less, when the squids surrendered. That means we've become too big in their eyes. Normally, they would destroy an upstart civilization like ours—but they can't spare the time or the firepower."

"Hmm… How do they plan to trim us down, then?"

I shook my head. "That's the part that's unclear. I know they're bringing along Nairbs and they plan to perform some kind of an audit."

"An audit… great. How, pray tell, did that other version of you manage to come by this information? It would hardly be something you could see with a body-cam."

I squirmed a bit. This was the tricky part. The part I hadn't explained to Graves and Harris, for fear they might take it the wrong way.

"Well sir…" I began, "my previous copy was known to have violent tendencies. In fact, I think he might have been a bad grow all along."

Drusus transfixed me with an intense stare. "Go on."

"Well… he might have… *might have*, mind you, coerced a Mogwa crewman into giving up this information."

Everyone's jaw dropped. It was like having three baby birds surrounding me, all waiting for dinner.

"You're joking," Drusus said.

"Nope… afraid not—but I wasn't there personally, so I can't swear to any part of the story as more than earnestly delivered hearsay."

Drusus began to pace. "You popped out there, broke into their ship, damaging an airlock. That was bad enough. But then, you dared to accost a Mogwa citizen—a Galactic citizen—and interrogate it?"

"Uh… that's about right, yes. Except again, it wasn't *me*, sir, who did this. Not exactly."

"Put a sock in it, McGill," Graves said. "Sir, I want to apologize on behalf of all Legion Varus for this unsanctioned activity."

Drusus laughed bitterly. "Apologize? You think that will be enough? They'll wipe us clean, Graves. It's as good as done now if it wasn't before."

"Now, hold on," I said. "I'm not as dumb as all that. According to that other James fellow, he killed the Mogwa and disposed of it before he left. The Empire can't prove who did this."

They gaped at me again. The Mogwa were our overlords. *Unquestioned* overlords, who ruled over a thousand craptastic planets like Earth. The mere concept that I would torment, question, and murder one of them on their own ship was so monstrous they could barely conceive of it.

"McGill," Drusus said, "the Mogwa are a lot of things, but they're not idiots. They know a spy struck their ship. Coincidentally, they're on their way out here to trim down an upstart civilization on the frontier of the galaxy. You think they'll believe that a damaged airlock and a missing crewman are all just a giant coincidence?"

I shrugged. "They have their suspicions, sure. But as someone who's been making his own rules for a while, I can tell you most people are blinded by their own adherence to the straight-and-narrow. I'd bet the Mogwa are blaming one another, or one of their Galactic enemies from the Core Worlds instead of us."

"Hmm…" Drusus said. "It could be true…" He heaved a sigh. "Well, what's done is done. Executing you for this would be cathartic, but pointless. Either you've doomed us all, or you haven't. Either way, you're dismissed—and that goes for all of you. Get out."

We high-tailed it out of his office. I, for one, was glad the day was over.

"Either of you gentlemen feel like a drink?" I asked. "I'm buying—it's the least I could do."

Graves shook his head and walked off. Harris glared at me, but he finally relented.

"You owe me McGill—and you're right, buying a round is the least you could do."

I smiled. Harris liked free booze just as much as the next legionnaire.

-12-

Harris and I had been at each other's throats for a long time now. I'd usually gotten the best of him more than my share of the time over the years. Strangely, however, we could get along fine when times were bad enough.

Sure, the stars hanging above us were full of approaching death and destruction—but the fleet wasn't here quite yet. When faced with war in the morning, a soldier's mind often turned to celebrating life on the evening before.

As we were well past the stage of youthful competition, I was determined to get Harris into a better mood. The ornery cuss had deserved everything I'd ever dished out, but tonight I felt that I'd clearly established myself as the tougher man. So I set out to make peace with the old dog this evening—who knows, it might even make him shine.

We were stacking beer bottles several hours later, and we refused to let the waitress remove them.

"That's a work of art, Miss!" I told her.

"I'm going to put the capstone on this pyramid," Harris added.

The waitress rolled her eyes at us and walked away, shrugging.

Harris stood and swayed slightly. I should have been watching him, but I was looking after the waitress instead. We'd chosen a bar where every girl was required to wear shorts that were paper thin and tight as your t-shirt after a buffet. That made it hard for a man like me to focus on anything else.

Harris made his move, placing the last bottle on the top tier—but he blew it. A cascade of glass, menus and coasters came crashing down. Somehow, we were both bleeding at the end of it, but we were laughing, too.

They threw us out after that, pausing only long enough to scan our tappers. The bill was high, and I thought they were probably ripping us off. Fortunately, we were both too drunk to care.

Once out on the street we began staggering back toward Central.

"McGill," Harris told me seriously, "you are without a doubt the biggest donkey-dick I've ever served with."

"Have you forgotten I'm a centurion now?" I asked, but I wasn't really angry.

"A centurion? Where's your unit?"

He had me there. "I guess I'm really more of a staffer," I admitted.

That set him off on a gust of laughter. "A staffer? You? No, sir! You're a born killer, boy. A killer set upon this Earth to commit as much destruction, murder and mayhem as humanly possible."

Finding his points impossible to argue with, I didn't bother. We both walked back into the military part of town without a care in the world. Sure, the Mogwa ships were gliding closer every second, but for right now, we didn't care one whit.

Now and then, one of us reached out a hand to steady the other. That prevented anyone from doing a face-plant on the puff-crete any number of times.

We heard a tram approaching at one point, but we didn't even take a look over our shoulders. So it came as a surprise when a round face poked out of a tram window to address us.

"Harris? McGill?" a familiar voice called out. "Looks like you two are in love. If you guys are going to bone, can I watch?"

I stopped walking and peered at the man in the tram. My eyes were blurry, but I could tell who it was anyway. It was Bio Specialist Carlos Ortiz.

"Carlos?" I asked. "What are you doing here?"

"Coming to look for you, sir," he said. "Graves said I was to round you up. The whole legion is being mustered, and I live to serve."

"They're mustering the legion? What for?"

"Might have something to do with that approaching death-fleet, but they don't tell me details. Get in, sir."

We climbed into the backseat and our heads lolled. The city lights blinded me as Carlos drove us back to Central.

I wasn't in any state of mind to be doing deep thinking, but if Legion Varus was mustering back in—well, that had to be serious.

When we got to Central, Harris and I managed to straighten up our kits a little. It wasn't enough to impress Graves, however.

"You guys are sloppy drunk," he said. "Ortiz, sober them up."

Carlos grinned. As a bio, he had all kinds of nasty brews in his medical kit. He shot each of us in the neck with an injection gun. Not only did that sting, but within ninety seconds, Harris and I were puking violently.

"Here, drink this," Carlos said, handing out squeeze bottles of something fizzy.

I did as he asked, but I spat it back out. "That tastes like horse-piss!"

"Close. It's anti-tox. You'll be clear-headed in half an hour."

It took less than that to put my mind into a murderous mood. The injection and the detox concoction had neutralized the alcohol in my system, but it hadn't done anything about all the normal effects of a hangover.

Sitting next to Harris with slumped shoulders, I listened to a briefing in Graves' office. There were a few dozen other centurions and adjuncts there. When they ran out of room and realized Harris was only a non-com, they kicked him out.

With an effort of will, I did my damnedest to pay attention to what Primus Graves was saying.

"The mission will be a special one," he said. "We're using a new kind of ship—an insertion ship. We'll be flown to an undisclosed location where we'll do some clean-up. When we're done with that, we'll head home the fast way."

I was still a little bit fuzzy, so I lifted my hand in confusion. "Primus sir? What's the fast way?"

"Are you still drunk, McGill?"

"Uh… no, sir. Sadly, I'm not."

He frowned at me. "I'm saying this is a one-way trip. We'll plant our device and blow ourselves up. We won't fly home— we'll die out there. Earth will revive us all as soon as the detonation is confirmed."

This had me confused and concerned. "What's the point then, sir?" I asked. "Why don't we just send a warship out to this target and blow it up from orbit?"

He shook his head. "That's not a bad idea, but it's been considered and rejected. The site is sure to be inspected. This is all your fault anyway, McGill. You should really stop complaining."

A lot of unhappy officers swung their attention toward me. Unfortunately, it wasn't the loving kind of attention.

"Just how was it my fault, Primus Graves?"

"You informed us of the intentions of the Galactics. They planned to perform an audit, remember? Well, there are some things we've been doing that we don't want the Galactics to see. Accordingly, we're going to erase these facilities before the Nairbs are able to document anything."

"I get it," I said. "We're flushing the evidence. I'm with you now, Primus. Please continue the briefing."

His lips formed a tight line, and he turned back to his desk. As he touched various points on it, the imagery displayed on the wall behind him flashed into being and swung around with startling rapidity. If I'd had anything left in my stomach, I might have hurled it up just then.

It was odd, listening to these details, to think that most of the members of Legion Varus would be completely in the dark until we were well on our way to our destination. That had been my lot in life until recently. As a Centurion, however, I ranked highly enough to be in the know ahead of time.

"McGill!" Graves shouted.

I realized I'd zoned out for a few seconds—or maybe minutes. It must have been the hangover combined with Carlos' evil brew of antidotes. Then again, maybe it was the fact I'd never been good at listening to lectures of any kind—by anybody—even when my life depended on it.

"Yes, Primus!" I shouted back.

"Are you listening to me? Your unit will come down *here* and deploy on these coordinates. Is that clear?"

"Uh... sure," I said, leaning forward and staring at the maps as if seeing them for the first time—which I was.

The depicted planet was a rocky, smoky hole-in-the-sky. It appeared to be slightly larger than Earth with a toxic atmosphere of corrosive gases. It was thoroughly unpleasant by human standards.

I took all this in, but they were still staring at me. Everyone was.

"Well?" Graves asked.

"Are we killing humans on this one, Primus?"

"No—not exactly. They're humanoids, but not humans. They're a subspecies the Cephalopods enslaved, but now they're on their own."

"And why again are we killing them, sir?"

His face darkened. "I didn't say what exact crime they committed. No one told me, and you'll be the last to know if they do at some point."

"But you must know something. Who *are* they?"

"All you have to know is that they need to be eliminated. This is a laboratory working on technical secrets. They call themselves 'tech-smiths' which sounds innocent enough, but they've gone rogue. Their entire installation must be erased before it's located by the Galactics."

"That's good enough for me," I said. "I've got the deployment point down, sir."

"Good," Graves said, "but what I asked was if you thought you could get your team from the drop point to the dome wall within thirty minutes or less. Timing is critical here, McGill."

Frankly, I had no clue if I could do what he was suggesting, but I put on my serious face to make him happy. I stared at the scenario depicted by the computers, which had green and red force-movement arrows going every which-way. As far as I could tell over the next seven seconds of stalling, I was supposed to get a group of troops from the insertion point at the bottom of a small crater up to some kind of dome-thingy. That had to happen within the span of a half hour.

The ground looked very rough, all spikes and pits. There were a few red boxes too, which I figured were probably some kind of defensive installation—but then I caught sight of the distance estimate in digital numbers. Four kilometers, it read.

I snorted and leaned back confidently.

"I can do four kilometers blind-folded, sir," I said. "No problem."

Graves nodded. "All right then. I'm going to hold you to that."

"Just one thing, Primus," I said. "What outfit will I be leading? I've been promoted, but I'm not aware of any assigned—"

"You've got my old unit. The 3rd is yours. Just have a heart and don't wipe them until this mission is complete."

Graves' announcement came as a shock, but it made sense. Since Graves had moved up to Primus, his old unit was in need of a commander. My follow-up promotion had plugged me right in.

All my old comrades would be under my command. They'd be saluting me now, sure, but at least we'd all know what to expect from one another from the start.

As I contemplated my first actions as a unit commander, my promotion to centurion began to feel real to me for the first time.

It's one thing to have some new doodad stapled onto your shoulders, but it's quite another to be put in charge of a hundred and twenty armed fighters who relied entirely on you and your judgment.

Despite my foggy state of mind, I resolved silently to behave as a man reformed. I had serious responsibilities now, and I wasn't going to shirk them. That old, shifty James McGill was a figment of the past.

Graves kept on talking while I entertained these thoughts, but I didn't listen much. I figured I'd pick it all up on the flight out to the targeted rock.

The whole operation looked like a cakewalk to me, anyways. After all, what could a bunch of science nerds in flapping lab coats do to oppose a professional force of legionnaires?

They were already burnt toast in my mind.

-13-

Stepping out of the meeting twenty minutes later, I found Harris waiting out in the hallway.

"Well, McGill?" he asked worriedly. "What kind of a bug-hunt is this going to be? Give it to me straight."

I looked at him seriously. Graves had admonished us, not five minutes ago, to keep our destination a complete secret. That said, Harris' question didn't seem out of line.

"It's not a bug-hunt, as far as I can tell. Looks like a pretty easy assignment."

He squinted at me. "Are you shitting me? All this prep and black-out—you're telling me it's going to be easy?"

"The target looks pretty soft," I said. "Sometimes, you're quiet because you're not so proud of your plans, not because you think the other side can stop you."

I began walking, and Harris fell into step beside me.

"What's your role then?" he asked. "Are you doing some kind of cowboy raid or something? Maybe teleporting in and playing commando?"

I stopped walking and turned to him, giving him my biggest, shittiest Georgia grin. "I've got great news, Veteran," I said. "I've been assigned a combat unit on this one."

"Really? A Varus unit? I thought you were special ops."

"Nope. Not today."

He looked at me thoughtfully. "But what unit? Has Winslade decided to…"

75

Suddenly, the light bulb went on inside Harris' fridge. He looked up at me, his eyeballs big and white all around.

"You're *shitting* me," he breathed.

"That's right! Your ship has come in, Veteran. You and I— we're going to be working together, tighter than two ticks in a dog's ear."

His jaw dropped, but he didn't get angry. He didn't start shouting or run back to whine at Graves. He didn't even turn away and leave. He just walked alongside of me. He moved like a man who was numb—a man who'd awakened from a nightmare only to find out it had all been real.

"Oh now, don't take it so hard, Harris," I said. "I'm an easy-going commander. I don't even care you called me a donkey-dick a few hours back. That's water under the bridge."

"Who's my adjunct… sir?" he asked quietly.

That almost broke my heart. Harris had sworn for years that if there was one thing in this world he'd never do, it was call me sir. His brain had been sprained when I'd become an adjunct over him, but this time, calling me sir and all… Well, he sounded like a broken man.

"Hmm," I said, looking at him with a frown. "Could you hold on here for a minute, Vet?"

"Here sir?"

"Yeah. Just wait right here."

I did a U-turn and went back to Graves' office. It took me maybe five minutes, and a string of promises longer than a tall girl's arm, but I wouldn't be denied.

Returning to the hallway. I found Harris with his eyes closed, leaning back against the wall. He opened them again when I came toward him, and I saw they were bloodshot like he'd poured bathroom cleaner into both of them.

Taking his hand, I placed a small box in his palm and closed his fist.

"What's this?" he asked suspiciously. "Are we supposed to swallow suicide bombs again?"

He was referring to an unfortunate incident we'd shared long ago. But I shook my head.

"Nah," I said. "Nothing like that. It's a present. Open it up.'"

He did so suspiciously. When he saw a shine coming from inside the box, his jaw sagged down of its own accord.

"Is this bullshit, McGill?" he asked.

"No, it's not some cruel joke."

"But I didn't take any tests. I didn't even apply to be an officer!"

He took out the single bars of an adjunct and looked at them wonderingly.

"Well, if you don't want them," I said, "I guess I could take this box back to Graves."

He put the insignia on his shoulders and snapped the box shut.

"No, I want this…" he said. "I think I've earned it, too."

I clapped him on the shoulder. "If you haven't yet, you will in the future. I guarantee it."

Harris and I had a strange relationship. Mostly, it'd been bad from the start. But today, I dared hope we could turn over a new leaf. Maybe we'd stop fighting so much of the time and act like a team. Well, a man can dream, anyway.

We spent a few hours organizing our new unit. With Harris as my sidekick, I felt more comfortable, honestly.

But there was another voice to deal with—two of them in fact. Adjuncts Toro and Leeson were frankly stunned by this series of events. What's more, Harris' promotion seemed almost as offensive to them as mine was.

"Let me get this straight," Leeson said. "I've been plowing shit for this legion for thirty years, and the most junior hick in the outfit gets promoted over me?"

"On top of that," Toro chimed in, "the noisiest veteran in the unit moves up into the officer ranks without so much as a memo appearing on my tapper?"

Harris and I glanced at each other. We'd both been insulted, but that wasn't too surprising. Leeson had always been a complainer—and Toro? Well, she wasn't the best officer even on a good day.

"I guess Graves calls them like he sees them," I said in an uncompromising tone. "Now team, we've got to pull it together right-quick. We've got a special transport, the *Nostrum*, coming to pick us up in the morning."

"What port?" Leeson asked. "Monrovian or New Dulles?"

I blinked. I realized I must have day-dreamed through that part of the briefing. "Uh… I'll find out. I got to the briefing late."

Harris bent over his tapper while I continued talking to my new adjuncts. They were suspicious, and a mite pissed off. They did seem to be listening, however.

"That's it, sir?" Toro asked when I'd finished.

I nodded.

"To get to the waypoint markers on the ground," she said, "we have to cross four kilometers of rocks—but what do we do when we get to the target?"

"We penetrate the dome, which is supposed to be defended by automated installations."

"Pillboxes? Drone turrets?"

"Something like that," I said, "we'll get past all that and enter the dome. Anyone there is to be arrested and removed. If they resist, we shoot them. The bombs will fall after we signal the all-clear anyway."

Leeson squinted at me. "McGill, why are they sending a legion if there's only a handful of scientists down there?"

"Well… there was mention of some secret weapons development. Earth gov gave them notice to evacuate, and some did. But others stayed behind. I think they might have delusions of seeking independence."

Leeson snorted. "There's no such thing—fools!"

"That's right, and we'll give them that message loud and clear. When they see us storming into their dome, I'm pretty sure the nerds will fold up and beg for mercy."

Mollified, my adjuncts stood to break up the meeting, but Harris spoke up. He'd been messing with his tapper since the start of the meeting.

"New Dulles," he said. "We ship out from there at 0800 hours."

I nodded to him. "Thanks," I said, and I meant it. Maybe Harris *would* be useful if he kept feeding me facts that I was too lazy to look up for myself.

"Wait a minute," Leeson said. "There's something I don't get."

"What's the problem?" I asked.

"This new transport is fast and light, correct? But we only have enough room aboard for our own troops on the way out. Are you talking about evacuating survivors? How many scientists are we talking about?"

"Uh…" I began, blanking out.

Harris was all over his tapper. Apparently, he'd already gotten access to the officers' briefing notes. "An estimated five to fifteen thousand of them stayed under the dome," he said. "That's according to our recent intel."

Leeson and Toro both looked suspicious. It was an occupational hazard when you fought for an outfit like Legion Varus.

"How the hell are we going to take that many prisoners off-world with us?" Toro demanded. "How big is this starship, the *Nostrum*?"

I felt just a tad of unfamiliar heat coming from under my collar. Although I knew the answer to this one, I didn't want to tell them they were going to be fried on the planet when the bombs fell. That kind of information wasn't helpful for morale.

"There's a contingency plan for that," I said firmly. "We'll find out more on the trip out there, I'm sure."

That seemed to satisfy Leeson and Toro, who moved off to get their people marching in the right direction. Standard operating procedure in these situations was to herd the troops aboard a sky-train to the airport and have them sleep on the lifter. They tended to get lost and go AWOL otherwise.

Assigning my adjuncts to the duty of keeping my unit together, I slipped out of Central as soon as I could. After all, rank did have its privileges, and I felt I'd suffered enough over the last few days to warrant an unscheduled break.

-14-

We had about twelve hours left until go-time when I finally got out of Central. That wasn't much time, even for an experienced legionnaire, but I was determined to make the best of it.

I called my parents and told them to hang on, because I wouldn't be able to help them for a few weeks. They'd made it home all right after the incident at the Mustering Hall, but they'd been worrying about me ever since.

The fortunate news I'd been promoted erased all their concerns. I assured them I'd come back home as soon as the mission was done—almost instantly, in fact.

They didn't get it, but that was okay. They carried on for a time, worrying about me in advance. I told them about my promotion and took a few shots of myself with my new shoulder-bling in place. That settled them down and got their minds onto a more positive track.

"You're *sure* you'll be back in a month?" my dad asked. "That's quicker than usual."

"I'm pretty sure."

"Don't worry about me," my mom said. "I'll be just fine. One more transfusion next week should keep me going until you get back."

She sounded and looked as weak as a cat on my tapper screen. I frowned at that. I might have to hurry my plans along.

"I'll see if I can speed things up," I told both of them, and I signed off.

Until that moment, I hadn't been sure where this version of James McGill might want to spend his last night on Earth. But an hour later found me knocking at the door of Anne Grant once again.

Anne opened it a crack and peered out into the dark. I knew there were cameras on me, but she seemed surprised to see it was really me anyway.

"James?" she said. "Why are you back here tonight?"

"Oh, come on," I said. "After yesterday, a man could hardly expect to be satisfied with a night alone."

She didn't open it any farther. "Struck out at the local bar, did you?"

"What? No way. Smell my breath, as God is my witness, I haven't had a drop tonight."

She heaved a sigh and opened the door. She was wearing a gauzy pink robe that went down just far enough to cover her butt. I followed her in with that formal invite and plopped myself on her couch.

"Hey," I said, "have you heard the Legion is shipping out in the morning?"

"Yes... they sent me a reenlistment offer."

"Really? You joining back up again?"

Anne shook her head. She had gripped her pink robe in her hands and wrapped it tightly over her breasts. She looked at me with continued suspicion. I was not yet feeling lucky about the situation here.

"Is that why you're here?" she asked. "To get me to come back to Varus?"

"No ma'am. I wouldn't dream of ruining an idyllic life like this one. I'm here for some company before I go off and die again."

Anne sighed and seemed to relax somewhat. That's about when she noticed the red crest on my sleeve and the bars on my lapels.

"You're a centurion now?" she exclaimed in obvious shock.

"That's right," I said. "Graves moved up to primus, leaving an opening."

"But you had to be the lowest man on the seniority list…" she said, thinking hard. "Leeson and Toro must be pissed off."

"They took it pretty well, all things considered."

She cocked her head, and I could tell she was thinking hard. I hated that look when it crossed a woman's face. It almost always meant trouble for the likes of James McGill.

"You had to have help to move up this fast… You're kissing up to Turov again, aren't you?"

"No ma'am!" I said. "She's not happy with me at all, let me assure you of that."

Anne chuckled. "All right. I believe you, I guess. It's a pretty easy thing to believe."

"Yeah…" I said, my eyes wandering around the place. "You mind if I dig in your fridge?"

She indicated I should take what I wanted with a wave of her hand. I jumped up and got to business. The contents of her kitchen weren't overwhelming, mind you. She was a single skinny girl living alone, but I made do.

Bringing back a pair of beers, I cracked them open and put one in front of her. Then I made a meal out of yogurt and cold chicken.

She talked while I ate—sitting on one corner of the couch, hugging her knees. This didn't bother me at all. In fact, I thought it was a good thing. Women often felt better about you after they told you a couple hundred things about their day.

But something she said over the next ten minutes caught my attention, a remarkable feat in and of itself.

"What's that?" I asked. "You're working for a private revival firm? I didn't think there were any of those."

She let her head roll back and stared at the ceiling.

"There are," she said. "I tried to run my own practice, but regs for civilian medical work are different than they are in the military. I could only get a job playing nursemaid. But then I found this deal. The money was too good to pass up."

I eyed her intently. "How can regular people afford revivals?"

She shrugged. "With cash, of course. It's still expensive, but there's money rolling into this planet now. All those squid worlds we took over—they need services. The tax-money isn't *all* going into the new fleet."

"Huh," I said, considering various scheming thoughts. "Anne, what if I were to make you a proposition?"

She released a puff of air. "I've been waiting for that."

"No, no, not like that. Not exactly."

Anne smiled at me, she got up and sat down next to me. Her butt, barely covered by that pink gauzy stuff, was right up against mine. Her legs were bare, and due to her sudden proximity, I found I had trouble thinking about anything else.

She kissed me then.

What could I do? What would *any* proper man do? I wrapped my arms around her and got to business. She felt good in my arms, and she smelled good, too.

My last night on Earth turned out to be a fine one, but I kept having nagging thoughts about my parents. I knew I couldn't help them yet. I just had to come up with the right angle to do it.

Pretty soon, I forgot about all that and just enjoyed myself. Anne seemed to be happy, too. We fell asleep together and dreamt of peaceful times.

-15-

My tapper woke me up in the morning. I opened one eye and looked at it. I was relieved that the caller was Della and not Graves.

"Why didn't you talk to Etta—or me?" she demanded.

"About what?" I sat up and blinked away the sleep.

"About our mission! We're leaving her again, and she didn't even know!"

It was never a good idea with the ladies, but I couldn't help it. I rolled my eyes. She caught that through my tapper vid, and she didn't like it. She was beginning to pick up on Earth gestures after all.

"Your attitude is completely selfish," she said, "I see it clearly. What kind of father doesn't tell his girl he's going off to die again?"

"Oh, come on, Della," I said. "My parents were supposed to tell her. I didn't exactly have time to go home for a tearful goodbye. I was kinda busy getting killed and revived a couple of times. Besides, I've been raising her, not you. She's tough as nails, in case you hadn't noticed."

"You're wrong," she said. "She was emotional when I told her we're both going. Earth is still new to her."

"Well, if you already told her, why are you busting me about it?" I demanded, but as soon as I said it, I knew the answer.

She was feeling bad about leaving her daughter. Sure, she didn't know beans about raising a kid, but she still had some of those mothering instincts buried inside somewhere. If there was one thing I knew well about women—besides the easy stuff—it was they didn't like feeling guilty. She was lashing out at me, making it all my fault.

Sucking in a breath, I forced a tight smile. "Listen," I said in a consolatory tone. "We're going to be back really soon. I'll call her right now and make sure she knows that."

"Don't even tell her that much. She's not dumb. The only way we could return in a month is if we die out there and get revived back home."

"Yeah… she might figure that out. Well, I'll just tell her not to worry. You're right, I should have talked to her myself already."

That seemed to settle Della down. While I'd been talking to her, Anne had hung out of sight. Now, she came forward and kissed me.

"It's hard to think of you as a father," she said. "Are you a good one?"

"No," I admitted, "but in my defense, Della isn't the best mother, and I haven't quite figured out how to get Etta to show affection."

Anne laughed at me, hugged me, and ushered me out the door with a wrapped up breakfast burrito in my hand. I hadn't even had time to shower. I had to get to New Dulles.

The skyways were full of stragglers and supply ships as I got to the lifter and my new unit strapped in. I'd taken the time to call everyone who I thought might care about my departure—including Etta. Just as I'd expected, my daughter seemed unconcerned about my prolonged absence.

"Can I sleep in your shack?" Etta asked.

"Yeah, I guess that'd be all right," I grumbled.

"Good, because Grandma said you wouldn't want me to."

"Uh… on second thought, maybe you ought to stay in the house."

She looked angry and stubborn. Here we go again. I sighed, because I knew what this meant. The girl was going to do as she damned well pleased.

After we said our goodbyes, I settled in for the flight up to orbit with the rest of the troops. One of the decks was sealed off from the rest.

"What's going on?" I asked Harris as I moved to a porthole he was staring through.

The porthole looked into the sealed deck. There were troops in there—and they looked mighty young.

"Don't you know?" he asked. "Don't you remember this part?"

"Remember what? These troops look like kids…"

Then, all of a sudden, I *did* remember.

"Oh… new recruits…"

"You've got it," he said, clapping his hands together joyously. "I'm here scouting out the best picks to flesh out our unit. We lost a few quitters after the Cephalopod War ended."

Nodding, I watched the scene with him. It looked like a high school bus full of band geeks to me. They were messing around, punching each other and playing with their newly issued equipment.

The lifter took off, and we began our assent. Harris kept watching the recruits, chuckling at them. He seemed to really be enjoying the thought of what was coming next. I began to suspect, in fact, that he wasn't really scouting at all. He was having a good time.

Finally, when we reached low orbit, there were odd sounds. The sounds of suction and hissing air.

The kids hadn't been issued helmets, of course. They were strapped in tightly, too. As the air was pumped out of the chamber, they began to suffocate. I found this hard to watch, remembering the terror I'd felt when they'd pulled this same trick on me.

A trio of enterprising recruits freed themselves pretty quickly and approached our position. As I recalled, I'd used my physical length of body to reach the bulkheads and attempt to escape. This group did it the more conventional way, using teamwork.

The trio must have seen us watching them, so they came our way. Harris grinned at them, but I felt a somber mood come over me. I knew I was wearing a stony mask, the same expression Graves had worn as he'd watch me die for my first time.

The three struggled mightily, but they were running out of air.

"Ha!" Harris laughed. "These kids have heart, don't they? They might even make it."

Two of them formed a pyramid for the third, who was a girl. She climbed on top and reached the bulkhead wheel. She gave it a good try, and she had leverage, but although it shifted on our side, it didn't open. She just didn't have the upper body strength to do it—or maybe the lack of oxygen was getting to her by now.

Behind these three, most of the kids were out cold in their seats, dead or dying.

The girl looked at me, eyes pleading. I knew what she was feeling too—she had to be wondering why this officer wasn't helping to save her? She had no idea it was a test, the first cruel test of many.

"Wow, does that little dynamo have the stuff or what?" Harris laughed. "She'll make specialist by the end of her first year, mark my words."

For some reason, his amusement rubbed me the wrong way. I put my helmet on and closed the faceplate. Harris didn't even notice. He was too busy giggling about the dying recruits.

Then, I reached out my hand and spun the wheel on our side of the hatch. It helped that the girl was tugging on it with all her fading strength.

The hatch sprung open and this took Harris by surprise. It wasn't supposed to work that way. Almost always, the entire chamber full of fresh recruits died. They were *supposed* to die. It was part of their training.

Harris hadn't bothered to put on his helmet. That was a safety violation all by itself, so I didn't feel too badly about what happened next.

The air in our small observation chamber depressurized explosively. I was braced for this, as I was holding onto the side of the hatchway. Harris was not. The hatch slammed open and took him by surprise. He pitched into the low-pressure chamber like a bug sucked into a radiator.

His face smashed onto the seats, and his body launched into the two boys who'd been holding up their companion. The boys were already convulsing and blue-faced by now.

As the girl was hanging onto the wheel which opened the hatch, she was the closest of them. I handed Harris's helmet to her—he'd left that behind when he'd flown into the chamber. She pulled it over her head with numb fingers. Stray blonde hairs were pinched off, almost blocking the seal. She didn't seem to notice.

Everyone in the chamber died in the end, except for the girl and Harris. The helmet had saved the girl, but the way I figured it, sheer cussedness had saved Harris. When air was finally pumped back in, he didn't look too good, but Harris was still kicking.

"McGill..." he gasped. He came up to me with his hands on his knees. "That was very unprofessional."

"What do you mean, Adjunct?"

"I mean you saved that girl just because she's cute! That sort of thing is poison for morale. Once the troops realize their leader is only interested in flirting with certain members of the unit, they won't respect your judgment. They'll realize there are pets and favorites who—"

"Now, hold on," I said. "I don't play favorites. I let you suffocate, didn't I?"

He glowered at me with bloodshot eyes. "I'm going to have to report this to Primus Graves," he wheezed.

"Yeah... You run along and do that, but consider this: maybe I have my own ideas about building morale. Maybe our best performers need to be rewarded with survival."

He eyed me angrily, puked, and glared at me some more. I grew tired of that, and so I helped the surviving girl to the infirmary.

The bio people looked surprised when I walked her into the med unit. They ran wands over her and clucked their tongues.

"I don't know," said the bio in charge. She was a big-shouldered woman with the disposition of a junkyard dog. "This recruit appears to have too many ruptured alveoli. We should recycle her."

"Aw, come on," I said. "Give her a few hours, and give her lungs a shot of that artificial surfactant stuff. She'll pull through."

The bio eyed me and put her hands on her hips.

"What kind of a centurion are you?" she demanded in a lowered voice. "You'll derail our training regimen if you baby these new grunts."

"You let me worry about that," I told her.

The girl recruit was named Sarah. She was still enduring bouts of painful coughing, but she gave me a grateful look. I have to admit, I'm a sucker for that.

The bio threw up her hands. "Suit yourself. It's your unit Centurion—but if you interfere, you own it—or her, in this case."

"Huh?"

"I'm recommending to Graves that this recruit be placed in your unit," she said. "If she lags, that's your responsibility."

"Oh... okay."

When I left the med center, Sarah followed me like a lost puppy.

"What do I do now, sir?" she asked.

"You head back to that chamber. There's lots of blood, puke and bodies that need to be cleaned up. The rest of your people will return to help as soon as they catch a revive."

Sarah shuddered a little at the thought of cleaning up a hundred dead bodies.

"Can you tell me something, sir?" she asked.

"Why we did it?" I asked. "It's all part of the playbook here. Part of your desensitization to death."

"No, no, I get that," she said. "I figured that out as soon as you wouldn't open the hatch for us. But what I'd like to know, sir... is does it get better after this test?"

I shook my head slowly. "Nope. Sure doesn't. This is only the beginning. It'd be for the best if you toughen up right now in preparation for what's coming."

Sarah looked dazed and lost, but I knew I couldn't coddle her any longer. I left her alone, standing in the hatchway. She stared at a mass of tangled bodies, all frozen in their last moments. Many appeared to be straining for life, even though they'd clearly lost the battle.

I felt a pang for her. I truly did. But Harris and that bitchy-bio did have a point. Everybody had to grow up sometime—especially if they'd made the grim error of signing on with Legion Varus.

-16-

The lifter took us to a waiting transport. Just one look told me Starship *Nostrum* was an entirely different class of transport.

The ship was beautiful. Her lines were sleek, whereas old *Corvus* had been lumpy and square-looking. *Nostrum* looked like a bird of prey built in flat planes and geometric shapes.

Soon after boarding, the officers for our cohort gathered together for an important meeting. I was new to being a centurion—but it seemed to me already that there were way too many meetings involved.

"Excuse me, Primus?" I asked, interrupting Graves.

He didn't even bother to crane his neck around to look at me. "What is it, McGill?"

We were in the middle of planning out our training regimen for the flight out to Arcturus. We had a large number of fresh recruits aboard who had to be taught how to handle snap-rifles in very short order. That was a valid goal, certainly, but I'd been having trouble paying attention to the minutia.

The source of my distraction was the amazing view the conference room afforded us of the universe outside the ship. The walls depicted space around us, which was nothing new. Most ships I'd been aboard had contained what we called "observation rooms." These were usually far forward in the prow of the vessel. Equipped with windows, they offered direct viewing of a star system when a starship was traveling at sub-light speeds.

But direct optics didn't work in a warp-bubble. When you were truly underway, traveling between the stars at a significant speed, the imagery was all interpolated from navigational data and displayed on the windows artificially.

I'd always liked observation rooms. The best part was the fantastically high resolution. Equipped with nothing better than human eyes, you'd have to get out a magnifying glass and start doing physics calculations on your tapper to find the slightest flaw.

This new ship didn't restrict such viewing pleasures to a single area, like an observation room. Instead, most chambers displayed the exterior view of the universe sliding past us to the stern.

"Sir," I said, staring at the gorgeous display around us, "who built this new ship?"

Graves actually moved his head when I asked this. He turned to look at me.

"Why do you ask that?"

"Well sir, I haven't seen a single Skrull running around. The crew seems human. And the tech—well, it's just more friendly and natural than I'm used to. Even this ability to see outside the hull—it's just plain fantastic. Not like the unimaginative Skrull at all."

Graves stared at me for a second before answering. "This ship was built by a new trading partner. That's the official word, and you're not going to ask that question ever again. Don't even bring that topic up."

Some would call me thick-headed, but I can tell when I've pissed off a superior.

"Yes sir," I said, and I lowered my roving eyes back to the briefing table between us.

The table was depicting the central exercising chamber. It was a lot like the region reserved for activities on every transport ship, but bigger. There were also new options for training scenarios.

"Here's the deal," Graves said. "The atmosphere will be toxic on this mission, but we aren't going to tell the troops that.

The plants and water features will all look healthy and safe. You can warn your troops one time to keep their helmets on—but that's it."

My lips worked, wanting to say something, but I resisted the urge. I can tell you—that was a real effort on my part.

"This is going to be a special drill," Graves said. "Several teams of new recruits will be facing each other in open battle. The difference is both sides will be unarmed as far as conventional weaponry goes. The primary purpose is to teach them how to deal with enemy humanoids who are hostile, but who don't possess weapons."

That was more than I could take. I cleared my throat.

Graves ignored me and pressed on. "McGill, you'll be assigned thirty regular troops with a few specialists in the mix. You're to lead your team from the northeast corner to the center of the exercise area. You'll have five full minutes alone in the room. You'll take the flag at the center, set up a defensive line, and prepare for an incoming assault."

"Sounds good so far," I said.

"Three teams of the same size as yours will enter from various angles," Graves continued. "These platoons are totally inexperienced, and they all need a good training. They'll be led by your own adjuncts. Now, is all that clear?"

"It sure is, Primus," I said, "but can I take along an adjunct of my own?"

Graves slid his eyes to Harris, then back to me. "You don't have to worry about bringing Harris. He's one of the new adjuncts who'll be carrying out this assault against your position."

"Say *what*?" Harris asked in surprise.

"That's more than satisfactory, Primus," I said loudly.

Harris crossed his arms and leaned back in disgust. He'd figured he was going to skate out of this one, but he'd thought wrong.

"But sir," I continued. "I'd like to bring along Leeson or Toro to help me as well. We need to gel into a single unit as a leadership team. We'll be outnumbered three to one already, so I don't think it will unbalance the contest."

"Right…" Graves said thoughtfully. "Okay, you can have both of them—as leaders for the other two teams against you."

"Well Primus," I said with a wide smile, "that's close enough. It'll have to do."

This announcement of their involvement shocked both Toro and Leeson. They'd been leaning back in their chairs until now. From that point forward, they became all ears.

"Primus Graves," Toro said, speaking up for the first time. "Involving experienced adjuncts such as myself might throw off the balance of this exercise."

He looked at her coldly. "All right. Since you're in the hot-seat, McGill, I'll let you hand-pick a few specialists to assist you. But no techs. Leave them outside."

Toro shut up and looked glum. She'd finally figured out that every time anyone complained, Graves made it harder on them with his adjustments.

"After five minutes of prep-time," Graves continued when everyone fell quiet, "we'll let the other teams into the chamber. They'll advance from every direction. At the end of thirty minutes, whoever has possession of the flag is the winner."

My mind wanted me to stay quiet, but I couldn't quite manage it any longer.

"Sir?" I blurted out.

"What is it now, McGill?"

"Not even a *little* weaponry?"

"Our mission at Arcturus IV is to capture lab people who aren't supposed to be formally armed. Accordingly, you'll all be issued shock-sticks and combat knives. You can also use whatever you find in the exercise chamber itself."

I grinned. "No way I could convince you to leave a rack of snap-rifles beside the flag, is there?"

He chuckled. "This isn't going to be fair anyway, McGill," Graves said. "Remember, these kids barely know how to fight."

I glanced at Harris and smiled. "I hadn't even thought of that, sir. Thanks for the reassurance."

"Can I be excused, Primus?" Harris asked. "I've got a pack of snot-nosed children to turn into killers overnight."

"Go for it, Harris," Graves said. "I wish you luck—I really do."

The meeting broke up after that. Harris had a determined look on his face, as did Toro and Leeson. I saw Leeson give the other two a private nod, and they left together.

I knew what that meant. There was going to be plenty of dying tomorrow, and they wanted it to be my team that got wiped out in the end. Well, let them plot—I wasn't going to just hand that flag over.

Their odds weren't that bad, actually. They'd be coming in from every direction and outnumbering us by three to one. All I had on my side of the equation was experienced troops and a five minute head start.

Legion Varus took a unique approach to training fresh recruits. We didn't sit around on Earth for six months having them do jumping jacks and whatnot. Other legions did that, but the masters of Varus considered that sort of thing to be expensive, antiquated thinking and a big waste of time.

Rather than paying some greenie on Earth to play around in a camp, we trained them on the job. The advantages of this approach were many. For one thing, other than the revival machines themselves, it was dirt cheap. For another, troops tended to pay real close attention to instructors when they knew they might die at any moment.

Plain old dying in itself helped out. The revival machines didn't bring you back exactly the way you went out. They restored your mind in an up-to-the-minute incremental way, so you didn't forget much about your final moments. But your body was stored in its prime. Dying could be a fountain of youth, effectively. Soldiers often lost years of age, injuries and the results of bad eating choices all at once. Undesirable details such as warts, cancer, excess fat cells and the like were all automatically edited out.

When we were returned to life, we truly were the best we could be. Every revival brought back a more finely tuned killing machine in its prime.

For all these reasons, our training was harsh. Most legionnaires died once or twice on their way out to their mission world. It was all part of service to the Legion.

In preparation for the morning festivities, I briefed my key troops. Of course, I chose Carlos and Sargon. They looked kind of sick, but they were game. They were almost always game.

After that, I turned in early to catch a good night's sleep. I'd let old Harris drill his kids until midnight if he wanted. I'd rather have a well-rested crew who were balanced and ready for whatever might be in store to come in the morning time.

-17-

That night, I dreamt about my momma. She was coming out of a bad revive, and she was screaming in my ear something awful—but I had to fight to wake up anyway.

"McGill!" shouted a familiar and slightly shrill voice. "McGill, we have to get to the exercise room!"

"What time is it, Kivi?"

"It's go-time!"

Heaving a sigh, I rolled out of bed onto my feet in one smooth motion. I stood and straightened up. Kivi had wisely skittered back out of my reach. I was well known as a man who didn't like to be shouted awake.

Kivi needn't have worried today, however. I was in a fine mood. My dream was just that, a dream. Sometimes I woke up from a nightmare all spooked—but this time was different. I was relieved my momma wasn't really dead. Not yet, anyway.

Slamming my hands together so loudly Kivi blinked, I followed her out of my private room.

I have to tell you, if there was one thing I liked more than anything else about becoming a centurion, it was my private room. Gone were the days of waking up with some clown like Carlos in my face every morning.

Sure, my door wasn't locked, and my troops often came in to annoy me when they felt like it. But they'd already learned a healthy respect for a closed door. That's why Kivi had bounced out of the way when I got up.

"You're not in this one, Kivi," I told her. "Not directly. No techs."

"I know that," she said, practically skipping to keep up with my long strides.

Kivi was short, cute, and nicely rounded all over. Don't get me wrong, I liked the skinny ones too, but a girl like Kivi always made my eyes rove over her more than other types did.

"I have to go over the shock-sticks," she said. "We've never trained with them before."

I frowned at her. "What? I've used a powered baton more than once…"

She shook her head. "I thought that, too. But these units are new. They're long, like spears. They have tips that deliver a powerful jolt."

"Are the tips pointed?" I asked.

"Yes, but they aren't sharpened like you would expect. The metal heads are charged and weighted, with a point that's a rounded surface about a centimeter across."

"Hmmm…" I said. "Sounds like the tip of a bullet. Not truly sharp, but still enough to hurt if you hit someone hard with it."

"Or if you hit them in a sensitive spot, like an eye," she agreed. "But that's not the real change. The main thing is their amperage. They do more than sting, they numb the body. You tend to lose the function of anything that's touched with a charged spear."

"Spears…" I said. "The oldest of weapons, except maybe for the club and the knife. Well, we'll make the best of it."

My hand-picked crew was waiting for me in the foyer just outside the exercise chamber. We were at the northeast corner, and I knew the three noob teams were gathering in similar spots at the other three corners.

"Do we know yet which group is gathering at which corner?" I asked her.

She gave me a sly look. "Not officially."

That made me smile. "Buzzers? You've got buzzers out there?"

"Shh!" she said.

98

"Why Kivi," I laughed. "You're cheating for your friends, aren't you? No wonder Graves said 'no techs allowed' last night."

"What good would I be as a tech if I didn't at least scout for my team?" she asked.

"What good indeed... Show me what you've got."

She lifted her tapper, and we viewed a few brief clips. Her tiny insectile drones had located and identified the enemy officers.

Each of them was haranguing recruits in their typical fashion. Leeson was making a dull speech. Toro was walking around making lots of noise and hand-gestures. Harris, being more hands-on, was lining his people up and having them all do stop-thrusts with their spears. He walked behind them, screaming in their ears and slapping anyone who did it wrong.

"They look scared," I said.

"They should be," Kivi replied. "What are you going to do to them?"

I gave her a little grin. "I'm not telling. You can watch from the observation booth."

Her full lips pouted, but she didn't complain. "Leeson is directly across from you, in the southwest corner. Harris is southeast, to your left as you walk in. Toro is on your right—northwest."

"Good work. Now, get out of here and hide your bugs before I'm disqualified or something."

She ran off, and Carlos walked up to replace her.

"Still lusting for my girl, McGill?" he asked. "Isn't it a violation to pork your noncoms now that you're a centurion?"

"Nope," I said firmly. "Not in this unit, anyway. Are the troops ready?"

"We're here, and we're ready to die pointlessly at your command."

"Good."

Carlos was the only bio I had in my hand-picked group. Partly, I'd chosen him because he was a capable hand-to-hand fighter as well as a medical type. Most bios were soft, but not him.

The rest of my crew consisted of the most vicious fighters in my unit—among them were Sargon and Della. She was small, but she was a natural-born killer with a knife in her hand.

"Okay team, we're going low-tech this time around. When we get in there, follow my lead. Della, you take point."

She looked surprised but didn't complain.

"The terrain is set for jungle-rough," I told them. "It'll be hot and hazy. Greenery will block vision more than ten meters in most places. Della, I want you to run to the center, grab the flag and hide it."

She looked confused. "Um…" she said, "aren't we supposed to fight over it?"

"We're supposed to be the last team holding it for thirty minutes," I said. "Fighting is purely optional."

Several of my team nodded thoughtfully. They weren't arguing at least, and I liked that.

"Okay," I said, "the rest of you follow my lead when we get in there."

"No hints, Centurion?" Sargon asked.

"Nope."

He shrugged and began stretching near the closed hatchway.

"Wait a second," Della said, coming up to me as I stood next to Sargon. "That's the whole plan?"

"Nah," I said. "I have some other thoughts, but I'll tell you about them when we get inside."

She narrowed her eyes at me. "Are you worried about spies?"

"Yes, indeed."

She nodded and looked around suspiciously. "Wise. I must ask you though, what if the flag doesn't come free from the center? What if it's stuck in a puff-crete base?"

That made me frown. I hadn't considered such a possibility. "Well… you've got a knife. Cut the flag off and run away with it. Sit in a tree or something."

She made a face that indicated resignation and took her place at the front of the pack.

A digital counter began running on everyone's tapper at once. It started at fifty-nine and began counting down.

-18-

When the count reached zero, the hatch opened, and we all sprinted inside. Carlos was whooping like an ape, and I almost felt like joining him.

Our legs churned, and big ferns slapped them wetly as we charged through the tangled rainforest. The trees were quick-grows with spindly roots, but they were good enough to fool me. Damn, this biotech was amazing. They'd grown an honest-to-God jungle in here overnight.

I knew the trees were weak, about as tough as stalks of witch-grass, but they looked great and felt solid enough when you slammed into one.

The moment we all got into the jungle, the hatch clanged shut behind us. We were locked in now and committed. Today it was do or die for the hundred and twenty odd lost souls in this cage. Even I had to wonder how many of us would walk out on two feet.

"Listen up!" I said, trotting to my left. We soon parted ways with Della who ran light-footedly for the center of the arena. "We're going to set up an ambush. It's critical that we gain utter surprise. Stand well back and lay low—half of you hide with Veteran Sargon, half with me. We'll watch the rookie group rush in, then hit them in the tail feathers the second they go by us."

We rushed through the ferns and vines, leaping over fallen logs and splashing through boggy areas. It only took about a minute to reach the next hatch—the southeast one.

Carlos puffed up to me and stood at my side.

"Find a hiding spot, Specialist," I ordered him.

"I will, but I have a suggestion first."

"Name it, quick-like."

"Someone should play bait in case they come in cautiously. Someone should stand in the direction of the center, and run off when they come in. That way the rest of you can hit them from behind."

"You know," I said, "that's a damned good idea. You're the bunny-rabbit. Get out there ahead of them and hide."

"What? Me? No way, I'm too slow."

My spear tip wandered close to his face, and he ducked away.

"Get out there bunny," I told him. "Lame bait is the best kind. They'll figure they can catch you easily."

Cursing in a steady stream, he headed toward the center. About a hundred meters in, he stopped and crouched.

The rest of us melted into the landscape. All we had to do was wait until our five minute head start ran out. I hoped Della had stolen the flag by now, or this mock-battle was going to go down as my first disgrace as a centurion. The other teams only had to walk in and take it.

The hatch groaned open on massive hinges. A group of nervous-looking punks walked in, holding their spears like they were hunting a saber tooth.

"This way," Harris said, taking the lead.

He didn't have much choice with this crew. They had to be led, or they'd freeze up.

For the next few seconds, everything went pretty well. Harris got about halfway to Carlos' position when the bio specialist jumped up and bolted. Harris roared and gave chase as did his crew.

All around us in the jungle, my own hidden people tensed, ready to spring up and charge into their rear line—but then Harris went off-script. He threw his spear after Carlos.

It was a mighty cast. Even I was impressed. Both accurate and hard-hitting, the spear caught Carlos between the shoulder blades. There was a snapping sound and a bluish flash—wow, these sticks could give a mean jolt!

Carlos spun around and went down. I couldn't see him in the underbrush, but I could see the spear sprouting up out of his back. He'd been gigged like a frog.

Already, I could see my plans were falling apart. I needed a new plan. Instead of charging off into the jungle after Carlos, the recruits were cautiously advancing behind their hero, Harris, who was bragging about the first kill of the day.

It was up to me to make the next move. I decided to take a page from Harris' book. I stood up, trotted a few feet, and chucked my spear at Harris himself.

One of the recruits stepped in the way at the last second, and the spear went right through his neck. He fell onto his face, gargling and such-like.

The stunned recruits were too green to respond properly. They looked at their fallen comrade, not back at me. It was only a split-second, but that was enough. A dozen more spears rose and fell. Recruits were taken out with jolts and impalement. Apparently, my troops had decided we were throwing our weapons away today as a group.

The tactic seemed insane at first, but it turned out to work pretty well. Any group, especially rookies, can only take so much. With a third of their number knocked down all at once, some broke and fled into the jungle. The rest listened to Harris and circled around him.

Sargon and his troops advanced on their flank with confidence, while my well-rested regulars approached them head-on. We had the eyes of killers, and the greenies in the middle had the eyes of prey.

"McGill!" roared Harris. "You did this just to screw with me, didn't you? Don't you even care about winning? This is a sorry attempt at revenge."

"Not so, Adjunct," I shouted back. "I'm in it to win it!"

We marched forward, half of us with spears leading the way. We outnumbered them by about three to one now. They didn't want to toss any more spears. They knew they'd be torn apart if they had nothing left but knives.

The lines clashed, flashing shock-sticks slapping at one another—but this is where Sargon's superior training really came into play. He was confident and accurate. He'd fought with any number of weapons. Like a wildman, he beat aside the opposing team's spears and jolted their bellies with impunity.

Harris was the one and only problem. He grabbed up fallen spears behind his retreating line and threw them with deadly effect. Three of my troops fell, but at last, Harris' line crumbled. One poor bastard even tried to surrender.

"You frigging coward!" Harris screamed at him, "get up off your knees!"

The man refused, so Harris planted a knife in his skull. The second he did so, Sargon shocked him down, and a brutal butchery began. Harris and his people had been beaten.

"A few of them got away," Sargon told me.

"Yeah, but they'll probably hide in the bushes like rabbits until this is over," I said. "Let's move toward the center."

I checked on Carlos as we passed him by, but he'd bled out during the battle. That was just as well, I figured. I picked up his kit and tossed it to the nearest troop who was scratched up. She began smearing medical salves over her bloody legs.

We grabbed up spears, most of us had more than one by now. The throwing tactic—I liked that.

Moving forward with caution, I had Sargon do the scouting. We couldn't afford to walk into an ambush like the one I'd just sprung on Harris.

At the center of the jungle, we found a ring of some sixty spearmen. They were organized into two ranks, with the back rank standing and the front rank kneeling. They'd gathered around whatever cover they could—but that wasn't much. There were only a few dozen stone blocks and squatty palms here, with knee-high grass all around.

In the center of the spearmen was a staff-like stick about three meters high. I could still see a scrap of red cloth from the banner that had once flown there.

From a range of about fifty meters or so, I stood fast and waved to Leeson. He was standing on the tallest block in the center. Toro was lower down, walking among the recruits and no-doubt telling them encouraging things.

"Leeson!" I shouted. "What are you doing out there?"

"Winning," he boomed back at me.

"I don't think so. That's not the flag—that's a stick."

"The flag is a place, McGill," he said confidently. "A location, not a—"

"Do it, Sargon," I whispered to my side.

Trotting forward in a crouch, Sargon advanced in the tall grass. He was like a leopard or something even more impressive.

Jumping up on top of a block myself, I stood as high as I could and laughed at Leeson. "That's a *stick*, man. Not a flag. You're losing! We've got the flag."

"You're so full of shit, McGill," Leeson said hotly. "I don't know who you blew to get centurion—wait no, on second thought—"

He never finished the sentence. His nervous recruits had been busy looking back and forth between me and Leeson like a crowd at a tennis match. They never saw Sargon until he sprang up about twenty meters out and cast his spear.

It was a beautiful thing to watch. Sargon had been a weaponeer before he'd reached Veteran, and those boys have to work out every damned day to carry their heavy guns around. You wouldn't think that a man of our day and age would be good with a spear, and most weren't, but some still believed in the old sports such as the javelin. All of us had trained over the years with various pieces of improvised weaponry anyway, just in case.

This was the day it paid off. The spear went a little bit low, catching Leeson in the belly—but that did the trick. He pitched off his perch and went down, howling.

Shaken, his recruits didn't know what to do. The front rank stood from their kneeling position, and to me, it looked like they might turn chicken and run.

To her credit, Adjunct Toro instantly recognized that she was in charge of two terrified platoons now.

"Charge!" she roared. "They cheated! Kill them all!"

Legion recruits, even the fresh ones, aren't generally wimps. They're usually at least jocks, if not true soldiers. A few of them were probably pissed off at seeing their commander taken out by surprise.

They came at us then, but it wasn't quite a charge. It was more of an organized trot. No one wanted to be the first man to come up against us.

They caught up with Sargon, however. He'd just been a little too close. He took a dozen thrusts in the back, but still managed to hamstring one recruit with his knife before he gave up the ghost.

"Single-rank!" I ordered, and my people formed a sharp line. "Thin them out at twenty paces!"

Everyone on our side with a second spear threw one at the advancing line. About a dozen of the recruits went down— Sargon wasn't the only one with good aim, if I do say so myself.

Taking casualties is never what a line wants to see, but they still outnumbered us badly. They came in, and our two lines clashed.

It was a mess after that. Screams burned through the air. We stung, stabbed, and slashed at one another. I realized along the way that whole battles in the distant past had been fought just like this.

The roman legions that were our namesakes must have warred this way. So close up and personal. It wasn't like shooting from a crouched position in a foxhole at a target you could barely see.

The smell, the noise—it was terrifying and mesmerizing all at once.

The battle didn't end the way it would have in ancient times, however. Those brave warriors of the past only had one life to live. They would have broken—one side or the other running away before half of them had fallen.

But that wasn't the way with modern legionnaires. We knew that running would mean the enemy would stick us in the back. Bearing the curse and privilege of knowing deep inside that we would be coming back to bear consequences for our actions, we were less willing to take that chance.

So, we stuck it out. Even the opposing recruits, God bless them, didn't break until there were only about fifteen left.

Finally, exhausted and bleeding, they turned tail and fled for the forest. My troops made to follow, but I called them back.

"Let them go," I said. "They did well."

Tiredly, my last handful of survivors returned and laid out flat on the rocks all around the stick that was our prize. It hardly looked like it was worth dying over, to be honest.

Della appeared a few minutes later and brought me my flag. She tossed it to me, and I used it to wipe up blood on my ribs.

"I wasn't sure if I should come back or not," she said. "I watched the whole thing from that tree over there."

"You did it right," I told her.

Della came close, fussing over my wounds. I let her.

"It felt wrong," she said, "not fighting with you down here on the ground. Did you send me away to keep me safe?"

"If I did, I'll never tell."

She smiled, and she kissed me.

I slept with Della that night. I hadn't planned to do so, but a man like me rarely plans such events. We just take whatever opportunities arise.

It felt strange as I hadn't been with her in a long time. We'd sort-of raised a child, and we'd tried to connect and make a life out of it—but in the end, we were just too different.

We had a mutual physical attraction, of course. That had never been the problem. But Della was a true wild-woman. She was the kind of person that I figured Etta would grow up to be.

My father had always said that some dogs were just too wild, too mean and ornery to keep around. That was how it was with Della. If most women were poodles or beagles, well, she was more like a purebred wolf.

After a night in my private officer's quarters we parted ways with a smile and a kiss. There were no promises to mend our feelings and make a fresh go of it. That part was kind of refreshing. There was a deep honesty underlying our failed relationship that most people could only dream of.

Sarah came to me later that morning in my office. That was a surprise.

"Centurion?" she asked me timidly.

Normally, a centurion didn't talk directly to recruits. That was for the veterans. They served as mother, father, nursemaid and angry primitive god for the recruits.

But she was cute and young. I'd seen her lying dead in the grass the day before. Somehow, that made me feel soft on her this morning.

"What is it, recruit?" I asked.

Sarah touched her blonde hair. It was shorter now, but there was still enough to encircle her face nicely. The modern legions weren't as rigid about buzzing off new people's hair as they once were. The creation of discipline through making everyone look alike wasn't as necessary as it used to be. After they died a few times, the recruits tended to listen to you very closely.

"I fought like an animal out there," she said quietly. "I didn't know I could be like that—that other people I knew could kill me, and I could kill them."

"Unfortunately," I told her, "the only way we know how to train troops to fight like experienced soldiers is to give them actual experience in combat."

"I know that, sir," she said. "But something happened to me out there. Something strange—I felt wild. I had a dream when I died, too."

Her eyes came up and met mine. Big baby blues looking right at me. "Is that normal?" she asked, her voice down to a near whisper.

Right about then, I began wishing I *had* sent her to her veteran. I thought about doing it now—but I didn't.

"Sometimes that happens," I admitted.

"How *could* it?" she demanded suddenly, loudly, staring at me. "Was it *real*?"

"I don't think so," I told her. "It's like *deja-vu*, it's an illusion.

Sarah looked down again, but she didn't leave. "You want to know what I dreamt about?" she asked quietly, stepping closer.

Suddenly, I sensed I was in danger. I was a centurion now, not a regular soldier or even a noncom. To take advantage of this poor girl's obvious distress, which had clearly turned her into a seductress in some kind of cruel psychological twist...well, it would be plain wrong.

Still, she *was* pretty. I knew myself well enough to know I'd succumb to the situation eventually if I didn't unload her sweetness right-quick. Maybe not today, as I'd already spent the night with Della… but eventually.

Accordingly, I smiled big and stepped past her out of my office. I walked toward the main chamber of our pod.

Sarah was surprised, but she trotted after me.

Every unit had its own pod for use during transport. They were generally cubical in shape, about a hundred meters square, and built to house troops comfortably enough.

"You've given me an idea," I told her. "Let's gather up the whole unit."

Using my tapper, I alerted my adjuncts and noncoms to gather the unit for an immediate assembly. They hustled troops out of their beds, bathrooms and hallways in a hurry.

When they were all organized, lined-up and looking bewildered, I stood in front of my collective command.

"Yesterday was a tough day for many of you," I told them, "especially those who died. That probably wasn't your first death, and it won't be your last."

They looked at me. The recruits were bleary-eyed from a bad night's sleep. The regulars ranged from bored to curious.

"Normally," I said, "a unit is given a day off to recover after an exercise like the one we just went through. I, however, don't ascribe to that theory. I think unit cohesion needs to be reestablished. Therefore, we'll drill today on the shooting range all afternoon. You have until lunch to get your shit together and turn your new brains back on. Dismissed."

Stunned, the unit wandered off. There were some mutters and curses. That was fine with me. I watched them melt away until most were gone.

Sarah was one of those who left dejectedly. I felt a little bad for her, but I figured we were done with introspection, sympathy-sex and navel-gazing for today.

Harris was one of the few who stuck around. He walked up to me, narrowing his eyes.

"What is it, Adjunct?" I asked him.

He shook his head as if wondering at something. "I don't know what to think," he said.

111

"Yeah? You want to talk about it? Maybe you had a bad dream when you were dead?"

"Say *what*?" he demanded angrily. "Hell, no. My problem is I don't know what to think about you. Yesterday—that was plain dirty. The dirtiest move I've ever seen played out in that scenario."

I shrugged. "I wasn't promoted for my personality."

"Damn right you weren't," he said. "You picked *me* out to ambush, didn't you? Or was it chance?"

"Which way would make you feel better, Adjunct? I'm all about feelings."

He squinted at me again and shook his head. "Graves himself couldn't have been more heartless, and I doubt he could have been more cunning. Why didn't you just sit in the middle of that damned jungle like any normal centurion would've done? Why'd you have to screw with the flag, knock out an enemy group—all that shit?"

I shrugged. "To win."

Harris nodded. "All right," he said. "I can accept that. A new centurion needs to demonstrate he's an ass-kicker…"

As Harris continued talking, my mind began to wander. It seemed that he was trying to figure out my angle in the training. The God's-honest truth was I hadn't been thinking about any higher-level of learning for my command. The contest was a game of sorts, and I'd wanted to win. I always wanted to win. It was that simple.

Leeson or some other similar officer might have stood his troops around the flag, fought hard, and possibly won anyway against a pack of green recruits. But that wasn't my way.

Listening to Harris vaguely, it occurred to me that telling him the truth about my motives wouldn't expand my mystique in his mind. So I let him carry on trying to fathom my alleged genius without help.

"One last thing," he said finally, forcing me to pay attention again, "what about today's drill? Why hit them hard right off? Is there something I need to know? Are we going into action earlier than planned?"

"Nope," I said, "I just got tired of seeing my people mope around. It's best to keep them busy. Forget your troubles, don't dwell on them, that's my motto."

He nodded seriously. "A good motto... That's all, sir."

After lunch, my unit hit the shooting range. There was an inspection going on when we got there.

Leading my unit to the lines, we took up our assigned weapons and began practicing. The recruits were given snap-rifles, standard issue for our greenest troops. The regulars were given plasma weapons. We formed two groups and began firing.

There were two other units using the chamber. A group of higher level officers walked along, reviewing their performance.

Graves and Winslade were among the officers performing the inspection. They seemed surprised to see my group when they approached.

"I believe these men are part of your cohort, Graves," Winslade said. "I'm surprised they aren't shooting my men in the next field by accident."

"McGill?" Graves asked. "Why are you drilling your troops today?"

"To clear their minds, sir," I said crisply.

I worked a plasma rifle charging pod out of the stock and replaced it with another. I rammed the spent pod into a slot in the rail that ran between me and the firing range to recharge. Flipping the rifle back on, I heard the weapon hum. It was a sound that rose in pitch until it became an inaudibly high singing sound. That meant it was good to go.

Graves didn't say anything for a second, but soon he nodded in approval. "Carry on."

I turned and fired at the target. A robotic monster flailed as it was taken down. After about five seconds, it got up again and began moving in random circles. I shot it again.

Sensing a presence at my side, I glanced to my left. It was Winslade.

"Can I help you, Primus?" I asked him.

Winslade peered up at me. "You're bucking for more rank, aren't you?" he asked.

"Excuse me?"

"Who ignores a day off to go shooting after an ordeal in the arena? Only a man with unbridled ambition would even think of it."

"Uh… Think what you like, Primus, but my men do best when they keep busy."

"Yes… I can see that. I'll keep an eye on you, McGill. You're a dangerous man."

"Thank you, sir!"

He left me then, and the inspection ended. I went back to shooting, and I actually found it cathartic. There was something about firing a powerful weapon and knocking down an alien over and over again—even an artificial alien—which I found very enjoyable.

-20-

After Drusus had been promoted up to Imperator, and then Equestrian, he became too high and mighty to run a Legion like Varus.

Accordingly, a new Tribune was appointed. However, that honor didn't fall to Winslade, who'd disgraced himself early-on in the Battle for Earth. Friends from high places on the Ruling Council had kept people like Winslade and Turov from being run out of town on a rail, but they hadn't managed to get them any new rank.

Instead, people of worth were advanced. In my opinion, Tribune Helena Deech was one of them.

On the one hand, she was a real piece of work. She wasn't pretty, and she wasn't nice. But she *was* effective.

Looking to be around thirty-five, she had tight curly hair and lots of freckles. Most people had edited that kind of thing out by the time they had reached a high rank—but not old Deech.

"You know what they say about our new tribune?" Carlos asked me during our general assembly.

"What? That she's Deech the Peach?"

He made a face of disgust. "Nah, that's lame. They say she's a ball-buster. That she hates men and attractive women. She only likes ugly old battle axes like herself."

"Huh," I said, gazing across the open expanse of the transport's upper deck. "I don't think she looks all *that* bad."

Under my unit's feet was our home pod. The whole legion was in the hold, standing on top of a stack of identical pods. The hull of the big transport arced overhead and the ribs of the ship loomed near. Each one was ten meters thick and forged with pure crystalline steel.

Deech didn't bother to walk in front of the whole legion and inspect us. She floated on a flitter above the cohorts, staring down from her whirring platform at us.

"Officers, veterans and recruits," she said. "This is my first action as the overall commander of Legion Varus. I'm proud to serve with you."

"This is bullshit," Carlos muttered. "Varus should be led by someone from Varus. She's from Iron Eagles. They don't know shit about us—about our culture."

"Culture?" I asked. "We kill stuff for a living. What's there to know?"

Carlos looked sullen.

I wondered why people always disliked outsiders from the first minute they ran into them. For my part, I was more than willing to give this old battle axe a fair shake.

"This operation should be a simple one," Deech went on. "In fact, we shouldn't even be deploying an entire legion for such a small matter. A group of renegade lab workers have refused to abandon their facilities. They've been warned and warned again. Earth can only tolerate so much defiance."

We stared up at her, listening, frowning. So far, she did sound like a hard-ass—I wasn't disappointed.

"Legion Varus has always served in special-duty cases like this one. It might get messy if they try to actively resist. It's even possible they'll use specialized, experimental weapons against you."

"Are they going to throw beakers and microscopes at us?" Carlos demanded aloud.

"Shut up and maybe she'll tell us," I told him. I'd let him get away with talking to me because we were friends, but I knew that couldn't continue in front of the troops. I was a centurion now, not a recruit in the back row.

To Carlos' credit, he did shut up.

"Now that we're underway," Deech continued, "I can reveal some details about our mission. First of all, it is important. The Galactics have outlawed weapons research of the kind that's been taking place at this facility. When Earth took over the Cephalopod worlds, it took us some time to figure out what we'd gained—and what we'd taken responsibility for."

She swept the crowd with a stern gaze. Nobody was laughing now. We knew trouble when we heard it. Galactic legal violations topped the charts in that department.

"Our government let the work continue in secret for a time. But when the Galactics were detected returning with their battle fleet, it was decided such efforts must be shut down and expunged. That's our true mission, to not only remove the scientists, but also to delete all evidence that might be incriminating."

Deech began praising us as a legion after that. She listed our accomplishments and talked about how respected we were. She then applied the old saw about doing the dirty work that needed doing. That's when I knew she was wrapping it up.

"Your individual officers will brief you on operational objectives. Train hard, don't assume the mission will be easy— even though it probably will be. Dismissed!"

The legion melted back into their pods over the next several minutes. I didn't go below decks, however, I watched a knot of officers approach Deech. Most of them were centurions, and there was a primus or two.

Taking my new rank seriously, I walked toward them and joined the circle.

"That's right," Deech was saying. "There is no comprehensive list of their security systems, or their experimental weaponry."

"But sir," Winslade whined. "How are we supposed to fight effectively against unknown weaponry? Surely, someone took notes during their initial surveys of the Cephalopod worlds. If only—"

"No," Deech said firmly. "The answer is 'no,' and it will continue to be 'no' until you stop asking."

I almost said something rude, but I contained myself. Winslade was getting beat up by the tribune enough on his own without me chiming in.

"We see security installation references on these maps," Graves said. "We've never gotten any details concerning them—are they classified as well?"

"They're all classified. The very existence of the target planet is classified. However, I can tell you the pillboxes are automated and of Cephalopod manufacture. They aren't particularly innovative—but they're doubtlessly effective."

That caused a bit of a stir. I'd sort of been envisioning a guard post manned by security men in space suits. It would be a lot harder to take out hardened bunkers with some kind of squid AI shooting at you.

"Can we turn those defensive mechanisms off?" Graves asked.

"They wouldn't be terribly effective if that was easy to do," Deech pointed out. "Their power lines are buried in solid rock underneath the pillboxes. They're fed from generators inside the central dome itself."

"Couldn't we just bomb the dome from space and have done with it?" I called out from the back row.

A dozen pairs of eyes swung to look at me. "I mean," I continued, "if we're going to blow the whole place up anyway, why not do it right off?"

Deech stared at me. "I'm not sure I've met you… Centurion McGill?"

"That's me, sir."

"Well McGill, there are some things we wish to retrieve from the dome intact before we destroy it."

"Like what kinds of things?"

Her demeanor shifted from open but measured, to downright annoyed. I'd seen that happen before any number of times in different folks.

"Last time Centurion…Your team may not be targeting one of them, and thus you haven't been briefed on that part of the operation—which is classified."

There were some freckle-faced daggers with that last part. Still, I almost asked another question, until I caught a simultaneous glare from Winslade and Graves. They couldn't both be wrong, so I paused. It occurred to me that up until my questions, only the primus-ranked individuals had asked anything. Accordingly, I shut up.

The informal meeting wrapped up after a few more minutes, and I was left wandering back toward my unit's pod.

"Why do I always feel the urge to cringe when you open your mouth, McGill?" Winslade asked from behind me.

"Well sir," I said, looking back at him and giving him a grin. "Sometimes a big man's voice will make a small man jump. It's nothing to be ashamed of. It's purely natural."

He huffed and walked away. Primus Graves caught up with me next.

"You shouldn't talk to a superior officer like that, McGill," he told me.

"Didn't you execute him once a few years back?" I asked him.

He shrugged. "I've executed you as well—several times. The problem is I can't seem to get it to stick."

He gave me a tight smile, and I realized he'd made a joke. I laughed politely. That was hard, because Graves had killed me *lots* of times. It could be hard to forgive a man for that.

"Have you got any more info?" I asked him. "Anything on the mission I mean. Who is going after the classified stuff?"

Graves jerked a thumb over his shoulder. "Winslade, for one. Go ask him about it."

I stopped walking and let Graves continue on. Frowning, I looked around but couldn't see where the weasel had gone. He'd vanished into one of the hatches on top of the pods.

Like a rat down a hole, he'd disappeared. I didn't like the idea of Winslade being in charge of collecting secret weapons and the like. I couldn't even comprehend why, with his record, a man like him would be trusted on a mission like this at all.

That was the problem with Earth, in my opinion. The government was blind to so many injustices and absurdities. One man might go to jail for espionage, while his office-mate might get a promotion.

119

The government types had a way of making things even more unfair in nature than they already were. By trying to keep an open mind, they often let the wolves in with the sheep.

-21-

Two days later, we arrived in the vicinity of Arcturus, coming out of warp a long way from the central star. This came as a surprise to me, as Arcturus was pretty near in astronomical terms to Old Sol herself, I would have thought it would be safe to warp in closer to the target.

Wanting to know what we might be dealing with, I sought out the smartest person I knew. Calling upon my own best tech, Natasha, I didn't get a helpful reply at first.

"Arcturus is a K-class star," she said, "not all that much different from our own sun."

I made a great effort and did not roll my eyes. "I *know* that. I'm wondering why we're here, because we're supposed to be checking up on a Cephalopod world. This planet is too close. We're well inside the borders of Province 921. This is a long way from squid space. It can't be a star system we conquered during the war."

She shrugged her shoulders and went back to studying something with a virtual nanoscope. "That's politics, not science. You'll have to ask someone else more qualified."

She didn't seem to care about what I considered to be a technical mystery, which was odd in itself. There she sat ignoring me, peering at her work. I decided to get a good look at what was so doggone curious.

121

"What's visible in that scope that's so damned interesting?" I asked her.

"Nothing. Just manufacturing marks."

That raised my interest level right off. I knew that any manufacturing marks which took specialized equipment to identify must be Imperial in nature.

"You're looking for an Imperial stamp?" I asked her.

Her head came back up from her scope, suddenly alert. "What do you know about that?"

"I know the Galactics stamp the things they make themselves with tiny identifying collections of molecules. It's common knowledge."

"No, it isn't," she said, staring at me suspiciously.

Immediately, I knew I'd blown it. I'd learned about Imperial stamps because they identified the most valuable kind of equipment I'd come into contact with. The teleport suits, for example, were very advanced and originally of Galactic manufacture.

The reason such items were a big deal was because lowlifes like humans out on the fringe of the known galaxy weren't supposed to have access to that kind of goods, ever. What's more, I'd once had a Galactic Key among my personal possessions—an extinction-level offense if it was discovered.

"Why are you looking for stamps, anyway?" I asked, seeking a fresh dodge. "Does it have something to do with the coming audit?"

Her mouth opened, then closed again. She turned back to her nanoscope.

"I know I'm in your unit, James," she said. "Technically, I'm under your command. But I've been asked to examine various items to see if they had certain markers—and I can't talk about it."

Curious now, I sidled close to her and stared at the item she was examining. It didn't look all that special.

"Is that some kind of actuator?" I asked. "Looks like it connects to something big."

Natasha quickly moved the flat of her hand between the object and my prying eyes.

"I thought I was questioning *you*," she said, looking over her shoulder at me.

"Apparently, you thought wrong."

She looked around the lab. It was pretty empty, except for a few bored-looking techs who were working on unimportant stuff. Mostly, they were equipment-checking for tomorrow's planned deployment.

"All right," she said. "You tell me why you know about Imperial stamps, I'll tell you what I'm examining."

I thought about that, and I nodded. "Okay."

"You first," she said.

"Wait—"

"This was my idea," she insisted.

Heaving a sigh, I gave in and lied. It was only a partial lie, which meant it was one of the best kind.

"The teleport suits are Galactic-made," I said. "At least, the original ones were."

"My God..." she said, staring into space. "That makes sense. No one told me. But how did you find out about that?"

"Well," I squirmed a little. "I was in the early teleport-attack program."

"Yes, so? How did that get you into the loop on manufacturing marks?"

I paused to gather my thoughts for a moment. The truth was, I'd possessed a Galactic Key—a powerful hacking tool that was strictly forbidden for humans to possess. It could bypass alien security, even if that security was built by the Galactics themselves. That's when I'd learned about the stamps.

I couldn't tell Natasha about that, though. Only a few people knew the keys existed at all—and I thought it should stay that way.

"Well..." I finally said, "during the teleport-trials I met a tech. Lisa was her name. She knew about the Imperial stamp on the suits and told me about it."

"Why would she...?" Natasha began, then she stopped and made a wry face. "Oh. Let me guess, Lisa is attractive?"

"She's a fine-looking woman," I admitted, "but she doesn't hold a candle to your aristocratic cheekbones."

She heaved a sigh and shook her head, going back to her work. "I should have known. Pillow-talk is dangerous."

"Your turn," I said.

"All right. But you can't tell anyone that I told you. This is part of our warp-bubble generation system. It's a specialized part that maintains a perfect balance between numerous high-energy emissions."

"Huh?"

"It's a critical component of warp engines. We only have so many of these, and the Skrull aren't sending us any new ones. We—we might have to build our own someday."

"Ah..." I said, catching on. "So, you're trying to copy the design. That's a serious violation of Galactic Law, you know."

"We perform more and more such violations all the time."

She was more right than she knew, but I couldn't tell her about it. Hell, she wouldn't be able to concentrate on her work at all if I did.

"But what about Arcturus IV?" I asked. "Why are we here?"

"I seriously don't know. But there are planets here. None of them are inhabitable, but they were first catalogued long ago."

I squinted at her. "So... is it likely one or more of these worlds would be rocky with a toxic atmosphere?"

"I would assume so," she said. "The new tribune stated in her briefing that we were heading to such a planet. That would make sense, given this star's high metallicity."

"Pretend I skipped that day in astronomy class," I said, "what the hell is metallicity?"

"A measurement of how much of a given star's mass is anything other than hydrogen or helium," she said. "Stars with high metallicity levels produce rocky planets. Life itself would be impossible without them."

"Yeah..." I said thoughtfully. "I think I'm going to go talk to some other people now."

Her hand shot out and caught mine. I stopped and looked at her in surprise. It had been a long time since she'd touched me at all. We'd had a serious relationship once, and we still did, but it was all in the old-friend category now.

"Don't get any ideas," she said, retrieving her hand. "Remember—you can't tell anyone what I've told you."

"They'll never know where I got it," I assured her.

Her eyes searched mine. She heaved a fresh sigh.

"What's wrong now?" I asked.

"I realize that you're promising to lie. That means what you've been telling me about Imperial markers was a lie, too."

"Oh come on," I said. "What I said wasn't a *total* lie. It was an adjustment. I was only trying to protect you."

"Whatever. You haven't changed a bit."

Troubled, I frowned at her. "I did it for your own good, Natasha. Believe me..."

She looked troubled right back at me, and then she stopped asking questions.

Natasha was right about one thing: we'd come to Arcturus for political reasons, not technical ones. That realization gave me the impetus to head upstairs to Gold Deck. That's where the real answers to my questions were.

-22-

In the old days I would have stormed into Turov's office. After a little bargaining, I'd have learned whatever I needed to know.

Unfortunately, Turov was back on Earth, and Tribune Deech was nowhere near as inviting. In fact, I couldn't even get in the door.

"Sorry Centurion," said a veteran guard, shaking his head. "The tribune isn't taking walk-ins today. Her schedule is full."

"Not a problem," I said. "If I could just talk to her aide—"

"I'm afraid he's left specific instructions on that score, sir."

I blinked. "He what? You mean he told you not to allow me into this door—me by name?"

"I'm afraid so," he said, consulting his tapper. "Yes… Centurion McGill—that's you, right?"

This unexpected resistance flummoxed me. For years I'd been told by countless adjuncts and veterans I didn't rate a direct audience with superior officers. Now, however, I'd attained the rank of centurion myself. Hell, Deech was only two steps above me in the command chain.

"Who is this new aide working for Tribune Deech?" I demanded. "Unless asking for that much is against the rules?"

"Not at all, sir. Primus Winslade has been newly appointed to the post."

Winslade. That worm. He'd already managed to wangle a key staff role working for Deech.

My mind raced. Winslade was like me in a way, but much more slippery. While I'd been drilling my troops and prepping for battle, he'd been throne-sniffing his way to the top of the lapdog-list. The moment he'd achieved his goal of avoiding hard combat, he'd set himself up as a gatekeeper to kick away rivals like myself.

Compared to Winslade, I was a political dunce. But I wouldn't have had it any other way.

"All right," I told the veteran. "I'm leaving—but I'll be back."

When I returned to my unit, my adjuncts were arguing. That's the trouble with having three of them—they all wanted to run the show when I wasn't around.

"Leeson?" I called out.

"Yes sir, Centurion?" he said, wheeling around.

I liked that. No matter what kind of an unimaginative ass Leeson had been in the past, he'd never seemed to resent my promotions like the others did.

Toro was clearly irritated about my rise through the ranks. Even though Leeson had been around longer than both of us, she took it personally that she was senior and should have gotten the promotion long before yours truly.

And Harris? Well… Harris and I had been at each other's throats for years. Only in combat did we gel and cooperate. Whenever we were at peace, and the revival machines were idling, he complained about every frigging thing I did.

"Leeson," I said. "As my senior adjunct in this unit, you're officially in charge when I'm not on deck. Is that clear?"

"Very clear," Leeson said proudly. "I *am* senior."

Due to our long lifespans and terms of service—which could go on damned near forever—seniority was less important than it had been in traditional military structures. People didn't get drafted, or get old, or retire out at a certain age. In fact, a chronologically older person might even be physically younger than their juniors because they'd been recently revived. The end result was a command ladder that was less rigid when it came to years served.

The other two adjuncts looked glum, but they'd quieted down. It looked like order had been restored—but that was just an illusion.

"In your absence this morning, sir," Harris said, "we've been discussing what we should do training-wise. This is, after all, our last opportunity to get these recruits ready for action."

"Harris wants to kill them," Leeson said flatly. "But I'm against any extreme action for our final day. The men won't be any good if they're traumatized when we face a real enemy."

"With all due respect," Harris said angrily. "That's the whole point. Recruits are going to die in the field anyway. They need to get their fears hammered out of them right now."

Harris was one of those guys who liked to say "with all due respect" when he actually meant you could go screw yourself.

Thoughtful, I turned to Adjunct Toro. "What do you think we should do for our last day?" I asked her.

The left side of her mouth twitched. "I'm surprised you're asking me," she said in a snotty tone. "You're the centurion. Don't you know what the right play is?"

I was finally getting pissed off at all of them. They were bickering still. It was less open, but it was still there. To my mind the whole thing was an insult. None of them figured I was a legit commander, so they were trying to take over by putting out their own ideas or downright foot-dragging.

Well, there were ways to get the attention of underlings. I'd seen Graves handle similar situations on many occasions.

"Thanks for the thoughtful input, Adjunct," I told Toro. She frowned in confusion, but I pressed on. "We're going to have ourselves another contest. This one should be less deadly, but still a teachable moment for the whole unit."

They looked at me with vague curiosity.

"First off," I said, "we'll break out shock-batons for everyone. Not those spear-things, they're too deadly. To make it interesting, we'll have three troops in each heat. One man from each of your three platoons. We'll start with the lower ranks and work our way up with winners going to a second round. Let's get started."

"Uh… just one thing, Centurion," Leeson said. "How far are the troops supposed to go? To the death?"

"Nah. Death might happen, but the point here is to beat the hell out of each other and get to the top of the pyramid."

He nodded thoughtfully.

"You mentioned shock-batons," Toro said. "What about armor? Will our heavies be allowed to wear it?"

She was asking because her platoon was made up of heavy troopers. In our previous exercise, they'd all led greenies from around the cohort. This action would be only for people in our own unit, who were mostly regulars.

"No," I said firmly. "In fact, we'll strip everyone down to their skivvies from the start. No equipment advantages for anybody."

Finally, Harris began to smile.

"This *does* sound like fun," he said. "My lights are trained to fight with nothing. They might do better than people expect with a level playing field."

Leeson looked glum. He was in charge of the bio people, techs and a few weaponeers. Sure, his weaponeers were tough, and the others were experienced, but most of them weren't front-line troops. To his credit, he didn't complain about it.

In past operations, we'd often deployed and fought with full cohorts of light troops or heavy troops. This time out our units were all mixed. We had so many specialized tactical objectives, and so little understanding of what we were going to face, the higher-ups had decided to organize us that way.

We decided to hold the contest in the main exercise room when it was unoccupied. We could only reserve it for a few hours, so we had to get moving right away.

Each platoon chose an individual combatant, and I let my adjuncts make the choices themselves. The atmosphere was like that of a sporting match. The adjuncts marched among their people, evaluating, giving advice and encouragement.

"All right, send in your first man," I ordered.

The ring was about thirty feet in diameter. Stepping out— or getting pushed out—meant you were disqualified. Otherwise, the last trooper on their feet was the winner.

Harris picked a capable-looking man with long arms and shifty eyes. Toro sent in a girl in response, and to my surprise, I recognized her. It was none other than Sarah, that young girl I'd shared a moment with back at Central.

Leeson chose last. Despite his mediocre leadership skills, he was a cagey devil when it came to strategy. He ordered Sargon into the field.

I thought about that, and I nodded in approval. He clearly saw Sarah as weak and the rangy-looking guy as beatable. If he played Sargon now, he was almost sure to win and send him on to the second round.

The fight began when I whistled. The three stepped into the ring, looking wary. Sarah looked downright scared and there was a certain look of desperation in her eyes.

Sargon roared and charged at her right off. She skittered backward and almost walked out of the ring.

Seeing his opportunity, the shifty-eyed light trooper rushed in toward Sargon's flank. He was *fast*.

Unfortunately for him, Sargon was vastly more experienced. Sargon seemed to know where the man was and exactly how he would attack. He whirled around, ducked, and thrust his baton into the man's belly. There was a crack of electricity and a flash of blue-white light. The recruit ate dirt, puked, and passed out in convulsions.

Sarah, to my surprise, darted in and actually landed one on Sargon's shoulder. His left arm went limp, and he spun back to her, howling in pain. I winced, knowing what was likely to happen next.

But Sargon didn't destroy her—not utterly. Instead, he kicked out at gut-level and she was tossed ass-over-teakettle right out of the ring.

It was over, and the crowd cheered. They'd been making quite a bit of noise during the contest, and they went wild when Sarah landed her baton. Even after she was kicked out, her team gathered around her and congratulated her on a good battle.

Of the three adjuncts, only Leeson looked worried. He'd won, but his man was hurt. The numbness of a shock-baton would fade, but it might take as long as an hour to do so. Sargon might have to fight his next battle with one arm hanging down limply.

I whistled again, and new combatants trotted out. This time, the light trooper won. That was another surprise. Maybe Harris was right about his people being underrated.

It soon turned out it wasn't so. The heavy people started winning consistently, only losing when a weaponeer dared to set foot in the ring. Those troopers that I was most familiar with were wiped out one at a time as well. Carlos lost, Kivi lost, and Natasha lost badly.

Natasha looked at me from the deck, gasping for breath and showing her teeth. I knew she didn't approve of this whole business of training by combat. As a tech, it was usually beneath her.

Soon, everyone in the enlisted ranks had gotten their chance in the ring. The survivors were still around, caring for the others. We'd only had one death, and one serious injury.

I stood over him and eyed him. He couldn't hardly breathe right. "Carlos?" I asked. "Prognosis?"

Carlos limped over and ran instruments over the badly injured trooper. He was one of Toro's heavies.

"He'll be okay in a week or two," he said.

"A week or two? You sure?"

"Yes sir, Centurion."

"Okay, get him down to Blue Deck. Tell them it's a code green."

"Will do, sir," Carlos said, helping the man onto a floating gurney. He guided him toward the exit doors.

My adjuncts exchanged glances with me, shaking their heads. A code green meant he was to be recycled. That would be tough on him, but I couldn't afford to have a trooper who was broken up on our drop-date tomorrow.

"Second heat!" I announced. "Winners only."

The mood had somehow turned from jubilant to grim. The survivors now realized they were in serious jeopardy. The more they won, the more they knew they might be too banged up to survive until morning.

Still, these were Varus legionnaires, not earth-bound hogs. They were tough-minded and naturally mean underneath. A poor mental outlook was a requirement for all our recruits.

131

After a series of vicious fights, we were down to our third heat.

"This is our last round for this stage," I said. "Let's go."

Sargon was thrown into the ring for his last go-round. His arm was still hanging. I didn't even understand how he'd won the second heat, but the third time was just too much. The other two troops rushed him after giving each other a nod.

I knew what that meant. They'd made a private deal, probably on their tappers, before the contest had even begun. They beat him down and then went for each other.

I didn't even pay attention to who won. Instead, I circled around and checked on Sargon. He was stone dead. They'd both shock-batoned his thick skull, and he'd suffered a massive stroke as a result.

"It's for the best," I told Carlos. "He'll be fresh as morning rain when we invade the target."

"Agreed," Carlos said. "I'm sure he'll be singing your praises when he comes out of the oven, sir."

At last, it was over. I declared all those who'd won three heats to be winners, with a hundred-credit bonus pay each. There were hoarse cheers, but they sounded exhausted.

As the day had worn on, several onlookers had come by to see what we were up to. Among them were Graves and a few others sporting the insignia of higher level officers.

None of them chose to disturb us. Most shook their heads in bemusement and left after watching a few of the beat-downs. Now that we were finishing up, we had quite a crowd of onlookers. I dared hope I'd started a new trend among the cohorts.

"Now," I said, looking around at the three platoons. "It's time for the officers to step-up."

"What?" called out Harris. "Did I hear that right? You didn't say anything about officers participating in this exercise, sir!"

"I said it was for the whole unit."

He glowered at me. "Is this going to be a four-way?"

"Nope," I said. "A three-way. We're going up by ranks, remember? Three adjuncts first. I fight the winner."

"That's bullshit," Harris muttered.

I didn't admonish him, mostly because he was right. Whoever won was likely to be injured. They'd have to face me, and I was as fresh as a daisy.

Harris, Leeson and Toro stripped down and took up fully-charged shock-batons. Through squinched eyes, they peered back and forth at each other.

At first, the whole thing proceeded with great caution. They all kept their distance from one another, reluctant to engage. Their platoons hollered and slammed their gauntlets together, creating a hammering beat.

At last, something happened. It took me a second to figure it out. Leeson had caught Toro's eye and given her a nod in Harris' direction.

It was kind of a dirty trick, but it was understandable. One-on-one, neither Leeson nor Toro stood much of a chance against Harris. He was probably the best hand-to-hand fighter in our unit.

"You bastards!" he shouted at them when they came after him together, but he didn't back up. He stood his ground.

As they came in, Leeson faltered in the final rush. Toro got there first, and Harris got down to business. Two blows, that's all it took. She was stretched out on the dirt by then.

Leeson had circled around Harris, however, during the exchange of blows. He landed one on Harris' back, and the bigger man howled.

Dropping his baton, he grabbed Leeson with both hands and brought him down on one knee. His spine crackled, and Leeson rolled off onto the ground mewling. He was as good as dead.

"That was quick," I told Harris. "You ready for the finale?"

"Bring it on!" Harris told me, breathing hard and picking up his baton again.

I stepped into the ring, and we closed together for the final battle.

-23-

Harris had never been easy for me to take out in a fight. Even today, when he was clearly winded and hurt, I didn't expect things to go easy.

Still, I'd invented this contest. I couldn't chicken out in front of the whole unit. Instead, I walked toward him confidently.

In response, he eyed me without moving. When I got to within a few meters, he suddenly cocked back his arm and threw his baton at me. The weapon spun end over end. It seemed to flare with a nimbus of energy as it flashed toward me.

I was too close to dodge. The fraction of a second it would take to duck would be greater than the fraction it would take to reach me.

My second instinct was to throw up my left arm to block. I didn't want to lose the use of my right, or worse, drop my baton.

The shock coursed through me. *Damn*! I'd forgotten how much these batons hurt when they landed on bare skin. Right about now, I was wishing I'd thought of some other form of training rather than this hellacious competition. My forearm was on fire, as if it'd been branded. It wasn't numb to pain, but it was unresponsive. I couldn't even flex my fingers.

Getting my baton around and putting it between Harris and myself, I gave him a little smile.

Harris roared at me, and I blinked, bracing myself for a fierce charge—but it never came. Instead, he hopped nimbly out of the ring and shrugged.

Lowering my weapon, I nodded. He'd played me.

Sure, the whole unit was groaning in disappointment, but Harris was grinning. He didn't care if they thought he was chicken—at least not in a sparring match. He'd landed a good shot on me and taken no injury in return.

"Well now," I said, "that ends today's contest. To the survivors, I want to offer my congratulations. Whether you won or lost, you learned something today."

"Yeah," called out one of the Weaponeers, "how to be a pussy."

There was a gust of laughter and hisses from the group. I frowned around at all of them. Harris was angry, too.

I knew what the problem was. Harris had made a mistake as far as leadership was concerned. He'd only been thinking of pulling a fast one on me, as I'd done to all the adjuncts when I'd announced the officers would participate. He hadn't been thinking about how his actions would look to the troops.

But all that was water under the bridge now. I had to pull these people together. We had to operate as a team in the morning.

"Wait now," I shouted. "Hold on. Adjunct Harris didn't piss his pants and beg for mercy."

Harris' face split into a snarl at the very idea.

"He wouldn't do that in the field—would you, Adjunct?"

He looked around at the group and blinked. "Nah... I'd have killed McGill if this were for real."

A few scoffed, but I didn't let it go at that.

"Harris demonstrated strategy," I said. "He was injured in the first heat. That meant he was at a disadvantage facing me one-on-one. He threw his weapon—yes, that was risky, but what if it had caught me full in the face? Or, if it had numbed up my weapon-arm?"

I looked around at the group seriously. Harris did the same. He spoke up at last, catching on to the situation.

"That's right," Harris told the group. "I might have won with one surprise strike. If I'd gained the upper hand, then I would have charged in and finished the job. But I failed, so I cut my losses and retreated. It's all a matter of strategy."

"Exactly," I said. "Unit, dismissed. Hit the flesh-printers and the showers after."

We broke up and melted away. Harris hung around to talk.

"That whole thing was a bullshit exercise, sir," he told me.

"Oh, I don't know," I grinned. "I had fun until that last minute."

He muttered something unintelligible. Then he spoke up. "Thanks for covering my ass—at the end."

"I didn't do it for your pride," I told him. "Your platoon has to feel you won't turn and run out on them in battle."

"I would never do that, McGill! You know that first hand."

"You're right, I do. That's why I told the troops what I told them. Now, let's get their peckers and their minds right. We've got to land on a rock in the morning."

"Right you are, sir."

We marched together down into our unit's pod, and we made a show of laughing off the day's contests. That caught many strange glances from the troops, but they seemed to take heart.

It was good for troops to know their officers were reliable, and that we didn't hate each other—at least not to a degree that divided us.

* * *

That evening, my door chimed just after midnight.

Sore and troubled, I'd turned in early. There was nothing better than a shower and a good night's sleep before you were fired like a bullet at a strange world.

My finger clumsily brushed my tapper, and the door slid away. A woman's figure stood there.

I sighed, worried that I knew who it was. I sat up, scratching. This girl Sarah was trouble, through and through.

"Can I help you, Miss?"

The woman stepped into my quarters, out of the darkened hallway. I rocked my head back in surprise. It wasn't anyone I'd expected. It certainly wasn't Sarah.

"Tribune Deech?" I asked, shocked. "What can I do for you, sir?"

The old battle axe herself strode in and looked me up and down. There she was—all polish and creases at this hour. I stood up, but she waved me back down onto my bunk.

"Were you expecting someone more to your liking?" she asked.

"Uh… no sir. I'm just surprised, that's all."

"I didn't have time to come down here to the pods until this late hour, I apologize," she said. "But I did see some of that nightmare you perpetrated on your unit today. Are your people in any condition to make the jump tomorrow?"

"We'll do more than that, sir," I said. "We'll be using rogue scientists as mops by noon."

"See that you do," she said. "Anyway, I was impressed by how hard-bitten you and your group are. When I asked Winslade which cohort had the toughest troops in the unit, he directed me to Graves. When I talked to him, he pointed the way to your door."

"That's mighty considerate of both of them."

She chuckled, catching the irony in my tone.

"That's what I thought. In any case, I've got an additional mission for you in the morning."

"What's that?"

"I want to you to shut down that dome, not just blow a small hole in it."

I looked confused, because I was. "How do we do that, sir?"

"First, you have to get to the dome. If you survive that long, your mission as it stands is to puncture it and stand guard over the hole until the rest of your cohort gets there and enters."

I nodded, that was pretty much the way I understood that things were supposed to go.

137

"But instead, I want you to press onward. We've calculated that after your early strike passes their automated defenses, you might be in disarray—"

"How's that, sir?"

"I mean that a large portion of your unit might be dead by then."

This statement surprised me. I'd gotten the impression all along that the mission was supposed to be a cakewalk. Now, I wasn't so sure.

"But you want me to continue to penetrate the dome—after my mission goals are completed?"

"That's right. Instead of guarding the entrance, I want you to press on into the dome."

"What's the reasoning behind this change in orders, sir, if you don't mind my asking?"

"Well, it's only logical. The element of surprise is a big factor in this operation. Some of the exotic weaponry they have presumably won't be ready to operate at a moment's notice. If we can strike them hard and fast, we might actually reduce our casualty count."

"I see... so we're to press on into the dome and—how do we take it down, sir?"

"The dome isn't entirely physical. The base is more or less a puff-crete wall. But reaching upward from that root is a field of pure energy. All you have to do is find the power supply and switch it off."

"Hmm," I said, "Sounds simple enough. Is this to make it easier for the final bombardment?"

"No," she said. "Planet-busters would sweep away their dome whether it's on or not. What I'm hoping to do is capture more of these rebellious lab people alive. You see, we can't save the lab itself, but if we can get any of these tech-smiths off the world and put them to work later, after the Galactic audit, we won't lose everything they've been working on."

"I get it," I said. "If they built it once, they can do it again."

"Hopefully so. If you take down the dome, we can use pinpoint shots from orbit to destroy any resistance that's effective. These rogue scientists should give up all the faster, and we'll gain more through their survival than their extermination. They'll gain more from their survival as well."

"Okay then, Tribune. I'm your man."

Deech smiled then. It was a thin smile, but it was indisputable.

"Good. Your mission parameters will be fine-tuned by morning. Have a good night, Centurion."

"You too, sir," I said. "Uh… could I ask you a few questions, since you're here?"

"Certainly."

"Did you know, Tribune, that Primus Winslade gave specific orders that I wasn't to be allowed into your office for any reason?"

She blinked in surprise. "No, I didn't."

"Well, he did. Then sir, he proceeded to recommend me for this special mission. Don't you find that combination of events odd?"

She thought about it and cocked her head to one side. "Thank you for that information. I gather that you attempted to contact me."

"Yes, only yesterday. That's how I discovered the roadblock."

"Are you in the habit of visiting your commanders personally?"

"I am," I admitted. "I've always found it's conducive to the most frank of discussions."

"Indeed," she said. "Just the kind we're having now. What did you want to tell me, McGill?"

"Huh?"

"When you came to my office and weren't allowed in."

"Oh, right. Well sir, I wanted to discuss with you why we're hitting Arcturus IV. This star system is not in the Cephalopod Kingdom. It's part of Province 921. Imperial space, well within the frontier."

"My stellar geography is up to date, McGill," she said coldly.

"Right… I'm only a centurion, but can I assume the reason for this operation is political, not strategic?"

"It's both—but as you say, you're only a centurion."

"Uh… right sir. Sorry sir."

Deech left me conflicted, and I found I had trouble getting back to sleep.

It had been one thing to contemplate a planetary invasion. It was quite another to worry about having superior officers who were dumping obviously suicidal missions onto my head at the last damned minute.

-24-

The morning of the invasion came, and we ate heartily in the mess hall—the experienced troops did, anyway. The recruits looked kind of green. They picked at their food and worried about dying.

To entertain themselves, the older troops told the newbies horror stories about their own first jumps. The recruits were universally referred to as "splats"—which was the sound these kids were expected to make when they rained down on the target world.

"Listen up, splats," Harris told a group of five big-eyed light troopers. He was eating and talking fast. He was also obviously enjoying himself. "When I went down the first time, I didn't tuck-in right when they dropped us. In those days, they fired us out of the bottom of the ship and encapsulated us on the way."

Knowing where this was going, I sat down at the end of their bench. The recruits looked at me in alarm, but then when I didn't say anything, their attention went back to Harris.

"When the encapsulation shell slammed shut on you, if you didn't have your limbs tucked in right, well… Something could easily get cut off. In my case, it was my left foot."

He chuckled and stared off into space, shaking his head at the memory.

"So there I was," he said, "one foot in, one foot out. By the time I landed and the capsule opened, my toes were missing along with about an inch more of meat, and I recall the brown-looking stain of burned blood all over the outside of the capsule."

"Did they recycle you right away, sir?" Sarah asked. She was one of the five attentive listeners.

"Nah, they didn't have to. One of those big farty giants from the Rigel system caught me hobbling around not ten minutes after I landed. I couldn't run, and my snap-rifle was a joke against a serious monster like that—it just seemed to piss him off. *Wham!*"

Here, Harris banged the table with such force every plate and recruit jumped in response.

"He clubbed me down. Must have been buried a foot deep in that muddy soil of theirs… Anyway, you just have to get used to the idea that your first jump might go badly."

"Or," I said, interrupting at last, "it might not. I came down without a problem. We were scattered, but we found each other soon enough on Steel World and formed up."

Harris grunted at me. "As I recall, your specialist got killed when you ran a saurian back into the group."

I gave him an icy stare. "Scouting is an iffy business. We took down the monster, and we won the day in the end."

Harris chewed his breakfast methodically, falling quiet. I could tell he didn't like me horning in on his story-hour, but I didn't want him petrifying my recruits right before we deployed.

"The word is this mission should be a relatively easy one," I told the group. "We're coming down in a crater outside the field of fire of their auto-cannons. We'll advance, taking out the AI in the bunkers until we reach the dome. At that point, things should be even easier. We'll be going up against scientists and lab workers, not real fighters."

Harris eyed me doubtfully, but he didn't say anything. I knew what he was thinking, of course. If this was supposed to be a slam-dunk, why'd they send out the entirety of Legion Varus?

No one who was talking had an answer for that, so I chose to believe the good word from Gold Deck. Anyway, to me it sounded like it was high time to change gears and move on.

"Our new injection system is different on this ship," I told them. "We won't get our feet chopped off when we drop. Instead of slamming together two halves of the capsule, you'll be loaded into the tail end, like a bug being dropped into a tube. The key is: don't resist, fall fast and hard to the bottom of the tube. The lid will slide into place and seal off the tube a split-second after you drop. Then you'll be ejected at speed and it'll be time to enjoy the ride."

Standing up, I left them with a nod and joined the next table. I liked the idea of personally checking in with each team before this new drop procedure was tried out. Graves wouldn't have done it, but I didn't like to think I would ever be as heartless as he was.

Time ran out about ten minutes later. The lights lowered, then the floor blazed with colored arrows. We got up as a group and charged out in squads to the launch deck—Red Deck.

The splats went first, followed by their squad leaders. The idea was that if the enemy had anti-invasion turrets, these splats would draw fire and be shredded in their capsules. Hopefully, there would be so many targets coming down the AI aiming systems would be overwhelmed and unable to shoot them all.

The most experienced troops brought up the rear. That's when we had our first accident.

Being a tall man, I noticed an alarming problem with the revamped delivery mechanism. The new ejection system was supposed to be rated for a man my size—but sometimes, capacities are overestimated.

Sargon was the first to discover this. He was the second tallest man in the unit, after myself. He dropped like a pro into the hole in the floor, and I watched, being up next.

The damned thing took the top of his helmet and scalp clean off. It was the damnedest thing I'd seen since our last deployment. That top sliding cap—it came across like a blade and gave him more than just a haircut.

"Shit!" I said. That was all I had time to say aloud.

"Better duck, sir," Harris told me, barely holding back his glee.

I stepped up and dropped. There was no time to fool around. The capsules were timed, and missing your slot was unacceptable.

The best I could do was bend my knees and scrunch down as much as I could. The cap slid into place overhead with the sound of a guillotine rasping home.

The interior of the capsule was more than cramped. I'd been in coffins that felt more roomy.

Then the capsule swung around, and I braced myself. Like being fired out of a cannon, I was hit with tremendous thrust. The hammer-like blow hit my boots, but I'd been expecting it.

I was out in space now, although I couldn't see anything other than a few indicators and a tiny screen measuring my progress. The capsule was inverted again, aiming my feet toward the planet, and I soon felt the punch as I entered the density of its mesosphere.

Arcturus was a fairly stable sun, and the target planet had a significant atmosphere for a specimen of its size. Unfortunately, the air wasn't breathable. There was too much methane, carbon dioxide and even a sprinkling of sulfuric acid for spice. As a result, the skies were a permanent gloomy brown.

Plunging into this deadly stew, my capsule was buffeted by powerful high-atmosphere winds. We were inserted at an angle, otherwise the capsule would have burned up due to friction.

None of this mattered to me much right now. I was in the hands of the techs and the gods at this point, and I knew it. All I could do was try to control my breathing without hyperventilating. I wished I could talk to the rest of my unit, but that was impossible. The burning atmosphere around us caused a blackout that lasted nearly a minute.

At last, we punched all the way through the clouds and came down in our final approach. My capsule linked up with others, and I caught the general broadcast feed of information.

"Cohort three is down, light casualties," said an emotionless female voice. The voice might have been human or AI—it was hard to tell the difference these days. "Cohort six is taking fire… Casualty rate acceptable."

144

That line made me think the voice *was* from an AI. Most humans wouldn't calmly describe death and terror as acceptable under any circumstances.

Mentally, I tried to visualize where six was landing. As I recalled, it would be in the mountainous region overlooking the dome itself. Why would they get shot up? It was only speculation, but maybe the gear-heads down there had set up an AA battery on the cliffs overlooking their lab.

Whatever the case, my number came up next. "Cohort nine is landing now—light casualties."

There was barely a chance for me to sigh in relief. About a second after the voice announced how we were doing, I hit the ground. It felt like someone had taken a sledgehammer and hit me across the tread of my boots with it.

The capsule tipped over, and it felt like I was slammed onto my face. Then, I began to roll. That lasted for maybe six or seven revolutions, just long enough for me to start wondering if I was on the edge of a cliff, rolling down into an abyss.

Then, blissfully, the capsule hit something harder and stopped rolling.

There was no time to say a prayer. I punched the release and a loud hissing sound began. The capsule opened, and I slithered out of it.

I was wearing a vac suit, of course. The air was poison, and we were going to have to get used to living with full protective gear.

Temperature-wise, the air wasn't too unpleasant. It was maybe twenty five degrees Celsius, and there was almost no breeze. The sunlight was dimmed by the brownish hazy air. I couldn't even see Arcturus in the sky—the clouds were too thick.

The landscape around me was wet-looking rock. There was some kind of viscous mess covering every rounded black stone under my boots, and they shifted under my feet as I walked. The going was rough on this planet.

Looking around, I saw more capsules with their occupants crawling out of them. I switched my radio to the tactical channel and demanded their attention.

Soon, a half-dozen troops were following me. I found Leeson and handed him his people. After about seven minutes, we were all assembled—except for Sargon. He'd died of blood loss on the way down.

"We splats made it," one of the light troopers pointed out, "but our veteran didn't."

"That's right, those are the breaks," I told her. "Leeson, you'll have to babysit Sargon's team personally."

"Wouldn't have it any other way, sir," he said with false enthusiasm.

"All right, we've got about twenty-three minutes left to reach the dome walls. Mind your pace—we're going to head straight up, double time."

"What?" Harris demanded. "There's no *way*, sir!"

"Not if we stand around here, there isn't."

We charged up the crater walls to the crumbling lip and went over the top. Several troopers seemed to trip and tumble back down into the crater again—it took me a second to see the blood.

They'd been met with a silent hailstorm of bullets.

-25-

The first casualties on Arcturus IV were two light troopers. They'd reached the top of the crater first, and they wore almost no armor. Their ravaged bodies were sent sliding and flopping back down past us to the bottom of the dish-like formation.

"Take cover!" I ordered. "Harris, scout the ridge. Pinpoint and mark the source of enemy fire."

Grumbling, he led a team of lights up there. They crawled through their last steps. The weird thing was we'd never even heard anything—could their turrets have silencers on them?

Not taking any chances, Harris had a tech send up a drone first. It buzzed around above the crater for perhaps thirty seconds before it was silently blasted from the sky.

Kivi picked up the twisted body of her buzzer and looked at it in concern.

"This isn't good, Centurion," she said. "The turrets were supposed to be a kilometer away. Either they have fantastic aim, or there are defenses we don't know about."

"Yeah…" I agreed. "Time to send up crawlers."

The techs rushed the crater wall and began launching more drones. This type squirmed among the wet sands and dark rocks like mechanical worms.

The crawlers lasted longer. It was nearly three minutes before they were blasted to scraps.

"I've got some good video," Kivi told me.

"Feed it to everyone on command chat. Upload it to the whole cohort."

The fire turned out to be coming from several directions. There was more than just one large AI-driven turret out there. The bullets were small caliber, but they were coming at us in silent and deadly sprays from multiple angles. It was a good thing we'd landed in the cover of this crater.

Deciding it was time to report in to my primus, I called Graves.

"Sir?" I said, "we've got a problem. We're pinned down already in that crater."

"How many have you lost?" he demanded.

"Seven, sir, including splats."

"That's pretty good, as it turns out. The enemy has set up numerous small stations to pick off anyone who isn't under cover. You're one of the closest units to the dome, but you've actually suffered the least."

"What are my orders, sir?" I asked.

"To perform your mission, McGill. Knock out the turrets and report back when it's safe to move up my rear units."

"Will do, Primus."

My heart sank as I looked over the tactical situation. The techs had pinpointed fourteen small turrets, and that wasn't even counting the big gun a kilometer off. I didn't want to know what that was going to do to us.

"Natasha!" I boomed. "Over here! Kivi too."

They were my two best techs. I let them work on a solution while I placed my troops along the rim strategically. In case these so-called "lab workers" had more surprises for us, I wanted to be ready for anything.

"Ladies," I told them a minute or so later. "I need a miracle."

"We haven't got one," Natasha said, "but we have a risky strategy."

"Give it to me."

"We have to weaponize our drones. Normally, that wouldn't work as they're too small to carry a charge that could kill an armored man. But this is different. If they can reach those small guns and blind the AI's sensors, we should be able to move forward."

"Are we talking buzzers or those wormy things?" I asked.

"It has to be buzzers—and they have to reach the targets very fast."

"All right... I'm working on a backup plan—but it's not going to be popular."

They worked to reconfigure their buzzers to carry small explosive charges. While they did so, I met with the unit weaponeers. We were down to five of them, since we'd lost Sargon.

While I explained my plan, I dug Sargon's belcher out of his capsule. I tried not to look at the mess inside. Carrying the belcher and some charging pods with it, I led the weaponeer team up to the lip of the crater. We crawled there, and we didn't dare do so much as peep over the rim.

"Now," I told them, "this is phase two of the plan. We'll have to be quick and accurate. When the buzzers fly, stay down. If the techs say the buzzers are getting hit, we'll pop up and fire at the turrets. One shot, that's all you get. I'll mark your targets on your HUDs. You won't be able to hear them, but you should see a puff of smoke. Aim there, fire once, and duck."

When Kivi and Natasha were ready, they released their buzzers. The tiny black robots swarmed up and split off in multiple directions. For several seconds, nothing happened.

Then, Kivi called out. "One has been destroyed—two!"

"Now!" I shouted. "Up, aim, fire, cover!"

We surged over the lip of the crater, putting the long heavy tubes of our belchers on it. Finding a puffing spot, one that looked like it was pumping out pulses of white smoke, I fired and immediately dove back down.

A few seconds later, we were all down, breathing hard.

"Everyone okay?" I asked.

They were all good. I dared to grin.

"I think the buzzers got three," Natasha said, "but it's hard to tell if they struck their target and destroyed it, or they were knocked out at the last second."

I nodded. "Kivi, fly one buzzer straight up. Let them all shoot at it. I want to count the surviving guns."

She did so, and we soon had our number. There were only seven left.

"One more time," I told my team. "Mark your targets… Go!"

The buzzers went out, sailing high into the brown sky. They soon plunged down again on Kamikaze runs.

"The buzzers are taking hits!" Natasha called out.

"Up!" I shouted, and my weaponeers popped up to play our little trick again.

I sighted, I pulled the trigger—and something hit my belcher. The man next to me cried out, and spun around with a hole in his faceplate.

"Down!" I roared. "Everyone down!"

We scrambled back down from the rim again, and no one else was taken out. But I was left shaken.

"How's that possible?" I demanded. "It should have worked even better the second time—there were only half as many turrets."

Natasha looked at me strangely.

"James," she said, "I think they adapted and changed tactics."

I squinted at her, understanding what she meant.

"You're thinking these turrets are smart?" I asked.

"Yeah. They learned—from one mistake, they learned."

"Hmm…" I said. "I know plenty of troopers who wouldn't have figured out what to do that quickly."

She nodded and stared up at the ruddy brown sky. "Yeah," she said. "They're quite impressive."

I phoned in the report of our progress to Graves, and he listened quietly.

"We're getting similar reports," he said. "Automated defensive systems that change tactics—but this is the first I've heard of self-learning weapons. Isn't that an advanced machine function?"

"I'd say so."

"Well, have you got any troops left?"

"Yes sir. Most of them."

"Then what are you waiting for? Finish your mission, McGill, or I'll relieve you of your command."

"On it, Primus."

Harris came crawling over to me. His eyes were big around, and I could tell right away he didn't like this planet, or the sneaky machines guarding it.

"What'd he say?" he asked me.

"He told us to stop pissing in our pants and get on with the show."

"Yeah... that's what I thought he'd say."

"McGill?" Kivi called to me. "We're all out of buzzers."

I looked at her and nodded. "That's great. What have we got left?"

Harris looked around and shrugged. "Well... We've got recruits."

That gave me a chill for some reason. Mind you, it was a normal thing for a Varus officer to say. Graves would have given the order without a qualm. But somehow, when it was my turn, it felt different. This centurion business was cold-blooded.

-26-

It took about thirty seconds to steel myself enough to do it. During that time, I made double sure my techs were out of buzzers—and fresh ideas.

"All right," I said, "I want all my light troopers to advance to the top of the ridge. When I give the signal, rush forward. Spread out, keep low, try to scramble for cover. You can crawl if you want to."

Sarah and her comrades looked sick. "What are the rest of you going to do?" she asked.

It was something the old James McGill would've gotten in trouble for asking, so I didn't yell at her.

"We're going to knock out the turrets while they're shooting at you guys."

The light troopers were almost hyperventilating by the time they snaked their way to the top of the crater and waited for the word. The rest of my people didn't look all that happy, either. After all, if the turrets had learned the last time, what would keep them from realizing the more heavily armed troops were the bigger threat?

"This plan depends on the light troopers drawing fire from those turrets," I broadcast to the group. "Don't worry if you go down, all that means is a quick revive back on the transport. Frankly, this might be excellent timing. We haven't got a revival machine operating down here on the surface yet, so for the foreseeable future, you'll be on vacation."

Sarah's eyes were big, her lips were parted, and she was blowing steam on her faceplate.

"Harris!" I said, "issue every light trooper a single grenade. If you get within throwing range, take your best shot."

They nodded and we all moved up close to the ridge, muscles tensing.

"On the count of three," I began, "I want every light trooper up and over the rim. On a count of five, everyone with a heavy gun is to stand and unload on the turrets."

No one said a damned thing. That was fine with me—Legion Varus for sure wasn't full of whiners.

"One... Two... Three!"

The light troopers, God bless them, did as I ordered. I was amazed and humbled. I wasn't even sure I would have done it back on my first deployment.

They scrambled up, showers of black dirt coming off their boots and knees. Most ran forward in a crouch and dove flat behind the nearest sizable rock.

I kept counting, and I knew by the shouts of pain that the turrets had come alive again.

"...Five!" I roared, and the heavy troops and weaponeers stood. We all sighted on turrets and blazed away. Even before we got them all, two of the lights managed to throw a plasma grenade that struck home. Before it was over, we had five dead recruits, but every single enemy gun was knocked out.

"Okay..." I said. "Harris, take what's left of your platoon and scout. The rest of you, fan out and follow me. Be ready to drop if we find another ambush."

We advanced a few hundred meters over the rough landscape, but no more turrets lit us up. We could breathe again.

"Centurion," Natasha said, "we're in range of that big cannon up there. We have to be—but it's not firing at us."

Peering, I zoomed in with my faceplate optics. She had to be right. I could see the thing now. It was shaped like a cone at the base, all shiny bluish metal. The turret on top was a big, ugly tube that swiveled around steadily. Past the big turret was the dome itself.

The dome wasn't glass, and it wasn't just an energy screen, either. It looked like some kind of crystalline surface—but that wasn't possible, to the best of my knowledge. Who would make a dome out of a single sheet of—whatever that was.

Putting the dome out of my mind, I focused on the turret. We had to get past it first.

"It's just sitting there," I said. "Did someone blind it, or knock its brains out? Have we had an orbital strike I didn't hear about?"

"No, I don't think so," Natasha said. "It looks fine, and the dome would be damaged if there had been a wide scale attack. They aren't dropping any bombs because the big turrets are too close to the dome walls. They didn't want to rupture the complex entirely and kill all the people inside."

"I'd welcome a little retribution from above right about now."

Natasha shook her head. "It's not coming. The tribune has ordered the ship's planned bombardment to stand down."

When we got closer, I could see the cover had been cleared from about five hundred meters out. There was nothing bigger than a fire hydrant to hide behind all that way in.

"It's waiting for us to get close," I said, feeling certain I was right. "It's holding its fire, baiting us in close. Once we advance into the open—maybe a hundred meters in, it will slaughter us."

Leeson walked up to me, peering at the alien-looking machine through his own optics. "I think you're right, McGill. That damned thing *is* smart—I can feel it too."

"We need something heavy," I said.

"I don't know, sir," Leeson said. "The dome is right behind it—if we miss, we'll knock a hole in that sucker as big as a truck."

"Yeah… I don't care. Who's your best weaponeer? What do you have with you?"

"Belchers. We're traveling light."

"We're in range. Set up every weaponeer you've got, everybody is to melt that tube from here with a focused, four-second burn."

"That might damage their weapons!" Leeson complained.

"We're going to get wiped if we don't do something quick-like."

He didn't grumble. He shook his head a little, but he followed orders. I was beginning to see what Graves had liked about the man.

The rest of the unit halted and stood around while the weaponeers adjusted their tubes.

"What the hell are you doing?" I demanded. "Keep moving. Advance slowly. Head toward cover. When we fire, dive low and stay down. You can't do anything from here against a hardened target with rifles."

They began shuffling forward again. No one wanted to get closer to that big turret. We all knew it was watching us, and no one liked it.

"Ready!" Leeson called out.

"Burn it!"

The weaponeers shouldered their tubes—and the turret reacted at last.

Had it been waiting for this precise moment? Or was it just triggered because one of my men had moved in too close? I would never know, but the evil machine came to life and began to move with unnatural speed.

"Fire dammit! *Fire!*"

Several beams lanced out together, converging on the structure. They all hit the target, and it began to spark and burn. Not everybody knows this, but metal burns just fine if you can get it hot enough. Multiple belchers generated a lot of heat when concentrated on a single point, and that did the trick.

The turret, however, had its own ideas. The barrel of that big gun started unfolding and rolling around, and it swept a beam over my advancing troops. Many of them had taken cover immediately—but not everyone.

Some men had nowhere to go. Like troops in a musical chairs contest, they dove and scrambled desperately—but the big blue beam of energy reached out and burned them down.

Such power! That cannon had the kind of impact I'd only seen on gunships up in space. It struck with so much force and heat that the dirt itself exploded under our feet. Eyes were blinded right through tinted faceplates, and troopers had the skin on their cheeks smoke, bubble and curl up—clean off the bone.

A massive roaring sound was all I could hear. That had to be the beam sweeping over my unit, annihilating my troops.

To their credit, the weaponeers stood their ground. They kept up that barrage of focused counter-fire for the full four-second burn I'd ordered them to release. By the time that short period was over, one of the weaponeers had ceased to exist. He'd quite literally been turned to ash.

The rest of us, though, were spared. The turret continued rotating, but the beam died. We'd knocked out the projector.

"Advance!" I roared. "Let's finish it!"

Charging, my men bounded up and rushed the turret. We felt like ants coming out of our tiny hill to bite a giant's foot. The turret reacted, moving and trying to target us—but we'd fried that big gun on top. It couldn't get out a beam to stop us.

When we got close, we threw grenades and destroyed the whole thing. It was pretty tough, but we managed it. Inspecting the smoldering crater we'd created, we found no operators, no rogue scientists were present.

"It was fully automated," Kivi said. "Just like the smaller ones."

"It was too clever by half," I told her. "It should have burned us the second we got into range, but no, it got all cocky and figured it could wipe us *all* out if it drew us in."

Kivi nodded. "Maybe the next one will be even smarter."

That idea disturbed me, because it was a real possibility.

-27-

We reached the dome's lower edge. It really was an impressive structure. At least three hundred meters high, it encompassed a vast area inside. Through the bluish-tinted crystal, I could see buildings, vehicles—but nothing was moving.

"Where are they?" Carlos asked, walking up to stand next to me. "They must not be total morons. They're not out in the open."

"That's right, they're hiding. Probably below ground level. The briefing indicated the lab complex was more extensive under the surface than it is up here."

"Why don't we just crack this dome, then?" he asked reasonably.

I shrugged. "Tribune Deech said *no.*"

"Sounds like our tribune needs some of your special magic, McGill. Why didn't you put the make on her when she came to see you last night?"

He'd caught me there. I'd hoped no one had known about Deech's visit to my quarters.

I blinked in surprise but recovered quickly. Upon reflection, I realized that within a small tight group like my unit, secrecy was pretty hopeless. Worse, if Carlos knew about it, then *everyone* did. He wasn't a man who could hold onto a bit of gossip for more than a few seconds.

"Deech isn't a very good listener," I said. "But she gave me clear orders. We're getting into that dome without leveling it. We're to arrest everyone we can, and kill only if we must."

"Those are pretty words," Carlos said. "It figures we're hamstrung by rules while these killer turrets chew us up and shit us out of the revival machines."

"Well then, you know the score. Now, shut up."

We walked to the base of the dome while we talked. According to common sense we weren't going to be circling around looking for a door. That would only lead us into more turrets—something I wasn't anxious to do. We'd already suffered a thirty percent casualty rate.

"You looking for a secret entrance?" Carlos asked. "Or…?"

I was freshly reminded about how much of a pain in the ass he could be when you were trying to do something serious.

"Natasha," I called out repeatedly over the unit channel.

She showed up, and we examined the situation with her equipment. Finally, she shrugged her shoulders.

"I guess we could climb up onto the metal base and burn our way in," she suggested.

"With a belcher?"

"Sure, it's worth a try. We could plug the hole with some smart-fabric and hope it holds without depressurizing the whole thing."

Nodding, I called in the idea to Graves. He roared back at me.

"No, no, no!" he told me. "Under no circumstances are you to damage that dome, McGill."

"What are we supposed to do to get inside then, sir? We reached our waypoint, and we're already ten minutes late. We can't get in."

"Did you check the destroyed turret?" he asked.

"Check it for what?"

"For a service tunnel or something!"

"Oh… uh, no sir."

"Get it together, McGill! Graves out."

Sending a few light troopers over to scout the damaged turret, they gingerly investigated the structure. Heading around to the far side, they vanished from sight.

"Centurion!" Harris called out to me a minute or so later. "They found something. There might be resistance."

"What kind of resistance?" I asked.

"The kind that just wiped out three of my recruits."

"Got it. Toro, deploy your heavies and advance. Search and destroy."

"On it, sir."

She trotted out there, flanked by a full squad in armor. At least she was game. Heavy troopers had powered armor and plasma rifles instead of accelerated projectile guns, otherwise known as snap-rifles. They were our regular troops, the backbone of any legion.

Advancing, they encircled the dead turret, looking for an opening, a downed light-trooper—anything. As they split now into two groups and continued to advance, Carlos shouted behind me. "McGill—Centurion, I see them!" Carlos wasn't with the rest of us. He was way back, behind me in the rear of the formation. He was pointing into the blue-glass dome.

I followed his gesture, and I saw them too. Several humanoids had pulled up inside the dome with a power-truck. They were unloading basketball-sized objects from the bed of the truck.

Frowning, I walked back toward the scene, straining to see them clearly. The glass—if it was glass—was very thick. The blue-tinted figures inside looked translucent.

These tech-smiths were tall. From what I could see, they were at least my height—some of the males were even taller. And they had long limbs, longer than was normal for a human.

I thought that would make them gangly and slow. But instead, they were graceful, and I watched as they dumped their globes into a chute on the far side of the glass.

That chute could only go to one place that I could imagine.

"Team!" I shouted. "The enemy seems to be deploying some kind of unfamiliar device. They can't be explosives—not unless they want to destroy themselves, too."

"Kivi," I said, "report this to Graves. Relay video of those packages they're using."

While she worked to comply, I watched the enemy drop the last of their spheres into the chute. Then they got into their power truck and zoomed away.

Graves called me personally a few moments later.

"McGill," he said, "I've got reports back from the far side of the dome. Get your men well back, form a wide firing field. They have drones. Don't let them get too close."

"Drones, sir?" I asked. "What kind of drones?"

"They're spherical, ground deployed drones. They'll attack with startling speed. Get your men—"

"Toro!" I roared. "Where is she?"

"They went inside," Natasha said. "They found a crawlspace or some kind of duct that accesses the dome."

I began to run toward the disabled turret. I didn't see Toro or any of her heavy troopers. "Back!" I shouted at the rest of the complement. "Fan out. Light troops, weaponeers—Harris, Leeson, get your people to form a half-circle around the base of this turret."

They were confused for a moment, but they moved to comply. Varus people had faced any number of nasty enemies on countless worlds. Even the freshest recruits quickly hustled to follow my command.

"Where's Toro?" Kivi demanded. "I can't get a signal from her. There's some kind of interference—that tunnel is shielded."

There was no more time for thought or talk. The drones began to boil up out of the duct and into the open field.

My troops didn't need any encouragement. Their weapons blazed. Only a few of the drones were able to reach our line. We wiped most of them out.

They were *fast*, just like Graves had said. Shaped like roly-poly bugs nearly a meter long, with churning tracks underneath, they were armored with segmented plates on top. It took a lot of firepower to stop them.

When we had a chance to examine them, we saw exactly how they were dangerous. They didn't blow us up, or bite anyone. Instead, they had what looked like stingers.

"That nail-like thing came right out of the shell," Carlos said to me, panting and staring at the smoking mess of parts at his feet.

Sure enough, I saw other drones repeating the trick. They ran in close, opened a segment of curved metal like a tank opening a slot in its armor, then out lunged an arm with a nail at the end.

But these weren't just nails. They were dribbling venom— or acid. Something that bubbled and flowed like thick glue, or fresh snot. Whatever it was, people who got stabbed by these nails crumpled to the ground in agony.

They writhed, screamed and died.

-28-

Our formation saved us. We were back far enough to destroy most of the nasty metal bugs before they could reach our lines. But by the end, we'd lost three more people.

"Harris, how many went in with Toro?" I asked when it was over.

"At least five," Harris said, "plus the three light troopers I sent in. They suckered us."

"Look at them!" Carlos called out, pointing toward the dome.

We craned our necks. The rogue scientists stared back through the blue glass.

"We can reach them if we rush through right now," Carlos suggested.

"No, that's what they want," I said. "They're baiting us. They've been doing that all along. Tricky bastards. Somebody loan me a belcher—mine burned out when we took down the turret."

A weaponeer approached and handed his over to me. I'd been a weaponeer back in the day, and the weight of the weapon felt right at home in my hands.

"McGill…?" Leeson cautioned. "Graves said we weren't supposed to damage the dome."

"Stop worrying so much," I said, cranking open the aperture on the belcher to its broadest setting. "Stand clear!"

Troopers scrambled out of the way. Perhaps sensing their danger, the on-looking dome-dwellers began moving back toward their vehicle.

I didn't give them any more time. I fired a blast—a widely dispersed flash of energy.

Beaming through the blue dome like a lens, it wasn't enough to damage the glass. But it did light one guy's hair on fire and set another one's clothes to smoking. They reached up and clawed at their eyes.

"You nailed the bastards!" Carlos whooped. "Now can we go into that death-tunnel?"

"I'd make you go first, but I need you," I told him. "Harris, take a team of lights down there and try not to lose them all."

"Damn you, sir!" he said. "I was just about to volunteer, but you beat me to it!"

We watched as they hustled into the hole. The recruits looked sick. There were only a few left alive. Most were back on the ship above, getting puked out of a revival machine.

Shortly after Harris' lights reached the entrance and began poking their way into it, I noticed something funny.

As I kept an eye on things, at first I didn't see anything but rocks and blue glass—but then, I spotted it. A puff of dust and dark smoke coming up out of the ground. I contacted Graves.

"Primus, something is happening" I said. "There's a disturbance in the area—a gas release I think, about four hundred meters west."

"Roger, McGill—keep an eye on that. We've got similar reports elsewhere. Report back any developments."

Frowning, I looked back at the men entering the service duct. All the light troops were in there by now, and Harris was ducking inside. He caught me watching, and he flipped me a quiet bird. I smiled at that.

By chance, I turned to look at the three lab-monkeys I'd injured earlier. They hadn't run off into the interior the way I'd thought they might. Instead, they were hunkered around some kind of equipment on the ground.

On a hunch, I walked closer to them and peered inside. The glass was more than thick—it had to be a meter of transparent material. That's probably why it looked colored, as anything transparent takes on a hue if you stack up enough of it.

The dome was so thick I couldn't really see their features, just their shapes, but they were definitely up to something.

"Harris," I called out, "what's going on down there?"

There was no answer, so I yelled for Kivi.

"Run a line down there. I want contact with that team, I don't care if you have to set up two cups and a string!"

She got to work on it, and it wasn't long before I could talk to Harris, shielding or no.

"We're in some kind of duct full of wires and pipe, sir," he said. "These power cables are as thick as fire hoses. You want us to cut one?"

"Nah, we already knocked out the turret they were powering. Keep advancing."

"Right," he said in disappointment.

I knew he wanted any excuse in the world to halt and screw around with something technical. The man who advanced slowest lived longest, that was his motto—unless he got pissed off. After that, he fought like a demon.

"Centurion?" Carlos said. "Uh… what's that?"

Following his pointing arm, I squinted at the region I had warned Graves about. The smoke was billowing out now, but it wasn't rising. It was flowing all over the place, getting closer.

"We'll soon be enveloped in that shit," Leeson said. He came to stand next to us. "There's another outlet over there."

Looking north, I saw what he meant. Another spot was gushing out dark vapors.

"This can't be good," I said. "Harris, in case we all have to come down into that pipe with you, tell me what you've found."

"Found Toro. She's been shredded. Looks like the same drones that attacked us."

"Roger that. Push in until you find the way out."

"That might not be a good idea, Centurion," he said. "I'm seeing a grate ahead, thick bars, no way through."

"Blow it up, cut it away, do your job!"

He grumbled, but he pushed further. I got his helmet feed now, as Kivi's set-up was finally working right. I could see what he saw.

The situation was grim. There weren't just a few finger-thick bars of steel in the way. The grate in question was more like a perimeter fence on a fire-base. Each bar was as thick as a sapling and as black as cast iron.

He shoved aside panicky recruits, attached a charge to the central bar, and ordered his people to retreat.

That's when they got him. Those drone-bugs slithered right under the bars in large numbers through the gaps. The bars were spaced perfectly for those critters to slide through while a man couldn't get more than arm deep.

The light troopers blazed away with their snap-rifles, but that just set up a deadly splattering pattern of ricochets in the pipe. Harris, in the meantime, was pinned by two drones that clamped on his boots, and six more that crawled over his armor, chewing up hoses and fabric wherever they found it.

He roared and cursed the whole time, and I didn't blame him.

"Centurion, I need help!" he called out.

"Harris," I said, "I can see the charge is set. Blow those bars!"

"I can't get out of range, sir!"

"I know that, dammit. You recruits, get out of there. Run for your lives!"

Harris' gloves were coming apart now. They were woven mesh, but these drones had teeth like buzz saws. They got through his left gauntlet, spraying blood all over the place.

"You're dead anyway, Harris," I said. "I order you to blow that grate."

"I hate you, McGill," he said in a labored voice.

Then, the signal cut out. A blast of soot and dust shot out of the service duct at our end.

Harris was on a one-way trip back up to the transport.

The last of the surviving light troopers came rushing back out of the duct a minute later. They were injured and desperate. Sarah was among them.

165

Seeing her crawl over alien rocks made me feel sorry for her. The faceplate on her helmet was cracked, and she was choking on the toxic atmosphere that was getting in.

Walking up to the last of them, I nodded. "You did well," I said.

"We didn't do shit," Sarah coughed. "Our weapons were useless, and most of us died like rats in a trap."

"That's right," I told her, "but you followed orders. That's appreciated. You saved the lives of others who are advancing after you, too. You are a crucial part of this battle."

She said something, but it was drowned out by a desperate coughing fit.

Deciding that now was as good a time as any, I executed her and her companions. They all had ruptured suits. It was only a matter of time before they died, and we didn't have time to do any babysitting.

Standing up again, I ordered my troops to gather around.

"Attach lines," I said. "That vapor will be here shortly."

"What if it's acidic?" Carlos asked. "What if it eats our suits?"

"Then we're screwed," I told him.

It took a few minutes for everyone to hook up. Our suits were equipped with filament lines with clips at the end. They could be used to attach troops to one another. Usually, we used them on worlds that had no light or any kind of dense atmosphere. They allowed us to communicate and find one another without vision or other sensory input.

Before we'd even managed to hook everyone up, the black cloud of dense smoke roiled over us. It looked like the kind of thing an oil-fire would emit. It absolutely erased our vision.

"Natasha?" I called out. "Analysis on this smoke—what have you got?"

"It's not breathable…" she called back.

"No shit?"

"It's not corrosive, but it is adhesive… I think it's meant to coat us with a dense film."

Already, I could see what she was talking about. I took a step, and I almost fell.

"It's some kind of slippery substance!"

"A fine aerogel. Clingy, slippery, sensory clogging."

I tried to wipe it away, but it was pointless. "All right people," I said, "we're going into that damned pipe. I'll lead the way."

Having started off near the entrance, I felt around until I found it. Others crowded behind me, complaining and bumping into one another. A few of them became disoriented and weren't able to get attached to anyone else.

"This stuff is preventing my sensors from operating," Kivi complained. "Not even sonar penetrates it."

"That's why we've snapped lines on. Let's go inside."

I tried to contact Graves, but the radio was out.

Crawling into the service duct, I felt a profound sense of claustrophobia. It's one thing to crawl into a sewer pipe, but it's quite another to do so when you can't see a damned thing.

Once I was in a ways, it widened out and I was able to almost stand. Behind me, my troops were tugging on the line as they fumbled their way in my direction.

"Come on, come on," I called out to them. "Quit playing with yourselves and get in here."

"How's it look down there, sir?" Carlos asked.

"It's great. Like a picnic on a sunny beach."

"That's what I thought."

I wiped an area on my faceplate repeatedly until I was able to see through the gunk. It was like having dirty oil smeared over your windshield, but with my suit lights on and wiped in a similar fashion, it was better than nothing.

The crawlspace was littered with dead troopers and fried drones. Apparently the drones curled back up into balls when they died. I kicked them out of the way.

The number of troops I'd lost down here—it was a crying shame. I told myself that if I ever commanded a legion, I'd flatten any dome full of rebels I met up with, and damn the casualties.

Behind me, the crawlspace began to fill up. About ten of us got inside before something else went terribly wrong.

Near the end of the chain was Carlos. He'd managed to crawl inside, and he'd just begun to wipe his faceplate clear.

"You're right sir," he told me. "This is like Heaven in here!"

He grinned, but then his line went taut behind him. It jumped, and so did he, jerking backward a foot or so.

He threw out his arms to catch hold of anything he could.

"Shit-damn! Something is yanking on my six!"

"Leeson!" I shouted. "What's going on out there?"

"I don't know, Centurion, but something just drew hard on our line. Maybe a vehicle hit our last man—there's been no gunfire, but I'm showing yellow circles on my HUD."

I activated the full unit locator, and the inside of my helmet filled with graphic data. I didn't always use the system as it was distracting in combat. But when you couldn't see anyway, it was more useful.

I saw right off that several of our people were dead outside, or I could hope they were out of contact and just reading dead on my HUD.

"Has the line been cut?" I demanded. "Sound off, who have we got out there who can tell me—"

That's about as far as I got before the filament connecting all of us jumped again. This time, Carlos was sucked right out of the service duct along with the next two guys in the sequence.

Everyone looked shocked, and we heard horrible noises being broadcast by the troopers outside. Screams, gurgles, and puffing, desperate breaths.

I'm not much good at complicated plans, but I do take action when it's appropriate. I rammed my way past several troops, banging them down on their backsides and into the walls of the pipe. I reached the man I was looking for. He clung desperately with a failing two-handed grip to an uneven spot on the tunnel wall. The tether behind him was as tight as a piano wire. I had my combat knife in my hand.

He looked up at me in shock, sure I was about to kill him. I grabbed for the slack line between us and held it up. I bid the man a solemn nod and shrugged as I cut the filament through— the ends slithering out of my hand. The poor bastard looked back and forth at the two pieces falling and then snapped

168

away—vanishing with tremendous speed into the utter blackness behind him.

-29-

"What the hell was that?" Kivi demanded.

She was clinging onto me. That wasn't like Kivi. We'd faced death together any number of times, and she could be as tough as nails. She didn't like dying, don't get me wrong, but she'd never seemed so afraid of it before.

She just kept staring into the black, roiling smoke outside. It wasn't coming into the crawlspace with us, possibly there was an air-pressure difference that was pushing it back.

"Specialist," I told her sternly, "you're a tech. Reestablish communication with the rest of my unit."

"Right... Okay..." she said, letting go of my arm and working on her tapper.

Techs had tools the rest of us didn't have. They carried a rucksack full of devices and a better computer than any tapper.

"Uh..." she said as I gathered up the last handful of troops I had with me and headed toward the bars where Harris had last reported in. "McGill? I can't raise anyone. Either that smoke is interfering with our communications, or—or they're all dead."

"Vital signs?" I demanded. "Anything?"

She shook her head. "Nothing. Not even dead-red location markers. We're cut off from fleet, and the unit."

"Should we go back outside and look for them?" asked one of the heavies.

"Nah," I said. "If they're alive, they'll make it in here. If not—well, we have to press on—we can't afford to lose this

170

precious ground. Our mission is to penetrate the dome and knock out any power source we can locate."

The whole team went quiet. They looked at me like I was insane. That was nothing new for me, mind you, but it annoyed me just the same.

"Come on now," I said, "this is Legion Varus. We're not some hog outfit. Sure, we're probably going to die, but I'm not going to hunker down in here and wait for it."

No one said a thing. Their bravado was spent. I understood. Historically, there were very few outfits that didn't break and run long before they reached a fifty percent loss rate. You couldn't help it. Even if you wanted to be brave, the back of your mind kept doing the math and declaring you a loser.

"Let's get this over with," I told them, taking point. "At least we might get a chance to roast one of those skinny friggers."

Harris' body was strewn over the deck, partially draped over the jagged bars he'd blown apart in his last, suicidal act. The drones that had been chewing on him lay scattered all around the place.

"Pick up some extra charging pods," I told them. "Who knows, maybe we'll get a chance to shoot something."

We made quick time after the broken grate and shortly came upon a round, blue disc of light. Before advancing further, I made another fruitless attempt to contact Primus Graves. I wiped my view clear one more time and advanced.

Coming out of the pipe and into the dome proper, I looked around. My rifle was up to my faceplate. Vac helmets always made it harder to handle a rifle, but we were trained for it.

"Clear!" I called back to the team after looking around cautiously.

They advanced timidly into the open space behind me.

The area under the dome was impressive. As I'd expected, the light here had a bluish cast to it. There were buildings nearby. They got bigger and bigger in a stair-step formation as they moved away from us. The largest buildings were under the peak of the dome, almost scraping it. Those nearby were necessarily squatty.

171

The weirdest thing was the smoke outside. It encircled the dome completely, reaching about ten meters up the side of the dome on every flank. We were in a sea of inky darkness, but the sky overhead could still be seen.

The power truck we'd seen earlier was still parked nearby, but no one was around to drive it. I found the first of the enemy dead a few meters off.

"Looks like this guy was killed when Harris set off his bomb," Kivi said.

"Yeah, looks like. Kivi, get into that power truck and try to get it running."

She did so effortlessly, and we climbed in. The power truck was bigger than a pickup truck, but there wasn't enough room in the cab for everyone. The troops in the back had their rifles balanced on the basket-like rim that surrounded a flat bed.

I wasn't sure that going for a ride in the truck was a good thing or not, but it stood to reason that we'd be pinpointed by their security no matter what. I figured we might as well move fast and have a look around before they sprung their next trap on us.

We headed into the center of the "city" without hesitation. I drove, because I pretty much knew everyone else was going to take their time.

Squeezing what appeared to be an accelerator-rod, I had the machine revving down streets and shaking as it made hard random turns. The streets were deserted and quiet. If I hadn't known there were people here watching for us, plotting to kill us, I'd have thought the place was abandoned.

"Where are we going?" Kivi demanded.

"We've got to put some distance between us and the original scene of the crime," I told her. "Haven't you ever run from the cops before?"

She looked at me in shock and shook her head.

"Have you got anything on your radio yet?"

"Yes," she said. "That black vapor was definitely interfering with our transmissions. We can talk to the ship if you like."

I didn't like, but I pulled over and shot a beam up to *Nostrum*. To my surprise, Graves himself answered.

"McGill?" he asked. "Are you still in the field? What's your status?"

"Yeah, I'm down here all right. I'm inside the dome."

"That's great… Yes, we're getting location data on you now. There's a power station about two hundred meters south of you. Head that way, and have your weaponeers knock it out."

"Uh…" I said, looking around at my handful of troops. "We're fresh out of weaponeers, Primus. I've got four heavies and one tech left."

"Shit… All right, you have to try anyway."

"You got it, sir. We'll do it, or die in the attempt. Just one thing: how'd you get back up aboard *Nostrum*?"

"I died, of course," he said, sounding irritated.

"Right sir, but your command unit was way back in the mountains. How'd they get to you?"

"That thick vapor you see outside is hiding an enemy force of automated defense vehicles."

"Hiding what, sir?" I asked.

"Crab-things. Some kind of biological combat system. They used the cover of the vapor to approach our units and destroy most of our troops. We've lost a lot of good equipment down there today."

That was classic Graves. He considered human bodies to be cheap and easily replaced. A good rifle, however, was another matter entirely. A gun or a space suit was harder to replicate than a soldier, and that made such things more valuable to him.

We followed his directions and made it to a building that was pyramid-shaped. We climbed out of the truck and approached the structure with our weapons at the ready.

"They can't use black smoke and giant robots on us in here," I told them. "They don't want to wreck their precious living environment."

"I have to admit," Kivi said, "I'm starting to want to blow a hole in this dome and finish them all."

"Yeah, I don't blame you Specialist. But we've got orders. Take down that door."

As my tech, she approached and tried it first. It was locked, and hacking it turned out to be hopeless.

173

"Good security," she commented.

"That's why I said to take it down. Do we have to use plasma rifles, or do you have a better trick in that bag of yours?"

She made a face at me and pulled a small charge out of her rucksack. She stuck it to the door bolt, backed up, and set it off.

Maybe the enemy had been waiting for this moment, watching and hoping a sealed, hardened door would stop us. But the second we knocked it down, they sprang up and went for broke.

They fired a shower of accelerated rounds down at us from every neighboring building. They'd come out of nowhere, from our point of view. The buildings had no windows—but they did. They weren't there one minute, then the next they were all over the place.

Fire-colored tracers streaked down, connecting my troops with the muzzles of enemy weapons now and then. Many missed, but several of my last troopers got hit. Two of them lived through the initial barrage, and we all returned fire.

The good news was the enemy had no armor. They weren't the best shots in the world either. Five, ten, fifteen of them went down, while we blazed back plasma bolts and ducked for cover.

"Science nerds my ass!" Kivi exclaimed, ducking down under the power truck with me. "These guys are fighters. We should put them down right now!"

"Agreed. When I'm a tribune, this kind of bullshit will end. All the resources we have at our disposal and here we are dicking around in a fire-fight under this dome."

She gave me a brief, searching look. "What makes you think you'll be a tribune someday?"

"It has to happen. Nothing would make Harris angrier."

Kivi chuckled and returned fire again. I could tell by my unit vitals we only had two other men left, and they were hugging the big wheels.

It was really hard to have a firefight with people up above you, especially while you're lying under a truck. Just ask anyone who's done it.

Although they'd lost their initial element of surprise, I could see we weren't going to win this. They were pulling up vehicles now, makeshift power trucks with higher powered guns mounted on the back of them. These blazed away, damaging the power truck we hid under. It might not run anymore, by the look of it. A trickle of fluids came down from the engine, staining my already smeared faceplate.

"We've got to make a break for the building," I said.

"We can't," she said. "It's too far, too open."

I glanced over to my right, and I saw what she meant. The door hung open, but it was a good ten meters away. That was too far by half with all the incoming fire raining down on us.

"Here's the deal," I told her. "I'm getting into the pilot's seat, and I'm ramming that wall. Crawl fast, and go under the truck to the doorway."

"You're not sending me?" she asked. "Why would you want to die that way?"

"You've got the bombs in your ruck," I pointed out. "Move! Everyone else, covering fire!"

The last two troops I had that could lift a rifle poked their noses out and shot at the enemy wildly, on full-auto. We didn't hit much, but we made them duck. These rogues had seen a lot of losses on their side already, and they may not even be trained to fight.

I got into the pilot's seat and rammed forward the power-bar. Cranking the steering mechanism to the right, I slammed the power truck into the smoldering doorway.

Along the way, unfortunately, I felt a hard bounce as I went over something solid. It could only be a body—one of my troopers.

I hoped that it was one of our dead. If it was one of my last survivors, it better not be Kivi. She'd be mad at me for years.

Regardless, I scrambled out of the truck and rushed the door.

I didn't make it. To be honest, I hadn't really *expected* to make it.

A big round caught me in the back and dropped me straight on my hands and knees. This one had gone through my armor—I saw the exit at the edge of my shoulder plate. Maybe it had hit a weak spot that had been hit before, I wasn't sure. It didn't really matter. I was lanced through, a sensation I knew all too well.

Getting hit by a hot bolt, rather than a solid kinetic like a bullet, caused a very different kind of wound. The heat burned you clean through. There wasn't as much bleeding, because the vessels were cauterized to ash. But it wasn't a pleasant way to go down. The tissue damage was tremendous, making more of your body non-functional immediately.

Knocked off my feet onto my face, I scrambled up—or tried to. Blood ran down, and the left side of my body didn't work so good. My arm dangled loosely, and I had to lever myself up with my right. Fortunately, my right side was up to the task, and my rifle was attached to my suit.

Crawling, my armor took several more hits in the back as I made it under the vehicle and then into the power station. I took a second to look back.

Kivi was dead in the street. I'd be damned if the power truck hadn't run right over her. Checking my HUD, I saw the others were dead-red, too.

Cursing, I did an about-face to go get her rucksack, but I knew it was no good. For one thing, the enemy was cautiously approaching from every side now. For another thing, Kivi's ruck was crushed under the same wheel that pinned down her broken spine.

Not knowing what else to do, I staggered into the dark building and managed to get square onto my feet. A few twisty passages and rooms led me to something that looked important. It was a glowing light surrounded by water. A Geiger counter on the wall indicated dangerous levels of radiation. These rogues might have evolved over time to take more rads than we could.

Not seeing anything else to do, I shot the glass encasement, hoping to rupture it. To my surprise, it broke, releasing a spray of hot steam.

As my faceplate had cracked and my suit was no longer in one piece, I was good and seared by that heat. I did a little screaming, but I kept firing until my rifle was empty.

Lying on the floor to avoid any more steam, I tried to ram another charging pod into my weapon. It was harder than it should have been. I knew I was dying, and my fingers were fumbling. Doing it with one hand was damned near impossible.

A face loomed close to me then. It was a female face.

She was lovely. So long and thin, with high-cheekbones like a fashion model back home. She had eyes that were tight slits. A small mouth, a long neck and long hair.

To me, she looked very human, but almost surreal. It could have been my blood loss, but I didn't think so.

Why do skinny women look so much better to me than skinny men? I don't know, but they do.

"You're lovely," I croaked at her.

She pointed a rifle at me and crept closer. Her face took on a curious expression.

"You live?" she asked, speaking with a soft, sing-song voice. "Do you yield?"

"Yield? You mean give up?" I laughed at that. Blood bubbled out of me as I did so. "No, Legion Varus people never give up. I'll die now, but I'll just come back tomorrow and finish the job."

"The tech-smiths simply wish to work unhindered to further our research," she informed me.

As she spoke I noticed some sort of badge bearing crazy symbols on her clean white garment and wondered if it was her name or title or maybe some company logo.

"Why would you work so hard to end us?" she asked.

"End you? We're just trying to get you off-planet. To evacuate your people, if possible."

She shook her head bitterly. "No," she said. "We have devices. We talked to those who agreed to leave—but now, they are no more."

That made me frown. *Damn it.* I knew my people. I knew the hogs, including their leaders and those above them who ruled all of Earth. The decision-makers back home were perfectly capable of such deceit and cruelty.

"I'm sorry about that," I said, "if it's true."

"Will you stop your madness, then?" she asked.

"No."

"But why? We did not expect you to get this far. Such determination… Why fight and die just to kill us?"

"Because…" I said, my words interrupted by a disturbing gurgle. Air was beginning for form up around my lungs inside my chest. Soon, I knew, I wouldn't be able to breathe at all. But that didn't matter much.

"Because of the Galactics," I told her. "They will erase all the human worlds if they find out what you've done here."

"Ah," she said, brightening. "You've spoken the first words I've heard from a human that I actually believe. All of it makes sense, if you are acting out of fear."

"We are," I said. "We always do that. My apologies."

"It's all right. I must apologize as well. We all have unpleasant acts we must perform."

Then, she shot me dead in the eye.

I couldn't blame her for that. In some ways, it was a relief.

-30-

When I came out of the revival machine, I wasn't angry. I was reflective. I was still thinking of the tall, dream-like woman I'd met, and the things she'd said.

After escaping the prodding of the bio people, I headed for the tribune's office. I skipped right by Graves, even though I knew that was rude.

Graves was in my direct chain of command, but I knew that telling him about what I'd learned would earn me nothing more than a shrug from him. He'd gladly put out a dozen blazing suns, freezing over planets teeming with people, in order to keep Earth safe. Hell, he'd do it just to nudge the odds in our favor. Death meant little to him.

It was only fools like me, in his view, that went around trying to find a less severe way to do things.

Before I could reach Tribune Deech, however, I had to get past Winslade. He personally intercepted me as I stepped foot onto Gold Deck.

"And what business might you have here, Centurion?" he demanded.

Winslade stood with his hands behind his back, no doubt clasped together. I suspected he might have a needler back there as well, hidden in his palm.

"Hello Primus," I said. "I've got a report to make."

His eyes became narrower and even more rat-like than usual. "Is that so? Under whose orders?"

"By order of Tribune Deech, of course."

Winslade gave me an unpleasant chuckle. "Nice try, McGill, but I know you're lying."

"Did you know she visited my quarters the night before the drop?"

His snide demeanor faltered for a second. Normally, a man in his position would laugh off such an assertion, but he knew that I'd had a very special, and very inappropriate, relationship with Turov when she'd been running the show.

"That simply isn't possible!" he snapped. "I would have known about it."

"Impossible, huh? Just as unlikely as you managing to weasel your way into the graces of yet another high-ranking officer?"

At the mention of his "weaseling" his eyes flashed with dark anger. His hand came around from behind his back.

He was quick, and sneaky, but I was ready for him. I caught his hand with mine and clamped onto him.

"Let go of my hand, Centurion!" he said angrily.

"What? Sorry, sir, I thought you wanted to shake."

As I said these words, I squeezed his hand for all I was worth. His face changed from rage to pain in a single moment. Then I heard a crackling sound. For a second, I thought maybe I'd broken a bone, but I quickly realized it was something else.

When I let go of his hand, there was blood and a small, crushed device between our hands. The wrecked needler was no bigger than a fifty credit piece. They tended to be a little delicate.

I smiled as the broken weapon clattered onto the deck between us. My grip had crushed it. They were built to be hidden, not to endure abuse.

Apparently, one could say the same thing of Winslade's hand. He shook it and cursed me through his clenched teeth. "Insubordinate little…"

"Well, Primus! It sure is lucky that weapon didn't go off unexpectedly—one of us might have gotten hurt."

"I'll have you arrested and permed!" he shouted furiously. "You can't assault a superior officer on this ship, McGill. I'll—"

"That would be a mighty big mistake, sir," I assured him. "I'm liable to confess all my sins if I get arrested now. That would be a crying shame. There are plenty of experiences you and I have shared in our checkered past which I think we'd both rather leave forgotten."

He glowered at me, but after a moment, a look of alarm crept into his expression. After that, he narrowed his eyes again with a new sneaky thought.

"Wait—what are you talking about? No one would believe you. All those claims of treachery and collusion—they were all disproven years ago at hearings on Earth."

"I'm sure they were," I said, "but there might be proof of contradictions. Facts are stubborn things, Primus. There may be a few out there you wouldn't care to have come to light."

The truth was Winslade was guilty of a raft of crimes, most of which I was no doubt unaware of. But *he* knew all the things he'd buried over the years. He also knew that if I was going down, there was no reason for me to keep quiet, even if I implicated myself.

"Very well," he snarled, clutching his hand. "Go talk to Deech, you'll get nowhere. She makes Turov seem angelic by comparison."

As I passed him by and made my way through the passages of Gold Deck, I had to admit I agreed with Winslade on one point. Turov was much better-looking than Deech.

"Centurion McGill..." she said as I entered her office. "Fancy meeting you here. I've heard quite a number of stories about you since our last encounter."

"All good, I trust," I said, looking around her office.

"Some of them were—some were quite the opposite."

You can tell a lot about an officer by the look of their office. Tribune Drusus had adorned the walls with the heads of slain enemy aliens. Trophies from a dozen campaigns on far-away planets.

Graves always sat in the center of his steel box. He didn't believe in fancy-ass decorations. Just tactical maps and other practical tools of war.

Deech was different. Her office held plaques, awards and gaudy star maps. These items were proudly presented, and each one indicated some kind of step in her career. This woman was a bona fide go-getter and a legend in her own mind.

"Huh," I said and walked over to finger a tiny purplish globe. "If I didn't know better, I'd say this was Ross-g, a misty world full of swampy principalities."

"Very discerning, McGill."

"Didn't you serve with the Iron Eagles? Originally?"

Deech assumed a posture of rigid pride. "I did indeed. Ross-g was one of our top assignments. No warlord was ever assassinated under my watch."

Nodding, I pretended to be impressed. Iron Eagles, Victrix and Germanica were all prissy legions, in my opinion. In years past, they'd liked to operate as color-guards. Usually, they'd spent years following some lordling around to impress other local petty tyrants on one planet or another.

Those times had passed all of us by, of course. We were all hard-fighting outfits now, but she seemed nostalgic for the old days.

Deech watched me as I poked at her trophies. Since she didn't demand I state my business, I kept exploring her office.

"Looky-here!" I said. "This is from the Galactics!"

"My greatest possession," she said pridefully. "A plaque from the Core Worlds, commending the service of the Iron Eagles."

I whistled at that. The only attention I'd ever gotten from a Galactic was the negative kind—as in an official demand that I be executed.

"Have you ever met the Mogwa in person, Tribune?" I asked her.

"I've never had the pleasure."

"Well, I have—several times. They're kind of snotty. They don't like it out in the provinces. They call us dark-worlders."

Deech stared at me. I took a glance and saw her mouth was slightly open, and she had the kind of squint to her eyes that indicated she wasn't sure if she believed me or not.

"Anyways," I said, "I'm here to report to you what I learned down on Rogue World."

"Something, I trust, that would be so critical you thought it was worth bypassing Graves to tell me about it?"

"Exactly. I learned this whole invasion is a waste of time. We should just bomb the planet now and cut our losses."

Deech frowned at me. "Are you accustomed to making large-scale strategic decisions for your superior officers?"

"As a matter of fact, that's come up before," I admitted. "Please hear me out before you dismiss me."

Then I told her what the lady scientist from the dome had told me. The scientists were fighting because previous Earth ships had promised to rescue them but ditched them in space instead. I didn't know if these cold facts would matter or not to Deech, but I figured I might as well give it a try.

"That's very interesting..." she replied. "But the Mogwa fleet is coming directly here—you knew about that, didn't you?"

"Yes, sir," I said, my heart sinking.

Her lack of surprise in response to my story told me two things: first off, she already knew, and secondly, she didn't care.

"Think, McGill, why would they travel directly here, rather than stopping off at Earth to question our officials?"

"Uh... maybe they want to catch us in the act of developing illegal tech out here?"

"Exactly," she said. "Now, if we don't care about these rogue scientists, what possible reason might we have for taking such great care not to destroy the dome?"

"Hmm... maybe we want to steal their data core, or something?"

She smiled. "This has been an interesting chat. I thank you for the report, and the tenacious way you brought it to me. Next time, it would be more helpful if you brought me something I truly needed to know instead."

I was starting to feel like I was in the principal's office.

"Just one more thing, sir," I said. "If we do find what we're looking for, will we let those lab folks live after that? I mean... maybe we can talk them into giving it up for their own safety."

"An interesting and very charitable idea. Unfortunately, we can't really afford to have thousands of angry civilians carrying around information that could get Earth erased, can we now?"

"Right... Thanks for being so honest with me."

"You're welcome, Centurion. Dismissed."

I left her office, my mind whirling.

Everything the lady on the planet had told me was true. The brass had lied to the troops again—but that was nothing unusual in my legion. In fact, it was downright commonplace.

But no one really likes genocide, not even the perpetrator. What my mind was chewing on now was the idea that something else could be worked out…

I kept thinking of that unearthly, fine-looking runway model down there on the planet below. Sure, she'd offed me without a qualm, but she'd done it for a good cause. I felt like I could reason with her if I was given a half a chance. It was more than I could say about my own people.

-31-

Winslade hadn't kept quiet. While I was talking to Tribune Deech, he ratted me out to Graves. By the time I got back to my quarters, there was a note on my tapper. It was red and blinking.

"Report to the Primus—immediately," I read out loud.

A few more of my unit's troops had been revived by then. One of them was Natasha, another was Carlos. As we weren't under attack in space, the algorithm had queued up the senior non-coms first.

Carlos was helping out with the revives and deciding who should be recycled in case there was a bad grow. Natasha was reviewing our cam data to see what had gone so horribly wrong.

"Natasha," I said, "come with me. We're going to see Graves."

She joined me as we headed to the cohort command office. Gold deck was reserved for fleet-types and legion brass. A primus like Graves was on the border-line in this situation. Depending on his assignment, he might get an office on Gold deck like Winslade had, or he might not. Since he was involved in direct combat ops, he'd been assigned to a cube just like we had.

"Centurion McGill," he said when I reached his cold steel walls. "Fancy seeing you here, instead of running around over the top of my head."

"Huh? Oh, right sir. Sorry about that. Deech asked me to report anything funny I found on the planet."

His demeanor changed. He had been reviewing summarized video of enemy capabilities from Natasha's vast collection of vids. Every trooper had cameras on their suits, but they generated too many hours of material for any one person to watch them all. It fell to techs like her to create highlights of the interesting stuff for the officers.

Graves stood up and gave me a stern glare. "McGill, I'm not going down this road with you again. You're not to bother the tribune with any wild, hare-brained scheme you come up with."

"I swear on my momma's grave that I would never even consider such an action."

"Your mother is alive, McGill."

"I didn't realize you took such an interest, Primus. I'm honored."

He heaved a sigh. "Look," he said, "when it comes to Deech, keep your pants on and your mouth shut. Is that clear?"

"Crystal, sir. Wouldn't have it any other way."

Natasha and Graves exchanged glances, and I could tell neither one of them trusted me. I wasn't sure if that was something to be proud of or not.

"All right," Graves said. "As the tribune hasn't complained to me personally, I'm going to assume you haven't set her off into a rage yet. You have your instructions. You're going back down with the first lifter in the morning. Assemble your troops."

"Uh… we're going down again, sir? What's our mission this time?"

He frowned at me. "What have you been doing all day? You were revived two hours ago. Check your logs, man. Tactical plans were distributed before those new lungs of yours took their first breath."

"Oh, that. Okay, Primus. I hadn't had time yet to review the documents."

"Well, do so. There will be no general briefing. We're going down, setting up a fire-base on the mountains above that damned dome, and we're going to take it. I don't care if every civvie inside dies in the process."

I nodded without argument. I knew personally that Deech didn't care if they all died either. Apparently, that might well make her mission easier.

"McGill," Graves went on, "your first unit action ended in a full wipe. Not a single survivor crawled out of that dome. Don't you want to avenge yourself and your troops?"

"It's a little more complicated than that," I said.

"How so?"

Natasha cleared her throat then. We both looked at her.

"I might be able to help clarify," she said, using her tapper to scroll through countless vids. She took us to the endpoint, a few moments before I was killed by that rogue lab-chief under the dome.

The imagery flashed up on the walls, and we all stared at it. Graves snorted when he heard her soft voice and saw her fine-boned face.

"Really, McGill?" he asked. "You found an alien girlfriend? It doesn't even matter to you that these people viciously slaughtered your entire unit?"

"She had her reasons, sir," I said. "You should listen to what she says. I mean, I don't agree with her, but I can understand."

He reached out and made a snuffing gesture with his hand. The vid faded and vanished.

"I don't need to," he said. "What I need is your assurance that you can complete your mission."

It takes a long time for a man like me to get mad—usually. But Graves was doing the trick today. Even Natasha was pissing me off. She shouldn't have played that vid and gotten Graves sniffing down the wrong track.

"Primus Graves," I said loudly. "Sir, how many other units were assigned to penetrate the dome?"

"Three," he said.

"And how many managed it, sir?"

"Just one—yours."

I nodded. "That should tell you all you need to know," I said. "The other teams might have had more survivors, but we

187

came closer to accomplishing our mission. We're the only ones that got in there, we reached the power plant, and I damned near shut it down myself."

He tipped his head back thoughtfully for a moment. "You did more than that. You did knock it out for about two hours. Rupturing the cooling jacket did the trick."

"Then I rest my case—mission accomplished, sir."

He sighed. "All right. You did well. The other units chickened and were devoured by the machines inside that black vapor. I'm just never certain how things will go when I deploy you into the field, McGill. It's a crap-shoot every time."

"I'll take that as a compliment, sir."

"You're dismissed, Centurion. And read those damned tacticals."

"Will do, sir. I swear it."

On the way out, I felt like strangling Natasha, but I controlled myself. "You've got a new duty to perform, Specialist," I told her. "Read all these tactical docs. Summarize and brief me before midnight tonight."

"Tonight?" she asked.

"Damn right," I said. "We drop in the morning."

"But I've got thousands of hours of suit-vids to review."

"Take a stim," I suggested. "Make Kivi help—and give her a stim, too. Hell, everybody gets a stim."

"Sir? Is this because I embarrassed you by showing Graves that vid of the girl?"

"Not at all," I said. "I'm neither petty, nor vindictive. I'd no more do such a thing than you would."

Natasha looked sullen. She knew I was calling her jealous as well as petty and vindictive. Clearly, she was still hauling around some baggage from our past relationship.

"Point taken, Centurion," she said. "May I be excused? I've got a lot of work to do."

"Get going.'"

She trotted off, and I watched her run. She had a nice shape to her. She'd lost some of her tone over the last year or so on Earth, but dying had been good for her. She'd regained her old body in top condition.

Sometimes, we all had to look at the bright side of death.

188

Along about midnight Natasha returned with her summary. I'd been sipping synthetic whiskey and relaxing, but I managed to stash the bottle before she walked in.

Her hair was a mess. It looked like she'd been running the palm of her hand through her bangs. She looked tired, but triumphant.

"You were meant to spend all day on this—it's a full dossier," she told me.

I nodded, keeping my face neutral. I realized that she'd mistakenly read the whole thing. That would include orders and plans for the entire cohort. As a centurion, I was only responsible for reading my own unit's mission plan, or maybe others I was likely to come into direct contact with.

Sensing that telling her that now would be another mistake, I listened as she described the briefing. She did a great job.

"Okay," I said when she was done. "We're dropping at dawn on the biggest rock formation that overlooks the dome. We'll try to probe—to bait them into doing some of their tricks. We'll destroy their defensive machine and biologicals then invade when the vapor disperses, about an hour later."

"That's the gist of it," she admitted. "But you got all those other details, didn't you?

"Certainly," I said. "I've committed them all to memory. You did fine work here, Natasha, above and beyond. Why don't you take the rest of the night off? You can process the vids from our first action later. There won't be any time for the troops to review them tonight, anyway."

She looked troubled by that, but she smiled gratefully. "Okay," she said.

Then she frowned at me and cocked her head. "Do I smell alcohol?"

I grinned. "A drop of it, yes," I admitted.

Revealing the squeeze bottle, I poured her a dollop and handed it over. She looked at it dubiously and sniffed it like a cat with a new food dish.

"Is this stuff safe to drink?"

"It's sterile, if that's what you mean."

She actually took a probe from her kit and dipped it into the cup. I shook my head as she read the chemical analysis.

189

Natasha always had been the smartest girl in the unit. She was more of a brain than an emotional type, but she could be both under the right circumstances.

Finally, when she was satisfied she wouldn't be poisoned, she sipped the drink. Making a face, she sipped some more.

We talked, and a few minutes later I gave her a fresh cup. That was it—after that, she was stone drunk.

I was getting pretty happy myself. We laughed and made sloppy love about an hour later. It felt just like going home again.

"I missed you," she said when she was lying on my bare chest.

"I missed you too," I said, and I meant it.

"Are we going to die again tomorrow?"

I hesitated, but I didn't see any advantage in holding back the truth from her now.

"Yeah... probably."

She heaved a sigh after that and went to sleep.

-32-

The next day was even more of a shit-show than usual.

I didn't even get a solid night's sleep. Usually, before a drop, they fed us well and let the food settle in our guts an hour or so before we boarded the lifters. Sometimes, if the ride was expected to be especially rough, they'd just give us this disgusting liquid-protein stuff and some motion-sickness patches.

Today was different. About an hour before we were supposed to be awakened by the ship's computer, a klaxon went off.

"What the hell...?" I asked, heaving myself up to a sitting position.

Natasha was an experienced soldier by now. She rolled right off of me, sat on the floor and started working her tapper—hangover and all.

Yawning and pulling on my boots, I saw the floor light up.

"Uh-oh," I said. "Looks like an alert. What's on the feed?"

"We're under attack."

Now, that surprised me. The rogues had shown they were resourceful, but I hadn't figured them for the kind who might be able to strike at us up here in orbit.

"What have we got?" I asked.

"Some kind of missiles are incoming."

"Dammit. I hope they don't wreck this nice ship. We're still breaking it in."

"Orders, Centurion?"

I pointed at the flashing arrows on the floor. Every recruit knew they were to follow them in an emergency. "We're a combat team, so we follow the red ones."

Kicking it into gear, we suited up and grabbed our rucks. Fortunately, legionnaires were permanently packed. The smart ones even kept their toothpaste ready for action.

Clanking and banging our gear on the walls as we moved, we trotted through the passages of the ship. As a unit centurion, I no longer had the task of babysitting recruits and regulars. I had noncoms to do that.

Instead, I communicated with my adjuncts as I ran, telling them to get their platoons to the lifters on Red Deck pronto. At the same time, I listened into command chat—picking up what was going on with the whole legion.

At my side was Natasha, to whom I'd given the task of monitoring ship-board data coming from Gold Deck.

"It's not good," Natasha told me. "They launched five missiles—it doesn't seem like much of an attack, but we haven't been able to take any of them down. They're punching through our countermeasures. Lasers are bouncing off—it looks like some kind of new reflective coating and an aerogel shield surrounds them."

"Hmm…" I said as we reached the main hatch on the lifter. "How long have we got before they deliver a payload?"

"About seven minutes—but it could be less."

"How could it be less?"

"Not all missiles carry conventional fusion warheads."

I didn't really know what she was talking about, but I figured *she* did, and that was good enough for me.

"Okay, listen up," I said. "Since we're supposed to be the first group off the ship, we're supposed to load-up last. Stand aside and let the other units board ahead of us."

A modern lifter held a full cohort, about twelve hundred troops altogether, plus a lot of gear. It was able to carry more in a pinch, but the brass didn't like to overload them if it wasn't entirely necessary.

We watched as two more units straggled in and boarded. There were three units aboard plus mine which was standing around outside on the dock. There was nothing else here other than a big pile of equipment for everyone. We took our portion and stood milling around.

Beyond the lifter, I could see the stars outside. They caught my thoughts for a moment. From here, they didn't look threatening, but they were blazing nuclear furnaces when you got up close—chock full of radiation too. Space was always deadly, no matter how peaceful it appeared to be from your viewpoint.

"What's the damned hold-up?" Harris finally shouted in my headset.

"Don't know," I admitted. "Is Graves aboard yet?"

"Yes sir," Natasha told me.

That's what I liked about her. She kept tabs on everything. If you weren't paying attention, she was. She functioned like the extra brains I'd somehow missed out on at birth.

"This is bullshit…" Harris said.

"I second that motion," Toro added.

I glanced around, and they were all looking at me. I was getting an odd vibe… Could they be expecting me to take drastic action? Was there some particular thing they were hoping I'd order them to do, so I would take the heat for it later? It seemed to me that they were.

Instead of answering, I sniffed loudly and checked my tapper.

"Invading a planet without breakfast…" I said. "It just seems barbaric."

Leeson sidled up to me. I couldn't recall ever having seen him do that before—at least not to me.

"Sir," he said in a low tone, using private tactical radio only. "Let the next unit climb over our feet. This lifter might get orders to eject any second."

I shrugged. "If it does, I'm not going to be the one who wasn't where I was supposed to be. Not this time. I have been awarded new levels of responsibility, and I intend to behave accordingly."

Leeson looked confused and a little pissed off. He'd always been a man who had a short temper.

"What's gotten into you?" he demanded. "Since when have you followed a petty order to the letter when circumstances dictate you could get away with something else?"

I shrugged. "We stand until we're ordered to move, or until everyone else is aboard."

He squinted at me suspiciously. Toro tapped his shoulder. She flashed me a look of disgust.

"It's no good, Adjunct," she said. "I heard our centurion here is infatuated with these rogues."

"What?" Harris shouted. "Are you kidding me? Centurion, did you bang one of those skinnies down there already? I mean, seriously?"

Heaving a sigh, I looked down at Natasha—who was quite red-faced. That told me all I needed to know. She'd apparently spread around some version of yesterday's events that was less than flattering.

"Sorry sir," she said. "I—that was before last night. I misunderstood the situation, and others must have embellished upon what I said."

"Gossip..." I said, shaking my head. "It's just too good to pass up."

I couldn't be too mad at her. After all, there was some truth to the claims. I hadn't touched the scientist in question, but I *did* feel like slowing this invasion down a little in her favor. I wasn't in any kind of all-fired hurry to go down there and slaughter anyone.

In fact, I'd been entertaining a highly treasonous line of thought over the last few minutes. If—just *if*, mind you—the transport was about to be blown to fragments—so what? We'd all be okay. Legion Varus would be revived back on Earth when the mission failure was reported. That sequence of events was about the only way I could think of that would allow the people on the planet below to keep breathing.

And who knew? If these rogue research techs could trash an Earth Legion, maybe they could knock out the Galactic ships that were reportedly in transit to Arcturus, too.

Alas, my subtle plan of stonewalling was demolished by Graves.

"McGill!" his voice boomed in my ear.

"Yes, Primus!"

My eyes darted around my team. Someone had ratted me out and kicked this upstairs. It could have been any of them, or all of them. Only Harris was meeting my eyes, and he looked pissed. That didn't mean anything, as he almost always looked pissed.

"What are you doing standing around on the ramp with your thumb up your butt?" Graves demanded.

"Sir, I've been ordered to be the last unit to board."

"You *are* the last unit!" he shouted. "The others were knocked out."

"What...? How, sir?"

"Didn't you feel a strike just moments ago?" Graves demanded in my ear.

"We didn't feel a thing, sir."

"Really...? It must be the new dampeners. I guess they're working even better than expected, Centurion. Anyway, the enemy warheads got within ten thousand kilometers when we met them with kinetic countermeasures. Rather than being knocked out, their onboard AI must have set off their warheads."

"Isn't that way too far off to affect us?"

"Normally, yes, but they were X-ray bombs. Atomic-powered lasers. That kind of tech only works once, but that's good enough. Extremely powerful X-rays beamed through the ship with precision. Every trooper who was still in the hold—still inside their cubes—died within a short time."

My mouth dropped open. So that was it. The missiles hadn't been intending to knock out the ship, they'd been going for our troops.

"How many did we lose, Primus?" I asked.

"About sixty-five percent. Command chat hasn't released any of this info yet, by the way as we didn't want to cause a panic."

I snorted. "A panic? There's no such thing in a Varus man's heart, sir!"

"Good to hear. Now, I'm sending some pigs loaded with extra gear. Every lifter has a revival machine aboard. They'll work non-stop to rebuild the legion. But the fresh troops will need gear, and it's your unit's first mission to load the ship with everything you can in the next ten minutes."

That's when I remembered there was a big pile of extra equipment in the lifter bay already. Battle-suits, beamers, snap-rifles and rucksacks filled with every type of gear were stacked high.

While I spoke to Graves, I pin-wheeled one arm. Troops began grabbing the extra gear and rushing up the ramp. They vanished in the dark maw of the lifter.

A pig came in with more, and we kept loading.

"Take the first section," I ordered my men. "Right here at the hatch."

To fit aboard as many troops as possible, a unit would normally press deeper into the rows of jump seats to the very back before sitting down. That way, the next load of troops wouldn't have to trip over boots and gear while coming aboard.

Graves contacted me again several minutes later. "Are you aboard yet?" he asked. "I can't see your suit cam online."

"All present and accounted for," I said, and I twiddled my body-cams back into the "on" position. I'd turned them off the night before when things had gotten interesting with Natasha.

"There you are," Graves said. "Tell your people to hang on. We're decoupling now."

After we got everyone aboard, the ramp began to close. A few stragglers had to climb and scramble to get inside. They managed not to get crushed as the ramp slammed shut.

As we cast off, I felt a distinct sense of motion. The big, fat ship slewed around and began to immediately plunge toward the planet's distant surface.

I had to hand it to those dome-dwelling rogues, they were resourceful. I couldn't help but wonder what other surprises were awaiting us when we got down onto their home turf again.

-33-

"X-rays?" Harris demanded incredulously after I relayed the facts to my command team. "You mean, like, what they use to shoot me in the mouth once a year?"

"Not exactly," Natasha corrected him. "These X-rays are much more powerful. It's not just radiation passing through the body to form useful images. Think of radiation that pierces every living cell in many people at the same moment. The organs are lethally damaged, and death quickly follows."

"That's crazy!"

"I think the attack makes sense," she said. "Kill the troops and the crew first, and you don't have to worry about an invasion. We're lucky they didn't wipe Gold Deck as well. If the missiles had gotten any closer, they probably would have killed everyone aboard all at once, wiping our legion in a single strike."

"Makes sense to you, maybe," Harris grumbled. "You techies love mass-death. It's just not an honest way to kill a man. Can you tell me this: why didn't they strike our ship with these missiles the second we showed up in orbit?"

Natasha shrugged. "Maybe they take a long time to target. Maybe we moved inside their effective range too quickly. We rushed straight in and dropped on their planet, remember. With our troops all deployed on the ground, using anti-personnel missiles on the transport wouldn't have been as effective."

"Huh…" Harris said, turning to me. "So, what's the plan, Centurion?"

"We *did* have a plan," I said, "but losing two thirds of the legion has probably changed all that. Command chat indicates that all six of the surviving Primus-level officers are discussing it now."

"Say what?" Harris said. "What about Deech? She's in charge."

"Not for the moment. She was reviewing troops in the cubes, and she was killed with them. The revival machines back on Blue Deck are pumping people out stat, but by the time she's back in the game we'll be down on the ground."

He frowned at me. So did Toro, Leeson and even Natasha.

"Who's in charge then?" Leeson asked the question that was on everyone's mind. "Tell me it's Graves."

"It should be," I admitted, "but the word is that it's Winslade for now."

There was a collective groan heard among my officers and noncoms. If there was an officer who was more reviled and less respected than Winslade in this legion, I didn't know who it was.

Serving the legion in the past, he'd been a pet-project of Turov's. When she'd bailed out on Varus and joined Hegemony—which everyone in the legions called the hogs—he'd followed her.

But after that, there'd been some shenanigans during the invasion of Earth by the Cephalopods, and Winslade had been sent back to Varus again. Their loss was our loss on that deal, the way I figured it.

About then, as if to reinforce my intel on the command situation, a familiar voice penetrated our helmets. It was none other than Winslade himself.

"Citizen-soldiers," he said. "We have been horribly wronged. Our rescue work here has been rejected by the rebellious lab-dwellers on the planet below. They have struck a great blow against the legion, one that cannot go unpunished."

I had to admit, old Winslade could turn a pretty phrase when he wanted to. It was all bullshit, of course, hot air about how mean the renegade scientists were for defending

198

themselves. He persisted in the myth we were here to save the locals despite themselves, and he was so convincing it sounded like he believed it himself.

After speechifying for three long minutes, he finally got to the point.

"Now, things are different," he said. "We can't afford further losses. Our generous hand has been turned into a fist. These rogues have forced us to act harshly."

"Here it comes," Leeson said, "and it's about damned time someone took the collar off this dog."

"Naturally," Winslade continued, "we'd rather isolate and arrest the malcontents and bring them to formal trial. Due, however, to our reduced numbers and the persisting resistance of the local population, that's no longer feasible. Every legionnaire is hereby ordered to use deadly force in the face of any opposition. Any hostiles who do not immediately surrender upon making contact with legion personnel are to be shot without hesitation."

My troops looked around at one another. We wore grim expressions. The enemy was tenacious and mean, but they didn't seem to have revival machines. When they died, it was permanent every time. It seemed a little unfair, when all things were considered.

Winslade signed off after assuring us with a promise of swift victory. We muttered glumly and reviewed the new mapping data being transmitted to our tappers.

Instead of dropping in three strategic locations in the highlands surrounding the dome, we were now going to be placed in a single spot of rough terrain. The LZ was about a thousand meters above the dome, and due north of it.

"All they have to do is get one more of those missiles to fly over our camp," Harris complained. "Then it's lights-out for everybody."

I slammed him on the shoulder, earning myself a glare.

"We're not going to let that happen, Adjunct," I told him. "When that lifter ramp drops, I want every jackass on this bus racing down there and seeking cover. When we've swept the immediate area, we'll get fresh orders, probably to mount an attack. Time to gear-up soldiers, and don't forget to say your prayers."

We rode down through the atmosphere with our teeth grinding. Only the good Lord knew what these people had in store for us today. The one thing I was sure of was they'd never go down without a fight.

When we struck ground the ramp dropped, and we rushed outside.

The planet looked much the same as it had when I'd last been here. It was all black stone, and mist lay over the landscape like a thick coat of teargas. Over my shoulder, Arcturus was big but very dim in the sky, visible through a shroud of thick brownish clouds.

"Take up defensive positions!" I called out.

Carlos came up to me and waved. "Good to be back on this shithole, Centurion," he said.

"It's like an April picnic in Georgia," I agreed.

"I got myself reassigned," he told me. "All the bio people were being called up to work the revival machines aboard the lifters. We've got to churn out a new legion."

I nodded. "Any news about Deech?" I asked. "Has she been revived yet?"

"No sir. She's staying in limbo."

My eyes narrowed. I knew what that meant. "Winslade likes the taste of command, eh?"

"Seems like it."

Harris came near, cursing. "Is this for real, Centurion?" he asked me. "Winslade's going to get us all killed—like ten times over."

"Nothing I can do, Adjunct."

"The hell you say," he retorted, looking me over. "That doesn't sound like the James McGill I know so well. Why don't you go have a talk with Winslade in his command bunker?"

"He has a bunker?"

He gestured off to the south, at a low point that was sheltered from the dome and everything else. Working with heavily laden, supply-hauling 'pigs', a team of men were building a structure out of puff-crete.

"He's got himself a well-stocked cave," Harris said, "I want to spit, but can't do it inside a faceplate."

"You can," Carlos interjected brightly, "but it would be messy."

"And you," Harris said, turning on Carlos. "You're one of McGill's butt-monkeys and a bio to boot. Get over there and poison Winslade's soup or something."

Carlos shook his head. "He's following protocol. Winslade was designated second in command by Deech. With the legion under fifty percent strength, it's regs to revive only combat people. You don't print out brass in the middle of a firefight."

Harris gestured wildly. His hands rose up on long arms, and they flapped at the sky. "Are you blind, Ortiz? Do you see any approaching enemy armies? We're on this rock alone, it's a quiet day in paradise out here!"

"I've got a solution," I said. "Why don't *you* go over there and settle the matter?"

Harris looked at me, suddenly calm. "Is that an order, sir?"

"It certainly isn't."

He grinned. "I see—but I have to refuse. I'm just not good at that sort of thing. I—I'd get caught right off. You don't want to see me permed, do you sir?"

"At least it would be quieter around here. It's put up or shut-up time, Harris."

He looked at me, then the ground, then me again. "Nah," he said, and he walked back downslope to his light troopers, muttering. They were all squatting around, taking a break. He began kicking ass and shouting orders the moment he reached them.

"What if he'd gone for it?" Carlos asked me.

"Well, then the problem would have been solved, one way or the other."

Carlos began chuckling. "That's cold, McGill. Real cold. I like it."

He left then, heading into the lifter. He had lots of work to do in a cramped revival chamber. I didn't envy him that. Giving birth to a chain of angry troopers—I'd rather stand out here and die clean.

Leeson had the weaponeers, and at this range they were our most important troops. He set up three 88s along the ridge overlooking the dome, building puff-crete bunkers around them. I hadn't operated light artillery in a long time, and I was glad to see them deployed today.

While I walked the ridge, there was some shouting and pointing downslope. Turning, I was immediately alarmed.

"That black slop again, Centurion," Leeson said. "They're farting it out of the ground all around the dome. Here we go with round two."

From this angle, I could see the phenomenon much better than I had when I'd been in the midst of it. There was no way it was natural or by chance. Every hundred meters or so, on what looked like a hexagonal grid, the vapor was chugged up out of the ground. It soon grew into a billowing cloud that filled the valley surrounding the dome itself.

My secondaries all looked to me. "Orders, sir?" Leeson asked.

"I don't know," I said. "I'm not getting anything useful from command, either. Just a lot of chatter."

We continued to watch as the vapor filled every square inch of low terrain. There was no doubt it was heavier than whatever passed for air on this world. It clung to the ground and soon smoothed over. It stopped rising and resembled a black pond of oil after twenty minutes of bubbling.

"There's no wind," Leeson said, checking his tapper.

"That's probably why they deployed it."

"No sir, that's not what I meant," he said. "There was wind a few minutes back. Now, it's dead calm. Do you think they have control of the weather on this rock?"

I thought about it, and what we knew of these people.

"It's a possibility," I admitted.

"What do you think is down there in that vapor? They wouldn't fill up the whole damned valley for nothing."

"You're right. It's got to cost them something to do this. It could be a defense against an attack from us, but we're just setting up. I've got an idea."

Calling to Leeson's weaponeers, I had them man the 88s.

"As a test, we're going to try to cut swathes through that vapor," I told them.

"Centurion," Leeson said. "Have we got orders to start hostilities."

"Who said anything about mounting an attack?" I asked him. "We're just going to test our guns. We can't do that without burning a few rocks, can we? Let's fire down there and see if we can't find something under that black smoke."

Leeson grinned, and he turned to do it.

Harris sensed something big happening and he called for his lights to set their weapons to sniping mode. Snap-rifles could be reconfigured for various types of combat by changing their barrels, sights and trigger mechanisms. They weren't powerful weapons, but they were versatile.

Seeing this, Toro got into the act. Harris had lined up his people, widely spread apart as snipers on the ridge overlooking the valley. At the same time, she moved her heavies up to crouch below and behind the snipers—just in case.

I looked it all over, made a few adjustments and was about to give the order to fire the 88s.

A message came in on my tapper at that exact moment. I could tell from the tone and the urgency of the vibration, it was from the command group. That could only mean one thing: my behavior had been noticed by some Primus or another. My operation was about to be shut down, even before I got it up and running.

Waving for Leeson to speed things up, I was grateful to see him turn and order his weaponeers to fire.

Now, an 88 is a weird weapon. In an experienced gunner's hands, it blazes out in wide swathes. It has a long cool-down, and once the gunner begins a sweep, he's kind of locked in. He has to complete the beam's path, trying to keep it even and steady, and afterwards he's down for several seconds while the cannon cycles through and recharges.

The weaponeers were all experienced troops. They handled their big guns like pros. Not an inch of overlap was to be seen anywhere on the valley floor. Vast, hundred-meter runways were cut thru the black mist, which recoiled as if it were alive and stung by the sizzling heat.

And there they were, under that covering mist. At least fifty monsters had been revealed.

They weren't robots. They weren't human. They were actual *monsters*. Beings such as I'd never seen before. They had twenty or more multi-jointed limbs each, and they scuttled around like crabs.

When the beams of the 88s struck them, they reacted as if in pain. Gray smoke wisped up from their bodies as furrows in their flesh turned to ash. An unarmored man struck by such a beam was converted to dust immediately, but I didn't see a single monster go down.

Instead, they scuttled into regions of black smoke that hadn't been burned away yet. They looked to me like giant roaches seeking cover when the lights suddenly flickered on.

And all of them—every last one—was rushing toward our lines.

-34-

As soon as my troopers got over their shock, they began peppering the crab-like monsters with sniper fire. At this range, it was hard to tell if it was having much effect.

My tapper buzzed my wrist again. It somehow seemed to me that the buzz was angrier than it had been just a moment ago.

"Sir?" I asked, answering the call. "Are you seeing this?"

"McGill, what the hell are you playing at?" Winslade demanded. "No one ordered you to fire at anything—"

He broke off at that moment as I streamed vid playback from my helmet to his tapper. Since we were already connected, he didn't even have to approve the incoming stream, it just started playing in his face.

"What have you *done*?" he demanded, his voice cracking high for a second.

"Nothing, Primus. I just saw something in that smoke down there, and I thought we should take a poke at it. Well sir, turns out I was right."

"Why is it always you who starts these things, McGill?"

"Just dumb luck, I guess."

"Are they attacking?"

"Uh…" I said, hoisting myself up to the ridge again to have a look. The ribbons of bare rock were vanishing again as the vapor closed over them. "The creatures appear to have all vanished into the smoke again. It's hard to tell, but they were surging in our direction when we uncovered their presence."

"You mean when you provoked them," Winslade said. "We'll have to step up every element of the plan. These damnable rebels. If I wasn't under direct orders, I'd burn their dome out right now."

"Your orders, Primus?"

"Keep those creatures from overrunning us. Those are your orders. Winslade out."

Nodding thoughtfully, I had another peek down at the field. Was that a feeler poking out of the smoke at the very bottom of the slope, at the edge of the smoke-filled region? It seemed to me that it just might be.

"Leeson," I said, "what are the other units up to?"

"Looks like they're setting up 88s now in a panic," he said, chuckling. "They should have done it first thing. What's the point of high ground and an open field of fire if you don't exploit it?"

"What's the point indeed... Leeson, what would you do if you were a bug that loved smoke, but were planning to rush out of it and kill something?"

"Well... I'd probably move to the edge of it and mass up right there under cover."

"My thoughts exactly," I said. "Let's get those 88s tilted straight down, shall we? We're going to be burning their forward perimeter in about thirty seconds."

"Thirty seconds? On it, sir!"

He began yelling at his men to hustle. They did so, piling up charges and cranking their field of fire more steeply, so they could hit the bottom of the ridge below with ease.

I liked Toro and her heavies just where they were, but I frowned when I considered Harris and his light snipers. They seemed useless against this foe. An enemy that could withstand an 88 was going to shrug off a snap-rifle without feeling a thing.

"Harris!" I called. "Get your lights off that ridge. Have them retreat to the lifter and pull out three more 88s. Set them up right in front of the lifter itself."

"Huh? Uh... right sir."

Surprised, he withdrew and kicked his people into gear. They raced past me toward the lifter. When his own butt was on the line, he tended to follow directions very well, as long as they didn't directly result in his own demise.

Long before the light troopers could pull out a fresh 88, however, my thirty seconds were up and Leeson laid down a fresh set of criss-crossing burn-lines in the smoke directly below us. The monsters hidden by the smoke were thus revealed, and their tough carapaces were left ash-gray by the searing beams.

Some of them actually ignited when they were hit by multiple beams. A few even went down and died, flopping and flailing.

But the majority appeared to go absolutely mad. They charged up the slope toward our lines, and even I was impressed by their ferocity.

Without being told, Toro ordered her heavies to advance to the ridge and blaze away. They already had their plasma rifles in assault mode, set for rapid-fire at short range. As the monsters came clawing their way up the rocks, Toro's team blasted away limbs and sent the leaders tumbling back into the roiling mass behind them.

Joining in, I found myself chugging out power-bolts like there was no tomorrow—and I seriously doubted that there would be if those things got to our lines.

Seeing that our part of the defensive line was being unfairly singled out, neighboring units had joined the fight. They sprayed the advancing line with all sorts of fire. 88s, snap-rifle rounds and power-bolts flew in a wild display of energy and heat.

Such was the tenacity of the enemy, however, that they reached our lines anyway. Our 88s died first, the weaponeers plucked free from their tiny bunkers by extremely long, powerful arms that whipped and moved with alarming speed. These unfortunates were beaten to death on the rocks, their faceplates cracking and blood spraying everywhere.

"Fall back!" I roared, and Toro's heavies hustled toward the lifter all around me.

The monsters dragged themselves, smoking and crippled, over the ridge and reached out to snap up men by the feet. Troops were killed in a variety of gruesome ways. The monsters seemed to favor tug-of-wars with the fallen, like terriers with prey animals between them. They ripped them limb from limb and left them to die on the rocks.

Running toward the lifter and firing back at them whenever we could, we continued retreating. If they hadn't been thinned out and slowed down by injuries, the monsters would have swept over us in an instant.

Up close, I was able to fully appreciate the size and power of this new foe. They reminded me of the Wur we'd fought on Death World in a way, but they were much lower to the ground. They stood no more than five meters high, but their span of legs was more than twice that.

"McGill!" my helmet buzzed. It was Graves this time. "Under no circumstances are you to allow those creatures into my lifter!"

"Got it, Primus," I said wearily. Turning to the heavies and lights around me, I gave them a grim nod. "We stand here."

They looked shocked. Several were already heading up the ramp, seeking safety. Even as I spoke, the ramp began to retract, shaking them off like fleas.

I'd hoped Harris' light troopers might have set up an 88 by now, but they'd failed. They weren't trained to use the equipment, and they were almost in a state of panic anyway.

"Hug up under the ship," I shouted to my troops. "Watch for the anti-personnel guns. They'll be poking out overhead any second now."

As I expected, Graves deployed the ship's last ditch defense. The ship's external guns were automatic and not very discriminating. They began spraying deadly bolts at the approaching enemy the moment they were deployed. In several cases, light troopers were slow to catch on. They died when they were caught between the turrets and their targets.

This last effort finally did the trick. The monsters were cut down. When they'd been reduced to shivering piles of smoldering meat, the gun turrets retracted back into the lifter.

Less than half of my troops had survived. Curious, I advanced and poked at a leg the size of a tree branch. It squirmed weakly at the contact.

"They *look* dead," I said.

Natasha advanced to my side. "They must be some kind of artificial life."

"Yeah..." I agreed. "You're something of an expert in that field, aren't you?"

It was a sore point for her, so she gave me a twisted grimace in response. She'd once engineered her own AL pet in college and been expelled for it.

"They've definitely been designed, I can tell that much. No sex organs. No variation in individuals at all. They were genetically edited together and cloned."

Giving the crab leg nearest me a stomp, it cracked open. I could see cooked meat inside. It was all red and white with thick cartilage wrapping the muscle.

"They'd probably taste good with some butter and garlic."

Natasha shook her head. "They're almost certainly toxic. If they can breathe this atmosphere, not to mention the vapor down there, they don't belong in a human gut."

"I wasn't serious, you know."

She smirked at me, then went back to poking at the dead. "What I don't get is where they're keeping these things. They're big, they must eat... There's no way they can all live under that dome."

"Maybe they come from underground, like that smoke," I said, thinking it through. "They can't have come out of the dome itself. It doesn't make sense."

"Which indicates," Natasha said thoughtfully, "that there must also be a way in and out of the dome from underneath."

"Hmm," I said. "Dangerous talk. Let's keep that one to ourselves, shall we?"

"What? Seriously, Centurion? It's my job to report something like this. Are you ordering me not to tell the Primus what we've deduced?"

I sighed. "No, I guess not. Go ahead."

She walked away, building up her after-action report, which would have to be melded into mine. I seriously considered editing her section out, but by the time I got it, Graves was demanding to see it.

Carlos came out and smirked at me. He had a tired look to him.

"You just had to stir the shit again, didn't you, Centurion?" he asked me.

"It's in my nature," I admitted.

"Winslade has to be hammering on his dinner table somewhere in that bunker," he said, gazing up and down the ridgeline. Here and there, the enemy was still fighting with various units. We'd gotten the worst of it, I figured, but it was hard to tell.

"What's the word on Deech?" I asked him. "Is she still on hold?"

Carlos nodded. "Indefinitely. In fact, you might have just given Winslade some help in that department. We just lost about five percent more of our troops. We're seventy percent down, and we're facing serious attacks. No one would pop out the brass now."

"Not unless they wanted a more experienced officer running the show."

"If that was the goal, Graves would be in charge right now."

"I'll take that as a vote of confidence, Specialist," Graves said, walking up behind us.

"Sir," Carlos said, turning in surprise. "That's exactly how it was meant, Primus. Anyway, break's over. I'm back to the sweatshop. The undercarriage on the revival machine has sprung a leak, and it's pissing itself every time it gives birth. It's 'all hands on deck' down there."

Having worked with the equipment before, I couldn't help but grimace and shudder. "Give me a rifle and a giant crab to shoot at any day," I said.

"McGill, where's your report?" Graves asked me.

"Right here on my arm, sir. You want me to send it to you first—or do I broadcast it?"

He looked at me for a second. "I'm not a schemer like you. Fire it off to all-points, and let the chips fall where they may."

"Your call, sir," I said, and I sent it.

The second I'd done so, I felt a pang of regret. I hoped my fears wouldn't materialize—but the hope was a faint one.

-35-

Not more than two hours passed before my report—
especially the parts written by Natasha—began to have their
inevitable impact. Winslade himself came to talk to me.

He at least had the balls to come out and stand on the
ridgeline with me. When he arrived with Graves in tow, I was
supervising the removal of the monstrous carcasses that littered
our encampment. Always having been a man who takes the
easiest course, I simply had the men use the robotic pigs to
drag them over the ridge and roll them back down to where
they'd come from. A ghastly, twisted pile of the dead lay at the
foot of our mountain.

Winslade peered down over the side at the mess, and he
made a tsking sound.

"Up to your usual hijinks I see, McGill," he said.

"That's right sir. Defeating the enemy and cleaning up the
mess afterward."

"That's not what I meant. You're a glory-hound. A man
bent on endangering his troops for his own personal
advancement."

I turned to look at him with my brow furrowing. Graves
had positioned himself directly behind Winslade, and he gave
me a slow shake of the head.

Forcing myself to relax, I smiled at Winslade. "That's right
sir," I said. "Men like you and me really know how to climb
the rank ladder."

It was Winslade's turn to frown, and even Graves winced slightly. Sure, Graves had been worried that I'd toss the little bastard off the cliff that was so temptingly near, but apparently needling him with remarks wasn't nice enough to suit either of them.

"Insolent, as always," Winslade said, then he glanced over his shoulder at Graves. "I don't know how you've put up with him all these years, Primus Graves."

"I'm not sure myself."

"Never mind," Winslade continued, "I have a solution for all this. A clear method that will allow you to redeem yourself, McGill."

Knowing what was coming, I forced myself to look interested.

"I've had every legion tech in the field analyzing the ground here," Winslade told me, "they've been using sonic wave equipment and the like. Even the *Nostrum* has been in on the work. They've found large hollow regions beneath the valley floor."

"Those caves had to be there, Primus. I just knew it."

"Yes… very intuitive. As a just reward for an ambitious man, I've decided you're going to be given the honor of leading a new expedition with the purpose of exploring—"

"Into those caves, sir?" I asked suddenly, excitedly.

"Exactly."

I slammed my gauntlets together, making a resounding bang in his face. "Hot damn! The troops said we'd never pull this duty, but you proved them wrong. Thank you sir! Thank you."

Winslade looked confused and a little put out. Graves knew me better. He was shaking his head again.

"Well," Winslade said, "if you're so eager to go, you'll be even happier to learn that I've stepped up the reproduction of your unit. I've got every revival unit on the lifters churning out your troops first. You'll move out in two hours' time."

This last announcement took me by surprise. We'd barely eaten and hadn't slept since we landed. My face faltered.

"Is there a problem, Centurion?" Winslade demanded with a glint in his eye.

"No sir, not really, but my boys are getting bored. I guess we'll just have to wait around for the bio people to get their jobs done."

Winslade nodded then left. Neither he nor I were satisfied with the encounter, and we both probably hated one another more than ever.

Harris showed up shortly after the brass had left. He looked like a man who'd been drinking all night and was only just getting to the hangover.

"Total bullshit," he said. "Complete, total bullshit. They can't send us into any frigging caves! How do we get down there in the first place?"

"I've figured out a way," Natasha said.

Harris and I turned to face her. Harris shook his head and exhaled loudly in defeat.

"Little miss prissy-pants. Of course you did. Let's hear it. Tell this old soldier how he's going to die on another fool mission for McGill."

I wanted to tell him to shut up, but I didn't quite have the heart. He had good reasons to bitch and gripe. We were all being screwed, and candying that up wasn't going to solve anything.

"How do we do it, Specialist?" I prompted.

"We've found the gas-release nozzles," she said. "They're very carefully hidden, but by reviewing the vids from *Nostrum* as the gas formed, it's obvious. About every hundred meters, a source has been pinpointed. It stands to reason that the exits from the caves must be nearby."

"It stands to reason?" Harris demanded. "That's it? You're sending us down there into Hell itself on a hunch, aren't you? Just admit it, girl!"

Natasha licked her lips, I could tell she was slightly nervous. "The rock density at those points is clearly lighter. The tunnels must be there—but they're hidden from us somehow."

Harris walked away, grumbling and kicking at alien fragments. The men had already stripped our dead and hauled them into the lifter for "recycling" but the enemy corpses had provided plenty of blasted scraps of meat for Harris to abuse.

214

Natasha and I gazed down into what could only be described as a valley of death. The black vapors had largely dispersed now, and the winds were blowing again. In the center of the scene, as the sun set, was the dome itself. Lights came on inside, and we saw movement within.

"They're as bold as brass in that blue-glass bottle," I said. "By now, they must have figured out that we're not going to blow up their dome. So, they're ignoring us."

"We're in a full blown siege," she said. "I wonder how long it will last."

"What if they fire X-ray missiles at us out here?" I asked.

"They really can't. The beams can be directed, but we're too close now for that kind of attack. They'd risk burning themselves as well as us."

I nodded. "If they don't have revival machines, they know we'd be called the winners in that scenario. We'd come back and they wouldn't."

"Precisely."

After a moment's quiet between us, I asked her the next thing that was on my mind. "Natasha, if I lead my unit down there, are you gonna find those cave entrances?"

"If those entrances are there, I'll find them," she said firmly.

Figuring that was the best I was going to get, I let it go at that.

With a couple of hours to rest, I checked on the battle lines and took a break in the lifter. I ate a cold meal with a single, sour bottle of synth-beer.

Della joined me. She'd died in the battle and come back in a daze.

"It's been a long time since I've died," she said. "I forgot what it felt like."

"Hey," I told her, "on the bright side, you're sporting a younger version of your body. Those creases I saw beginning to form in your face the other day—they're gone. It's a miracle!"

She glanced at me sidelong. "Is that detail important to Earth women?"

"Usually," I admitted.

Della was different. Being from Dust World, she wasn't always in tune with human norms. She was like Etta that way. Neither one of them cared much what other people thought of them, or their appearance. Dust Worlders just weren't wired that way.

"It's nice of you to say, anyway," she said.

Experimentally, I slipped my hand out and touched hers. She gave me a tiny shake of the head, and I retreated. It just wasn't to be.

I understood. Her recent death had left her thoughtful and apprehensive about the future. That happened to the toughest of us.

Dying and coming back from the grave a few hours later—it just wasn't natural, after all.

-36-

The hours flew by. Night fell, and the sky turned just as black as the ground. Gathering my glum troops, I marched them outside.

There was no moon swinging around this rock of a planet, and not much in the way of standing liquids like oceans. The sky itself should have been full of icy stars, but they were hidden behind cloud cover. In short, it was as dark as a coal-pit out there.

The only vision we had was artificial in nature. We were running purely on night gear, which let us see something, at least. The landscape blazed green when seen through our scopes. The oily rocks glimmered, reflecting a wet, poisonous sheen.

"Formation as follows," I ordered, "light troopers up front with Harris. Leeson will take the center, Toro the rear. Lights, move ahead about a hundred meters and fan out."

"You heard the man!" Harris boomed. "Spread out! No sense in letting some demon eat our sorry asses all at once!"

Ahead of us, I could see the light troopers forming a double-line and moving downslope. When they were a hundred meters away, Leeson and I advanced after them.

Leeson's weaponeers looked sad. They didn't want to abandon the relative safety of their 88s to climb down into the dangerous valley. I couldn't blame them for that. They carried nothing but belchers and some smart-missiles on their shoulders.

Toro's heavies followed us down at the rear. They moved warily, slowly. I had to keep contacting her to speed up and close the gap between us, which she never did do to my satisfaction.

Picking my way down various trails on spiked boots, I had Natasha on my right, and Leeson on my left.

Adjunct Leeson was a bitter man on the best of days, but today he was downright irritable. He'd died in the last battle, and I think he was still annoyed about that.

"This thing between you and Winslade," he told me on private chat, "that shit has to stop, McGill."

"Maybe you should inform the primus of your deepest feelings about it," I suggested. "Maybe if he knew how hurt you are when we pull an assignment like this, he'd be sweet on us forever."

Leeson chuckled and grumbled a little more, but then he finally shut the hell up.

"I'm getting a reading, Centurion," Natasha said when we reached flat ground and began to climb over giant, crab-like corpses.

"Give it to me," I said.

I displayed the datastream I was getting from her on my faceplate. It was distracting, and possibly deadly in combat, but I was used to it. Since we were doing nothing other than walking, I figured it was safe enough.

I noticed an indicator on my HUD—about a hundred meters south, a portion of the ground was lit by a smoky golden circle. The golden circle wasn't really there, of course, but it was superimposed on my faceplate by my tapper. It was a way of letting me know where something interesting was located.

"Might as well investigate," I said, and I relayed the stream to all my adjuncts.

They stopped advancing and threw up a hand to signal their troops to halt as well.

"The Light platoon would like the honor of investigating this find, sir!" Harris called out.

I grinned. He knew he was going to have to go first. I gave him the order and he sent three of his luckiest people to the spot.

I expected black gas to come pumping out at their approach. I seriously did. But nothing happened.

"Maybe they're all out of smoke," Harris said as if he'd read my mind.

A few more recruits dared to gather around the spot, useless snap-rifles in their tight grips. The searched the rocks carefully.

Natasha raced up with her equipment when the all-clear was sounded. She began setting it up, and she quickly got a confirmation.

"The caves are definitely under us," she said. "There must be an entrance. It has to be close."

Like a pack of fools, we began looking around. We were all daring to feel hopeful already, I could tell. After all, nothing had attacked us yet. Maybe we'd find a way to sneak into these caves. Maybe, those tall skinny bastards in the dome were all out of monsters and traps.

The human spirit is damned near unstoppable in its own way, and rare is the man who truly believes he's about to die— even when it's frigging obvious.

Natasha's machine let out an audible hum. It had found something—some kind of gap in the ground, perhaps.

That's when it happened. The rocky valley floor simply opened up and swallowed us down.

Not just Harris and his light troopers went in, mind you, but me and Leeson's people too. The only ones who were outside the deadly radius were Toro and her overly cautious pack of heavies.

I hated them as I fell. I hated Toro herself most of all. Somehow, when a man is dying, he oftentimes hates those who were lucky enough or smart enough to avoid the same awful fate.

The fall itself didn't kill me—although it should have, by all rights. There were bones grinding in my chest and both my legs had snapped.

How far down was I? There was no time to check. Fifty meters, maybe. My suit had caught some of it, and it hadn't been a straight plunge. As a bonus, I'd bounced around against some rocks on the way down. Only my armor, which was like a shell on a beetle, had kept me alive and gasping for breath, if only temporarily.

Some around me groaned, and I knew they were still alive, but only a few of them stirred.

I forced myself up into a sitting position. I was proud of that. My rifle came around, but it was dead. Something had killed it in the fall—maybe I'd landed my fat metal-covered ass on it.

My pistol still glowed green, however, and it was easier to operate anyway.

There was something in the dark with me. I could sense it. My night vision was out, so I kicked on my suit-lights.

Now, that's against the rules when everyone else is running their night gear, but I was beyond caring about that at the moment.

Harris saw me then. He had his helmet off. He was coughing and sitting up like me. One of his eyes was crushed shut, or maybe torn out. It was hard to tell.

"Put that damned light out!" he yelled at me.

"I can't see without it."

"They'll find us if you don't turn it out!"

"Have you seen them?"

"No... but I heard something."

"Harris," I said, getting to my knees. It hurt like a son of a bitch, but I found I could crawl. "Harris, we're dead anyway. Let these crabby, spider-monsters come."

"Toro is up there. She can lower ropes. She can get us out."

"Nah," I said. "We're all broken up. Even if they did get us out, they'd just recycle us anyway."

He stared at me, knowing the truth of it, and went into another coughing spell. His suit was still pouring oxygen up into his face, but without the faceplate and a good seal, he wouldn't last an hour.

"Okay," he said, accepting reality. "Back to back, like the old days."

I crawled over to him, put my back against his, and we waited for the monsters to come. When they finally did, there was a moment of terror in my heart, I don't mind telling you. The Devil himself never looked scarier than these crab-things did in that black, dusty pit.

We fired our weapons. We knew it wouldn't do much, but we were going to go out fighting. A few other troops stung them too, from here and there around us. Maybe my own troops were smarter than I was—seeing as they'd kept quiet and played dead until the crabs found us.

When one of them loomed near, I saw the underside of its shell. That's where the mouth was. A six-pointed star, with six squirming teeth, or spines, that served as little hands to shove the food into that lowering orifice.

That's when Harris showed his true genius. He had a plasma grenade in his hand, and he held it straight up in his armored fist, which rammed home into the lowering maw.

Apparently, these things fed by kind of squatting on top of their prey.

Harris had great timing—either that, or my tapper didn't update fast enough. I had no memory after that. Either his grenade went off and killed us both, or we were chewed up and swallowed.

Whichever was the case, I have to say it wasn't my favorite death. Not by a long shot.

-37-

I soon experienced one of my more unpleasant reawakenings.

"Get him out of there!" a rough voice ordered. "Right now!"

"But he's not fully formed yet," a female voice said. I figured she had to be a bio. "We should just abort."

"Forget it. He can fight. I don't care if he's deaf, dumb and retarded—he can fight."

I recognized that voice now. It was an old acquaintance of mine—Claver. I couldn't fathom why he was giving anyone orders. He was supposed to be in prison.

Knowing who was talking didn't help me much. I felt *wrong* inside. Kind of sick, like my guts were twisted up in cramps. A revival usually left me bleary-eyed and confused— but this was worse than normal.

"Is he a bad grow?" Claver demanded. "He's tucked up in a ball, shivering. That's not the McGill I know."

"He's trying to pull it together—I told you it was too early. He's not fully-formed yet."

Those words alarmed me. If they were birthing me early, there had to be a reason. I attempted speech, but it came out as a croaking sound.

"He's a dummy," Claver declared. "He's normally as shit-off stupid as a tomcat anyway, but this is even worse."

"You want me to recycle him and try again?" asked the bio.

"No, there's no time. Try to quicken another seed from his combat team. You'll probably never get finished—but try it anyway."

The bio went to work, and I heard the goopy sounds of thick chugging liquids as the machine was refilled with supplies for a new job.

Something told me I should keep my eyes shut, but I tried to open them anyway.

Pain! Blinding white light—then a vague shape loomed over me. I could feel his heat and smell his breath.

"Get off me, Claver," I managed say in a raspy voice.

"There! See that? He's awake! The bastard was just playing possum on us, that's all."

He laughed harshly then, but he seemed relieved.

I tried to think, but it was harder to do than usual. Why was Claver in the Arcturus system? Why was anyone listening to him? Something had to be wrong. These thoughts danced in my mind, but speaking them aloud was too much effort right now.

Groaning and straightening out my body, I coughed and puked up some gunk. That was worse than usual, too. Fresh lungs always started off with a coating inside that evaporated over time—and it was just as irritating as it sounded.

"That's it," Claver said, "get up, boy. We need you!"

My spine straightened slowly, popping every single vertebrae into place as it did so with an audible click. It was weird and a tad disconcerting. I didn't think I'd ever been brought out this early before. I hoped all my parts were there.

Hands caught under my armpits and helped me sit up. A warm spray of water gushed over me, washing some of the gunk out of my face.

"Hey, you have to do that outside," the bio said irritably. "I'm charging the machine, here. Extra water can mess up the next grow."

Claver chuckled at her. "Yeah… good luck with that, little lady. Come on, McGill. Spit, shit, and git off the table. I need you, boy. All of Earth does."

"Why?" I managed to say.

"We'll talk about that. Real soon. I promise—nurse, I need you to clear me for a quick exit. I'll take care of James here, personally."

The bio came near. "I'm not a nurse, sir."

"I'm sorry your majesty—can you check him out, please?"

I felt her hands running over me to perform her final inspection. "Apgar scores are surprisingly good. Cognitive functions are slow, but acceptable."

"That's par for the course on this model," Claver said.

"Physically... his breathing is labored, but I don't see any reason not to—whoops!"

My eyes opened a notch wider. Hearing your midwife say "oops" was never good when you were freshly reborn.

"What's wrong?" I asked.

"Look at that—that's a new one," she said. "His toes aren't fully formed. I told you we shouldn't pull him out early. We're lucky he has hair and ears at all. Those get printed last by these units."

Alarmed, I lifted a foot to see what she was talking about. Sure enough, my toes were tiny pink bulbs—way too small. They looked like a child's toes. There were no nails, no hair growing out of the top—nothing. I wasn't even sure they had bones inside.

"Freaky," Claver said. "Can you walk, boy?"

Experimentally, I climbed off the table and moved around the room. The toes weren't only shrunken, they were tender.

"They feel like the skin has been peeled off," I said.

"That's a bad break," Claver said, shaking his head.

I could see him clearly now. He was in a uniform—a Hegemony uniform. He had rank insignia, too.

"Who made you a frigging Primus?" I demanded.

"God did, as far as you're concerned," he told me sternly. "Now, if you can't walk, we're going to have to trim those off. Bio?"

She approached, looking worried. "I'd suggest a regrow, but something's gone wrong with the revival machine. It seems to be idling. I've punched in the next order several times."

"You don't say?" Claver asked her. "Well, try a full cold reset, and I'll report it up the line. We'll send some techs down here to fix it right up."

The bio looked offended. "We don't let techs touch these. Only our own people are rated to work on them."

"Ah, right. Well, good luck with that. McGill, come on. Crawl if you have to."

Unsure of what the hell was going on, I dressed and pulled on boots. That was agony, but I did it anyway and followed him out of the bunker in a stumbling gait.

"Damn," Claver said he led me outside, "getting pulled out early really messes a man up—or maybe it's just you. Are you some kind of weak-sister? Some kind of—"

I'd had about enough of him by this time. Actually, I had enough for five minutes or even five years by then. Grabbing him by the shoulder and spinning him around, I pulled him close to me and got into his face.

"What the hell are you doing here, Claver?" I demanded. "You'd better start talking to me, and you make sure you give me a damned good reason not to strangle you right now."

"Be careful you ape," he said. "This rank is real."

"I'm a bad-grow," I told him, "you said it yourself. I'm liable to do damned near anything. Now, start talking."

He tried to pull a weapon, but I batted it away.

"Nice reflexes," he said. "You really are McGill, toes or no toes."

"Talk!"

"All right, settle down. It's kind of complicated. Just let me say that I have the best interests of you, Earth, and all humanity clearly in my mind today."

"Bullshit. Why are you really here?"

"To talk to you, like I said."

"Why pull me out early to do it?"

About then, a bio rushed by us in the passageway. I saw him racing through the bunker back toward the room we'd just come out of.

"See that?" Claver said in a hushed tone. "That's why. The revival machines have been shut down. The bio people are panicking."

225

I looked around, still a little confused. I let go of him, and he smiled.

"That's right," he said in a soothing voice. "Just let old Uncle Claver take care of everything. It's going to be all right."

"This isn't my cohort's lifter," I said, looking around. "It's a bunker… How long was I gone?"

"About six days as I understand it," he said.

My mouth fell open. "Why? Why'd they wait so damned long?"

"I think you pissed off Winslade—or maybe it was Graves. Could have been either of them. You always have to give people the finger, don't you boy?"

Peering up and down the passageway, I was beginning to catch on. "This is Winslade's bunker, isn't it?" I asked him. "You revived me here, because this whole thing was unauthorized."

"You see that? Even a monkey can get one right now and then. You're right on the money."

My toes throbbed, and I hissed in pain. "But why didn't you let them finish growing me?"

"Couldn't wait any longer," Claver said. "Everything is being shut down. If I'd waited for you to get one of those all-natural, massage-therapy kinds of births, you'd be stillborn back in that chamber, dead and down the chute to the mulcher."

He began walking again, and I followed him. I didn't have much choice. What he was saying was perfectly possible. Winslade was a vindictive man, and he might have decided I'd failed twice in a row. Pushing me to the back of the queue— that could have taken six days, easily.

"What about my unit?" I asked him. "Are they back yet?"

"Oh sure. They've been up and fighting and dying for days. They only iced you."

"Wait a second," I said. "Where are we going?"

The lights flickered then went out. We were cast into darkness. Our suits automatically glowed with LEDs to show the way.

"You see that?" Claver asked. "We've got to secure the power station first. They have a backup that's not Imperial, but it won't provide enough juice to run everything."

I grabbed him again, and he looked at me with a weary expression.

"Why did you want *me*?"

"Because the Galactics have arrived in orbit, boy. Not the whole battle fleet—not yet. But the Nairbs are here. They're scouting for the fleet. You didn't think they'd send the whole battle fleet out here blind, did you?"

"Battle Fleet 921?"

He sighed. "Am I speaking English, here? Are you really that addle-brained? Maybe I should have let them dump you down the chute after all."

"All right," I said, trying to think clearly. "The Nairbs are here, I get that. They shut off all our Imperial gear—I get that too—but what do you think I can do about it?"

Claver smiled, and I began to understand as I looked into that devious face of his.

-38-

Claver and I went a long way back, all the way to Tech World. That had only been my third major campaign, but I'd been much the same man as I was today.

Claver, as far as I could tell, had been a wily, henhouse-thieving fox from the day he was born.

One point of conflict that had come up between us during our frequent—and often violent—encounters, was something known as the Galactic Key. He'd stolen it originally, and I'd taken it from him. We'd repeated that process any number of times since then, with Galina Turov taking a turn holding the key here or there.

The Galactic Key was a total secret to most humans as it was an extinction-level violation in physical form. It was a hacking device that allowed the user to bypass security on any technology that was made by the Empire—which included just about everything worth having.

"You want the key, right?" I asked. "Do you think turning off a few machines is going to make me cough it up?"

Claver narrowed his eyes. "Now, what's this new tone and attitude I'm seeing? Don't be thinking you're going to out-scheme me, McGill. Don't even go there. You're not smart enough for that."

Claver had never had a high opinion of me. He thought of me as cunning, rather than intelligent. In his mind, I had good instincts and tended to get awful lucky sometimes, but I wasn't anything like his equal. I'd never bothered to correct him on this since his arrogance had given me an edge from time to time.

"I'm just asking questions," I told him.

"Sure… well, here's your answer: I know you have the key, yes, and I think you're capable of comprehending how important it is right now. The Nairbs are in orbit. They've been watching the whole shit-show down here. We can reasonably assume they know the full story."

I frowned. That could be bad. "Why haven't they done anything yet?"

He shrugged. "You know the Nairbs. They like to hide and get a full accounting first. Every violation they see runs a little thrill through their bloated, slimy guts. They're up there all right, probably having too much fun to lower the boom on us yet."

"Maybe…" I said, feeling my brain finally beginning to work, "or maybe they're waiting for the full battle fleet to arrive."

"Could be," Claver said, shrugging. "Doesn't matter much to us."

"How can you say that? You know what they've seen. You know what they'll do—Earth won't survive."

"That's possible," he admitted. He made a sweeping gesture, encompassing the bunker, the legion and presumably the whole planet. "This is all as good as gone. Graves, and Harris and all your Varus turds. Those… *people* in the dome, too. The battle fleet will arrive, get the report from the Nairbs, and the Mogwa captains will melt this world down to bedrock inside of an hour. Hell, we'll be lucky if they don't burn down all of humanity for this stunt."

"How do we stop all that from happening?" I asked. "Even with the key I don't see how—"

I stopped talking, because Claver was laughing at me. He wasn't just chuckling, either, he was belting out a full-fledged belly-laugh.

"You dumb-shit," he said, "I'm not trying to save any of these rubes! I'm trying to help you and I. That's it. That's the deal. I have teleport suits, and I—"

"Suits?" I asked. "Plural?"

"That's right," Claver said in a sly tone. "The new kind that are made for humans."

"I thought we'd lost them all—and I thought you were in prison."

He chuckled. "How do you keep a man imprisoned if he's in several places at once? Especially if he has teleport suits and knows how to use them better than any hog does?"

I nodded slowly. Claver was a strange, slippery man. I'd always suspected he had a secret lair somewhere. A cave, maybe, on some forgotten corner of an uninhabited world. He must have his own revival machine there and other tech gadgets like the teleport suits. I reminded myself that the first time I'd seen a suit, it had been on Claver's back.

"Okay," I said. "Let me see if I'm understanding your offer… You'll get me off this rock, and we'll both live. In exchange, you want the Galactic Key."

He smiled. "I wronged you, boy. I've often compared your intellect to that of a gibbon. But you've got—at the very *least*— the brains of a chimp. One of those smart ones that can do sign-language, even."

My hand came up slowly to rub at my chin, as if I was having myself a think—then I shot out a nasty hook with it, nailing him.

Claver had never been able to take a hard right to the jaw. Today was no different. He spun around in shock and went down. I gave him a couple more blows to the head, and he stopped moving.

Disarming him carefully, I found all kinds of interesting gear, including two needlers. I kept everything. Then I dragged his sorry ass into a side passage full of ammo and water cans and sat on the floor.

Damn, my toes were hurting! While Claver gurgled and bled throughout his nap, I took the time to dig out a small first aid kit and used up all the bandages to bind up my ridiculously small toes. That helped a lot. They weren't happy, but at least I'd be able to walk with less pain.

Claver groaned awake a few minutes later.

"I was wrong," he grumbled. "You *are* a gibbon."

"Sorry Claver," I said, adjusting my boots on my feet. "But your plan is unacceptable."

"Why?"

"Because I don't have the key, you shithead. I don't have it on me—it's not on this world at all."

"Failure," he grunted. "Give me a needler."

"Right, sure," I laughed.

"You can hold it under my chin if you want. This 'Claver' is a failure. I'm taking him out of the gene pool."

"Suicide? Just like that? Is that how you gather all your toys—by offing yourself if you fail?"

"Precisely."

I chewed on that for a second. Claver seemed dejected. I came close to feeling sorry for him. He crawled up into a sitting position and looked at me. "Well?"

"I'm thinking..."

"We don't have that kind of time, boy!"

"Listen," I said, "I'm not going to use threats or torture. That won't work on a head-case like you. But even though you are a sneaky, black-hearted son-of-a-gun, I'm willing to offer a deal."

"You just said you have nothing."

"That's not exactly true," I said. "I stashed your two teleport suits nearby. Don't you want them back before the fleet blows this rock to glowing slag?"

He smiled at me. "You think I didn't consider that, dummy?"

I didn't let on, but my hopes sank a bit. He seemed to have thought this all through. Maybe, if he didn't return in time, another Claver would come along and retrieve the suits. Or maybe, all this talk of teleport suits was just bait to get me to give up the key.

Whatever the case, I knew this version of Claver wasn't going to help me any further. I lifted one of his needlers and aimed it at him.

He didn't even complain. He just watched me with this creepy, knowing smile on his face.

After I shot him dead, I ripped the rank insignia off the uniform he wore and tucked the body under a pile of junk. I didn't know if he really was a primus or not, but I had a lot to do, and I couldn't afford to be arrested for killing an officer.

My first call was to Natasha, and she seemed relieved to hear from me.

"James," she said. "I'm glad you're back."

"Where are you?"

"The same ridge—the same camp," she explained in a weary voice. "We need your help. We've sent down troops, but we can't get through the caves. So many of us have died… so many times…"

Her report made me angry. "Winslade can't mistreat my unit like that," I said.

"Well, he's doing it."

"I'll fix that soon, but we've got to tackle some more serious problems first."

"Does this have anything to do with these power outages and equipment failures?" she asked. "The weaponeers say their 88s are dead."

"I can't talk about that online."

She fell quiet, but only for a second. "I understand," she said. "I'll meet you on the ridgeline."

I fitted myself with a helmet and sealed my suit. Making my way out of Winslade's dark bunker, I found it was brighter outside, but not by much. Dawn was breaking, and it was cold.

Natasha met me along the ridgeline. We talked in person, faceplate-to-faceplate. No radio transmissions could be considered safe. I quickly explained the situation to her, and she filled me in as well.

Winslade had ordered various elements of my unit to keep trying to penetrate the dome. With me gone, Leeson had led the troops. He'd sent in Harris' light platoon, mostly, and many of them were close to breaking.

"I want to show you something," she said.

Quietly, she led me to the side of the mountain nearest Winslade's bunker. I saw Harris lying there, facedown. He was dead and flat-looking, like a housecat on a highway.

"Why hasn't he been recycled yet?" I asked. "That gear looks good."

"I marked the body as lost when I called it in," she said. "Take a look at this."

She showed me the back of his helmet. A tight cluster of snap-rifle rounds had punched through it. The signs were unmistakable—this was murder.

"Huh…" I said. "He's been making friends again, I see."

"The light troopers are breaking. This is their first deployment, you know."

I nodded, thinking that over.

"All right," I said, "you go see if you can find where those teleport suits might be hidden. Look for a signature that matches the ones we built at Central. I'm going to go have a talk with the troops."

She nodded and went to work.

When I met up with the light troopers, they were huddled around a rock-heater. They stood up at my approach.

"Sir," Sarah said. "I'm so glad you're back."

"Me too," I told her. "Sarah, would you take a walk with me, please?"

I turned away, and she followed me on quick feet. While we walked I checked on Natasha every minute or two. So far, she'd had no luck finding Claver's stash.

"I just found Harris," I told Sarah. "He's stone dead. It wasn't an alien monster that did that to him, either. The back of his helmet was so full of snap-rifle rounds it looked like a porcupine's ass."

"Is that right, sir?"

Something in her tone made me turn around to face her. She stopped in her tracks, and her eyes were guilty. They looked down, then to the left. They were darting everywhere, but they weren't meeting mine.

As a near-famous liar myself, I knew a guilty person when I saw one. Sarah knew what had happened.

"Who did this?" I demanded. "I know you have the story. Let's hear it."

Sarah sighed. She met my gaze at last. "He called me *skinny*," she said in a weak voice, "and he volunteered my squad for *everything*."

"You?" I asked angrily. "*You* fragged him?"

233

"He laughed when I requested he send another squad," she said. "I died three times yesterday. *Three times*! He thought that was funny! He ordered us to scout again this morning—and I couldn't take it."

"Yeah... Harris can be like that," I told her. "He's new at running a platoon, but he's a good man under serious fire. He was better as a veteran, if you ask me...but what you did was still wrong."

She stared up at me. "What now?" she asked. "Are you going to perm me?"

"I'll tell you what," I said after a moment's thought. "I just checked on my tapper, and Harris came out of the oven before the machines shut down. He'll be back here soon, wanting blood."

"The revival machines have shut down? What do you mean?"

"Never mind... the short version is, he'll soon come back to this spot and figure out what happened. It's only a matter of time."

Her eyes looked full and wet. I didn't allow myself to feel sympathy—at least, not much. I'd killed Harris plenty of times myself, often just because I was pissed off like Sarah was.

"Okay," I said with a sigh, "look, we're going to call this a bad-grow-day. You were a little off this morning, and you took it out on your commander. The next time we revive you, I'll move you into Toro's group."

"Don't," she said. "Everyone will think I can't take orders from a man."

"Leeson's platoon, then."

She nodded, looking stunned, sorrowful, and a little crazed.

"But..." she said after a moment, "I'm still alive."

"Yeah... about that... we'll need to fix it."

She stared at me. "Are you going to shoot me?"

"Can't be me. That wouldn't play into the narrative of the bad-grow."

"Well then... you want me to shoot myself?"

"No, girl! You'll simply have to follow Harris' last orders and march down into those caves again, solo. That should do the trick."

234

She turned slowly and looked at the rocky valley below. There was no way to cross it alive. She nodded with sober resolve.

"I'll remember this, Centurion," she said, without meeting my gaze. She began to run downslope into the open.

"In a good way, I hope!" I called after her.

Sarah didn't answer. She just jogged down into the smoke and rocks. She soon reached the valley floor. Fifty meters later she was caught and ripped apart, just like that.

After she was gone, I had to wonder if I'd done the right thing. The revival machines weren't working for now. There was no way to bring her back unless that changed.

Still, it was the only solution I could think of. If we could stop the Nairbs and the battle fleet, we'd revive her later on and all would be well.

If we *didn't* manage to do all that... well... in that case we were all as good as permed anyway. At least Sarah had died quick, free of guilt, and with happy thoughts in her brain about the future.

What more could a legionnaire ask for?

-39-

"James," Natasha whispered in my headset. "I think I found what we're looking for."

"Great, I'll be right there."

Harris was standing in front of me with his big hands on his hips. We were standing over his fallen body. I knew how he felt. Being faced with your own unjust death was a hard pill to swallow.

"This is unacceptable!" he said for what had to be the fifth time in a row. "I want this taken to the top. I want Primus Graves, Primus Winslade—even Deech to know about this."

"Look," I said, "she's awfully young. She lost it, that's all. She said she'd been revived three times yesterday alone. That's a lot for a rookie to take in. A bad grow could have—"

"Don't even start with that 'bad grow' bullshit on me, McGill. Don't even go there. I know all about your 'bad grow' murders, and I'm not buying any of it today."

"Well," I said, "your vendetta will have to wait."

"Why's that? You sweet on this girl? Another one, McGill? Isn't she a little young this time, even for you?"

"Nope. But she's dead anyway, and she's not coming back anytime soon."

"What the hell are you talking about, Centurion?"

"The revival machines—they aren't working right now. Almost nothing is—most of our Galactic-made gear has been shut down."

Harris stared at me for a second, then he looked up at the skies. "They're here?" he said, lowering his voice to a whisper. "Already?"

"Not the whole battle fleet—just the Nairbs."

"Those green snot-bags? They shut us down right off? How are we supposed to clean up this mess without guns? Why don't they just drop the bomb on us right now?"

"They might just do that, Adjunct. They just might. Anyway, support Leeson. You're one of the last people to catch a revive. Enjoy life while you can."

"Where are you off to, sir?"

"I have to fix this—if it can be fixed."

He squinted at me suspiciously. "I don't know whether I should wish you luck or not. You could save us—or kill us all."

"You're right about that, so, you'd best wish me luck."

Harris muttered, but he never did wish me luck. I headed toward Natasha's location. She was a green contact on my tapper. I reached her about six minutes later.

"Where are they?" I demanded when I found her. "The teleport suits can't be here."

We were standing in front of Winslade's lifter. Not a hundred meters off, his bunker yawned open. A few robot pigs stood around, frozen like statues. They were ugly, mechanical things on the best of days, like headless bulldogs the size of draft horses. But today, they weren't buzzing and walking around. They were as dead as our guns.

"Don't tell me the suits are down there in the bunker?"

"No," she said. "It's worse. I'm getting a reading from this lifter."

I took a look at the looming vessel. "Where?"

"Upstairs—on the lifter's Gold Deck."

"Winslade rode down on this thing. How could he not have known Claver and those teleport suits were aboard?"

Natasha shrugged. "You can ask him, if you want."

"I'll pass. Let's go."

Marching into the gloomy interior, I led the way. The rank of centurion had already made my life easier in any number of ways. For one thing the odds of being randomly stopped and ordered to leave an area dramatically dropped off with each new level of rank I'd attained.

Aboard this ship was no different. The veteran guards and occasional wandering adjuncts who served as aides didn't say a word. They looked at us, sure, but they didn't stop us. They assumed we knew what we were doing simply because I outranked them.

All the way up through the hatches to the lifter's Gold Deck, I sweated about running into a primus. Any of them would have questioned me for certain. Even another, more senior centurion might have given me trouble—but we didn't run into either type. I figured they were all busy in the bunker, or marshaling troops—or dead.

Whatever the case, I managed to get onto the lifter's small Gold Deck unchallenged.

"Where to now?" I asked Natasha.

Silently, she pointed down the narrow passageway to the end.

I headed that way, but I halted at the door. "Not in here?"

"Yes," she said. "It's got to be the tribune's office."

"Damn…" I rattled the door, but it didn't open.

Normally, a noncom would have intercepted us. But since Tribune Deech had been dead for quite some time, and everyone was short-handed, there was no one to greet us or to tell us to piss-off.

"Hack it," I told Natasha.

She compressed her lips and crunched up her nose like something stank, but she did it. I could tell it bothered her. She was one of those rule-following types of girls. I never could understand what she saw in a man like me.

The door clicked and opened. We hustled inside—and found a corpse on the floor.

It wasn't just any corpse, and it wasn't fresh, either.

"That's her—that's Deech," Natasha said.

"Yeah… I've got a bad feeling about this. She was supposed to have died back onboard *Nostrum*."

"McGill," Natasha said, "there's someone coming."

We stepped away from the door, standing on either side of it.

238

A sharp rapping sound began. Someone was knocking on the door.

Natasha and I exchanged confused, wide-eyed glances. She gestured, as if wanting to know if she should open it. I shook my head vigorously.

"Come now, McGill," Winslade called out. "Aren't you going to invite me in to the party?"

"Sure thing, Primus," I said, and I flung open the door.

Winslade stood there with a shitty grin on his face. There was a veteran standing on either side of him, and a female adjunct just behind his shoulder.

"Hmm…" he said. "This is very convenient. We have the victim, the murderer, and the motive all in one spot."

"Motive?" I asked. "I was lost, looking for the head. Isn't that right, Natasha?"

She didn't even bother to answer.

"Yes, motive," Winslade said. "You're here to steal the teleport suits. Most likely, you planned to run from this doomed world because the Nairbs have arrived."

"Uhh…" I said, "that wouldn't be a bad idea, actually. But we came here to check on Deech. Did you kill our tribune and take her place, Primus?"

His eyes flashed at me angrily. The two veterans shifted uncomfortably. I didn't know them personally, but they knew who I was well enough—thanks to many long years of building up my particular reputation.

"It is *you* who are under suspicion here, McGill. Drop your weapon. You're under arrest."

I smiled. "I surely will. This is all a misunderstanding."

Carefully, I lowered my plasma rifle to the deck. It was useless anyway. Natasha slowly drew her laser pistol and dropped it as well.

The veterans made a mistake then. They moved forward confidently to handcuff us. One upward stroke with my combat knife—that was all it took. The lead veteran lost his hand just below the elbow.

He looked at his arm and the blood pouring out. He was in a state of shock. Everybody was, I think, except for me. My blade shifted and came up through his guts next, slashing his diaphragm and heart in one stroke.

"Sorry," I told him as he sagged down to the deck.

The second veteran made another serious error. All his training told him to make a bad move—he stepped back, raised his rifle, and pulled the trigger.

But nothing happened. The plasma rifles we used in this legion were Empire-made. They didn't work anymore.

"Idiot!" Winslade hissed, seeing the mistake and scrambling out a needler.

Earth made her own needlers, so I knew it would operate as intended. Rather than trying to kill all of them, I slammed the door shut again, and rammed my knife into the bulkhead, spiking the door.

It was a temporary fix, and it had pretty much disarmed me, but it was all I could think of.

"What now?" Natasha asked, breathing hard.

I grabbed her and kissed her. I don't completely know why—it just felt like the right thing to do.

"What's that for?" she asked.

"For trusting me. Now, get into one of these suits. They'll pry the door open pretty soon."

Looking harried and confused, she helped me climb into a teleport suit. It was technologically complex, but simple in appearance and operation.

"It's charged," she said. "Should I get into the other one?"

"Yeah," I said. "Hurry."

She didn't quite make it. By the time she had her legs in and the zipper in her hand, the door went down.

Winslade burned a neat hole in her throat then flicked his wrist horizontally. The beam sliced through her soft neck and took her head mostly off. She sagged down to the deck and died.

"Now McGill," he said, stalking forward, "get out of that suit. I don't want to damage it, but if I have to—"

That was all I heard. Rather than hanging around to find out what he had planned, I touched the jump button on the suit.

The room wavered. It blue-shifted downward, then up. Winslade fired his beam, but I was no longer completely in the same space he was.

I teleported out without the slightest clue where I was going. Sometimes, my whole life felt like it did in that moment.

-40-

There wasn't much time to regret or celebrate my move. About a second after I'd launched, I landed again.

I knew right off I was aboard the starship *Nostrum*. Everything around me looked like our new, sleek transport. She'd been decorated in dark purple, beige and puke-green, with plenty of steel tubing to accent everything.

Activating my tapper, I tried to contact the crew. The only crew members who'd been left behind when the legion had been fully deployed were still on Gold Deck.

They didn't answer my call. Not even the AI beeped at me. I didn't like that one bit.

Running through the ship, I saw systems in operation everywhere, but no living people. There were plenty of dead ones, though.

Still in vac suits in many cases, they were sprawled out or curled up in fetal balls. They were very dead, a week-gone if I had to guess—and I've seen more than my share of dead people.

Apparently, no one had bothered to clear the dead from the cubes. They'd been left here—not to rot exactly, because the microbes in their bodies were as dead as they were, but to chemically age at least, like freeze-dried meat.

When I reached Gold Deck, I found more dead—everyone was dead.

242

My eyes flashed over the scene, I have to admit, it left me ill at ease. How could so many have died without me hearing about it? Had this happened recently, or hours ago?

Checking the chronos built into the tappers, and the public logs, I read that the ship had suffered a recent attack from the ground. It was another round of missiles from our friends under the dome, of course. They'd used X-rays again, and they'd neatly killed the crew.

At that moment, I felt hope slipping away. The rogue scientists down in that dome were tough, mean, resourceful, but they had no idea what they were up against. Battle Fleet 921 was coming, and the Galactics were here right now with their scout ship. The tech-smiths couldn't hope to beat them all, even if they could take down my legion.

Making a fateful choice, I reached for the comm systems. I'm no tech, but our systems aren't built to be hard to use. Centuries of design advancement had made most computers fairly accessible to any person with decent skills. They all had the same kind of interface, you just had to know what you wanted to do and how to search for it.

"Native people of Arcturus IV," I said, beaming out a general call. "This is the starship *Nostrum*. We wish to discuss terms to end this conflict."

They didn't answer right away. In fact, they weren't the first to answer me at all.

The big forward screen on the bridge lit up instead. It was Winslade, and his face was bigger than it had any right to be. His teeth were each a meter across, and his hairy nostrils were flaring as big and black as tractor tires.

"McGill!" he screeched at me. "Get off this channel. You've got no authority—"

"Excuse me, Primus," I said, "but are you aware that everyone aboard Starship *Nostrum* is stone dead?"

"Stop broadcasting immediately!" he ordered. "You—"

I was tired of him by now, so I muted him and continued to hail the planet below. At last, a signal came back in response.

Another face loomed, and this time I found it a pleasant one. The sad, lovely visage of the woman I'd met inside the dome looked at me curiously.

"Why are you calling us, James McGill?" she asked.

"I'm glad to see it's you," I told her. "I never asked your name when we met before."

She blinked slowly, then answered me after a moment's thought. "I'm Floramel, she said."

"Floramel..." I said, letting the name linger on my lips. "A lovely name for a lovely woman."

"I'm not strictly a member of humanity, McGill."

"No ma'am," I agreed, "but I'm hoping you have compassion and good sense to go along with your natural beauty."

"I don't understand why you've contacted us."

"I really wanted to talk to the leader of your people..."

"We're researchers. We have a lot of independence, and we operate with a loose framework. That said, I'm an allocator of resources."

"Um..." I said. "Does that make you a leader? A decision-maker?"

"Yes, as far as we have such functions."

"Okay then, let's talk. We need to end this conflict."

"Do you wish to surrender?" she asked. "To beg for your life?"

"Normally, that might seem like a good idea. But you don't fully understand the situation. There's another ship here, in this system. It's hiding, but they can see us even if we can't see them."

Floramel nodded. "We know of this vessel. It lingers back, out of our reach. We have made no move to attack or establish contact with it, as it appears to be a harmless observer—unlike you and your legion."

"I know," I said, "it looks that way, but looks can be deceiving. The ship is from the Empire. The crew are Nairbs, agents of the Galactics."

"I see... Why are they here, visiting this remote lab colony?"

"Because you represent a violation of Galactic Law. The advances in technology you've made here are illegal."

"We had no idea Earth cared about such a distant power and its laws."

I smiled. She was wise, thoughtful, and out of her depth all at once.

"Like most people," I told her, "we humans have our masters, too. We serve the Galactics. They've dispatched a fleet to this system—a vast armada of ships known as Battle Fleet 921. When it gets here, they will destroy you utterly."

She blinked again, and she looked troubled. "This is grim news, if it is true. Why wouldn't the Galactics visit destruction upon Earth instead of our world?"

"They might," I admitted, "when they get around to it. The bigger problem right now is your survival."

"And what would you suggest that we—?" she began, but there was an unexpected interruption.

A beam sang past my ear. I'd just moved my hand up to scratch, as my faceplate was off for the first time in days. A man can build up a powerful need to scratch after spending a long time in a vac suit.

That small movement, combined with the low accuracy of a needler at a range of some twenty meters, saved my life. As it was, the beam burned a line into the rubbery material of my neck guard and slashed downward, drawing a hot line across my teleport suit.

Fortunately, Earth techs had seen fit to construct these valuable suits with very tough materials. The suit was scorched, but it wasn't burned through.

My first reaction was to drop to the floor. The consoles and crash-seats provided me cover, and I scrambled on all fours for the nearest exit.

Cursing, Winslade gave chase. He had his needler out and ready.

God never saw fit to give me much in the way of brains, but for reasons of his own he made me a tougher fighter than most. When I scrambled around a console, I doubled back and hunched there. When Winslade rounded the corner where I crouched, I kicked him hard.

It was a low blow, and it wasn't entirely accurate. He was wearing the second teleport suit, of course, and therefore his balls had a certain degree of protection.

Still, the force of the kick and the sensitivity of the region gave him some trouble. Hissing, he staggered away from me and raised his needler.

There was murder in the man's eyes. I'd seen it a thousand times before.

Having little choice and no real weapons, I grabbed his arm. His hand, his beamer, and even a portion of his wrist vanished inside my larger grip. I felt numbing heat—he'd burned me.

But my hand still operated. I yanked him down on his face, and I beat him with my good hand until he stopped moving. It wasn't clean, or pretty, but I stood up panting in the end and he lay still on the deck.

All this time, the lovely, watchful eyes of Floramel hadn't missed a beat.

"That was savage," she said in a wondering tone. "Isn't he one of your people? Why would you mistreat one another in this way?"

"It would take quite a bit of explaining," I admitted, still heaving deep breaths of air. "The brief version is that I don't really include this little rodent as one of my people. But what really matters is that other ship out there, and the battle fleet behind it."

She cocked her head and stared at me blankly. I'd noticed that her people seemed to do that when they were thinking. While she did so, I stripped my teleport suit down to the leggings and began to bandage my wounded hand and wrist.

"McGill…" she said eventually. "Your conversations intrigue me. *You* intrigue me. How can an intelligent being be simultaneously barbaric and civilized? How can you be part animal and part sentient?"

I chuckled at that. Shaking off the sweat that had beaded up on my forehead, I got out a tiny flesh-printer from the bridge emergency kits and sprayed cells on my injured arm.

"That's a good question," I said, "would it surprise you to learn I've heard it before?"

"No, not at all."

Just about then, I noticed a blue light. It pulsed and shimmered. My eyes widened in fear. The suit on the floor—Winslade's suit—it was teleporting out.

In a panic, I dropped the flesh-printer and tore at the suit that still wrapped me up to my knees. I hadn't bothered to pull it off completely until just now.

My suit also began to shimmer. A few seconds later they both vanished.

"Where did the body go?" Floramel asked. She was still watching from the forward wall.

I stared down at the empty deck at my feet, panting hard. Both teleport suits were gone without a trace. That had been a very close call.

"I have no idea where it went," I admitted, "but I'll bet it was somewhere far away from here..."

-41-

Floramel told me she'd be in touch, and that she had to go attend to other matters. Before she closed the channel, I asked if her people would attack our transport ship again.

"As long as you don't attack us, we have no quarrel," she said. "This has always been true. Each time you've been injured it was due either to a trap we set to discourage invaders, or a counterstrike in response to your relentless aggression. Is it possible that your leaders never understood that?" Her expression was puzzled and sincere.

"Yep," I told her. "It's perfectly possible. Humans are good at a lot of things, but logic in the face of adversity isn't one of them."

"I see…" she said. "We thought our position was self-evident. Perhaps we should have issued warnings—but we feared you would only use the delay for further opportunity in attempting to bypass our defenses."

"Bingo," I said. "You're right again. You see? You *are* beginning to understand us."

"So strange…" she said, and her lovely face faded away to pixels.

The next call I made was a difficult one. I called Primus Graves.

He was a stern man under the best of circumstances, but as I attempted to explain the events of the last several hours, his face grew positively sullen.

"I knew something was going on between you and Winslade, McGill, but I failed to grasp the depths of this series of mistakes. When the legion is restored to order, I'm going to recommend you be stripped of your rank. You're not centurion-level material."

"Okay, Primus," I said. "That's fine. But right now, we have problems. The Nairbs are out there, and they're likely to eradicate every living thing in this star system."

Graves sucked in a deep breath and let it out. "You've put me in a grim situation. I'm the most senior officer left alive by both experience and commission date—meaning I'm in active command of what's left of Varus."

"Right sir, that's why I called you first."

"You're sure Winslade was involved in all this? And Claver? Again?"

"It sure looks that way, sir. I can't be certain of what his motives might have been, but—"

"But it doesn't matter," Graves finished for me. "We can't revive him anyway—we can't revive anyone—and you're sure the entire crew aboard *Nostrum* is dead?"

"They're freeze-dried, sir. I'm the sole breathing occupant. On the plus side, the rogue scientists have promised not to nail us again as long as we stop attacking them."

"That's very considerate of them," Graves said in what I assumed was a sarcastic tone. With Graves, it was sometimes hard to tell—his sarcastic mode sounded exactly like his dead-serious mode. "I take it you've got a girlfriend among the locals? Is that safe to say?"

"Uh..." I said. I'd neglected to identify Floramel by name or description.

"That's what I thought. Fair enough—we'll try to get off-planet. It's time to bail out of the Arcturus system. You stay put and wait for us. Try not to get into any more trouble. Can you do that, McGill?"

"I'll swear on a stack of bibles if you want me to, sir."

"Fine. At least the lifter engines are still working. The Nairbs will have to clean up here. We failed in our mission, but at least we didn't all get permed. This will be the biggest black

249

mark on our legion since the Teutoburg Forest debacle—but we might survive it."

Sometimes, when Graves made remarks like that, I wondered just how old he was. I knew he was older than Legion Varus itself, but to be referencing ancient Rome… Well, it was a little bit creepy.

"Just a second," I said as he moved to sign off. "What do you mean the Nairbs can deal with this?"

"Exactly what I said. They can drop their hell-burners for all I care. I'd kiss each one on the way down if I could. We've lost too much blood and treasure on this Godforsaken rock already. These rogue scientists have signed their own mass death-warrants, and I'm willing to make my peace with it."

"But sir, that's not really fair. I found out that if they'd surrendered, we were planning to dump them all in space anyways."

"Is that right?" Graves chuckled. "That has Winslade and Deech written all over it. Well, the rogues had their fun at our expense. Quit crying about it. They aren't even human, McGill, get a grip."

Before I could argue further, he cut the channel. I cursed and fretted for a time, uncertain as to what I should do.

Finally, I took action I knew I was going to regret. I recorded a warning on the bridge comm system, and set up a timer for it to be transmitted down to the dome later, when we were already underway. I hoped that Floramel's people wouldn't retaliate with more missiles if we were retreating. If we had a head start, there wouldn't be time for those deadly X-ray warheads to catch us.

The message was simple. I provided Floramel with an explanation concerning the Nairb ship, its capabilities, and its primary goal of bombing out the surface.

When I'd finished the recording, I sensed a presence behind me. I whirled around, fully expecting to see Claver in a teleport suit, or maybe one of the lab-people looking distant and ethereal.

What I saw instead surprised the heck out of me—even though it shouldn't have.

"A Nairb?" I asked. "What are you doing on our ship?"

It was indeed a Nairb. They were strange creatures. They amounted to greenish bags of protoplasm shaped sort of like earthly seals. They even had flippers.

"I'm documenting your infractions," the creature said to me with the aid of an interpreting device. "Please continue with your activities, human. My list is already impressive, but I'm hoping to achieve even greater merit when you're expunged."

I gathered from its odd statement that the more violations I confessed to, or performed while it watched, increased the Nairb's status in some way.

"It makes too much sense that you'd be more interested in brownie points than justice," I said bitterly.

"Assuming these 'brownie points' are a measurement of success, your statement is essentially correct. Please continue."

"I'm finished."

"But you haven't completed your treacherous act toward the Empire. You must send your message to the rebels on the planet below."

"I was just *thinking* about doing that," I lied. "I wasn't going to send it. That was never my intention."

"Interesting…" the Nairb said, slithering forward with a humping gait to investigate my settings on the ship's comm console. "Ah-ha! I see your plan. The message will be transmitted after you've begun your escape. That adds several new counts."

"What?"

"Premeditation has been confirmed. What's more, you performed this latest deception while in the presence of a duly appointed officer of Galactic Law. That adds to the severity of the penalty, if not the crime itself."

"But I never knew you were here until now!"

"Irrelevant," it said, "…but again, intriguing. Your statement amounts to another admission. You lied when I first asked you about this message, didn't you? More violations! Please attempt further complications, human. I'm not certain, but I believe I'm reaching a new threshold in bonus points."

"You vile bag of snot!"

"Yes, like that! Well done! Verbal assault has now been added to your robust list of infractions. You're a most compliant being. It will be a shame to erase you from existence. Now, let's get down to details. I require your DNA for individual identification—"

At that point, I knew this had to stop. The Nairbs had ordered me permed several times in the past. On each occasion, they'd been tricked into believing their orders had been carried out. That had worked for many long years because the Galactics usually couldn't be bothered to track individuals out on the frontier. We were like fish in the ocean to them: we were all the same and therefore almost without value.

But if he scanned my DNA and ran a search, he was sure to discover I'd been tried and convicted of serious violations on any number of past occasions. That would reflect poorly on Earth and all of humanity.

Whether he knew it or not, the Nairb had forced me to do something I knew I'd regret later.

Nairbs are the very definition of soft creatures. Even their hides are relatively thin—and their bones? They're like rotten sticks.

I didn't even bother using a weapon. My fists easily smashed his skull in, and goop flew everywhere.

"Ugh… damn… You stink inside."

The Nairb didn't answer, because he was as dead as a snail under a farmer's shit-kickers. I watched for a moment as he settled on the deck, slowly flattening and glubbing out nasty juices all over the place.

-42-

The next twenty minutes or so weren't my finest.

I felt truly screwed. Worse, I felt like I'd possibly screwed whatever chances Earth had for survival as well.

"Why, McGill?" I asked myself. "Why'd you have to go and slaughter a Nairb—again?"

My momma had always said I'd had trouble with authority figures—starting off with her. I'd just never fully grasped the concept. Even today, this flaw seemed to haunt me.

The slime from the Nairb spread far and wide. It was slippery at first, when it touched your boots, but it turned sticky as it dried. I didn't think that was any kind of improvement.

Many possible options occurred to me as I pondered what to do next, but none of them seemed feasible. I could, for instance, try to clean up the Nairb and toss his flappy corpse off the ship. But the Nairbs weren't sloppy about investigating such things. They'd demand a full accounting, and certain Legion Varus officers would be only too happy to hand me over to the Nairbs.

Other possibilities seemed equally far-fetched. Aiming guns at the Nairb ship, asking Floramel's people for help— even begging for mercy. None of these things would matter to the Nairbs or my commanders. In fact, in the case of the Nairbs, they'd probably wet themselves with happiness to get their hands on a creature so undeniably guilty as I was.

To pass the time, I watched local space on the sensor screens. The Legion vacated the siege upon the dome as I watched, the lifters formed a chain of disks that rose up out of the atmosphere and came toward the transport.

Watching them, I got a scare. Something else loomed—something dark, oblong and distant.

Was it a ship—a Galactic ship? It wasn't an Earth-design, I knew that right off.

I watched helplessly. The Nairbs had come out of hiding. They were on the far side of the planet, swinging around into view now. Were they stalking the lifters, or the planet itself? Or even me in the transport? I couldn't tell.

"What in the nine hells were you thinking, boy?" asked a voice from behind me. "If you don't get yourself into the damnedest predicaments..."

I whirled around to see Claver standing behind me. He was wearing a grin and a teleport suit.

"How much did you see?" I asked him.

He laughed. The sound had a cruel edge to it. "Enough to know there was a country bumpkin in this woodpile somewhere—and here he is!"

"Why'd you come back?"

"Back?" he asked me, squinting his eyes.

That's when I noticed he had a laser pistol aimed at me. I glanced at it once, then looked back at his beady eyes.

"So," he said, "you met me before. I wasn't sure. Imagine my surprise when Winslade showed up dead! No McGill, no Claver—just a deceased Winslade."

"Yeah," I said. "That must have seemed odd." I was stalling and fishing for clues.

He walked around the consoles to get closer to me. He seemed to be worried I might try to duck, or dive out of easy range. Nothing could have been further from the truth—but he didn't know that.

"So how did you get along with the last Claver you met up with? And would you mind telling me what happened to... the other me?"

I shrugged. "Sure. He came to me, and he told me he'd trade me a ride out of this hellhole in exchange for the Galactic Key."

"Good, good," Claver said, just out of reach now. "So, what happened to my brother?"

"I thought that was obvious. Winslade caught on, and he killed you."

Claver narrowed his eyes and waggled the gun barrel at me.

"You wouldn't be trying to pull one over on me, would you? That'd be a bad idea—but we both know you're dumb enough to try."

"Think about it. There were two suits. I'm here, Winslade and the other suit came from here. We teleported to the ship, then we had an argument. Afterward, I took off my suit, and they both teleported away."

Claver chuckled evilly. "An argument? That's funny. You always argue with your balls and your fists, don't you boy? Looks like Winslade lost this argument, and somehow he managed to die in the process. Most unfortunate."

"That's what I said."

His face worked. He didn't seem sure what was true and what wasn't. It burned him that he couldn't nail me down any further. My story was backed up by certain facts, but there were also holes in it you could drive a power-cart through.

"Okay," Claver said. "I don't care what really happened here. I take it I'm dead, Winslade tried to steal everything, and you clocked him. I'm okay with all that. Let's call it a sketchy deal gone bad."

"Agreed."

"But I still want the key. There's no way things would have gotten to this point unless it was somewhere at hand. Why else would you teleport back up to the ship?"

My face went slack. I looked as dumb as a bag of hammers.

"Don't try that on me today," he said. "I know you're a moron, but people keep dying around you. Even a moron has to have an edge to keep breathing for this long when you play so close to the fire. Now, where is the key, boy?"

"Winslade seemed to think it was here," I said, compounding my lies now into a big sticky ball of nonsense.

"That's why he ported up. I don't know where exactly it might be on the ship itself."

He narrowed his eyes again. "Wasn't it in your possession?"

"That's old news. Winslade and Turov took it off me years back—I died for a long time, remember?"

"That is true…" he said, thinking it over. "Right… but why did Winslade take you for a ride up here if he was just looking for the Galactic Key—which has nothing to do with you? And if he knew it was safe, why come at all?"

"You were hunting for it," I said. "I think Winslade wanted to make sure it was still where it was supposed to be."

"Why bring you along, though?"

I shrugged again. "No one said he brought me. Maybe I followed him."

Claver grinned at last. That's when I knew I had him.

"That's it!" he said. "You got greedy! That's the first thing you've said that I fully believe. You knew this ship was up here, dead—so big, quiet, and full of nothing but echoes. Winslade was up here alone, looking for that key like a little girl in the dark… so you followed him up and nailed him."

I didn't move. My face didn't change expression, either. When a fish investigates your bait, you don't start cheering him on. You just let him sniff and nibble it, hoping he'll take that fatal bite.

"We've got a problem, anyway," I said, pointing to the forward screens. "Two of them, in fact."

On the screens, the returning legionnaires in their lifters were growing closer. It wouldn't be long before the first of them docked. Behind them, the shadowy cylindrical shape of the Nairb vessel had shifted too, approaching at a cautious pace.

Claver's boot nudged the Nairb's corpse on the deck.

"And here's problem number three," he said. "Do you still piss the bed every night, McGill? I think you must. There's never been a giant mess made in this universe that can't be at least indirectly traced to you."

"What do you suggest we do to solve all this?" I asked.

He scratched his face, putting one finger through his open faceplate to do it. He had visible stubble on his chin—a week's worth, maybe. That seemed strange to me, and I realized the last version I'd seen only hours before had been clean-shaven. What's more, newborns always came out of the revival machines without any facial hair.

This version of Claver had been around for a while. That meant he was making clones—copies of himself. I wondered vaguely just how many Clavers were drawing breath right now.

He withdrew the finger, and he turned to me.

"I should kill you right now," he said, "but you might know where the key is."

"I might."

"Shut up and let a man think," he snapped. After I was quiet for a second, he continued. "Obviously, trading teleport suits for the key and such failed to work. Since there's no other Claver around—not even a body, that line of fair trading failed. Why?"

I pointed to the screen. "What good is running home in a teleport suit to anybody? The Nairbs are pissed off, and the battle fleet is almost here. They'll just follow us to Earth and kill everyone."

"You see, that's your problem," he said. "You've got no imagination. Earth is just a planet. Don't be such a home-boy. The universe is a big place. There are even humans, if you want companionship, on dozens of other worlds."

"I'm loyal to Earth."

"Bah! You're just provincial. Small-minded. But never mind, there's no time to argue the point. We have to do something about these Nairbs before they order all these fools in your legion to self-execute."

I opened my mouth to say something, but whatever it was, it died in my throat and my mind.

Claver stepped up to the console and punched the send button on my message. I stared at him in shock.

"Yeah, I saw what you did..." he said, "and yeah, I sent your message early. Someone had to get this show rolling. Just relax—let's see what happens."

-43-

My eyes were as big around as saucers. Events outside the ship were playing out, and I felt helpless to affect them.

The lifters arrived, one at a time, and legionnaires began tramping over the decks. I didn't bother to leave Gold Deck and hide someplace. Graves would hunt me down and demand an accounting no matter where I went.

"Look at that!" I said, pointing at the forward displays. "Those are missiles!"

"Don't worry," Claver said, looking over the instruments. "They aren't targeting this ship—they're going for the Nairbs. These dome-monkeys have more balls than I'd figured..."

"Hey look," I said. "The Nairbs are running!?"

I stepped up beside Claver, and we stared at the big screen. We watched as the Nairb's oblong ship stopped moving toward us or the planet. Instead, it veered off and dove away at an angle.

"Chicken-shits," Claver chuckled.

"The good Lord hates a coward," I said.

"Well, he must hate *me* then. This is where I cut and run, McGill."

"Where are you going?"

He jerked a thumb down at the dome below us.

"Isn't it obvious? The only gain left in this system is the tech they have under glass down there. I'm going to see if I can scoop some up before they all get themselves killed."

258

"Leave me a teleport suit," I said.

He had a second one—it was poking out of the top of his satchel bag. He'd come back with it, perhaps hoping to implement his original plans to get his precious Galactic Key.

Taking a short glance down, he tucked the exposed bit of suit back inside of the bag. "Oh, come on James. Why would I do that?" he demanded. "Give me something good enough to consider it, at least."

"Good enough? Like what?"

"Like the key. Or something equivalent. I'm a trader, boy. Trade me something I can use."

I shook my head. I had nothing.

"Fine," Claver said, and the room wavered and shifted blue.

A moment later I was alone and uncertain. I found myself staring for a spell—unfocused on anything. Graves showed up not long after that.

"You're just standing around on the bridge, is that it, McGill? Innocent of all crimes?"

"Very perceptive, Primus. I'm pure and clean. Like wind-blown snow on a mountain peak."

He chuckled. "All right. I see the remains of our Nairb friend, here. You know you've possibly doomed our entire homeworld by killing him, right?"

"A crazy suggestion, sir. He was like that when I got here. Maybe the rogues got him. They've got some pretty fancy tech—and they're mean when they use it."

Shaking his head, he stepped up to the console and examined the scene. "All this is related to Claver somehow?"

"And Winslade. He's involved in this up to his bushy eyebrows."

Graves made a show of inspecting the premises. "There's only one trouble, McGill," he said. "I only see you and a Nairb corpse here. No Claver. No Winslade. Just McGill, as usual. Now, as you know I'm not an overly suspicious man but—"

"Far from it, Primus!" I chimed in.

"But, there are strict limits to my gullibility. After having listened to countless fabrications and half-truths from you, I'm inclined to doubt this latest tale—which lacks a single scrap of evidence. Do you understand me, Centurion?"

"Loud and clear, sir. But I think there is *some* evidence."

He crossed his arms and narrowed his eyes in my direction. "Explain."

"First off, there's my physical presence aboard this vessel. I didn't take a lifter up—they're all accounted for. Teleportation plainly stands to reason."

"All right, go on."

"If I teleported, where's the suit?"

He looked around. There was nothing, of course. Claver had taken both his suits with him.

"I fail to see how—" he began, but I put up a finger to stop his suspicions.

"Someone must have taken the suits away," I told him. "Someone was here, therefore, and now they're not."

"I need proof, McGill. This isn't holding water."

My eye crawled over the bridge and the console. Sure, there was a little damage. The Nairb was stone dead—but I'd done that myself. Then I saw a splatter of blood on the deck and smiled.

"That," I said. "That's where Winslade was standing. Get a bio up here to run a DNA test on it."

Graves frowned at the spot and called up a bio. She frantically arrived a short while later, took a sample, ran it through the ship's computer and declared it a match.

"A match to who?" Graves demanded.

The bio looked startled. "To Primus Winslade, of course— I'm sorry, sir. I thought you knew."

His eyes slid from her face to mine, then back again. "I just wanted to hear it from your lips," he said to her, "dismissed."

When she was gone, he turned to face me. "This is a serious situation, McGill."

"Uhh…" I said. "Which one, sir?"

"You're practically standing on the remains of both a Nairb and your superior officer. I really thought you'd changed, you know. This mission felt different. You seemed mature, and you functioned as a leader ought to."

While he spoke, Graves took out his laser pistol, checked the charge, and slammed the breach closed again.

"Hold on, Primus," I said. "You've got this all wrong."

"I don't think that's possible. I've caught you with a dead Nairb, evidence of a dead superior officer, and hell, a dead ship all around you."

"Right, right, you've got a point there. But Winslade killed the Nairb, not me."

He hesitated. "Why?"

"Why'd he do it? Because he's a greedy snake, sir. He planned to trade away the tech these rogues came up with to advance his own designs. Claver is here to make his own secret deals."

"Why?" Graves asked me. "Why should I believe anything you say at this point?"

I threw my hands wide. Graves flinched in response, but he didn't shoot me—not yet.

"Okay," I said, "let's try applying some logic here. Why would I come up here in a teleport suit? How did I get one?"

"It makes sense that Claver or Winslade gave it to you," Graves admitted. "But that doesn't—"

"No, no, it doesn't mean I'm innocent. But come on now—what's in it for me?"

"You had a girlfriend on the planet. You're real sweet on her. You warned them about the Nairbs, and they're attacking because of that."

"Actually, Winslade warned them."

"How?"

I quickly showed him the recording, and I showed him the timer it had been associated with. The trigger had never gone off, but instead someone had sent it early.

"That was Winslade," I said, choosing to make him my scapegoat.

To be honest, I chose Winslade because I had physical evidence he had been on the bridge. There was no particular reason to hate Winslade over Claver—they were both bastards of the first order.

"Hmmm," Graves said. "I don't understand all this, and I'm not sure I need to. All I need to do is kill you and call it even."

"That won't satisfy the Nairbs, sir," I pointed out.

His gun and his face sagged a little. "No... No, it won't."

"May I make a suggestion, Primus?" I asked.

He looked at me. "I know I'm going to regret this... but sure, let's hear it, McGill."

I dared to smile. It was a small thing, but it was undeniably there—I could feel it curving on my face.

When I was done presenting my idea, I might have thought Graves looked a touch sick—but that couldn't be. He was too tough-minded of an officer to turn green over a little bit of adventure.

-44-

We contacted the Nairbs, and for once in his long, long life, Graves let me do the talking.

"What is this intrusion on our harmony?" droned a translation device. The Nairb that spoke pulsed toward the screen, filling it entirely. Suddenly, he slopped back and away, quivering with agitation in contrast to the bland words I was listening to. I couldn't help it—I thought of a Jello mold at supper when the table leg gets kicked.

"Uhh…" I said. "This is the starship *Nostrum*. We're an Earth vessel, charged with local enforcement of Galactic—"

"We know who you are, Earthman," the Nairb said. "Why have you set your lapdogs on us? They can't reach us with their missiles—we've moved out of range. Your unprovoked attack has been accounted and added to the growing list of—"

"You're right about all that, sir," I said, "except for one thing. We're not in control of the planet below our two ships. We're here, in fact, to exterminate these people."

The Nairb stared at me for a second then turned and barked at someone off-camera.

"Your claims are unverified and do not match observable data," he said.

"They certainly do," I replied, "we've been battling these rogues for days—weeks, even. Surely you must have documented that."

"It seems that you have assigned a derogatory label to the illegally operating technologists—either in a weak attempt to mislead us from your association or perhaps from sheer arrogance on your part. And yes, there was a plainly visible conflict on the world below, that's true. But we have no intention of taking up sides. We've been busy cataloging numerous—"

"I'm sure you haven't missed a trick, sir," I said. "The point I'm trying to make is that if the missiles came from the planet below, they have nothing to do with Earth. We've been hit by similar attacks over recent days."

"Are you claiming this world isn't under your control? That you're therefore not responsible for the actions of its inhabitants?"

"That's exactly right, sir. They refused to evacuate. They refused to stand down. Now that we've failed in our mission to negotiate our way out of this rebellion, we're asking you to put it down."

"How so?"

"Use your hell-burners!"

The seal-like being appeared to ponder my suggestion. "You want us to destroy this world?"

"We certainly do. We insist upon it, in fact."

"This isn't a warship," the Nairb complained in monotone. "We have only basic weapons."

"You've got bombs, don't you?" I demanded. "Use them!"

The Nairb looked upset. "We can't get that close. They've fired missiles at us, and our analysis indicates they're dangerous enough to keep our ship out of bombing range."

"I see," I said, nodding my head. "You're chicken."

"Your colloquialism is unclear through my translator...I am no variety of poultry animal."

"Cowards. Shirkers of duty. You're unreliable."

This last insult finally seemed to sting the Nairb. "Your offensive language is counterproductive," he said. "Nevertheless, it appears we have the same immediate goal."

"Good, now, let's get down to—"

"Just a moment," the Nairb said, interrupting. "We have orders for you to carry out before our cooperation can begin.

You must first provide a clear explanation concerning the fate of our field agent."

The screen changed, and the Nairb I'd beaten to death appeared. The vid was clearly streamed and stored from the point of view of their agent. He was looking around, and apparently his recording systems followed his senses.

Suddenly, a flurry of violent motion saw the Nairb knocked to the floor and savagely beaten by a tall figure. We couldn't make out the face in the dark.

Graves sighed and his chin touched his chest in defeat.

"I recognize that vicious creature," I said loudly. "It's a thing called a Winslade."

"What is this 'Winslade' you speak of?"

"A treacherous beast," I said. "An evil monster beyond calculation. Fortunately, he's dead. I killed him myself."

"That's unacceptable," the Nairb snapped. "We must have an accounting. We must mete out our own specialized punishments."

"Uh…" I said, thinking fast. "Well, we could revive him and turn him over—along with physical evidence that he was right here at the scene of the crime."

"That would be most satisfactory."

"There's a problem, however," I said. "Our revival machines have been switched off. In fact, most of our combat gear is inoperable. One of the reasons we had to retreat from the world below in defeat is because our guns no longer worked."

My statement seemed to cause some kind of fervor on their side of the channel. I saw the Nairb I'd been talking to speaking in alarmed tones in its native tongue to others out of sight.

But then, a truly shocking event transpired. The Nairb was collared and electrocuted—at least, that's what it looked like.

It had to be Claver. Could he have gotten down to the planet, procured deadly tech, then teleported it up to the Nairb ship to sabotage them so quickly? If so, it was an impressive feat by any measure.

But then, things became more clear. All throughout my conversation with the Nairb, I'd gotten the feeling it was listening to someone else off-camera. This being now made itself visible by gliding forward into range of the pick-up.

"Greetings, Earther." The translator spoke the alien's words. His glossy body, about the mass of a large man, was levered by six spidery legs to settle onto the ground. Two limbs swung before him, and the long, weird fingers steepled in a gesture of pretentious superiority.

I recognized it right off as a Mogwa. A familiar feeling hit me—like when you know not to put your hand into a dark place because a nasty critter is going to bite you.

The Mogwa were scary creatures. They might not be impressive to look at, but they were powerful. They were *actual* Galactics. Individuals from a superior race who lived at the Core of the galaxy on sophisticated planets of which we could only dream.

It didn't entirely surprise me that there was a Mogwa representative aboard the Nairb ship. They were the Nairbs' masters, after all, and this was a critical mission. A scout ship couldn't be left entirely to underlings.

"Huh…" I said. "Pleased to meet you, Mr. Mogwa. What happened to the fellow I was talking to?"

A flurry of ratcheting clicks funneled through the translating device. "He was substandard in performance," the Mogwa said. "He has been removed from my service."

"I see…" I said. "In that case, what can we do for you, sir?"

"What is your name, slave?" the Mogwa asked.

"I'm Centurion James McGill."

"Are you in charge of this local militia?"

"Yep."

Graves looked startled. He almost spoke up, but I gave him a tiny shake of the head. He deflated a little. We both knew I was the better liar. Our survival depended on my skills of deception at the moment.

"Who do I have the honor of addressing, sir?" I asked the Mogwa.

"I am the Magnate Slur."

"Great to meet you, Magnate."

"A polite slave, at least," Magnate Slur said. "As a reward I will treat you with undeserved kindness and explain my behavior. I executed the Nairb captain because it was his decision to turn off all your Galactic technology. That was a foolish mistake. Your pathetic ground forces were clearly in the thick of battle, attempting to expunge a rebellious force. After listening to your discussion with the Nairb, I found I couldn't contain my rage any longer."

I squinted at him. "What exactly got you so fired up, if you don't mind my asking?"

"Isn't it obvious? These rebels fired missiles at *my* ship! If we'd been a million kilometers closer, they would have killed everyone aboard. That would have included my eminent self. Such idiocy on the part of a Nairb—he was so sure you were performing some kind of violation of Galactic Law that he risked my person to prove it."

"Ah..." I said, catching on. "A natural response, Magnate. I completely understand."

Every Mogwa valued his own comfort and safety above the extinction of any dozen races in a frontier province—perhaps even more than that.

"So," Slur continued, "I will now provide you with new orders. These orders will supersede anything you've been instructed to do by Earth. Is that clear?"

"Crystal clear, Magnate."

"Good. First, we will restore the function of all your equipment so that you may defend yourselves. Then, you will revive and arrest the creature you referred to as a 'Winslade' and extradite this beast into our custody."

"So far, so good," I said happily.

"Lastly, before Battle Fleet 921 arrives at this dark, greasy hole, you will kill every living thing on the planet below us."

"Hmm..." I said thoughtfully. After hesitating for a second, I got an idea, and I brightened. "Okay. We'll do it."

"There is no need for you to agree with my commands, creature," Magnate Slur said sternly. "It implies you have the option of disobedience. My word is the word of your master. What is required of you now is action—not agreement or even acknowledgement."

I almost blew it then and said "Yes sir!" but I caught myself in time. Instead, I stood there and stared like a statue until he dismissed me and cut the channel feed.

When the Mogwa's ugly face finally faded away, I threw up my arms and let loose with a whoop of joy.

Graves twisted his lips up in disgust. "That was gut-wrenching to watch, McGill."

"What? We just got soooo lucky," I told him. "You don't even know the half of it, sir."

"Enlighten me."

"Didn't you hear? They turned all our weapons back on. We can revive our troops, and we can get the legion moving again."

"So what?" he demanded. "We had all those resources before, remember? We fought the rogues with everything we had. They beat us, McGill."

"Huh? No, no, no," I said. "You aren't getting my point at all, Graves. We're not going to kill the rogues. We're going to kill that hoity-toity Mogwa. It's the only way."

Graves stared at me after that, and his mouth sagged open a little. I felt proud at that fine moment. I couldn't recall ever having stunned him into silence before.

-45-

Graves started off by reviving Tribune Deech. I thought that was a mistake, but since I wasn't really in charge of the legion what I thought didn't matter much.

"We have to get our command and control working again," Graves said. "McGill, you promised to deliver Winslade to the Mogwa. I can't proceed until I hear from an officer who outranks both Winslade and I."

"We could revive him and ship him off—then just print a new Winslade," I suggested. "We don't even have to tell the second one there *was* a first one, for that matter."

Graves looked annoyed with my idea.

"We're reviving Deech first," he said firmly. "She can decide what she wants to do."

In the meantime, I left Gold Deck and became reacquainted with my unit. Leeson was the first man of rank I ran into. He didn't look too happy to see me.

"Centurion," Leeson said, giving me a slight nod. "What kind of fresh Hell are we stuck in now?"

"What are you suggesting, Adjunct?"

"Well… you disappeared. You didn't come up here on a lifter, and neither did Winslade. I can only surmise, sir, that there was some serious hanky-panky involved."

"That's out of line Adjunct," I reprimanded him. "I'm going to ignore your rude remarks, and I won't hold them against you, but let's not hear any more of that kind of talk."

269

Harris had come up during this exchange, and he crossed his arms and rolled his eyes when he heard my false outrage. He didn't say anything, however.

They were both right, of course. I'd been involved in all sorts of conduct unbecoming an officer today and it wasn't even dinnertime yet. But a man certainly couldn't run a unit with his subordinates giving him a hard time in public.

After handing out a slew of orders, I sent them off to clean up the dead all over the ship. Despite this gruesome duty, the troops were glad to be back aboard *Nostrum*. The planet below us had been anything but hospitable.

"Sir?" asked Harris a few hours later, "can I have a word?"

I was stretched out on my bunk at the time, and I'd just been starting to dream. The lights in my quarters were automatic, and they didn't turn off until the entire cube went into night-mode. Consequently, I'd had my arm thrown over my face.

"What is it, Adjunct?" I asked wearily.

Flesh-printing wands had been run over my various injuries, but I was still sore and worn out. One bad thing about command was how little sleep a man seemed to get.

"It's about my murder," Harris said. "Have they revived that recruit yet?"

"Sarah?"

"Yeah."

I took my arm off my face and looked at him.

"I thought we'd settled all that," I told him. "She had a bad day, and a bad revive. Let's not get—"

"I'm pressing charges, Centurion," Harris said determinedly. "I just wanted to let you know as I'm required to inform my immediate superior."

"Aw, now, Harris…"

But he was gone. I shook my head and sighed. My arm slipped back over my face and I dozed for a few precious minutes. It occurred to me that being in command was quite possibly more of a pain in the butt than it was worth. At least when I'd been lower-ranked, I hadn't had to babysit everyone who got into testy arguing about who killed who.

When I woke up, it was night. My tapper was buzzing, and I got the feeling it had been doing so for quite some time.

I groaned and sat up, pecking at my arm with bleary eyes and clumsy fingers.

Tribune Deech herself showed her face to me. She didn't look happy.

"Centurion," she said. "I'm awake and back in command of this legion. Graves has briefed me on a number of gross errors that have been made while I was on ice. Your name has been mentioned prominently, and I wish to talk to you."

"All right, sir," I said, "but can it wait until morning? I've had quite a day as well."

"I'm not interested in sleeping, Centurion," she told me sternly. "I've been doing it for days, and I'm ready to get things done."

"Yes sir," I said. I signed off, climbed out of my bunk and into the shower.

A few minutes later, I was back on Gold Deck. Deech looked different, I'll give her that. It must have been a while since she'd died and been revived. Her nose was smaller and straighter, along with the countless other improvements that come with becoming younger. I dare say her bust-line was riding a little higher in the water, too. I could only surmise that she hadn't died for at least ten years.

"You look great, Tribune," I said.

She sneered at me. "Is that all you have to say?" she demanded. "They told me you were a shallow man. A rutting beast of the field who thought of women as nothing but targets. Is that true, McGill?"

I was taken aback. "Uhh..." I said, holding the sound longer than usual due to my natural surprise. "Is there something wrong with noticing a woman's attractive appearance, sir?"

"I'm your superior. You will address me with respect."

"Of course, Tribune," I said, stepping closer to her desk.

She hadn't told me to sit down or anything, but I was getting annoyed already with her snotty attitude. I figured she was just cranky about having died. People tended to be like that when they weren't used to the process.

271

I plopped my butt down in the chair in front of her desk, and I leaned back a little. I didn't put my hands behind my head or anything, and didn't cross my legs because I don't usually do that. But I made myself at home and looked fully relaxed.

She frowned at me. "It has been explained to me that you performed a variety of unsanctioned actions on behalf of the legion," she said. "What do you have to say in your defense?"

"Defense?" I asked. "Am I under investigation, or something?"

"You're on report. You're permanently on report, McGill. I thought I'd give you a chance. I was a fool. The next time my subordinates warn me about a troublemaker I'll listen and take harsh action from the start."

"Permission to speak freely, Tribune?" I asked.

"Granted—but don't abuse it."

I leaned forward. "Sir," I said, "you've got the wrong idea, here. I didn't cause all these problems, I reacted to them. Someone else brought the legion out here. Someone else parked this ship close enough to get us X-rayed to death. And someone else left you dead for a week."

Deech glared at me. She clearly didn't like me, and I didn't think she was enjoying my little speech, either.

"Insolence, insubordination, risk-taking above and beyond…" she said. "Combined with a weak respect for women. Shall I go on?"

"Only if you desire to, Tribune."

"McGill, do you know what unexpected action I'm considering right now?" she asked me.

"Hmm…. Nope."

"I'm thinking of sending you to the Mogwa. They don't know what Winslade looks like since—"

"I know," I said, "they can barely tell one human from another. But why would you send me, sir?"

Deech had my complete and undivided attention at last. She began ticking off my crimes on her fingertips. I hate when people do that.

"Because *you* killed that Nairb agent, not Winslade," she began. "Then you teleported up here to this ship without

272

authorization. Lastly, you impersonated a commanding officer in a diplomatic crisis as well—namely, me."

"Hold on," I said, "Graves was in command when I represented myself as our legion commander, as you were dead at the time."

Deech waved away my words. "It doesn't matter. The situation is grim. We've been charged to deliver Winslade to the Nairbs and take out the tech-smith scientists under the dome. The first order is unfair, and the second order is probably impossible."

It was about then that I realized how Winslade had gotten ranked-up so fast. He'd romanced Deech before she'd died and straightened out her nose. That had to be it. I'd suspected something of that nature, but now, hearing her talk about how unfair it would be to march him into the lion's den, I felt certain about it.

I could have said plenty in my defense at that moment. Not the least of which would be accusing her of having an inappropriate relationship that had clouded her judgment on the subject of Winslade. The irony ran deep in her related accusations toward me concerning improper conduct.

I didn't bother to do any of that though—mostly because I knew it wouldn't have done any good.

"Primus Graves and I came up with a great solution to all this, Tribune," I said. "I'm surprised he didn't tell you about it."

Deech looked at me suspiciously. "*What* solution?"

Then, I told her about my ideas. She looked appalled, then thoughtful. Before I was done, she was white-faced and wincing as my words fell over her mind like gravel hitting a tin roof.

By the time I was finally done, she took a deep breath. She picked up an object from her desk—a trophy in the shape of a planet. The inscription read: *For exemplary service on Rigel-7.*

"You *are* different," she said thoughtfully. "You're *much* more dangerous than I'd been willing to believe."

"Aw, now, hold on—"

"Let me finish," she said. "You see this award? I've earned dozens like it. Do you know why? Because I get things done, and I do them by the book, McGill."

I shrugged. "So I take it my ideas aren't pleasing to your ear?"

"They're like a discordant hammering," she said. "Like the sound of an air car smashing into the ground. Speaking of which—didn't this rivalry between you and Winslade go back to just such an incident some months ago?"

"Oh, that? No sir. That was just a bump in our shared road. No... we've been hating on each other for at least a decade now."

Deech nodded slowly and returned the trophy to her desk. She set it down carefully, so it aligned perfectly with the others.

"I should have known," she said. "Do you know why I'm upset right now?"

"Uhh..." I said, unsure of the proper response. I'd gotten a similar if not identical question from women on many occasions, and they'd never been happy with any of my answers.

"Because, McGill," she went on, relieving me of the stress of having to come up with a response, "I'm beginning to listen to your insanity. Although I'd dearly love to send you in Winslade's place, it amounts to deceiving the Nairbs. I just don't see any other way out."

That cheered me up. I'd just begun to give up on her because I'd misread her signs. Instead of becoming sour and stubborn, she was seeing the light. That didn't make her happy, but it did make her smart.

"You won't regret this, Tribune," I told her.

She chuckled. "I'm very sure that I will regret it," she said, "but I don't know what else to do."

"You see that? That spot you're in now? That's when it's time to call up old James McGill. Drusus—back when he was our leader—he called me into his office to help him come up with something creative like this many times."

"Did he really?" she asked.

"Yes sir, as God is my witness, he did."

274

She nodded slowly. "That explains a lot. Dismissed, Centurion."

When I left her, Tribune Deech was looking long in the face, like someone had just run over six of her seven cats.

Conversely, I felt pretty good. We had a plan, and we had a chance. In my book, that meant we were better off than we had been just a few minutes earlier.

Things were looking up.

-46-

A few hours later, Winslade woke up on a pinnace. I was flying it, and there was a veteran pilot unconscious on the floor.

Winslade looked around blearily. "I… what's going on?"

"Don't concern yourself with the details, Primus," I said. "You're being delivered to the Nairbs for crimes against the Empire. Just relax, and you'll be processed in short order."

His eyes widened, and he looked around in growing alarm.

"You…" he said, "you knocked out the pilot? You're giving *me* to them instead? Why don't I remember any of this?"

"The mind's a funny thing," I told him. "It's liable to play all kinds of tricks on a man when he's fresh from a revive."

"Yes…" he said. "I remember now. You killed me. Let me go, McGill. Whatever mad scheme you've hatched, it will never work."

"Come on now, sir," I chided him. "You don't want to end things in a way that leaves you remembered as a coward."

He began thrashing around, fighting his bonds and making a racket. I gagged him with tape, and then I took my name patch off my tunic and slapped it onto his. It sank in and adhered to his clothing like it belonged there.

He kept straining, looking down at the patch saying "McGill" and straining to rub it off. I could have told him it was hopeless, but he wouldn't have listened.

When we docked with the Nairb ship, I carried Winslade over my shoulder like a kidnap victim and marched aboard. A suspicious pack of Nairb crewmen met me and escorted me up to their command deck.

There, I met with the first Mogwa I'd seen in the flesh in years.

"This is the prisoner," I said, setting Winslade on the deck.

"How can I be sure?" Magnate Slur asked. "One of you looks much like another."

I shrugged. "That's him," I said. "I'd swear on a stack of bibles *this* high."

"Your words are meaningless," the Mogwa complained.

It slithered forward to the squirming Winslade and ripped the taped gag from his mouth.

"Identify yourself, creature," Slur commanded.

"Magnate," Winslade said breathlessly. "I'm Primus Winslade. That criminal over there is James McGill. He's the one you want!"

"*You* are the Winslade?" Slur demanded, looming even closer.

"I am indeed."

The Mogwa shook, and its lobes puffed out at the sides. I honestly thought it was going to kill Winslade right then and there.

"Take this beast away," Slur said at last. "I'm having trouble controlling my temper in its presence. I don't want to damage it irreparably—not yet. The death must be drawn out over much time."

Winslade eyes widened, and he was dragged away. He looked back at me plaintively, and I have to admit, I almost felt bad.

He got one arm free and grabbed the corner of a hatch, holding up his captors for a second.

"Why'd you put that patch on me?" Winslade demanded, shouting at me.

"Because," I told him, "Galactics can't read English—but you can."

Shock and understanding filled his face. Then, he was gone.

277

All the way back to *Nostrum*, I felt a little low. I knew I had to give up Winslade, he was our scapegoat, and he deserved death a hundred times over. But to let a man be tormented to death by aliens—that was beyond the pale. Sure, he'd have done the same to me in a heartbeat, but I was the one who had to live with myself after today.

The flight back to *Nostrum* wasn't a long one, but I came to a decision before it was over. I reached out and switched off the radio. It was only going to start squawking and complaining. I didn't feel like listening to an endless stream of orders telling me to come back to base.

I tilted the angle of the vessel and dipped it down into the atmosphere. It was shaped like a tiny version of a lifter, with just enough space aboard for a squad to fit if they squeezed.

When I landed just outside the dome, I left the snoring veteran in his vac suit aboard the small ship and walked to the dome walls.

"Floramel?" I broadcast with my suit radio. "Are you here? This is James McGill. I've come alone, and I wish to talk."

It took a few minutes, but she finally answered.

"You shouldn't be here," she said.

"Why not? We're not enemies today. I'm not going to shoot anymore of your people."

"We don't have revival machines, James," she said. "The people you killed on your last visit cannot come back. Their families are despondent."

I understood, but I didn't care. I kept tapping on the dome and broadcasting her name until she showed up. A delegation of rogue scientists backed her up as they cautiously opened the dome and let me inside.

They encircled me, searched me, and took my weapons.

"Floramel," I said, "I'm sorry about our conflicts, but that's all in the past now. These Galactics in the sky—they mean business. We've managed to convince them not to burn Earth, but they are still determined to destroy you and this planet."

"Why don't they come near and do battle?" she asked.

"Because they're cowards. They'll either wait for us to defeat you, or they will wait even longer for their battle fleet to arrive and permanently exterminate you from the comfort of space."

"And what would you have us do?" she asked.

"Take me to your deepest tech vaults. To the places where you hide your best secrets."

She frowned, creasing her lovely face with lines. "What for? Do you still lust to steal our achievements? If so, we'd rather die with them."

"No," I said, "but I know someone who does."

Floramel needed a little more coaxing, but she finally led me underground. The lab was really located there, inside a dozen subterranean vaults. It was when we reached the deepest, darkest of these chambers that I saw what we were looking for.

"Where are the abercronders?" demanded an acolyte. He rushed forward, greatly disturbed. A spot on the floor was dust-free, and it looked like something large and heavy had once sat there.

"I don't know what abercronders are," I said, "but I take it that they're missing?"

"Yes—" he said, but then another man cried out across the dim-lit room.

"Warren! Over here! More theft!"

There were artifacts missing here and there all over the place. The rogues were outraged. At first they accused me, but I managed to reason with them.

"If I was stealing all this stuff, do you think I'd fly down here and parade myself in your face?"

They had no answer, but they were full of despair.

"What would you like to do to the man who stole your tech gizmos?" I asked them.

The acolytes and even Floramel quickly listed a surprisingly nasty series of abuses.

"Well then," I told them. "I'm the man who can help you out. Let's set up a trap for this sneaky bastard who's stealing your goodies."

We worked together, and it took several hours. We left our traps here and there all around the basements of various labs. Every passing minute was filled with fresh anger, as the tech-smiths kept finding new items that were missing. A tech trove to fill a king's vault had been stolen.

At last, as we were setting the seventeenth trap, Floramel shrieked.

I turned to her in alarm. "What's wrong?"

"We caught something. Back in bay five—how did someone get in there?"

Chuckling, I left her behind. "Stay here," I said. "This rat is dangerous and clever. Let me handle him."

Upset but uncertain, they let me go it alone. With vast care, I trotted to bay five, threw open the doors, and stared within.

There stood Claver in an odd, off-balance pose. His body had been ensnared in a stasis field. He wasn't entirely motionless, but he was vastly slowed down.

I could see his eyes. They blinked once, in slow, slow motion. By the time they'd completed the movement, I'd approached to where the stasis projector hummed, and I placed a hand on it.

"Gotcha, rodent," I said, grinning at Claver.

-47-

Naturally, I was overjoyed to have captured Claver, but I was even happier to gain a teleport suit.

"I don't understand," Floramel said, coming up from behind me and looking at Claver with curious eyes. "How can this man have stolen so many of our artifacts?"

"He's a dirty one, Claver is," I said. "See that suit he has on? It's a teleporting suit."

She stared. "I'm familiar with such technology," she said. "We've developed it ourselves, but it only works when you have a powered device at each end of a hyper-spatial link."

That got my attention. "*You* developed such a thing? Are we talking about projectors, maybe this high?" I gestured with my hands, and she nodded.

"I'll be damned…" I said. "That's what the squids used when they invaded Earth a few years back. They marched millions of heavy troopers onto our planet, and they nearly took us out."

"Oh…" Floramel said, looking down at the deck. "We must apologize, in that case. We were the primary developers for the Cephalopods when they ruled us."

"Right," I said. "Before Earth opened this lab here in our local space."

"No," she said, "not exactly. We came here using a gateway such as you describe. The Cephalopods gave us to your world as a form of tribute."

281

"Slaves, huh?" I asked.

The Cephalopod Kingdom had an odd culture. They didn't understand concepts such as individual rights, democracy, etc. In their universe, you were either a slave or a master—or both depending on what company you were keeping at the moment. There was no other social role possible between individuals.

"Of course," she said, "we served them as we served Earth, until we learned you planned to kill us all."

"Let's talk about politics later," I said. "What we all want now is to survive the day. To do that, we have to take out that Nairb ship up there."

"You can teleport to the ship with that suit," she suggested.

"True... But one man will have a hard time annihilating an enemy force so large. We've only got one suit—unless you can make more?"

She shook her head. "This is Galactic technology. We're good, but they're better, with a million planets worth of resources to draw upon for such an effort. Even if we could fabricate such a system, it would take months of research."

"Right, new developments won't help... We have to use what we've got now—and quick. A first strike, if you will."

During our conversation, Claver seemed to have finally taken notice of us. His eyes had finished a blink, and now they were sliding with infinite slowness toward ours. We probably sounded like buzzing insects to him.

Was his head beginning a long turn in our direction? Maybe... it was hard to tell.

"What about bombs?" I asked her. "Big bombs—anti-matter, maybe?"

She shook her head. I wasn't sure if she'd picked up that mannerism from me, or she'd always had it. She'd only begun to do it recently.

"No," she said. "Such devices were removed with the initial group of refugees. We have many curiosities, but few weapons. That's why we made so many fleshed drones to defend our compound."

"Right, a few powerful weapons... What about one of these gateways you talked about?"

She frowned, and checked her instruments. Unlike humans, the rogues didn't have built in tappers on their forearms. They had several devices instead that wound around their bodies on a central wire. It looked kind of creepy—like they had a snake hugging up to them. These harnesses even moved on their own to stay tight, reforming to the bodies twists and turns.

"We have a few gateway units left. An old, simple model. It only links two points in space—you can't reset it to a different destination without dismantling both ends."

My eyes grew big, just as Claver's were beginning to do. My mouth spread into a grin.

"That will do fine!" I said. "Let's get it."

"What about him?" she asked, pointing at Claver.

"He's all right for now. As long as his hand doesn't reach up to touch that dial on his chest. If he gets close—cut off a finger or something."

Floramel stared at the immobilized thief and again considered appropriate abuses. She then left instructions with a pair of guards to prevent Claver from escaping us.

We found the equipment she spoke of deep in the recesses of the dark chambers under the dome. She showed it to me doubtfully.

"What's wrong?" I asked her as I inspected it.

"I believe I know what you're planning—and the thoughts disturb me. We never wanted to release savagery upon others. That wasn't our desire. We invented things to expand the mind—to delight, and fill beings with a sense of wonder."

My mouth made a rude, blatting noise. "A sense of wonder?" I laughed. "What good is that? We're all about killing each other. You ever met a species that wasn't?"

She shook her head sadly. "Not many," she admitted.

"I bet not. Either you kick the other guy's ass, or he kicks yours. Cooperation is possible, mind you, but only as long as you've got a mutual enemy to struggle against. Look at the Galactics. They had it all, so what did they do?"

Floramel looked at me curiously. She had no answers. In some ways, her race was made up of innocents. They were smart, but they weren't very realistic.

"They got into a war for supremacy, that's what," I told her. "They all wanted to be King of the Hill. Imagine, ruling an entire galaxy and blowing it all for petty spite."

"You think such things are intrinsic within intellectual beings?"

"I guess," I said, messing with an actuator. "I'm not much of a philosopher. But I do understand the basic nature of thinking beings. Look at it this way, if you're competitive and mean, you rise to the top. If you aren't, you serve those who are. Or maybe, you're killed off. Who could possibly become the masters of the cosmos other than the biggest, meanest bunch of bad-asses among the stars?"

Floramel looked at me thoughtfully. "In that case," she said, "you humans might someday inherit everything."

"Nah… We're mean, but I've seen worse. The stars are chock-full of interstellar assholes."

We stopped talking philosophy then and got to work. She demonstrated the gateway—but it didn't operate.

"It takes a vast amount of power," she said. "We'll have to connect couplings under the dome itself—you damaged one of our generators last time you were here, you know."

"Yeah… sorry about that."

"If we weaken our shielding, you might take down our dome entirely. Or, you might have been sent here by the Nairbs to cripple us."

I met her eyes. She had a new look there, one of suspicion. I felt bad, having brought so much discord to her intellectual race. I wasn't sure if I was doing them a favor by explaining the universe in realistic terms—or performing an ethical crime.

"Look," I said, putting my hands on her shoulders and giving her a tiny squeeze. "We're not here to kill you—not now. We have to kill the Nairbs, or we all die. That's how true allies are born—in fear of a greater predator nearby."

She didn't look at my eyes, but instead at my hands. "Are you attacking me?" she asked curiously.

"Uhh…" I said, dropping my hands away. "Sorry. Sometimes, humans touch one another in order to make a point."

"I found it distracting. I barely heard what you said."

"I was trying to explain that allies—"

"Yes," she said, "I got your message. Our people only touch when it is time to mate. Were you attempting to mate with me?"

"No… as I said…"

My face turned red, but she didn't seem to notice. She was still staring at my hands.

"That was a very unusual, sudden, forceful contact," she said. "I've never been approached that way."

My ears thought they heard a little something in her voice. "Did you like it?" I asked.

Floramel thought about that, and at last, she nodded. "Yes," she said.

That was it for me. We'd been working in this dark tomb for hours. I was tired, and thirsty, and… It didn't matter. She was beautiful, and this version of James McGill was a virgin.

I just had to break him in, and I did so with relish. She seemed to like it too, but I think she was used to a much more stately process.

When I make love, a woman knows what happened—if you know what I mean.

It took a while, but Floramel finally melted and got into it. An excellent time was had by all, and it wasn't until later that I realized I was still thirsty.

Along about half-way through the love-making, I figured out Floramel *had* to be human. I mean, there are only so many ways to shape feminine body parts, but hers were just too similar to what I was used to for the whole thing to be some kind of evolutionary coincidence.

Quietly questioning her about it, she explained that her people were descendants of neuro-typical humans. Their ancestors had been stolen from Dust World, just as the litter mates, trackers and other types had been. Bred for brains, they'd come out looking a little different from the human norm, but no more so than one race varied from another back on Earth.

Somehow, I felt better knowing I'd just made love to a real live woman. Leaving her curled up on a cot we'd found in the chamber, I went searching for a drink.

-48-

Unfortunately, it seemed like the rogues had never discovered alcohol, or at least they didn't bother to drink it for fun. When I'd finally given up asking nerds about it, I headed back through the maze of equipment toward the love-nest I'd set up with Floramel—but I never made it back there.

"McGill!" hissed a voice from the dark.

I whirled and drew my pistol. I couldn't see who was talking, but I knew a snake when I heard one.

"Claver?"

"You fuck up," he told me. "How'd you get these lab-monkeys to catch me? They're smart, but not like that."

While I responded, I picked my way through the mounded equipment and junk that was piled high in the room. I circled a motionless drone, and I thought I had him—but he wasn't behind it.

"I told them what you'd come to steal next," I said. "They set up the trap."

"Hmm…" he said. "A simple appraisal of trading value? That's what it was? Am I that transparent, even to a man of your low intellect?"

"You're like a bay window drinking in a sunny morning," I told him. "As clear as glass. How did you get away from those rogue guards, anyhow?"

He made a snorting sound. "That was easy. They turned off their stasis field and tried to arrest me. Like most tech geniuses, they're gullible fools when it comes to practical matters—but I can't get off this planet."

"Why not?"

"Their stasis device drained the charge in my suit, and I can't jump. I can't even find a charging port that will fit."

I smiled. I'd taken the precaution of telling Floramel exactly what kind of fitting we used. I'd had them remove that connection point from every portal down here.

"That's a damned shame," I said. "What can I do for you?"

"It's what I can do for *you*," he said. "I can make you rich, McGill. I can get you off this rock in order to spend it, too. You'll live on even if every other human in the galaxy perishes."

"Sounds pretty good!" I said in an upbeat tone.

That's when he finally revealed himself. He stepped out into the open and gave me a big smile.

"I'm actually glad to see you, boy," he said. "These people give me the creeps. They're too honest and thoughtful. It's weird."

I took a step toward him, lowering my weapon. We were both smiling like it was our wedding day.

"Show me a matching power-coupling," Claver said, "and I'll give you coordinates to safely port out of here."

"Throw in a suit, and you've got a deal," I told him.

I stepped forward, and he reached out a hand to shake mine.

Now, I'm no genius, but my momma didn't raise no fool, either. Claver's suit was Earth-made, and I'd traveled using similar suits a number of times. The charging meter on his chest was clear and easy to read. It had a full charge, with a green LED glimmering on the front panel.

Accordingly, my hand moved forward to meet his—but it never got there. Instead, I grabbed his wrist and pulled him toward me. My other hand came up balled into a fist, and I punched his lights out.

It wasn't the first time I'd abused one version of Claver or another, and it probably wouldn't be the last. He fell, rolled over, and I checked to make sure he couldn't reach the teleport button. I stripped off the suit, and he groaned awake on the deck during the process.

"What was that for, you ape?" he demanded. "You just wanted to rob me, didn't you? I can't believe I fell for it."

"You got greedy, Claver," I told him. "You should have been satisfied with stealing tech and escaped when you could have."

"What are you talking about?"

"I'm talking about you planning to port me to the Nairb ship. What kind of reward are they offering for my capture?"

He looked at me with his right eye only. His left was swollen shut. "More than your damned carcass is worth, that's for sure!"

"Dead or alive?" I asked. "If you'd ported out the moment we shook hands, I'd have melted in flight."

He shook his head. "Nah, probably not. It's only a few million kilometers up to their ship. You'd be singed outside the suit, but you'd live."

I smiled at him again, because he'd just provided me with the critical information I was looking for. The suit *was* set to go to the Nairb ship next.

Still smiling at him, I buttoned up his suit onto my own, larger frame. It automatically stretched and cinched, reshaping itself.

"Aw, shit," he said, seeing my smile and catching on. "Just kill me now, McGill. I've been bested by a subhuman. Clearly, I'm a bad grow. I should be recycled, feet first."

"Sorry, no time for that," I told him, "I've got too much work to do—and I think the locals might want to deal with you in their own way."

I contacted Floramel and her people. They soon came and arrested Claver.

With a teleport suit at the ready, and a gateway system being set up for my use—I was feeling pretty good.

The first thing I did was test it. I popped up to the Nairb ship and had a look around. That was a ballsy move, even for me. I could have arrived in the midst of a firing squad—but I didn't. I was in a quiet hold with dim lit ceilings far above.

There were items there I recognized. Claver had been squirreling away his stolen loot aboard the Nairb ship. I had to marvel at that—he was gutsy. I didn't know if the Nairbs were in on that part of the deal or not, but either way, Claver was a criminal mastermind.

Heading back to my starting point was easy enough. Earth suits had a "back button" that took you to the last place you'd come from. Employing that, I found myself standing near a surprised-looking Floramel a moment later.

"Excuse me, Miss," I said. "You should really mark the spot where a man teleports out. If you stand right there, you might merge up when he comes back."

Alarmed, she did chalk the spot, and they all stayed well clear of it.

I had Floramel's nerds help me get the exact coordinates of the Nairb ship from the suit's memory. That wouldn't last long, of course. The computer on the suit was smart enough to match for drift, but if the ship got underway, I'd be left popping out into the void to no purpose.

Next, I had them calculate the position of *Nostrum* relative to where we were now. This wasn't hard, as they were constantly monitoring every vessel in the star system. Taking one half of the paired gateways in my hands, we recharged the suit, and I popped out again to the *Nostrum*.

This time, I didn't land perfectly. I came out about three meters above the deck, and I crashed down pretty hard due to artificial gravity effects. Fortunately, the gateway wasn't damaged.

I lugged the device into a quiet hold and plugged it in. The plug was of universal Galactic design. Smart, and easy to find. I turned the gateway on, activated it, and Floramel stepped out of a shimmering pink-white haze in the air between two poles.

"So fast…" I said, impressed. "The unit synched right up and found its mate instantly."

She smiled. "This is an improved model," she said. "It can't handle heavy equipment like the ones the Cephalopods used to invade your world—but it can transfer one person at a time reliably over short distances."

Short distances. She was talking about millions of kilometers of open space. I knew the teleport suits could do better—crossing lightyears without a landing spot predetermined at the other end. Still, this tech was very impressive.

Floramel did something odd then, she reached up both her hands, put them on my shoulders, and squeezed me lightly.

"Um…" I said, "are you trying to start something?"

"Maybe later," she admitted. "Right now, we should probably talk to your commanders."

Reluctantly, I led her out of the hold and up to Gold Deck.

Deech, Graves and a few other primus-level officers looked at me and Floramel with great suspicion. I couldn't blame them for that—after all, my companion had helped arrange the deaths of thousands of legionnaires in the Arcturus system already.

"Sirs," I said, "meet Floramel. She's a principal investigator in this system. A boss-lady scientist, you might say."

They still looked like they smelled something foul. I decided to press on without commenting about it.

"Floramel has decided to help us," I said. "She—"

"Oh, she has, has she?" Tribune Deech said, swaggering forward with her hands on her broad hips. "Investigator, you're under arrest. All your people are to report via radio, so they may be picked up for immediate processing."

Floramel looked at me in surprise. "Who is this person?" she asked. "I thought you were in charge of this ship."

"Uh… no," I admitted. "I'm an officer, but these people are my superiors. Let me explain—"

Graves made a rude sound and chuckled. "No need, Centurion. You're antics are well known and expected. You gained her trust, told her a pack of lies, and lured her up here. She's your collar, don't worry. No one else will try to claim this capture."

Deech glanced at him in annoyance. Then she turned back to me. "What about the rest of them?" she asked. "We saw you set up a gateway in our hold. Graves said we shouldn't

290

interfere, but I'm anxious for results. Get the rest of the rebels to march through and into our hold."

"Hmm," I said, "I think there might be a misunderstanding, here. The scientists aren't surrendering their lab—not yet."

"Then why have you been wasting my time?" Deech demanded.

"Perhaps I can explain," Floramel said. "If we surrender now, you will destroy us. You've already demonstrated this intent. On the other hand, if we on stay on the planet, the Nairbs will eventually lose patience and erase us."

"Not the Nairbs themselves," Deech said. "Battle Fleet 921 is on the way. When it gets here, your time—and ours—will have run out."

"I understand," Floramel said, "and I believe I have a solution that will allow all of us to keep breathing."

They all looked at her with squinty eyes. No one looked happy—and I figured after they heard her out, they were going to be even less happy than they were now.

After Floramel had explained her plan, they all looked shocked. I felt it was my civic duty to step in and clarify.

"You see," I began, "the key is that no one in Battle Fleet 921 can suspect that we did this—or that the lab people did it. The whole thing has to look like an accident."

"Why not blame it on the lab people?" Graves asked.

"Because we won't participate if you do!" Floramel stated flatly.

I knew that wouldn't buy any bacon with Graves, so I raised my hands and gestured for calm. "That's just part of the reason. Remember that the Nairbs are touchy, and the Mogwa make them look open-minded. If they think their representative—that guy Slur—died because of some kind of screw-up on our part… well, Earth might as well be toast."

"Are they really that unreasonable?" Tribune Deech asked. "All the time?"

"Yes," Graves admitted. "As a longtime member of Varus, I've run into our Galactic benefactors on several worlds. They're never friendly or forgiving. Quite the opposite."

"We just fed them Winslade so they could torment him to death," she said. "You'd think that would massage their egos."

"The Mogwa think a great deal of themselves," I said.

"All right then," Deech said. "I'm putting you in charge of this insane plan, Graves."

She stood up from behind her desk and walked out. Everyone watched in surprise. She turned back at the doorway.

"Make sure you don't screw anything up," she told Graves. "I'll review every second of this briefing if things go badly—otherwise, I'll delete it to eliminate the evidence."

Then, just like that, she was gone.

"What a cast-iron bitch," Graves said. "She's trying to disassociate herself—Earth be damned."

"There's always a good reason why a top officer has survived so long," I agreed. "You'd better get your troops rolling. I need a shower."

"Not so fast, McGill," Graves said. "You're going in with the first team."

My mouth sagged open. I hated when it did that, but I think it's just part of how my brain is wired.

"But sir," I said, "I don't have any technical expertise. This first move against the Galactic ship is just a matter of wiring."

"Uh-uh, you're not getting out of this one. They'll need security, and your unit will provide it."

"That's a lot of people. Our odds of being discovered will rise dramatically."

Graves turned to Floramel again. "How big did you say their central hold was? And what percentage of it was full of collected trophies?"

"The space enclosed is estimated to be three cubic kilometers. Approximately two-thirds of that volume is occupied by a wide variety of—"

"Of junk, right," Graves finished for her. "The Mogwa like to steal a few choice artifacts from every world they annihilate. I don't know why they bother—they don't seem to do much with it."

"Maybe they just like stacking it up," I offered. "Like packrats."

"Make sure you provide the next Mogwa you meet with that theory, McGill," Graves told me. "In any case, my point is that there will be plenty of room to land a team and invade the ship without sounding an alarm."

"We don't really know that, Primus," Floramel objected.

Graves pointed at me. "He just ported into that hold and messed around for a while—no one saw him. In any case, that's my price for agreeing to this mission. McGill goes along."

This insistence honestly surprised me. I wasn't sure exactly why Graves was pushing it so far. Maybe, he wanted me to watch the rogues, just like he'd said. Or maybe, he wanted me to die and play scapegoat. It was hard to tell which it was.

Anyway, there wasn't much time left for fooling around. We went down to my unit's cube, suited up the troops, and headed back to the floor of the open hold. The first trick was to get everyone positioned right. Floramel started off by walking through the poles of the gateway on our ship and transporting herself back to the planet.

That's when Graves showed up again. It seemed like he'd been watching me every second. He had with him a large power cart. On the back of it was a watermelon-shaped object with digital readouts on the sides.

I'd seen such things before—in fact, I'd carried them to their destinations and set them off.

The object in question was an antimatter bomb.

-49-

Just seeing the bomb made me nervous. I'd handled such weapons before. They were ten times as powerful as a good, old-fashioned H-bomb from Earth. They converted mass to energy on a one-for-one basis, which was a dramatic improvement over other explosive devices.

"Whoa!" I said to Graves, waving my gauntlets at him.

"Don't interfere, McGill," Graves said. "It's the only way. We'll roll this into the gateway, and their dome will vanish. We'll have completed the mission Magnate Slur set for us."

"Hold on," I said as he prepped the bomb. "They have stasis projectors down there, sir."

"What?"

"You know—the same things Claver used to freeze me when I tried to bomb him with one of these back on Earth."

He squinted at me. "You're bullshitting me again."

"I've got proof, sir," I said, and I shared my body-cam vids with him. They showed Claver being trapped as he teleported in.

"I'll be damned…" Graves said. "You think they've set these things up to catch anyone coming through this gateway?"

"Stands to reason," I said, using my best poker face. "We can't take the chance. We haven't got any stasis fields aboard that we can use to catch them in return. All they'd have to do is roll our bomb right back here, and KA-BOOM!"

I made wide circles with my arms. Graves got the idea, and he looked worried. Turning to Leeson, he handed him the bomb.

Leeson's eyes flew wide. "What do I do with this, Primus?"

"Take it to your techs. It's set to go off in a few minutes."

Alarmed, Leeson ran off, shouting for Natasha. Graves didn't even watch him run. He was a philosophical and fatalistic man. If we all died in a vast explosion, well, he knew he wasn't going to feel a thing, so he didn't worry about it.

"McGill," he said, "you just vetoed our best option. Now we're back to your original, cockamamie plan."

"So... who's idea was it to just roll in the bomb?"

"Tribune Deech came up with it, of course. She brought it up to me, and I immediately agreed to it. The plan was a brilliant scheme, if only due to its simplicity."

"But now you're switching back to my plan?" I asked. "Don't you have to approve that with Deech?"

"You heard her, she put me in charge. That's her standard mode of operation. She knows she can always fry me for failing later on. That's the key to upper management, McGill—always have a chosen sacrifice all prepped up on the altar in case things go wrong."

"I'll remember that, sir," I said, "but I'd feel better about this if I knew you believed in me."

He shrugged. "You're the best chance I've got left. You can't know how much it pains me to say that—but it's true. No one else has led commando missions aboard enemy starships. You're it."

I had to admit he had a point there. He left, and Floramel arrived with her team of nerds just in time to see him go.

"What was that about?" she asked, pointing after Graves.

"Nothing," I said. "He was just wishing us all the best. What did he say? 'Glory and Honor?' He shouted something like that, didn't he Sargon?"

"He sure as shit did," Sargon lied for me. I could always count on him to back up anything I said.

Floramel looked a little confused, but she stopped asking questions. I could have told her the truth instead, of course. After all, I'd saved her people from a quick ride up into the stratosphere—but I knew women well enough to know that wouldn't have earned me any points at all.

Her team came through, and they brought another pair of gateway units with them. The plan was to link the planetary surface to our ship, then link our ship to the Nairb vessel. That way, we'd chain all three locations together in two steps.

The whole thing presented an interesting set of tactical possibilities. As I thought about it, I better understood why Central had sent us out here to steal this excellent tech, rather than destroy it.

"The gateway is hooked to power," Kivi said.

"What about that… uh… *subsystem* Leeson gave to Natasha?" I asked her.

She gave me a sharp look. "We're still alive, aren't we? The situation was contained."

"That's a relief," I said. "I'm glad things worked out so easily."

Kivi gave me the stink-eye. "You have no idea what you're talking about. We should switch jobs sometime. Maybe you'd have time to appreciate all that we techs do for the grunts."

"Oh really?" I asked. "You want to switch places? I can let you play officer and take charge of this ride into hostile territory, if you want."

She balked at that idea. "Forget I said anything."

"Done," I said promptly, "now and forever."

Giving me a strange glance, Kivi rejoined her fellow techs, and I summoned the entire unit. They came bubbling out of the cubes nearby and gathered, fully kitted out. Many of them were so fresh from their revivals they still had wet hair. Sarah was one of these, and her eyes were looking kind of glassy.

Harris was glaring at me with his arms crossed.

"Oh… right," I said, "Leeson, Sarah is now part of your platoon."

He looked at her dubiously. "What am I going to do with a whack-job light trooper?"

"Put her on point," Harris suggested. There were twitters from the group at that.

"She'll be your stenographer," I told him in irritation. "Now team, huddle up."

Reluctantly, the surly group came together. Our defeat down on Rogue World hadn't done any wonders for our unit's morale.

"This is the finish," I told them. "We've been honored with the privilege of striking a blow for Earth."

They looked at me seriously. Most of them had no idea what we were going to do. Probably, that was for the best—but I had to let them in on it at some point.

"We're going on a very special mission," I said. "We're going to board the Nairb ship."

"*Excuse me?*" Harris said loudly. "Did I hear that correctly?"

"You did indeed, Adjunct," I told him.

He looked like he was barely listening. He was working his tapper, no doubt contacting Graves to rat me out. After a few seconds, he looked up again, shocked.

"That's right," I said to him. "This action is fully sanctioned by the legion brass. We're going to board the Imperial destroyer and immediately disable her communications module. There can be no signals going in or out of that vessel fifteen minutes after we board her."

"What if we fail?" Leeson asked.

"Then… Earth might well be screwed."

Harris pointed at the gateway. "That thing can carry a thousand troops!" he complained. "Why not flood their damned hold? Why not—?"

"Because," I interrupted him, "if they realize they're under attack before we knock out their communications module, they'll send a deep-link message to the battle fleet."

"Right…" Toro said, catching on. "Then the fleet will know we joined the rebels, and they'll bomb Earth instead of this worthless rock we're orbiting."

"Bingo," I told her. "There's no use holding any secrets from you people at this point. Everything depends on us being successful. We board, we move fast, and we take out the comm module. At that point, our mission will be complete. The rest of the legion will take care of the rest of the ship."

"The plan is insane," Harris said. "We're supposed to be commandos, but we've got no idea where we're going. Does anyone even know where the comm module is located?"

"We do," Floramel answered. "At least, once aboard we'll be able to detect it."

Harris laughed bitterly. "We're trusting the rebels? We were dying all over their dome like bugs on a windshield just yesterday!"

"This isn't an optimal solution," I admitted, "but command thinks it's our only shot. All right, I want everyone kitted up. Pack light, we'll do or die pretty fast. No sense weighing yourself down with useless gear."

As everyone moved to obey, Harris approached me. Seeing his move, Toro and Leeson joined him.

"Sir," Leeson said, "with all due respect, this plan seems half-baked."

"Half-retarded more like," Harris snapped.

I gave him a glare, and we locked eyes. He looked down at the deck after a second or two, but he still looked pissed.

"We've been chosen because we have more experience than any other group with boarding ships via teleportation," I explained.

"That's only because you went crazy two years back against the squids," Harris pointed out.

"Be that as it may, we're it."

"Centurion," Toro said, "I'd like a transfer. I've got no experience with this sort of mission, and I've got heavy troopers in my platoon. We'll just slow you down."

Harris laughed bitterly.

"Request denied," I said firmly. "We're sending a full unit. We're not sending more, or less. Our group has fought and died together now through some hard times. We'll do okay—and we might need heavy troops to win through. There's no telling what kind of onboard defenses those Galactic sludge-bags will have."

None of them were happy, but at least Leeson didn't argue with me. He beat his hands together until his troops were hustling to the second gateway unit, which was still inactive.

Floramel approached me next.

"It's time," she said, "who will teleport through and set up the gateway on the destroyer?"

Looking around the group, I shook my head.

I wanted to delegate this duty, but it didn't feel appropriate. When something's got to be right, you do it yourself—that's what my dad had always said.

"I'm doing it," I told her, and I suited up.

-50-

Floramel gave me a tiny kiss before I teleported out. That made me smile. She was human—mostly—but I'd only just taught her about kissing the night before. That made the gesture all the sweeter somehow.

Holding the heavy gateway unit in my arms, with my plasma carbine dangling from straps, I had her tap the start button on my chest.

The world shifted blue and wavered. It was a familiar effect to me by now.

For a second, I was in two places at once. That was the weird thing about short hops. If you flew over lightyears, teleportation gave you plenty of time to think and worry—but not when it was just a ship-to-ship jump.

One instant I was on *Nostrum* watching the lights waver and my vision dim, the next I was on the broad deck of the Nairb ship at the same time. Over a period of about a second, that transition changed again, when the deck of *Nostrum* and the staring faces of my unit faded away. At the same time, the hazy image of the Nairb ship grew stronger and more substantial.

Then, it was over. I stumbled, but my footing was only off a little. I looked down and saw my heel was fused with a cable.

Cursing, I put down the gateway unit and drew my combat knife. I'd have to trim my boot down, or the cable, in order to walk. Fortunately, my foot hadn't merged up, just my boot.

My natural instinct was to cut the cable, of course, but I hesitated. Where did this cable go? What was it powering? Who would come to check if I cut it?

Baring my teeth in a moment of indecision, I looked around. The hold was dim-lit and cavernous. It was full of doodads from a thousand worlds. There were odd machines, crumbling pottery statues and these weird baskets woven with what looked like strands of steel surrounding me.

Instead of cutting anything, I removed my boot carefully and left it there. Walking with a hobbled gait, I searched for a power coupling to plug in the gateway—but I wasn't finding anything.

I began to sweat in my suit, even though my exposed foot was stinging from the cold of the deck. Already, this mission was off to a clumsy start. I feared it was only a matter of time until it went tits-up completely.

Deciding to follow the power cable I'd landed on, I finally found a terminus. I unplugged an environmental meter of some kind that was probably meant to keep the atmospherics in the hold stable for the benefit of the trophy collection.

The coupling fit—that wasn't a surprise, as the rogues had known where I was taking this thing and counseled me accordingly. Both fittings were Galactic standard.

Shoving them together, I felt as much as heard a satisfying click in my hands. The gateway poles began to glow.

"Oh, shit," I said, realizing I hadn't set them up right.

I hobbled forward, trying to push the two poles apart. They were supposed to be aligned with a precisely measured meter of separation between them. Feeling an urgency of purpose, I kicked the farther pole away—and it fell over instead of sliding over the deck.

The two poles were now about a foot apart, and one was laying on the deck itself, sparking. A stream of curses and one hopping, frozen foot slowed me down, but I squatted and got a grip on the second pole to stand it upright again.

Just then, the poles interacted. There was a flickering of released energy. Someone—*something*—stepped through them.

Instead of a clean transmission, the traveler came through... *garbled*. There was a gauntlet holding a rifle, and a face, sort of. The face was merged up with its faceplate.

Dragging the squirming, smoking soldier out of the way in case more were coming, I righted the two poles and looked down into the still-living eyes of this mission's first casualty— it was Sarah.

Damn! That cold bastard Leeson had found a use for her, I guess. He'd sent her through as a scout.

She tried to talk, but her words never made it out of her throat. There was no air in her lungs to push with.

Fortunately, the girl died fast. I grabbed her left arm, which was relatively intact, and I worked her tapper. I erased her last minute of life from her memory.

That was a trick Natasha had taught me. In Sarah's case, I figured it was a mercy.

Pissed off, I picked her twisted body up and stepped back through to *Nostrum's* deck.

"Here," I said, handing Sarah to Leeson.

His face screwed up into a grimace. He'd seen plenty of gruesome deaths, but few soldiers had been twisted into a smoldering pretzel before.

"I wasn't finished setting up the poles yet," I said sternly. "The plan was for *me* to walk back, proving the connection was valid."

Leeson hung his head. "I'm sorry, Centurion," he said. "You were gone a long time. We've only got eleven minutes left."

"Wrong," I said. "The timer starts when we're all across. Let's not frig this up any further, all right people?"

No one argued. Leeson left Sarah on the deck for the bio people to dispose of.

Shoving on a fresh boot, I led the march back onto the Nairb vessel. Every member of my unit had a good look at Sarah as they passed through the poles.

It did them good, in my opinion. It sobered them up. This was no game, and it was time for everyone to act like the pros we were.

"Okay," I said on tactical chat. "Are we all through?"

Harris, Toro and Leeson reported their counts. We were all in the enemy ship's hold—minus one. The last to report in was Floramel and her team of rogue nerds.

"If we get separated by more than a hundred meters," I told them, "we'll have to use hand-signals. Our stealth transmissions won't reach further than that."

Our latest communications tech was pretty good for clandestine work like this. We'd long ago perfected radio packets that simulated background emissions. Our techs carried computers that could relay signals that were virtually undetectable. The system automatically linked us into a network that measured and mirrored our environment, making the whole thing dynamically adjust itself.

As a secondary advantage to our tech, the signals quietly jammed other communications coming into and out of our local area.

Taking a second to mark our destination, I put a green arrow on top of the chamber we were trying to get to. Fortunately, it wasn't far. We had about a kilometer of boxes to walk through, then we'd reach the communications module.

It was located on the belly of the ship, to the stern. There wasn't much of an antenna to worry about, just one big transformer and a power supply that could feed the deep-link.

Interstellar communications were possible, but expensive. The Galactics had a monopoly on the technology—no surprise there. They allowed worlds to talk to one another in real-time, but ships almost never had the tech—at least not among human starships.

What was too expensive for an Earth fleet was no problem for a Galactic ship. They'd never seemed to lack for budgetary funds until recently, when civil war had broken out among the Core Worlds.

Particularly in the case of a scout ship, there was no point to its operation without a deep-link. But even when you had one of these pricey gizmos that used entanglement theory to communicate over lightyears instantly, the systems took a lot of power and had a slow baud rate. The signal was thready, and messages were usually done with text and small low-resolution images rather than full-motion video.

"Okay," I said, looking over my team. "Toro, you stay here and guard the gateway. Harris, you take point with your light troopers. I'll be right behind you with Leeson's weaponeers and our techy guests."

"Got it," Harris said, trotting off toward the green arrow on the horizon.

I let him get ahead of me a ways before following. In the meantime, I left instructions for Toro.

"Don't break radio-silence once we're out of range for the stealth network. Not even if you get discovered. Just destroy everyone who comes at you and hold your position."

"You don't want to know if we're getting hit?" she asked me in surprise.

"No, Adjunct," I said. "The stealth will break at range. The enemy will then know there are invaders in more than one part of the ship, and with a little triangulation, they could figure out what our goal is. We can't afford for the deep-link to report they have boarders from Earth."

"Understood," she said.

Wheeling around, I ran after Harris. Leeson and Floramel followed me.

The whole mission felt crazy already. It was such a risk. We hadn't detected any automated surveillance equipment down here among the dusty trophies—but that didn't mean it wasn't here. The Galactics were advanced, after all.

But there wasn't any time for second-guessing now. It was time to do or die—or both.

-51-

We caught up with Harris in short order. Technically, his team was faster than ours, but since they were on point they had to advance more cautiously. My group moved with the relative certainty of being second in line.

"Harris," I contacted him. "Any sign of anything?"

"Not really," he called back. "There's lots of dusty junk in here, but most of it is inert. So far, I haven't seen a single monitoring system. But they could have flying drones or something."

"I've got Kivi laying out buzzers," I said. "They're reporting back nothing—so far."

"They're probably too snooty to run security systems down here," Leeson said.

"What do you mean?" I asked him.

"Well, you know the Galactics and the Nairbs as well as anyone, Centurion. They think they shit chocolate. Who would dare to come aboard one of their ships and sneak around?"

"I have…" I said. "A couple of times."

There was some snickering on command chat in response, but nobody called me a liar.

"McGill!" Harris hissed out about a minute later. "We've reached a hatch. There's no apparent way to open it."

"We'll be right there."

When we arrived, we realized he was right. The Nairbs had built a ship without a door handle on the inside of the hold.

"Now we know why they didn't bother to put security systems in here," Leeson commented. "Should I have Sargon burn it down, sir?"

"Hold on—Floramel? Have you got a way we can get through this short of destroying it?"

She examined the hatch with interest.

"We don't have much time, sir," Leeson said, "seven minutes."

"Floramel? Talk to me now, or the hatch is going down."

"That will make a lot of noise," she objected. "Any sensor in the passages beyond would register a change in heat, pressure—"

I waved my arm at Sargon. He was already shouldering his belcher and sighting on the hinges.

"Focusing tight," he said. "Stand clear, please."

Floramel continued to run her hands and an instrument box over the hatch, not listening to us.

"Maybe she's trying to delay us," Sargon said on a private line to my helmet. "I'll burn her right through, sir. Just give me the word."

"Stand down."

"You better get your girlfriend away from that hatch, Centurion!" Leeson complained.

"Girlfriend?" Della asked, looking back at them. Apparently, she hadn't heard the rumors yet.

"Floramel," I said, ignoring them all. "Either open that hatch on the count of ten, or I'm taking it down. We'll revive you back on *Nostrum*—if we get there again."

She kept probing, and suddenly she paused, reaching for her bag.

Sargon tensed up. "I bet she's blowing our cover. This smells like a trick. I don't trust these rebels an inch."

I put my hand on his shoulder. "Hold your fire. That's an order."

He relaxed slightly, and we all heard a loud click. That was followed by a groan of metal on metal. The hatch probably hadn't been opened in years. It swung wide, and we surged into the passageway beyond.

I caught up to Floramel in the shuffle. "How'd you do that?" I asked her.

"The hatch wasn't locked," she explained, "it was meant to be opened by touch. The temperature changes and aging—the hinges were bound up. I sent in nanites to worm between the leaves and lubricate them."

I laughed, and I thought about how we'd almost blasted her unfairly. All's well that ends well, I figured.

We rounded a bend in the passage, which was a good six meters wide, and ran right into something we weren't expecting at all.

There was a machine of some kind. A robot, I guess. It was bulky, built like a steamroller with arms. The arms were welding along the bottom deck.

"It's a maintenance drone!" Floramel called out. "Don't—"

But it was too late. Varus legionnaires are notoriously trigger-happy. I count myself as one of the worst, in fact. The light troopers scattered while weaponeers fired shafts of energy into the unit. It buzzed and ceased functioning, pouring out smoke.

"It's transmitting a distress signal!" Kivi told me.

"Burn it down!" I ordered.

Several weaponeers crisscrossed the thing with beams and plasma bolts. It finally died.

"What now?" Leeson asked me.

"Keep moving, that's what," I told him. "Double-time, we're really on the clock now."

We raced past the ruined machine and approached our goal. It was another big hatch—but this one was locked.

"Explosives," I ordered, "take it off its hinges."

A team of techs pasted nanite-gel and bombs to each hinge. They stepped back, and a pressure-wave rolled over us. The sound was deafening, even through my helmet.

Harris led a rush of light troopers into the chamber beyond, and snap-rifles began chattering on full automatic.

"All clear!" he called out.

I stepped inside and found three Nairb techs on the floor, leaking green fluids.

"They said something about us self-executing," Harris joked, "but we must have heard them wrong. Is this what it always feels like, McGill?"

"What?"

"To kill a Nairb. I know you've done it before, and now I get it. Feels great."

I clapped him on the shoulder. "There's hope for you yet, Harris. Floramel, shut down that deep-link."

She advanced into the room and pulled a power coupling. "We should retrieve this—take it back to *Nostrum*. It's very valuable."

"Not more valuable than this mission," I told her. "I'm not lugging anything with us other than our own dead—if we have any."

With our primary mission objective accomplished, we raced out of the module and back up the passageway. I'd marked a new, green waypoint on our HUDs. The gateway wasn't far, and time seemed to go by faster than it had on the way in.

"Sir..." Harris called to me as we picked our way through the vast stacks of goods. "I'm seeing smoke up here."

Concerned, I pressed forward. We were too far for the stealth communications system to work for sure, but I didn't care. With the deep-link down, the Nairbs couldn't call for help anyway.

"Toro!" I called. "What's your status?"

There was nothing. Just dead air.

"Toro? Do you read me?"

Nothing.

"Harris, fan out," I said, switching back to our tactical channel. "Leeson, take the center. Everyone advance with caution."

Jubilation had quickly transformed into fear. We had no idea what we were walking into.

"She's probably stepped out on us," Carlos said. "The second the mission timer was up, I bet she ran for it."

"Could be," I admitted, but I somehow didn't think that was the case.

Harris reached the open area where we'd set up the gateway first. "looks bad," he reported. "I see bodies—they destroyed the gateway, sir. We're cut off."

"Who did?"

"No enemy causalities. Whatever hit Toro took her out without a loss—either that, or they carry their dead away with them, too."

"Do a body count," I ordered. "Is Toro among them?"

"Yeah... you better come take a look, sir."

Cautiously, I moved up to where Harris was. The scene was grim. About half of Toro's platoon was there, dead. They'd been in a firefight—that much was obvious.

"Where are the enemy?" I demanded.

Floramel was kneeling to examine the broken gateway poles. "These poles were deliberately destroyed."

"And Toro is right here—her demolition pack is gone."

Her body had taken hard damage. A leg had been torn clean off, despite her armor.

"Floramel, Kivi, what happened here?"

Kivi looked the scene over while the rest of the troops formed a paranoid circle.

"Heavy prints—they scratched neutronium deck-plates," Floramel said.

"Galactic automatons," Kivi said, looking it over. "That's what I think this was."

"Where did they go?" I demanded.

"There's only one answer to that," Leeson said, squatting next to us. "They passed through the poles and invaded our ship. It was a two-way street, after all."

I nodded, getting it at last.

"And Toro managed to blast the poles to stop them—or at least to break the link. Do you think all of them got through? How many are we talking about?"

Kivi shrugged. "It's a big hold. There could be any number of them in here with us right now."

I stared at her in shock. "They're *here*? In packing crates or something?"

"They were," she said. "But we activated them—or the Nairbs did from the bridge."

Looking around with new alarm, I began to shout orders. Everything had changed. Our mission had been successful, but it was supposed to be only a first step in putting down the enemy ship. Instead of having the Nairb ship at our mercy, all we'd done was warn her and get our own vessel invaded.

I had to wonder what Graves and Deech were saying about me back on *Nostrum* right now.

-52-

The Nairbs hadn't put surveillance equipment in their hold because the hold was capable of taking care of itself. We found the broken crates, about a hundred meters from where we'd first landed. We hadn't seen them because they'd been placed in the hold in the opposite direction of our goal. As they weren't in our pathway when we stormed toward the deep-link module, we'd never noticed them.

"Whatever they were," Carlos said, whistling as he looked over the damage, "they were big."

"What makes you think they're all gone, Ortiz?" Harris demanded, poking through the wreckage.

"If there are more," Carlos said coolly, "they're not in this stack. They would have to be somewhere else. Makes sense the mass of them were right here in the center of the hold."

I didn't comment as I was too busy examining the evidence firsthand. The crates were weird-looking. They weren't box-shaped, or even cylindrical. They were polyhedrons. They had twelve sides, and they were about five meters tall. Blasted open from the inside, they resembled high-tech eggs that had hatched.

"What are they made of?" I asked Natasha as she pawed at the nearest of them.

She was running chunks of the crumbling foam-like material into an analyzer's input port as I watched. She examined the results and looked up at me.

311

"It's organic," she said, "but artificially grown."

"Eggs?" I asked. "They look like eggs, but on a grand scale and with the wrong shape."

"Right... Whatever laid these wasn't some kind of bird. It was an artificial life form—if it's really alive at all."

"Hey!" shouted Harris from a dozen meters off. "Hey, come look at this. Ortiz, I want you to suck on these prints and give me an apology!"

We moved over to where he stood and examined the floor he was pointing at. The scarred up deck in this spot showed a line of wreckage away from the center of the hold. It wasn't as large a region as that which led toward Toro's last stand, but it was undeniable.

Natasha rushed to the scene at my side. "I was expecting this," she said.

"You were?"

"I never bought your theory that Toro had destroyed the gateway poles. I think these guardians did it—which means some of them are still here."

"Oh..." I said, feeling dumb for not thinking of that.

"One..." Natasha said, squatting over the bizarre prints and counting them. "Two... Three? My best guess is that three of them went deeper into the hold instead of attacking our troops."

"But why do that?" Carlos asked. "Their chances were better hitting invaders all at once... Unless..."

"Unless what?" Harris demanded.

"Unless there are *more* crates, and some of them went off to release the others?"

We all looked alarmed.

"Natasha," I demanded, "how far does your stealth jammer system work?"

"Maybe five hundred meters. No more than that."

"They might be outside that region. Maybe they tried to communicate with the bridge, and couldn't. Some might have moved off to do that."

"Either way, Centurion," Leeson said. "We can't let them perform their mission."

"Right," I said, "we have to go after them."

312

Moving forward, an arm reached out and hooked mine. It was Leeson's gauntlet that gripped me.

"Sir," he said. "You're the only one with a teleport suit. No one else can go back to *Nostrum* and get another gateway set up. Without reinforcements…"

"You're right," I said, peeling off the suit. "Kivi, you put this on."

"Okay," she said quickly, seeing her chance to escape the hold.

She got into the outfit, set the coordinates, and powered up. Soon, her outline wavered, blue-shifted—then she was gone.

"Why'd you send her?" Carlos asked me.

"Because we need fighters here, not an extra tech. She knows how to run one of those suits better than you do—and we have Natasha in case we need something figured out."

He didn't argue, but he didn't look totally happy. Kivi and Carlos had had a long term thing going, and he always suspected me of putting a move on her. At times, he'd been right, but today I just wanted to complete our mission.

"Harris, have your people armor up with functional breastplates and try to give them all plasma weapons instead of those snap-rifles."

He did so, shouting and kicking rumps when they didn't move fast enough. The light troopers weren't fully rated on plasma weapons, but they were going to get a crash course today.

As there was nothing functional left to guard at the center of the hold, I ordered my entire force to advance along the trail of wreckage. Whatever these hatchlings were doing, it couldn't be to our benefit, and we had to stop them.

About two hundred steps later, we found something new. Three more torn open cartons, eggs or whatever we were dealing with.

"Six of them now," Carlos said. "Long odds."

"Nonsense," I said. "We'll take them out. Sargon, your people are our best shot. Go for tight, focused beams—using multiple cannons on each target. Just in case they're as tough as I think they are."

"I'm on it, sir," the veteran said.

He'd spent most of his years in Legion as a weaponeer, but he'd recently moved up to veteran in rank. In this situation, he was perfect to lead the hunt. I had the feeling we were going to need all the firepower we could muster to deal with this threat.

Advancing with increased caution as we got closer to the wall of the hold, we were all on edge. Each slight sound made the troops jump—including myself.

But when the attack finally did come, it was from an unexpected direction.

When we'd first located the evidence of the things from the eggs, we'd seen the deck plates scratched and damaged. I'd figured the enemy were of such weight and possibly made of metal, that they'd dented floor the way one might scratch a surface by dragging heavy furniture over it.

But that wasn't it at all. What happened to us must have happened to Toro's crew—the enemy dropped down into our midst from the ceiling.

Leeson, God love him, was the first to die. Something huge and dark with claws like the Devil himself fell from the roof and landed right on him, squashing him like a bug. He didn't even get a shot off, or scream, or nothing.

The monster was flesh, but not all flesh. It had metal boots with claws—or maybe that was just how the feet looked, it was hard to tell. Standing in a crouch, its fleshy body was mottled and lumpy, like an alligator or a stone-carved gargoyle come to life. A mouth opened, showing a pink interior, and it made an awful, low, rumbling sound.

My men didn't need any special orders after that first half-second of shock passed. They craned their necks to look up, rifles lifted—and sure enough the ceiling was crawling with these monstrosities. They began dropping all over the place.

Plasma bolts and laser carbines—even a few snap-rifles began to fire. No one was holding back. They were all on full auto, panicky and falling back in disarray in every direction.

"Concentrated fire!" I heard Harris roar. "Mark my target and take one down at a time!"

Sargon's group was near the monster that had flattened Leeson, and they lashed it with powerful beams. Surprisingly, it didn't go down right away. It smoked and lashed out with those black, crusty-looking limbs. Metallic claws on its feet swept a trooper up and pulled him close in a hug. The head dipped and came back up—the soldier's helmet crunching in those powerful jaws.

"The damned thing ripped Carlson's head off!" Sargon shouted. "Burn it down!"

The startled weaponeers finally got their act together and lanced it until it fell in a smoking heap.

The key strength of human weaponry has always been keeping the enemy at a distance and firing lots of lethal stuff at them in an organized fashion. This foe, however, had messed that all up. They were right in our midst, and it was hard to concentrate fire without hitting each other.

"Sargon," I shouted, "hit the ones on the roof. Half of them are still up there."

Three were down now, and three were on the ceiling. Sargon relayed my orders, marked his target on every weaponeer's HUD and one by one, the three on the ceiling were destroyed.

We still had two left in our midst, however, and they'd been busy. They'd each bitten large chunks of meat off a couple of troopers, while simply smashing down and walking over others, crushing them

Blood and smoke were everywhere. I ran up behind one of the monsters, placing my carbine where the spine should be and holding the trigger down. That made a smoking hole but didn't stop it. The thing didn't seem to feel any pain—I pissed it off, all right, but I didn't manage to stun it or get it to cower back.

Grabbing one of my sad-sack light troopers, it lifted her up and that maw opened wide. Everyone knew how this was going to end, and we winced, showing our teeth in sympathy.

The girl in question was screaming, but she didn't die easily. She had on a breastplate from the fallen heavy troopers Toro had been leading. She pulled out something blue and glowy.

"Grenade!" I shouted, hurling myself backward.

Others nearby scrambled for cover when the gravity weapon vanished. The usual blue-white light came, but it was muted.

The creature lurched in shock. Finally, something had gotten the full attention of one of these nightmares. He keeled over stone dead.

The rest of us looked around, but there were no more targets. They were all down.

Harris and I approached the monster which still clamped tightly on the girl in those claws.

Harris began to smile, then to laugh. "She rammed that grenade right down into its belly!"

"Yeah," I said. "Either that, or it snapped her arm off before she could let go of it."

"Either way, sir, that was a win for us. We outdid Toro, alright. Just wait until I tell her. She lost at least *twice* as many regulars, and I didn't see a single dead monster."

I looked around at the carnage thoughtfully. "Maybe she got hit by a lot more of them. We counted about twenty broken eggs."

"Yeah… maybe," Harris admitted. "If twenty had hit us— we'd have been toast. What now, sir?"

That was a damned good question. I looked around at what was left of my unit, and I saw every tired, desperate eye meeting mine at once.

Sometimes, command wasn't what it was cracked up to be.

-53-

To give myself a chance to think, I ordered everyone to patch up and cannibalize equipment from our dead. That took about five minutes, during which I desperately hoped I'd hear something from Legion Varus, or Kivi—or just about anyone.

It didn't happen. There was no relief column, and our communications equipment wasn't powerful enough to reach across a star system to talk to those still aboard *Nostrum*. I would have dearly loved a report from that direction, but it wasn't going to happen anytime soon.

"There are two options," I told my tired, haggard-looking crew. "We can sit here at the LZ and wait for Kivi to return—hopefully with reinforcements, or we can break out of this hold and invade the ship."

There were a lot of surprised faces looking at me now.

"Sir..." Harris said, "are you serious about that second idea? We're getting our asses kicked in the hold. Why would invading the ship itself be any easier?"

"Legionnaires don't look for easy paths, Adjunct," I told him. "We look for effective ones. By now, the crew of this ship has to know we're here. They have us bottled up, and they're clearly not without effective defenses."

"That's my damned point, sir. I vote we stay put and wait for the cavalry."

His position was typical of Harris, but it wasn't unreasonable. We'd been pretty badly beat-up already. Not even Varus people relished violent death. My unit was at something like half-strength and morale was breaking.

"All right we'll wait," I said, to everyone's relief. "But we'll have to set up a defensive position someplace else. They probably have this place zeroed by now."

That was an alarming thought, and it got them all up and moving again. No one wanted to see any more gargoyle things dropping from the ceiling. As it was, everyone kept looking up and peering over their shoulders into the dark.

Leading the way, I took them to a corner of the hold. There was no retreat from here, but we would be able to see an enemy approaching.

"Natasha," I said, "set up your stealth network in a chain back to the LZ. When someone comes back, have a buzzer tell us."

She went to work on that while Harris and I set up firing positions. As Toro's group had wiped, and Leeson was gone, I was shorthanded for officers. I took Leeson's platoon and Harris ran his light troopers around in circles. He had them all using plasma rifles like they knew what they were doing—but we both knew they were very green.

For about half an hour, nothing really happened. Every minute that passed left us feeling more and more worried.

"What's the hold up?" Harris demanded, haranguing Natasha for the tenth time. "Is Kivi taking a shower or something?"

"There's no way of knowing what happened to her, Adjunct," she told him.

"That's great. That's just great. We're screwed. You should have gone yourself, McGill. Kivi probably got lost."

I smiled at him. "I'll take that as a rare vote of confidence, Harris. But you're right, it's been too long. We can't sit here any—"

Right about then, we heard something. Something loud and deep. It was a massive clang of metal on metal.

Everyone stood up, looking around. Objects around us— light ones like cloth and paper, began to flutter and rise into the air.

We'd been in space for long enough to know what was happening.

"Faceplates closed!" I shouted. "Pressure readings, Natasha?"

"We're down to seventy percent of one atmosphere and dropping," she said.

"We've got a breach," I said. "Most likely, it's intentional."

"The Nairbs are getting smart," Harris said. "They've opened an airlock to vent the atmo into space."

He was probably right, and we all knew it.

"We can still sit tight, can't we Centurion?" A light trooper named Jenna asked me.

I shook my head. "No, probably not. They know we're here. They'll take action for certain now, and our relief troops are late. Time to get back into this battle, people. Shoulder your gear!"

As we marched toward the nearest exit, I thought about how grim our situation had become. We'd been an advanced force, a commando raid, really. But now we'd become the entire boarding party. The ship was being defended, clearly.

Things took an even worse turn once we reached the hatch. While we worked to open it, the air pressure went to zero in the hold. They'd opened an external hatch somewhere and let all the air out into space.

"Sir!" Natasha called out to me, her radio crackling. "Radiation levels are spiking!"

I looked back, and I saw a brightening glow. A white light had grown in the middle of the hold, and it looked like star-fire up close.

"What the hell...?" I asked.

Natasha was looking at it, too. "McGill," she said. "I think—I think we're in warp. The radiation signatures, everything matches. They've turned on their drive and opened a hatch."

I was finally catching on. The Nairbs had more in store for us than a simple suffocation. We'd be frozen, asphyxiated and microwaved before they were through. It was just a matter of picking our favorite form of death.

"Get this hatch open!" I roared at Sargon. "Or we're all dead!"

He was already working on it. No subtlety was required now—he burned the hinges off, melting away heavy metal like butter with the close-range application of his plasma cannon. Several other weaponeers helped him, and steel was turned into burning vapors and white-hot liquid.

Finally, the hatch clanged down. About then, they turned off the gravity.

Not all ships had artificial gravity, but the big ones normally did. This ship had been maintained at something like one hundred and twenty five percent of Earth normal. Very suddenly, that shut down.

The big hatch floated up, still red hot, and it flipped around until it struck a weaponeer's helmet. The helmet starred, and broke. The man screamed briefly as all the air was sucked out of his lungs.

Then his blood boiled and his eyes popped. Exposure wasn't a pretty way to go.

"Get through the hatch!" Harris was shouting.

"Help each other!" I called out as the survivors surged forward. "Grab and drag, people!"

We were weightless, but we had magnetic boots and plenty of training. We hand-over-handed our way through the hatch and into the passageway beyond.

It wasn't a big improvement. The doors at both ends of the passage had already slammed closed. Either the ship had sensed the breach and loss of air pressure, or the Nairbs were actively trying to box us in.

"There's no staying here," I told them. "Keep moving, I'm feeding a simulated ship's layout to your tappers. Follow it to the bridge if command is wiped out."

None of the troops responded. All I heard over the comm channel was labored breathing and cursing. I opened up the system to allow anyone to transmit. There weren't so many of us left that it would be all that confusing.

We advanced on magnetic boots, clanging and cursing as we went. Walking on magnetics always felt like you were slogging through snow with gum on your shoes.

The Nairbs sprang their next surprise on us at the forward hatch. It linked this cargo area to the upper decks, and apparently they'd decided to make a stand here with their defenders.

A dozen or so gargoyles kicked the hatch down as we beamed the hinges into slag. That crushed two men, as the gravity had been switched back on.

A gust of air swept over us, as apparently the next region was pressurized. The gargoyles began to smother and die, but they still had plenty of fight left in them. They tore up another man and bit the head off a third before we'd beamed them to the floor. Mostly, they died of asphyxiation.

"Ha!" I boomed, trying to sound hopeful. "The captain is an idiot. He's killing his own defenders."

With gravity helping again, we jogged forward at a steady pace. We scrambled over lumpy bodies and reached the next hatch. This one swung open as we approached, making us paranoid.

"Break it up," Harris shouted, "don't all bunch at the door!"

They scattered, with two unlucky souls chosen at random sent in to have a look around.

"It's empty, sir!" the scouts called back.

"Advance!" I ordered.

"McGill," Harris beamed me privately. "It might be a trap."

"Of course it is. But we need to get away from that radiation behind us, and there's nowhere else to go."

He sucked in a breath and said nothing. He knew I was right.

When the last man passed through the hatchway, it clanged shut behind us. Gas hissed, filling the space inside with air.

"It's breathable, sir," Natasha pronounced a moment later.

"Keep your helmets on," I told them all. "Unless you run out of oxygen, don't trust yourself to take a single breath."

Unexpectedly, a sound rang out, and then we heard a translated voice.

"Rebels," it said. "Your invasion has failed."

The voice was garbled and artificial, coming through speakers somewhere in the passageway.

"For the sake of your personal honor, I, Magnate Slur, demand that you self-execute."

We paused and I looked at the walls around us.

"Slur?" I called out. "Will you spare our world if we do as you ask?"

Harris came up to me and grabbed my shoulder, giving me a wide-eyed "are you crazy?" look, but I shook him off.

"No," the voice said. "You've gone too far. Your sins are too great, too unspeakable. Your very existence must end. You must be expunged from the galaxy like the plague you truly are."

"At least you're an honest alien," I told him. "That's good to know."

Then I led my troops forward to the next hatch. They followed me in a panicky rush.

-54-

There was no more pretending, or parlaying. It was them or us—it was that simple.

Magnate Slur, however, didn't seem to have gotten the memo. As we pressed on through brute effort and force of will, taking passage after passage, he continued to demand our surrender and orderly execution.

"I don't think this guy gets it," Harris told me. "We're not his slaves—not anymore."

"That's right," I said. "We've bitten the hand and tasted the master's blood. Like any pack of wolves—we only want more."

When we got close to the bridge, a new enemy faced us. They were Nairbs, armed with plasma harnesses.

These weapons were different than our rifles in that they were meant to operate when the trooper had no real arms or legs. Nairbs had flippers. They were semi-aquatic creatures, who in their natural habitat could live on land or in the sea. Using the harnesses allowed them to manipulate a weapon just by looking our way with their squishy heads and willing it to project a beam in our direction.

Three men went down moments after the hatch did, and it would have gone badly for us if the Nairbs had been better trained or equipped. They had plasma guns, and there were at least a hundred of them. Unfortunately, they had no armor, just simple vac suits and those weaponized harnesses.

"Wide beam, Sargon!" I shouted. "Burn them out of those suits!"

He cranked the aperture on his cannon to a broad cone and fired a sweeping beam. Enemy fire flashed past him, and a few bolts struck among our troops despite our best efforts. We'd all hugged up against the walls and the floor.

But Sargon's beam took out a lot of the enemy. At least twenty Nairbs popped and steamed like water balloons put to the torch. The rest began retreating in a near panic.

"Grenades, Harris!" I shouted. "Don't let them pull back through the next hatch."

"Don't worry, sir," he said, rushing forward with a trio of his people at his back. They all had plasma grenades in their gauntlets. "We're not letting them pull this shit again."

When there wasn't any other good choice, Harris could be extremely brave and effective. He lobbed his plasma grenade into the massed and wallowing throng of Nairbs. Two of his companions did the same.

But one man tripped and went down—at least, I thought he tripped, but then I saw he'd caught a bolt and been killed outright. The Nairbs were firing with wild desperation. Since we were bottled up one of them had been bound to get lucky.

The plasma grenade in the dead man's hand, unfortunately, was glowing and active. I gripped the armor of the two men nearest to me and pushed them both to the deck, calling out a warning.

The grenade went off. Harris and his companions were lifted up and knocked flat. They groaned, coughed, and crawled over the deck in agony.

"Advance!" I ordered. "Mow down the survivors!"

I walked up to Harris and knelt beside him as my men finished off the pack of panicked, humping Nairbs. It was a slaughter.

"Harris?" I asked. "Can you walk?"

He made an incomprehensible growl of pain. "Just do it, you fuck!"

I shot him, then I shot one other survivor who was similarly injured. I recorded their deaths on my tapper and advanced with about twenty men into the bridge itself.

324

Here, the chamber was as quiet as a tomb. One Mogwa sat on a throne of what looked like smooth stone.

"Magnate Slur," I addressed him. "You're hereby captured. If you cooperate—"

"Detestable scum," he said, interrupting me. "The battle fleet will scrub your race from the heavens. We'll kill every last human on every world in this province, and we'll determine which species aided you in this accursed act. You have no honor, no right, no—"

I shot him. I've killed a few Mogwa before, and they always die easily. This one was no exception. He flopped, and made farting noises, then finally slid out of his monolithic throne to curl up on the deck like a daddy long legs. A wide smear of indigo colored goo was left on the throne behind him.

"That, troops, is a Galactic," I announced. "Take a good look. They're nothing. You can kill them the same as anything else—maybe even easier. Remember that."

The survivors from my unit stood around in a circle and stared. They'd been bred their entire lives to think of the Mogwa as beings akin to gods. Like the pharaohs of ancient Egypt, these alien creatures were supposed to be above us in every way.

I knew from personal experience that this conditioning could be broken. Staring down at a dead god went pretty far in that direction, so I let them have a good, long look.

The next day or two was rough. We had to take the ship out of warp, turn it around and head it back to Arcturus. All the while, we were out of communication with our legion because we'd knocked out the deep-link. We had no idea whether or not Battle Fleet 921 had shown up and killed everyone.

"If we hadn't had Natasha," I told my haggard crew some forty hours later, "we'd have flown all the way back to Core Systems."

"Truth!" Carlos said, beaming.

He was happy just to be alive this long. Kivi, Harris, Leeson—they'd all bit the bullet on this trip.

Natasha basked in my praise, and I thought she really did deserve it. She was our last surviving tech, and our best. She'd figured out the interface, the navigational system—the works.

"I'd have blown this ship up like a monkey with a stick of dynamite in each hand," I told her.

"You can say that again—sir," Sargon chimed in.

After we were all finished praising her up and down, we got to the grim business of manning an unfamiliar ship full of dead Nairbs.

"If there's one thing I would change," Sargon said, "it would be that final, wide-angled blast of energy into the Nairbs. They smell so bad when you cook them."

"That's right, and their rations aren't much better."

As a semi-aquatic race, the Nairbs ate slop that stank of rotting fish. Unfortunately, old fish seemed to smell the same on their planet as it did on ours.

When we finally arrived at Arcturus, I had Natasha park us far from the central sun, or any of the planets. I wanted to see what was what before we moved in.

"I'm not getting much from these sensors," she complained.

"Well, our ship is pretty far from here. And there are time-effects too, due to the distance, right?"

She gave me a look I knew all too well. It was the look of someone smart trying not to call me a dummy.

"It doesn't quite work that way," she said, letting me down easy. "Light does take about four hours to travel from Rogue World to here, yes. But it's been doing it all along. So, we're seeing the planet as it was four hours ago from here, and it's been visible since the moment we arrived."

"Okay," I said, "makes sense—sort of. What do we have?"

"I don't see *Nostrum*," she said. "That's what worries me."

"Can they see us yet?"

"No, they can't see us until the four hours have past."

After thinking about it, I nodded. "Let's move in then. The only other thing I can think of doing is turning tail and flying this wreck to Earth—but I don't think parking a Nairb ship in orbit would make anyone at Central happy with me."

"I should say not. That would be clear evidence of an entirely new extinction-level offense against the Galactics. You've got to know, James, that we should probably just destroy this vessel right now."

326

"What?"

I couldn't believe I was hearing this kind of reasonable thinking from her. I'd expected her to be so fascinated with the alien technology all around us she'd skip right by such logical conclusions.

"Think about it," she said with sudden intensity. "If the battle fleet shows up in the next hour, they'll see us hanging around here and begin trying to contact us. Once they figure out that only humans are aboard…"

"Huh…" I said. "That would be bad."

"That's right. Every minute we spend in this system, we risk discovery and the extermination of our entire species."

I frowned. "What are we supposed to do then? Self-execute just like that piss-bag Slur told us to? I'm not interested in that."

"I know," she said, "but the risk… it's tremendous."

Her words concerned me. They gave me a headache, in fact. I'd already searched the entire ship's stores and found nothing in the way of alcohol, either. Apparently, the Nairbs had never heard of it.

That thought alone was almost enough to make me feel sorry for the arrogant green bastards.

Almost.

-55-

We spotted a starship about thirteen hours later.

I was dozing at the time, in that hazy state between dreams and wakefulness. I knew people were around me, becoming excited, talking faster with each passing second…

Snorting awake, I found Carlos looming over me.

"Wake up, McGill!" Carlos said. "We found her! We found the *Nostrum*!"

"Okay," I said, rubbing my face. "Okay, good—now get out of my face."

I sat up and shook myself like a dog. "Natasha? Where's Natasha?"

"She's on the bridge. She spotted the ship—it has to be ours."

Fixing Carlos with a sudden stare, all kinds of bad scenarios played out in my mind. "Has to be?" I asked. "As in, it's not confirmed yet?"

"Has to be," he repeated stubbornly.

I've known Carlos for a long, long time. He was one of the first men I'd ever killed directly, and he'd likewise offed me upon occasion. Sometimes, that sort of history builds a connection between two people. It was kind of like we'd been stuck in a bad marriage for decades.

One thing I knew about him was that he was more than capable of self-delusion. All men were, but he had a special knack for it. When he wanted something badly enough, well, in his mind it became an undeniable truth.

Lurching to my feet and snatching up my gear, I marched toward the bridge. Carlos followed me, muttering about something—but I didn't care what it was.

For all their arrogance and softness of body, the Nairbs didn't run a luxury ship. They didn't know about pillows, or beds, really. Someone had theorized this was due to their being an aquatic race. They had bathtubs in their quarters instead of beds, and I guess they were used to just filling them up and sleeping in there when they felt the urge.

That didn't work for humans, though. I didn't even try it. Consequently, I'd been sleeping in a dry bathtub for too long. If you've ever tried that, you know you wake up with a crick in your neck every damned time.

Thumping up to the bridge, I rubbed my neck and cursed the whole way. I didn't put on my helmet until I sighted Natasha. She didn't like people being out of safety gear while aboard an enemy ship. We were all in the habit of taking our helmets off when she wasn't looking, mind you, but we knew well enough to put them back on again when she spotted us.

"Hey," she said, giving me a hard look, "do you know how long it takes to asphyxiate in a hard vacuum… sir?"

"Uh… as a matter of fact, I've done it a few times. You might get a minute in there if you—"

"No," she said. "You get less than that. Your blood will boil within—"

"Look, Specialist," I told her, "have you spotted an Earth ship or not?"

"I *think* so," she said, sighing and turning back to her instruments.

She'd interfaced her mobile computer—which was about a thousand times more powerful than the tappers everyone had embedded into their forearms—into the Nairb ship's console. From there, she was able to work an interface of her own design. It was quite a feat of hacking, even if the ship was built along Imperial guidelines.

"You *think* so?" I demanded. "What's that mean?"

"I mean there's something out there, and it isn't an Imperial ship. I think it's ours."

"How can you not know?"

"It's… here, just take a look."

She transferred the imagery and data she was looking at to the main console. There, I saw the Arcturus system laid out in all its glory. The world of the rogue scientists was there, fourth from the star, looking as dark and unpleasant as always.

"You see that?" she asked. "Peeking out from behind the planet?"

"No—wait… Yeah, I see something. A little silver line. Is that a ship?"

"It has to be. It's not a satellite, natural or unnatural. I've plotted its orbit—and it's not orbiting. It's stationary in a position that can't be maintained normally without a prohibitive amount of thrust."

"Have you contacted them yet?"

Natasha looked at me. "I was waiting for you to make that decision."

Suddenly, I knew why Carlos had come to wake me up. No one could make this call but me.

The stakes were high. Her eyes watched me as I thought about it. I was glad she wasn't telling me all the pros and cons—they were obvious.

If we contacted this ship, and it wasn't from Earth, we'd be revealing our hand. It could be very bad if it was some element of Battle Fleet 921 that we didn't know about. After all, we hadn't seen the fleet in a century. The Galactics might do things differently now.

"Do it," I told her. "Contact them."

She nodded, clearly unsurprised.

"Done," she said, touching a spot on her screen. "We're not identifying ourselves, we're demanding that they do so. That way, if it isn't a human ship, they might not realize we aren't the Nairbs. It should buy us time."

"Good thinking. How long until we can expect—?"

The radio began squawking even as I spoke. While I'd slept, we'd been closing in on that troublesome planet where our earlier siege had cost us time and lives. Besides, it wasn't too far to go for communications traveling at the speed of light.

"Identify, or be destroyed," said a robotic-sounding voice.

I frowned at the console she'd hooked up. "That doesn't sound like Graves, or Deech."

"It's not," Natasha agreed. "Analysis gives a ninety-five percent chance it's an AI voice."

"Really?" I asked. "AI is running that ship?"

"Seems like it."

Narrowing my eyes with a new suspicion, I made a spiraling hand-gesture. She transferred the channel to my helmet, letting me talk to—whatever it was on the other end of the line.

"Unknown vessel," I said, "are you allied with the rogue planet you're orbiting?"

There was no answer, even after I waited twenty seconds or so, the length of time I'd waited before. I was just about to repeat my query when Natasha stiffened in alarm.

"They've fired missiles!" she said. "Two of them—we've got incoming, McGill."

That surprised me quite a bit. I've had missiles fired at me any number of times, of course, but I'd been under the general impression we were having a conversation. Apparently, I'd been misinformed.

"Get our defenses up," I ordered Natasha.

She threw her hands up in defeat, shaking her head. "I don't know how to do that! I've spent every hour figuring out how to fly this thing—not how to make her fight."

"Give me any info you have on those missiles," I told her. "Are they similar in design to the X-ray missiles that were fired at us before?"

Natasha worked her computer for what seemed like a very long time, but which had to be under a minute.

"Yeah," she said, nodding emphatically. "Same spectrography on their chemical trail. Same general size, acceleration—"

"Can we outrun them?"

She shook her head. "We'd have to go to warp again... I don't know. I'll start working the calculations."

"You do that," I told her. "Your timer here—is this accurate? It's says we've only got four minutes."

"That's a best guess."

"Great…"

Thinking fast, I opened the channel again. "Hostile ship," I said, "there's no cause to fire on us. We're from—"

"Your vessel has been identified," the artificial voice spoke up, interrupting me. "It's been classified as 'enemy' and will be treated as such."

"You're making a mistake. This is Centurion James McGill. We are allied with the rogues… uh… the scientists of Arcturus IV."

There was no immediate response, and I became a little nervous. This was my first time commanding a starship, and it looked like it might be my last.

The two missiles streaked toward our defenseless, stolen ship without pausing. They were going to go off when they got close and irradiate us all. We'd be as dead as fish sticks in a microwave after that.

"Contact the planet directly," I told Natasha. "Call up Floramel for me."

"Last I heard, she was aboard *Nostrum*," Natasha pointed out.

"I know that, but you have to give it a try."

Shrugging, she did as I asked.

The channel crackled, but we didn't hear anything.

"Floramel? Anyone down there? Your robot ship has gone mad. It's attacking us, and we haven't done a thing to make it hostile."

Finally, a blip came back. "Is this the man known as James McGill?" asked a male voice.

"Yes, it certainly is."

"If you're innocent, we suggest you run from our vessel. It is automated, and it will protect us at all costs. If you don't flee—you will be destroyed."

"Where'd you get this ship, anyway?" I demanded.

"We've always had it hidden in the system. We didn't reveal it because we weren't sufficiently threatened."

"Great, well, can't you switch it off?"

"It's a doomsday device. We've accepted our erasure, but we intend to greatly harm those who remove us from the cosmos."

"This action on your part is premature," I insisted. "Turn off your robot dog, and—"

"This conversation no longer serves any purpose," the guy said. "We wish you well. May your last two minutes of existence be enjoyable."

After that, the channel closed. I stared at the screen with my mouth hanging open.

"Well, shit a brick," I said. "They don't even seem to care."

"I'm charging up the warp engines, but we need time, James."

Contacting the AI ship again, I demanded that it answer me.

"Hey, one-two-three... wake up, robot!" I said.

Nothing came back, and I looked down at Natasha. "Can it hear me?"

"I think so, yes."

"AI ship," I said. "You've gone mad. Slow down those missiles, and we'll leave your system. You'll be a hero, having defended—"

"Your pointless communications are wasting my processing time," the ship complained. "You must cease this idle chatting."

"Wasting your processing time?" I demanded, incensed. "I'll have you know you're about to blow up an allied ship, one that would be willing and able to help you defend this system against the real battle fleet. I've never even *heard* of such a stupid AI system."

"This is the McGill?" asked the voice.

"I already said so, moron."

"Don't antagonize it, James," Natasha hissed at me plaintively.

"Your ship would do battle with the Imperial fleet that's expected to arrive shortly?" the AI asked.

"Yes, of course. We don't have much in the way of—"

Natasha reached up a hand, placing it over mine and shaking her head.

"Oh… let me repeat: yes, we will fight alongside you. We'd be glad to."

The AI ship didn't answer. Natasha's eyes were huge, hopeless. She reached up a hand again, grabbed mine, then stood and gave me a kiss.

"You always were an idiot, James," she said. "I don't know what I saw in you."

"Uh…"

That's when the lead missile went off. I saw a bright spot, like a star being born among the heavens.

Was that how X-rays looked when they fried you?

I didn't know, but I figured I was about to find out.

-56-

For about ten long seconds, I figured we were stone dead. I could tell by the way Natasha was acting all lovey-dovey that she thought we were goners, too.

But then, slowly, everyone relaxed. We *weren't* dead. There was no way the beams from those missiles could have taken so long to reach us.

"What happened?" I asked.

Natasha let go of my hands and sat down again. She checked over her instruments.

"The X-rays went off—but they didn't strike our ship. They were either aimed badly, or—"

"Or *nothing*!" I whooped. "The AI changed its mind. *Hot damn*! Winner-winner chicken-dinner!"

Carlos stared at me as I celebrated life.

"McGill…" he laughed. "That's got to be the most retarded thing I've ever heard come out of your mouth. Chicken dinner? What's that even mean?"

I gave him a hard look.

"Oh…" he said, "I mean: you sounded retarded, *sir*."

"That's better."

I would have smacked him, but I was too happy to be alive right now.

"Sir," Natasha said, "the lab people are trying to contact us."

Sitting down with a huge sigh of relief, I picked up a strange-looking headset. It looked rubbery—and crusty.

"What are you supposed to do with this?" I asked her dubiously.

"You're supposed to put it in your mouth," Carlos said unhelpfully. "It's like a suppository—but it goes in the other—"

I kicked at him, and he skittered away. Carlos was good at dodging well-earned blows. He'd had a lot of practice.

"You hold it up to your ear," Natasha said. "The sound comes out of that bulb. But I wouldn't, like, *touch* it to your ear."

"Yeah, it's sticky," I said. "These Nairbs are disgusting creatures. I'm glad we spaced all the bodies."

The bulb-thing began talking to me. Screwing up my face into a scowl, I held it close enough to listen.

"Hello?"

"McGill?" said a feminine voice. "Is that you?"

"Floramel? Yeah, it's me."

"You're still alive. Did anyone die?"

"Nope. Not yet."

"I'm so sorry," she said. "The defender is a doomsday weapon, you have to understand."

"Uh… how do you mean?"

"It's meant to fight on after we're all dead. We built it for the Cephalopods originally, but they never deployed it."

"Hmm… Why didn't you guys use it against *Nostrum* as soon as we showed up to invade?"

"We honestly didn't think we had to."

I found that somewhat offensive. She was saying that they thought they could beat us with one hand tied behind their backs. To be honest, though, they were probably right.

"Okay," I said, "why didn't it kill us?"

"We thought that it might have done so. We're not in complete control of it. The ship has advanced AI, and it thinks for itself."

"Huh… you mean you set a big dog on us without knowing if it would kill us or not? That's not very nice."

"You have to understand, James, you've been gone for days. When the Nairb ship warped out, everyone assumed that your boarding party had been lost."

Thinking about it, I could see how they might make that mistake. After all, there had only been my single unit aboard.

"How did *Nostrum* do against the invading gargoyle-things?"

"The guardians? They caused some wreckage and some deaths, but they were destroyed. Your legion dealt with them quickly enough. But they did serve to convince Tribune Deech that you'd all been lost and the mission was a failure."

"Yeah…" I said, trying to look at it from their point of view.

We'd been sent to board the enemy ship, but instead of returning, a pack of monsters had come back through the portal instead. Then, the target ship took off and vanished. That had to have looked very bad for us.

"So, they took the legion back to Earth?" I asked.

"That's right."

"And they just left you out here?"

"It sounds harsh, I know," Floramel said, "but I understand your people. They're hoping the battle fleet will come here and annihilate us, but then stop. They're hoping that if they're nowhere near the scene, Earth won't get blamed."

"But they must have been worried if they thought we'd failed. The Nairbs could have contacted the battle fleet by now, or joined their ranks."

"That's true," she said, "they didn't know what had happened, and they weren't happy about that."

"So… what now? Are you going to stay here and fight?"

"Yes," she said firmly.

"How about you and I get together and talk?" I asked her.

Floramel hesitated, and I caught sight of Natasha's reaction. She'd rolled her pretty little eyes at me. That wasn't too much of a surprise, because I knew she still cared about me that way.

"All right," she continued. "You're in range now, so I'm sending another gateway link up to you. You'll be able to move from your ship, to my planet."

Sure enough, a gateway kit appeared in the hold. It was kind of freaky, watching the backed-up vids of its arrival.

We set up the kit and soon had two humming poles a meter apart. Before I walked through, I had a chance to marvel at the tech. These nerds really *had* come up with some neat tricks.

What if the lab people had decided to send us a bomb instead? I supposed that if that had been the case, I'd never have known what had hit us.

When I stepped through, Floramel and a team of her aides in white suits were there to meet me. They looked like they were curious about me, but they were also wary.

Floramel smiled, but the rest didn't.

Taking this as an invitation, I stepped right up and gave her a hug.

Her eyes were wide in alarm, but her smile returned after a minute. I got the impression that hugging was weird to them, like one of those double-cheeked kisses French guys always handed out in the old vids from Earth.

In any case, she liked my personal greeting and led me up into the nicer, cleaner region of the dome.

"Where'd you hide that ship all this time?" I demanded, pointing up through the diamond-hard blue glass at the nighttime sky over head.

Arcturus was below the horizon, and the local stars were big and blazing through the relatively thin atmosphere of Rogue World. The ship itself was visible up there too. It blotted out a portion of the starscape and reflected the distant light of the central star. Like a silver-white triangle, it hung up there, motionless above the planet.

"It hides itself. It's been up there all along with a light-shield surrounding it. We activated it when *Nostrum* left us. The battle fleet will come now, and all will be lost."

I lowered my eyes back to hers. She was staring up at the sky. I could tell this was an emotional time for her, and I could understand why—but I didn't get all of it, like her people's strong motivations.

"Why'd you fight so hard to stay here?" I asked her.

"This is our home," she said simply. "I know it must look like a lifeless rock to you, but we were born here."

"That's it? You're defending your home turf?"

"It's not just that. We lived for a half century as slaves to the Cephalopods. We don't want to go back to being slaves to the Galactics now. All our life's works would be gone as well, even if we did submit to survive. Isn't that so?"

I thought about it and nodded. She had a good point. Her work was illegal. Even if, by some miracle of diplomacy, these rogues were allowed to live here under their bubble, they would never be permitted to continue inventing things that other star systems in the Empire no doubt had the patent on. The very idea was unthinkable to any Nairb or Mogwa.

"Yeah…" I said. "I get it. You couldn't even do the work you've dedicated your life to. So, how are we going to keep you breathing?'"

"You can't James," she said, then she pointed up into the skies again at her automated ship. "But the AI ship might. It's very powerful. It might just be able to stop the battle fleet."

I laughed in her face, but she didn't seem to get offended. She didn't smile, either. She meant it.

Floramel was a hard case. She didn't want to leave her world, even though I offered her safe transport out. She didn't want that, and she didn't want to admit she was going to lose this fight, either.

"We've got defensive capabilities we haven't revealed yet," she told me.

"Really? Why didn't you use them against us, then?"

"I have to admit, we didn't think you stood a chance against us. When you personally led a mission into our dome, we were shocked. All our predictions said it couldn't be done by an external ground force. We were wrong."

"You sure as hell were," I told her. "And you're wrong about the Mogwa fleet, too. They know how to fight. They won't do it fairly, either. They'll stand off in high orbit and blow this planet to fragments."

She kept gazing up at the sky as she talked to me. Looking up like that, her face was as pretty as a picture. I couldn't take my eyes off her, just as she couldn't take her eyes off the stars.

Seizing opportunities had always been one of my strong areas. Accordingly, I slipped an arm around her thin waist and put my head up close to hers, staring up like she did.

"What…? You're touching me again. Is this some kind of tradition on Earth?"

"It sure is," I said. "Do you like it?"

"I'm not sure. It's unexpected and provocative. Are you attempting to mate again?'"

"Uhh… Would you like that?"

She blinked at me. We were close, close enough to kiss. I already had one arm snaked around her waist, and for me, that's halfway to home base.

But I didn't pull her to me and go for it. I let her think about it first. This kind of girl was a thinker. Sometimes, you had to let that kind decide what was what for themselves.

She came around in the end and melted up against me. We kissed, and I held her close. We both looked up at the skies again.

"You're looking for that fleet, aren't you?" I asked her. "Waiting to see the moment it arrives."

"Yes."

"What will your people do when it shows up?"

"We'll fight. First, the AI ship will challenge them. It will do battle. We've analyzed Galactic warships as best we can. It was built to deal with them."

"You mean it has more tricks up its sleeve than just throwing out X-ray missiles?"

She laughed quietly. "Yes."

"Good," I told her, "because you're damned well going to need all the help you can get."

After that, I made my move. My patience had paid off. She was ready and interested. We soon moved to her apartments and made love there.

All the while, with the window open, we could watch a nighttime view of the overly-bright stars near Arcturus. The sky made our love-making surreal, like we were embracing in open space itself.

-57-

The next morning, I awoke alone. Arcturus was blazing in the heaven on a rare, cloudless day. I immediately had a sinking feeling, like I'd overslept on Easter Sunday.

Bouncing out of bed and pulling on my boots, I soon went searching for breakfast and Floramel, in that order.

I found her about an hour later working below ground in the dark labs. She looked at me with a pale, worried face.

"What's wrong?" I asked her. "Your people won't talk to me."

"They don't entirely trust you," she said, going back to her work.

"They don't? Well... what about you?"

She looked at me, troubled. "I don't know," she said. "Your people invaded our world. You take what you want, you kill, and you bed me like a captive."

"Now, hold on!" I said. "Did I misunderstand last night? Was I in the wrong?"

Floramel heaved a sigh. "No," she said. "I'm sorry. But the battle fleet has arrived, and it's not cooperating."

That froze my mind over. My mouth hung wide, and I spun around on the heel of my left boot.

There was a monitor displaying deep space nearby. It showed blank stars.

"I don't see them," I said.

"No, you're not meant to. They're not optically visible yet."

That was a stunner. Sure, we'd never seen the battle fleet except for that one day they annexed Earth. But they'd been very visible in the skies during that dark time. Every vid from a century back showed countless ships—plain as day.

"Are they stealth ships?" I asked.

"They have that capacity, yes," she said. "But they're also hanging back, far from our planet. They're at the very fringe of the Arcturus system, where our two gas giants orbit.'"

"Floramel?" I asked, turning back to her.

She looked up from her work, and I took her hand in mine.

"Come with me," I said. "Just you—or everyone. We can get aboard the Nairb transport. There's plenty of room. You don't have to stay here and die. There's no point in that."

She looked at me with those perfectly shaped eyes, and I could see I'd gotten through to her. At least part of her wanted to go with me.

"Where will we go?" she asked. "To Earth? We won't be welcome there."

"There are lots of planets in the universe," I told her. "The battle fleet has a weakness—it can't be everywhere at once."

After a moment of tortured thought, she pulled her hand out of mine.

"No," she said. "We'll fight."

"Girl…" I said, flummoxed. I'd given her the best shot of James McGill charm I had in me, and she'd shrugged it off. "You can't win. What's the point?"

"We don't know that. Not yet."

"Well, *I* know it. The Mogwa aren't running a quarter of the galaxy because they're a bunch of chumps. You might hurt them a little, but all that will do is piss them off."

"We'll see."

My eyes turned back to the monitors. They were still blank, as far as I could tell.

"How do you even know there are any ships out there?"

"We're using gravimetrics. No radar, visual or other light spectra will work to detect them—but they have mass they can't hide."

"I see… How many are there?"

"About four percent of this planet's mass was just added to this star system. That works out to… About a thousand large ships? It's a guess, I admit, but an educated one."

"A *thousand* ships?" I groaned. "Come on, girl. Let's run while we can."

"No, I'm sorry."

She'd left me in a tough spot. I eyed the others in her team. There really weren't a lot of people on this planet, but they'd done amazing things. It would be a shame to lose them all.

"I've got an idea," I said. "Have you got a data core? Something with all your knowledge stored?"

"Of course."

"Well? Give it to me. That way it won't be lost if the battle fleet wins."

They looked dubious, but logic won out after a few seconds of thought.

Floramel nodded, and her minions didn't argue. I'd gotten a weird vibe from the lab techs over the last few days. They weren't normal in the head—not by human standards. I got the feeling they were clones, but they didn't *look* like clones. Whatever the case was, by birth or conditioning, they followed Floramel around like she was their mother duck.

They gave me a copy of their data core, which was an organic thing in a box. It sloshed when I carried it, and smelled like a dirty fish tank.

"How can we interface with this?" I asked.

"I'll put an app on your tapper," she said, and she did so quickly.

Taking the data core back to *Nostrum*, I was confronted by Carlos and Natasha.

"Centurion?" Natasha asked. "Are you alone?"

"That's right, Specialist. They're not coming with us."

"Fools," Carlos said. "They don't stand a chance when the battle fleet gets here."

"I've got bad news on that front," I said, handing the data core off to a couple of wide-eyed recruits. "Handle that with care," I told them. "It's got a copy of their research on it."

They got a power cart and hauled it away like it was the Arc of the Covenant itself.

"What bad news?" Carlos asked me.

"Oh... just that Battle Fleet 921 is already in this star system and approaching. They detected it using gravimetrics."

Natasha turned white, and even Carlos looked concerned.

"How long do we have?" Natasha asked.

"Until they decide to start shooting? Who knows?"

She looked at me and bit her lip. "Should we run?"

"We can't run," I told her. "It's too late for that."

"Why?"

"Think about it. The Galactics have been in the system observing us for some time. They're probably trying to figure out what's wrong with this ship. Maybe they're sending us secret messages in code, and we're not answering."

Her eyes darted from side to side. I could almost see the wheels turning in that pretty head of hers.

"I should have thought of that. I should recommend action—but, I don't know what to do, James."

"We're screwed," Carlos said, throwing up his hands. "It's as simple as that. We're just screwed. Sometimes it's easier to accept death and hope for a revive back on Earth. Let's make something up, then transmit it home. If they get it in a few years, maybe they'll revive us."

"Hmm," I said. "I like part of your idea, Carlos, but it needs work. Natasha, check every channel to see if the Galactics are transmitting to this ship."

She looked at me oddly. "We're really *not* going to run?"

"They'll *know* this ship isn't controlled by a Nairb crew if we do."

"How are they not going to know that anyway, James?" she demanded. "We can't just slip into their ranks silently without making some kind of report."

"Normally, that'd be true. But we're about to see a battle. In the heat of battle, things can get confusing and protocols might be broken."

"Oh yeah," Carlos said. "I can see where this is going. Excuse me while I go inject myself with a quart of morphine, okay?"

"Stay at your post, Specialist," I told him without a glance in his direction. "Natasha? Can you hook me up?"

"All right," she said. "I'll try—but you're crazy, James."

"Always and forever," I agreed.

Natasha began her work, but she didn't finish before the battle started. About an hour after I'd first been shown the enemy ships by Floramel, the fireworks began. The Empire ships revealed themselves in all their glory—honestly, I wanted to crap my pants just a little.

Grabbing the comm gear and connecting to Floramel, I saw she looked relatively calm, if distracted, on the big screen.

"They're coming for you!" I told her. "Transport up here right now!"

"I'm sorry James," she said. "Win or lose, we're not leaving this place."

"Win or lose?" I asked incredulously. "They'll blot out your sun when they reach orbit. There are too many of them for your robot ship to handle, no matter how smart it is."

"You can watch, but you must stay quiet," she told me. "I can't afford to be distracted now."

I slapped the top of my helmet with a gauntlet. I didn't know what else to say to her.

The fight unfolded in an unusual way. It was a scary battle—if you could call it a battle. It was among the strangest operations I'd yet to witness.

Truly advanced technology is akin to magic—at least, that's what they'd told me back in officer training school at Central. This battle seemed to prove out the logic of that statement.

First off, Floramel and her lab people began to play some really cool tricks once the enemy fleet approached and revealed itself. A series of mines lit up in the middle of the Galactic's formation. How they got there, how they'd gone undetected—I didn't know. They weren't even explosions, exactly.

"Masers," Natasha told me in awe. "They've got functioning maser weapons, and they've deployed them right in the enemy fleet's core."

"What the hell is a maser?" I asked, but she didn't answer right away.

Violet streams of light came out of these pinpoints of origin. Like spines from a sea anemone, these beams lanced out in a hundred random directions at once. Many of them missed all targets—but some landed.

The enemy fleet was tightly bunched. They took hits to scores of their sleek vessels. The beams punched through hulls and ripped right through the skin of a stricken ship and out the other side. The masers didn't burn for long—only a split second before burning out forever, but in that time they were like landmines in a marching formation of troops. Ships were torn apart and destroyed. Dozens of them.

"Holy shit!" Carlos called out. "We are dead. We are so, so dead. We're so dead that they won't even be able to—"

"Shut the hell up!" I ordered, and he fell to muttering darkly.

"Masers are theoretical weapons," Natasha told me. "They're an older tech—developed before lasers on Earth. But this kind of power… They might be using fusion bombs to power them briefly."

"How'd they get them out there into the middle of the fleet?" I demanded.

She shrugged. "Maybe they were sitting out there all along."

More masers went off, but the Mogwa ships had shielding now. Either the Galactics hadn't had their shields in place before—or, more likely, they'd focused them all forward expecting a more traditional attack. Whatever the case, their ships stopped dying to the masers and they advanced steadily.

"Why didn't they use these masers on *Nostrum* when we approached?" I asked Natasha.

"You said yourself they didn't want to. Isn't that what Floramel told you? That they could have wiped us out, but they didn't take us seriously."

"Well…" I said, "I can now see why they—"

"The Mogwa are firing back," Natasha said, leaning over her instruments and making adjustments to our optics.

Now that the fireworks had begun, neither side announced itself or made any declarations of doom. Battle Fleet 921 slid forward, advancing despite their losses. They seemed powerful,

346

implacable. Just watching them made me want to freak out a little, like Carlos.

The Galactics opened up with some kind of freaky attack that had explosions popping all around the AI ship—which was still parked in orbit over Rogue World.

"What the hell are those strikes?" I demanded.

"T-bombs," she said calmly. "The Mogwa are trying to teleport bombs inside the ship. The AI ship must have good shielding, though, as it's not working."

"T-bombs…?" I said, my mouth hanging open again.

Thinking it would be a good idea to record this, I tapped the record-all button on my tapper and streamed it to the data core. There was a faint hope we'd see Earth again before we were snuffed out, and I wanted to take home a gift of intel.

Seeing as how we were probably doomed as a species, I figured it was the least I could do for those clueless bastards sitting home at Central.

347

-58-

The AI ship just sat there, like a spider in a web, waiting for the approaching Galactics to get closer. It was ominous.

"Pull us back around to the far side of the planet," I told Natasha.

"It won't help," she told me. "If they lay just one of those T-bombs on us, we'll be wiped out."

"I didn't ask for advice, Specialist. Retreat out of sight pronto."

She did as I'd ordered without anger or much in the way of hope in her face. Our big transport ponderously looped around the planet and slid behind it, out of direct sight from the approaching fleet. Naturally, we still had drones and the like reporting back visuals and other forms of data, so we could watch the battle unfold.

The Galactics seem to have given up on the T-bomb approach. They were moving closer to bring their main guns to bear.

The AI ship, however, wasn't cooperating. It had started acting oddly. Instead of being in one fixed location, it looked like it was blinking around into random spots every second or two. Even the timing on the movement was randomized.

"Look at that..." Natasha breathed. "It's phasing—shifting in time and space. It's got to be almost impossible to hit."

"They're sure trying," I said, watching the approaching fleet open up with their main batteries.

The big guns were going off. Much of the back-and-forth assault utilized radiations that would normally be invisible to the human eye, but our computers compensated when displaying the situation optically.

The AI ship was firing back, too. It had missiles at first, X-ray types like the ones it had used on us. But those were failing to penetrate now, so it shifted to a single, bright beam that was depicted as a lavender line on our screens.

This line stretched out with what seemed like a languid pace, but it was really moving at the speed of light. The distance between the two opposing forces was great enough to take several light-seconds to traverse.

But what I didn't understand was how this lavender beam was slicing laterally through the Galactic fleet.

"How's it doing that?" I demanded. "It looks like a sword cutting through space from one point to another…"

Natasha nodded. "The effect seems to be related to the random jumps the AI ship is making. It's slashing that beam in random lateral directions with each shifting of its position. Absolutely fascinating technology."

I glanced at her, thinking it was just like Natasha to get excited about tech, even when it was terrifying.

The AI beams were scoring hits as the Empire ships came closer. It slashed and danced, cutting apart enemy cruisers and battleships each time. It almost always got one, sometimes two. Once I even saw it kill three in one shifting sweep.

But the battle fleet was reacting, responding and taking countermeasures. I had to wonder if even those smarty pants, Galactic Core-dwellers had ever encountered anything like this. They weren't running yet, so maybe they had.

"They're widening their formation," Natasha said. "They're realigning their shields—there, see that? The AI ship jumped and slashed—but the beam didn't knock out the last battleship that was attacked."

I watched the ship in question. It had been hit hard, its shield sparked and dulled to a flickering orange color. That ship immediately pulled out of formation and retreated.

349

This became the new tactic. Each ship that was hit survived, as often as not, and immediately fled to the back of the line. As they became more scattered the AI vessel could only hit one at a time, and it was only getting kills rarely now.

"They're down to eight hundred ships," Natasha said. "There were over a thousand to start. The AI ship has performed magnificently."

"If one gets through, it will be too many," I said.

We watched tensely, and the battle shifted again. The Empire ships were no longer targeting the dancing phantom in orbit. They turned their weapons instead on the blue glass dome the ship was protecting.

"No…" I said, seeing beams lash down from space and strike the dome. "It can't hold, can it?"

Natasha shrugged. "I don't know. I wouldn't have thought the ship could have held out this long."

Bombs were falling now. Not all the way down from space—that would have taken hours. Instead, they were being teleported into the atmosphere itself and allowed to fall down near the dome by the attraction of gravity.

"Get Floramel online!" I ordered.

Natasha did so quickly, and I stared at the glare and looming mushroom clouds that now obscured the dome itself.

For a minute, I couldn't hear anything other than static. Then the explosions ceased and the EMP effect dispersed.

"Floramel?" I demanded. "Can you hear me?"

"James?" she said, her voice scratching due to static. "You should leave here. This can't last much longer."

"You have to gate up to our ship. We still have the poles set up here. Come through, and save yourselves."

"We can't do that, James."

"If you won't do it to save yourselves," I said, feeling desperate as more and more Empire ships came into range, "come along to save us. We need you. Earth needs you."

"No," she repeated. "The gateway transmission—even the fact we're in contact right now—it's all being documented. Earth could be expunged for that alone, James."

My shoulders sagged in defeat. "What do we do then?" I asked. "We're screwed regardless."

"I'm sorry James. This was never meant to include you and your people—but remember, you did come here uninvited."

"So we did," I admitted.

"Don't worry," she said. "We'll always be with you."

Then the screen went dark, and she was gone.

On the surface of the rogue planet, the skies lit up with one final dawn. A dawn so bright, so full of released energy and awesome power, that it would never be duplicated. The remains of the planet were expanding outward after that, gaseous, plasma—fire and dust.

"The whole world just blew up," I said, stunned.

"The crust has been vaporized," Natasha said. "But the bedrock core will still be there afterward. When it cools, it will look much the same, but without an atmosphere."

Her voice was deadpan and cool. She'd lost all hope.

I knew what she was thinking. Earth was next. I was too— how could we think of anything else while watching the end of another world that had dared to oppose the Empire?

Earth school children were taught about the fate of planets that didn't submit to the rule of the Empire. But all that had been talk and stories. I'd never actually *seen* it happen. Not like this. I'd seen a few planet-busters fall on a Cephalopod colony once, sure. But to see the surface of an inhabited planet shorn away and blasted into space like that…

Well, it was an experience I hoped I'd never have to live through again.

Natasha gazed at me in shock. I looked around the bridge of the Nairb ship. Most of my surviving unit members were here now, watching. They all looked like they'd watched their own deaths. No one said a word or cracked a joke—not even Carlos.

"Your orders, Centurion?" Natasha asked me.

"Hmm… I'm thinking."

Carlos closed his eyes and shook his head in defeat.

After a minute, I snapped my fingers and pointed at the helm controls. "We've got a gun on this thing, don't we?"

Natasha blinked at me in surprise. "We do, but it's only a small shore-bombardment laser."

"Doesn't matter. Power it up and attack the AI ship. Right now."

Her expression indicated she thought I was crazy. "We can't possibly—"

"Natasha, that's an order."

She turned back to her controls, and soon we were swinging around and accelerating toward the battle.

"Wait a minute!" Carlos complained. "We're going back out into the open? We should just run. Let's warp out of here."

"We can't," I told him.

"Can't? Why not? Something with the warp core—?"

I looked at him seriously. "The Empire knows we're here. We've been idling this whole time, standing around with our

352

thumbs in our butts. If we run now, we'll be marked as a rebel force. You just watched how the Empire deals with rebels. You don't want that for Earth, do you?"

"No, sir…" he said, and he finally shut up.

We came out from behind the smoldering planet and approached the AI ship from behind.

"Get closer," I said.

"We can hit them from here," Natasha said.

"Then start firing, and charge right in close."

White-faced, she did as I asked. The ship accelerated, pushing us all into seats that were better shaped to fit a Nairb's rear end.

At last, when we were alarmingly close to the action, our laser cannon flashed out shot after shot. They were short bursts, maybe a half-second long each time.

"We're missing!"

"The target is dancing around still, sir."

"Guess where it will be next. And get closer, so we can hit it before it can shift."

Natasha pressed on, taking us closer every second. The debris from the destroyed planet had now billowed out so far into space it was beginning to get into our way. Our shields flashed and alarms whined, informing us we were in some kind of meteor or dust storm.

We ignored all this and bulled our way closer, coming up on the stern of the AI ship. We were far closer than any of the Empire vessels, but so far the AI had ignored us utterly.

"It probably has calculated we're not a serious threat," Natasha said.

"It has calculated correctly," Carlos interjected, unable to contain himself.

"Get in there and shoot it right up the tailpipe," I ordered.

Natasha's hand shook a little as she followed my orders. All around me, my unit's finest looked like a pack of sick dogs. I knew they were thinking they'd fought hard, completed their mission, and now as a just reward they were about to die because of the suicidal actions of their sole-surviving—but crazy—officer.

I didn't argue with them or explain my actions. They were right to be worried, but we also lacked time to fuss about it.

As we rushed into the battle against a ship with about a million times our firepower, the people around me grew quiet. Not even Carlos had something funny to say. We knew we were about to die.

For all that, I have to give my troops credit. They followed my orders despite the fact they felt *sure* it was going to get them killed. If that's not loyalty, what is?

Our crappy gun began firing, and the computer colored in a thin line of yellow to show what effect it was having—the short answer was: not much.

"We missed?" I asked. "We missed again?"

"We're at extreme range still," Natasha explained.

"We're almost on top of them! We're not more than twenty thousand kilometers off her stern."

She shrugged helplessly. "The target is still shifting. My predictive software—"

"Open a channel with the AI," I said. "Then when it replies, lock on the beam. That should help give us a clue."

Wincing, she worked her computer, which in turn worked the Nairb boards. All the touch interface icons on the Nairb computers were huge, about the size of a human palm. I guess it was hard to delicately operate a touch-screen with a flipper.

"Channel opened."

"Hey!" I called out. "AI ship, your planet is burned away to dust. Why are you still fighting?"

"Mission parameters not yet met," the machine answered.

"What's your mission then, if not to protect the planet?"

"Primary mission failed. Secondary mission: destroy all intruders. Secondary mission in progress."

I turned to Natasha. "Did you get a lock?"

She nodded to me. Her face was ashen. I think she knew what I was going to say next.

"Good," I said. "Now, kick it in the ass."

She turned back to her boards, and she laid her hands directly on the Nairb icons. She used her entire palm, making large arm motions to reach high enough. After about five touches, the pencil-thin yellow line leapt out again—but this time, it connected our ship to the bigger AI vessel.

For about a second, no one breathed. But then, we relaxed a little as there was no immediate reaction.

"Do it again," I told Natasha.

"Hey, guys...?" It was Carlos. He'd come close and was pointing up at the big board.

The AI ship was turning. She was coming about. Perhaps her frontal gun port only aimed forward. Maybe the center-line gun emplacement ran the length of the ship and had limited flexibility when targeting.

Anyway, she was still dancing as she did a one-eighty to face us. It was a sight to see. All hellfire was blazing away at her stern, but the enemy fleet was a good million kilometers off still and spread out too. They were nowhere near as close to the AI as we were, so they were still missing.

But we'd landed a glove on the big vessel. Sure, it had been a paltry, glancing blow. No damage had been registered—hell, we'd barely caused the stern shields to flicker.

But she'd noticed us. That much was more than clear.

"Do we run, sir?" Natasha asked me.

"Dodge. Give it all you've got. Lay in a course to warp out in the meantime."

"That ship will toast us, James," Carlos said at my side.

We'd been together for a long, long time. He and I went so far back, I could hardly remember the first time I'd bashed him in the mouth. But he'd almost never used the voice he was using now or called me by my first name, either. He sounded serious, concerned and thoughtful. That made me give him my full attention.

"Look," I said, "we've got to take another shot. If we don't, none of this will look real."

"If it hits us," Carlos said, "we probably won't catch a revive on Earth for a decade. Maybe never."

"I know. Ride with me, Specialist. One last time."

He slapped me on the shoulder, but his lips were a tight line. "Okay, *cabron*."

Looking back to the forward screen, I saw the AI ship was fully aligned. That forward gun port—it was glowing a purplish color. Then, the gun port blazed, and a gush of energy lanced out. Natasha slapped at her controls—literally, like a seal beating on a drum—and our tiny ship moved in random jinks and swirls.

The AI ship phased, dancing, and the purple beam cut from one part of the heavens crosswise to another.

We were like a buzzing fly caught in the middle of that vicious, sudden slash of power.

-60-

I have to admit, I had my eyes squeezed almost shut. My gauntlets were gripping the back of Natasha's chair like they were welded there, but then the beam was past us. It blazed with blinding color over the screen, and we were angling off and accelerating past the AI ship's flank.

"Jesus…" Carlos breathed. "That thing shaved our fins off!"

"Going to warp!" Natasha shouted.

"No, no!" I shouted. "Hold on. Contact the battle fleet."

She glanced up at me with wide eyes. She had that expression I knew too well, the one that said she thought I was insane.

"Do it!" I ordered. "The AI ship took a few seconds to turn around last time. We're past her, and she'll have to re-orient."

As I spoke, she was obeying, connecting me up to a new, Galactic channel.

For about two seconds, our channel request pulsed and was ignored.

"Give it another—" I began, but then they answered.

"This is Grand Admiral Sateekas," an imposing Mogwa said.

He was on screen now, and he didn't look pretty. I doubted his own brood-mother could have approved of his bloated body and wattled, squirming limbs. He looked old and fat—even for a Mogwa.

357

"Hello Mr. Grand Admiral," I called out. "I'm Centurion James McGill, and I've assumed command of this vessel—"

"Put me in contact with Magnate Slur," the Grand Admiral demanded.

"Well you see, sir, the crew is all dead…"

"Rebel slaves!" Sateekas rasped out. "It is as I conjectured. We've been watching your—"

"Hold on, Grand Admiral, hold on," I said, throwing my arms high. "We're not rebels. We're just the last people aboard this ship. The crew was killed by the actual rebels on this planet. They used X-rays to kill everyone aboard."

Grand Admiral Sateekas fell quiet for a second or two, and his nasty cluster of eyes crawled over the unfamiliar faces of my troops.

"Animals run the ship?" the Mogwa demanded. "Is this true? Who ordered the attack on the enemy vessel?"

"I did, sir. We're your local enforcers in Province 921. We're—"

"Silence, creature. Here are your orders: you will wheel and strike the ship again. You are distracting it, and you're allowing our fleet to close. Continue your actions."

"Yessir," I said. "As long as we're able, we will do so."

"I did not specify—"

Frantically, I made a cut-off motion to Natasha, who caught on quickly and aborted the connection.

"Now," I said, "dance like a monkey on a hot stove. We'll take one more shot then we'll run."

"What if it cuts us in half?" Carlos complained.

I glanced at him. "Then, just *maybe*, the Mogwa will spare Earth due to our sacrifice."

"Oh. Right."

We could hardly breathe or swallow as the battle continued—if you could call it that. It was more like a teasing session. We felt like a Chihuahua trying to piss off a grizzly bear. Our ship danced and cavorted, while we held onto straps and seats shaped all wrong for our bodies. We didn't even bother to fire anymore. All Natasha's attention was riveted on dodging that deadly slashing beam.

358

It occurred to us all at once after about thirty seconds that the AI wasn't trying all that hard to hit us.

"Is it even shooting at us?" I asked.

"No," Natasha said, "it appears to have shifted its attention to the real threat, the battle fleet. It's killed twenty more of them—and James, I have bad news. The Mogwa fleet is in range now, they'll start saturating this area with radiation any second now."

We glanced at each other, and I nodded. "Time to pull out. Go to warp."

"It's not safe this close to a gravity-well. We're not aligned toward any destination. If we—"

"Go to warp, dammit girl!"

She did so, and we flashed out of existence. As far as the other ships were concerned, we no longer existed. We were inside an Alcubierre warp bubble, drawn through space itself inside a "low-pressure" pocket of space that sucked us forward at terrific speeds.

"Warp back in," I said about a minute later.

Everyone had just begun to relax, sigh, and open their helmets. They choked when they heard my words.

"Don't tell me we're going back into that shit-storm!" Carlos complained.

We promptly came back into normal space. We were far from Arcturus IV, far from the battle, but still in the same star system.

"Align our helm, Natasha. Take your time. Then, warp us out for home."

She smiled at me at last. "You think the Mogwa will buy all this?" she asked.

"Let's send a final transmission to Grand Admiral Sateekas to make sure."

When she had the channel open, it was a one-way transmission. We were too far out to hold a normal conversation. The radio signal would take several minutes to reach the battle fleet.

"Grand Admiral Sateekas," I said. "We're your loyal allies and enforcers from Earth. We fought closer to the enemy than any ship in your fleet. We are almost unarmed, and we are damaged. We had to retreat, as your other ships have done throughout this glorious battle. We wish you well from Earth, and we will no doubt celebrate your victory soon. Centurion James McGill, out."

"Ha!" Carlos shouted when I was done. He came forward, clapped me on my armored shoulder, and beamed into my faceplate. "That was grade-A Georgia horseshit if I've ever heard it, McGill. If we live, I owe you a beer."

"I'll take you up on that when we get home, Ortiz."

While Natasha sweated to figure out our navigational parameters, I took the time to watch the battle unfold. The AI ship had done incredibly well. It had taken out close to a third of the enemy strength. Now, however, the Galactics were in too close. They had their main batteries in play, and they were scoring hits.

It was clear the AI ship was doomed.

"Warp out!" I ordered.

"What?"

"Now, before the damned Mogwa win this."

Natasha didn't slow me down to tell me how she wasn't ready yet. She just jumped on it. That's what I liked in a trooper of any rank. Action under fire.

We vanished again, and left Arcturus in our wake. I hoped never to return to this star system, and I doubted I ever would. After all, there was nothing left here other than a ripped up husk of a planet and some floating probes.

As we slid away to safety, my mind drifted to think of Floramel. She'd said she would live on with us. I supposed she meant in spirit. I vowed to remember her, as I remembered so many I'd seen perish and die their final deaths.

Overcome with fatigue, injuries, and a sense of sadness mixed with relief, I fell asleep in a dry Nairb bathtub. With my faceplate open, I dozed while others chattered and high-fived each other. Everyone was relieved to be heading away from this whole mess.

Only Natasha seemed nervous, I thought as my mind slipped away to dream. She was still trying to figure out how to control this ship.

Hoping she could get it right, I slid into a quiet, dark dream.

-61-

It took us about a week to get home. It was a rough ride, if the truth were to be told. We didn't have any human amenities. No showers, no changes of clothing. We were stuck in our battle suits the whole time, and we were getting pretty ripe by the time we reached Old Earth.

Sure, we could have taken our clothes off to bathe in one of those Nairb bathtubs, but no one wanted to try it. You see, the Nairbs didn't seem to like clean water. Their water was more *swampy*, like something a manatee would feel right at home in. Particulate matter and an unfiltered, gray-green slime was our only option on hand to fill these tubs.

Fortunately, our suits were equipped with emergency filtration systems. We could draw enough moisture and process it to keep us alive indefinitely. We just didn't smell too good.

During that long week, I tried my luck with just about every girl left alive on the ship. For some reason, they weren't interested. Maybe it was the fact we weren't bathing anymore. For myself, I figured that shouldn't have stopped anybody. Hell, if both partners stank that pretty much canceled out the problem in my mind. But the women disagreed, so I was left frustrated and bored until we came into sight of our home star system.

"James!" Natasha called out the moment we came out of warp.

Right off, I knew something undesirable was afoot. Not only because she'd called me by my first name, but also because there was a twinge of fear in her voice.

"What...? Oh..." I said, viewing the screens.

Ships swarmed Earth. Hundreds of them. They were so thick in numbers and size that they looked like an asteroid swarm in a tight orbit.

"Is Earth...?" I asked her.

Natasha worked her boards feverishly. "No, not yet. There's no sign of radiation, and the atmosphere is no more stirred up than usual."

We all breathed sighs of relief.

"What are we going to do?" Natasha asked me.

I was no starship captain, but I knew I had to make some hard choices and act like one.

"You think they know we are in-system yet?" I asked her.

"Probably."

"Dammit, I'd hoped to beat them here. This scout ship should be faster than the battlewagons."

She shrugged. "It probably is, but I'm no master at operating a Nairb vessel. Those warships are built by shipyards in the Core systems. Even if they're outdated by Mogwa standards, they can still move fast."

"Right... Well, we can't just run off now. Move toward Earth like we own the place."

Natasha bent to her work. Soon, the big ship turned, lurched into gear, and headed toward Earth. It didn't take more than a few hours before everyone took notice of us, and old Grand Admiral Sateekas himself was on the screen again.

"Centurion," Natasha whispered to me before I had the chance to say 'hello,' "Central wants to talk to you too."

"Right... but I can't be rude. Conference-up the calls."

"What is this delay?" Sateekas demanded. "Why am I being kept waiting by beasts?"

"I'm sorry, Grand Admiral," I said. "We're not a professional starship crew."

"That is a lie," he said flatly.

Alarmed, I looked around the room. I'd told a lot of lies in my life, some only this morning, but this time I'd spoken the God's-honest truth.

"Uh… what did I say that was wrong?"

"We observed your maneuvering in battle firsthand. It was masterful and brave beyond description. I've had two of my own captains flayed and killed repeatedly while they were forced to observe your example. They will be revived when the process is finished with two steps lost in rank."

This was all news to me, and it was somewhat disturbing, but I've never been a man to pass up on praise.

"You think we did pretty well then?" I asked. "Did you hear that, Central? Are you recording this?"

"We are, McGill," said a pissed-off and very familiar feminine voice.

It was none other than Galina Turov. Seeing her again made me wonder how she'd recovered her rank and position back at Central after the failed invasion of Earth. That woman was twice as slippery as Winslade, but at least she was pretty.

Natasha put Turov up on the screen split with the Mogwa admiral. It was quite a comparison.

"Grand Admiral," she said, "I want to apologize for all of Earth, regarding any problems McGill might have caused you. He's a disobedient braggart, who—"

"Silence, creature!" the Mogwa boomed. "He is your best. He is your finest. He all but committed suicide before my eyes at my slightest whim—an exemplary minion. If I possessed a thousand like him I'd have won our recent conflict in the Core."

Galina shut up. Her face went red, and her lips were a tight line, but she stopped talking and shook her head in disbelief.

"Now, McGill," Sateekas went on, "I haven't been able to tell you how pleased I was with your attack. You single-handedly saved me a hundred ships, if my strategists are to be believed."

"Really?" I said. "I thought it might have been more like two hundred."

The Mogwa made farting sounds and quivered. I assumed he was laughing.

"Yes! That's the spirit! It makes my duty now all the sadder."

"Um... what duty is that, sir?"

"Why, the removal of your species, of course. It's always like this on the frontier. A promising, aggressive breed is identified. Rather than attaching the yoke and cinching it tight, the prissy beings from the home stars begin to flap their limbs and bleat about regulations."

I swallowed hard, sensing the importance of the next few moments of this conversation. Galina had changed her attitude as well. She'd gone white now, rather than the flushed red of anger. But she was still staying quiet. Her eyes studied me, and they were pleading.

Taking in a breath, I puffed out my chest and regarded Sateekas. To me, he seemed more grounded and reasonable than your average snooty Galactic.

"Well sir," I said, "perhaps we can work something out. What's the nature of the problem, exactly?"

"It's very simple, really. You've fought hard and well. But you've also spawned technology that is dangerously advanced. That AI ship—it was as good as our best back home."

"You've got that kind of tech?" I asked. "With the phasing, the lateral slashing of that beam, and—"

"Yes, yes, of course," he said. "Did you really think this collection of rust-buckets was the pride of the Mogwa fleet? Hardly. Battle Fleet 921 is a made up of outdated patrol boats. We don't need our main battle-line ships out here on the frontier, you see."

The funny thing was, I *did* see. Empires always operated like this. Back in Earth history, Europeans had their best armies arrayed along their borders in Europe. Out in the bush, they sent cast-offs along with soldiers that needed discipline. The Colonial officers weren't always the favored sons back then, either. They were people the rulers were just as happy to place in an outpost in the weeds.

It occurred to me that Sateekas himself had to be just such a creature. He was probably irritating to his fellows back home— an old warrior who was so blunt, so practical, and so intolerant of foppish behavior he was a liability in the Emperor's court.

Because he was effective, they'd given him a command, but he'd been assigned to the worst of duties due to his personality.

I could commiserate with old Sateekas. Under different circumstances, I might even have been able to call him a friend. But today was a special day, and I had to get my mind into gear.

"So," I said, "you're saying that because the rogues built that ship, we all have to go?"

"I'm afraid so. It's a typical situation, really. I must apologize for discipline that may seem strict to you. That display of firepower is unacceptable on the frontier. There are other violations, of course, but that one cinched your fate."

"Hmmm," I said chewing it over.

All around me, my crew was pale. They looked like they were already dead. They knew we couldn't fight the battle fleet. Sure, there were only about eight hundred main-line vessels left, but our navy consisted of less than a hundred ships. Not to mention we were easily outclassed by the Galactics in addition to outnumbered.

No, this had to be done without fireworks. The problem was figuring out how...

"Well then," Sateekas said, giving himself a shake. "Time's pressing. If you would be so kind as to fly your ship into your local star, I'd be grateful. I'll go so far as to put a positive footnote into my log about your species."

"Uh..." I said. "That's a mighty fine offer, Grand Admiral, but if you could indulge me for just a few more moments? I promise not to pester you for long."

He made a rasping sound. I thought it might be a sigh.

"Be quick about it."

"Yessir. Firstly, why didn't you dust off Earth already? Surely, you've got plenty of planet-busters on board for the purpose?"

"Thousands of them," Sateekas assured me. "We've plotted out the precise placement. Enough to be sure, but not wasteful. No more than fifty will do the job. The atmosphere will be gone, the oceans boiled off, but we don't have to dig down to the magma. That's inefficient overkill and I won't have it."

"Good thinking… but you didn't exactly answer my question, sir. Why'd you wait?"

"I thought that was abundantly clear, creature. Perhaps I overestimated your cognitive powers—but no matter. We waited for your ship to return here. Otherwise, we'd have needed to go off searching for it. Fortunately, you saved us that valuable time. I'll think of it as a final service on your stellar record."

"I live to serve," I said. "But there's another thing bothering me."

"Really? Be quick about it!"

"Why is Earth being blamed for the actions of the rogues?"

"Blamed? You're not being blamed, you're being credited. That's just as bad in this case, of course. The rogue animals were human, you're human, therefore all humans must be expunged."

"Ah!" I said, brightening. "I think I've put my finger on the source of our mutual problem, sir. The rogues weren't human. Not at all. They might have *looked* human, but I assure you they were not."

The Mogwa studied me for a second. I heard another chattering voice off to his left, and I thought to see just a flash of a green flipper. Could this guy have Nairbs aboard, telling him what kind of protocols he could and could not break? I bet he did. We all had our masters, in the end.

"You are in error," Sateekas said. "I've just gotten confirmation. My science team is ninety-nine percent sure you're a match. There are no preserved specimens to study, unfortunately, but judging by habits, appearance, and a dozen other parameters, my crew—"

"What about DNA?" I asked. "What if there is a significant variance in our DNA?"

Sateekas ruffled himself. "That would be conclusive, of course, but as there is no DNA to test—"

"Hold on," I said, "I've got some DNA. A small sample, but it might be enough."

Everyone aboard my ship stared at me. So did Sateekas. He looked annoyed, but it was hard to decipher the expressions of a Mogwa.

That green-flippered bastard off to his left began chattering again. Sateekas listened and then turned back to the viewscreen.

"Are you making a formal motion to stay action on the basis of new physical evidence?"

"I am," I said loudly.

"This is most unusual. It's more than that, it's troublesome. I'm almost ready to take back all the praise I so recently heaped upon you and your squalid little species, McGill."

"I'm really terribly sorry to give you trouble, Grand Admiral," I said. "But this is rather important to me and my people."

"Typical self-centeredness," he complained. "I'm seeing it everywhere. In fact, I'm going to strike the positive note from my log after your species is eradicated."

"That'd be a sad thing, sir," I said. "But I can understand how you feel. Now, what's the next step in resolving our motion for a stay?"

Things became technical after that, and I stepped back from the view screens. Lawyers showed up at Central, and they argued with the Nairbs. Each side filed briefs, codified rules, and all kinds of other garbage to certify the results of a DNA test as valid.

In the meantime, Natasha pulled me aside and whispered harshly in my ear.

"I don't know if I can do it, James," she said, breathing shallowly.

"You look like you're in a panic, girl," I said. "What's wrong?"

"Your promise to produce evidence we don't have, that's what. Earth can't do it. They'll quarantine this ship first, that's what they're talking about now. That means we'll have to rely entirely on what we have at hand. You've put me in a terrible spot, James—I mean, don't get me wrong, you did what you had to do, you lied, and—"

I gripped her arm. She lifted her eyes to meet mine. I could see that the weight of all the world was on her shoulders. She was in a full-blown anxiety attack, and she could hardly think.

"Settle down," I said in soothing tone. "We'll be all right. You don't have to do anything. I've got the evidence—at least, I think I do."

She stared at me without comprehension.

"You have DNA from the lab people? Where? Why?"

"Um…" I said, feeling slightly embarrassed. "Well, you know how we haven't taken showers for days…? I'm still wearing the same clothes I had on the day we left Arcturus IV."

I stopped there, and I stared into her eyes. I knew she was a smart girl. She would figure it out eventually.

When she finally did, she slapped me, and I smiled sheepishly.

-62-

Natasha's hand pulled back for another swing, but I caught her wrist. I did it gently, so I wouldn't break it. I actually had practice with that maneuver, having been slapped by any number of angry women on various occasions.

"You should be happy," I told her.

Still breathing hard, she dropped her eyes, and her hand fell to her side.

"You're telling me you've got Floramel's DNA in your pants, aren't you?" she demanded. "You pig."

"That's right. At least, it should still be measurable. We—"

"I'm not going to do it," she said, crossing her arms. "I'm not going to dissect your disgusting underwear to prove anything."

"Natasha, you probably won't have to. They'll send up some kind of expert or something."

She aimed a trembling finger at the viewscreen. "You haven't been listening, have you? You never listen!"

"Well… I heard some parts."

"Right. They've decided no representatives from either party will be allowed to handle the evidence on this ship, on the grounds it might introduce contamination. They want a joint delegation to come here and observe while we extract and display the test results ourselves!"

"Hmm..." I said, chewing that over. "That does sound indiscreet. But listen, we might be saving all of Humanity. You should be happy I've got an alibi for us."

"It's still upsetting, James."

"Yeah, I understand. I guess I've got a weakness for a pretty face. You know that. Everyone does."

Natasha sighed. She still wasn't meeting my eyes, and it made me feel bad. I'd had a thing for her for years. She'd felt the same way for much longer. I didn't want to hurt her, but I needed her to help make this thing go right.

"I'm sorry," I said quietly, "I'm a jackrabbit when it comes to women. I understand how you might hate that. But you and I haven't been together for a long time. And on this single occasion, my character flaw might actually help save Earth."

"I'm glad, in a way," she admitted. "Okay, I'll do it. But I'm telling you, James McGill, as God is my witness, if this doesn't work out, and they decide to dust off Earth after all—I'm going to kill you personally. As my final action."

Smiling, I took out my sidearm, handed it to her butt-first and nodded. "In that case, you can be my guest, Specialist."

"You realize this 'evidence' might not help us? The rogues were based on humans genetically. They appear to be adapted from our line, manipulated artificially, but who knows how the Nairbs will judge such a case?"

"If you've got a better play, you'd better make it known right now."

Natasha sighed. "Find a plastic bag or something. They're shipping up a genetics kit both sides have approved of. I'm going to do this as a professional."

"That's the spirit!" I boomed at her, but she gave me a dirty look.

Carlos was ordered to help her, as the unit's last surviving bio. When he discovered what the sample was—he freaked out a little.

"No way!" he exclaimed. "This has to be some kind of a joke. McGill is screwing with us again, isn't he?"

We painstakingly explained the situation to him, and he reluctantly aided Natasha in the procedure.

"You owe me for this, McGill," he said. "If Kivi and I ever have a baby, you're changing its diapers until he's potty-trained."

"You're on, Ortiz. Now, get in there and do it right."

Grumbling, he worked with Natasha. A few hours went by. That's all that it took. Our equipment was pretty good by now, with medical automation having reached advanced stages.

I would be the first to admit I was a little nervous when they finished up and turned in the sample with the preliminary results. Natasha herself looked sick.

"How'd it go?" I asked her.

Her face was ashen. She gave her head a tiny shake.

"I did what I could," she said. "But I don't know how this will go, James."

That concerned me. Natasha was a worrier of the first stripe, but she had a handle on technical things like this. If she thought the whole test was a failure—it probably was.

More waiting began as Grand Admiral Sateekas' crew went to work on the data we'd provided. They took longer to get back to us than Natasha and Carlos had.

"They have to be debating the findings," I said, daring to hope. "That's good, isn't it?"

Natasha nodded slightly. Something about her demeanor tipped me off. I began to question her about the nature of what she'd found. She responded with noncommittal, vague statements.

Before I could get anything useful out of her, Grand Admiral Sateekas finally got back to us. He glowered through the projected image. I didn't know much about Mogwa emotions, but the way his limbs were squirming he looked pissed off to me.

"I'm speaking to the McGill?" he asked.

"Yes, Grand Admiral."

"Good. I wanted you online to witness the first of many executions."

My blood went cold. So it was to be killing time. If he asked me to execute my crew, I knew I wouldn't do it. I'd order Natasha to flee or even attack. Sure, our transport couldn't outrun them or do so much as scratch a line on their smallest cruiser's hull, but I wasn't going down without a fight.

"This creature," Sateekas continued, "has bitterly failed us."

The camera view shifted to include the figure of a Nairb. The green blob of flesh looked deflated.

"I don't understand these findings, Lord," the Nairb said. "They're impossible to credit."

"Untrue," Sateekas bubbled. "It makes perfect sense. I should have known from the moment I saw these brave slaves risking their lives to aid my fleet. Who is forever whining about the incompetence and untrustworthiness of humans? Why, you are, Magnate."

"My grievances have been filed with good cause," the Nairb bleated through its translator.

"Silence!" Sateekas boomed. "I've heard enough of your worthless prattle."

So saying, he blasted a smoking hole through the Nairbs' head. This startled me, and I have to admit, put a tiny smile on my face.

"He will not be revived," the Grand Admiral admonished his crew. "His file will be purged, and every record of his existence is to be expunged from the Treasury of Erudition."

I cleared my throat, and Sateekas whirled back to the camera pickup.

"There!" he said. "Did you see? Did you witness justice being done?"

"That was a sight for sore eyes, Grand Admiral," I assured him. "I've never seen a Mogwa serve Galactic Law better than you do."

"And it will not end there. Your evidence was conclusive, if shocking. Who would have dreamt the Nairbs were handing Empire secrets to these rogues as you call them? Who would have believed such treachery was even conceivable to this servile race?"

"Who indeed?" I asked, catching on. I gave Natasha a glance which she didn't return. She was still white-faced and staring straight ahead.

Natasha was a rules-follower, born and bred, but it was obvious she'd given the Mogwa Nairb DNA instead of human. Or maybe it was some mix of the two. That she'd pulled it off was the surprising part. People often tried to mimic my trickery, but they typically didn't have the natural flair for it and failed miserably.

"It makes too much sense," the Mogwa continued in the tone of a creature talking to itself. "How could a collection of animals living in the dark out here on the fringe of the fringe build a ship like that? Impossible—without help. The Nairbs provided the guiding light. My only question now is whether they did it for profit or for worse reasons. Could they be rebels in disguise? Snakes hugged to our bosom for so many long centuries?"

"Best to be sure," I told him. "My advice is to torture it out of them. Don't let them squirm and lie, either. Give them everything you've got."

The Mogwa took a sudden interest in me. He stopped musing to himself and stared out of the screen for a moment.

"This brings me to my next, sadder duty. No doubt you've already surmised what it is."

"What?" I asked excitedly. "Is the battle fleet setting course for the Nairb homeworld, with a dozen planet busters cooking in your hold?"

"No," Sateekas said. "Only those Nairbs who were on station here in this frontier province will be exterminated. It's going on right now all over my fleet and throughout the province."

"What then, sir? I can't guess."

"Loyal, fierce—but stupid," he said, looking at me closely. "A perfect combination in any trained animal. Such a grim loss for the Empire. We could use more species like the humans, but so often we end up being forced to delete them."

My eyebrows furrowed. I was beginning to get a bad vibe again.

"Uh…" I said. "What are you talking about, Grand Admiral? Could you spell it out for your most loyal subject?"

"You humans are to be removed," he said. "From the cosmos, in your entirety. The rogue-creatures were human. The

Nairbs gave them illegal tech, that's true, they seemed to have mixed genetically with you—disgusting bestial cloning. But you humans aren't without guilt. Your species accepted this criminal gift. That was your doom."

I blinked at the big ugly face on my screen. The Mogwa was right—things weren't going my way today.

Looking around at my team, I saw shocked expressions across the board. We'd all thought we were in the clear, and learning all over again we were about to get snuffed out as a species was hitting them hard.

What I was really hoping for was a good idea, as I was fresh out.

Natasha was my first stop. I fixed her with a wide-eyed stare. She gave it right back to me—putting up her hands and shrugging in the classic "I don't know" gesture.

Next, I swept my gaze over the rest, still hoping. So many weren't on hand: Kivi, Leeson, Graves—hell, I'd even have welcomed a suggestion from Harris, had he been here to share this lovely moment.

But he wasn't. None of them were.

There was one party to this conversation, however, who'd been keeping uncharacteristically quiet. That was Galina Turov. She chose this moment to speak up.

"Grand Admiral!" she called out in a slightly shrill tone. Maybe panic was beginning to set in down there inside Central. "This person—James McGill—he isn't the only party involved. Please speak to us and let us make our case."

"That would be a gross error," Sateekas said, gesturing aggressively with his foremost pair of appendages. Flaps of his old skin wobbled where his legs met his lumpy body. "Only the McGill has saved your species until now. He performed optimally, and if there was any way to allow the continuance of this deadly variety of beasts, I'd support it. Unfortunately, Galactic Law is very specific about dangerous animals when they are identified on the frontier. They must be destroyed."

Galina didn't know what to think after that. She stared at Sateekas like a deer in the headlights, uncertain if she should argue or shut up to avoid making things worse.

"McGill," hissed a voice to my side.

I looked, and I was surprised to see Carlos. "What?" I whispered back.

"You remember when we faced our first Nairb? When we fought the saurian in hand-to-hand at the spaceport on Steel World?"

Blinking, I did recall the moment. We'd gotten into trouble then, and we'd all been ordered to self-execute. The saurian had done so immediately, but we'd argued until we weaseled out of it.

"McGill?" boomed the grand admiral.

I turned back to the screen, looking dumbfounded. "What is it, sir?"

"Do not besmirch your achievements. Accept your fate with honor. You will be given a footnote—I swear it—and it will be positive in nature. That will be your legacy, and scholars throughout the Empire will be able to find the item in the Imperial Archives... Should they choose, for some reason, to search for it."

"Um... that would be a great honor, your excellency," I said. "I thank you profusely for offering to bless me with such an incalculable gift. But unfortunately, I must file a grievance."

"A grievance?" growled the Mogwa. "What's this? My estimation of the quality of your species is dropping once again just upon hearing those words!"

"I'm sorry sir, but I feel I must do it. Justice must—"

"Justice?" the Mogwa demanded. "No, no, this is base cowardice. Self-serving malignancy. I've been deceived. You are *not* the servile creature I thought you to be."

"Nevertheless," I said, "as a citizen of the Empire, I have the right—"

"No… you don't," Sateekas assured me. "That regulation has been abused, and it is waived under these circumstances."

"Could you explain, sir?"

"I'm no Nairb, I'm the Grand Admiral of Battle Fleet 921. You can't file a grievance only to obstruct justice being meted out against your person, I hereby disallow it. Your species will be exterminated, and now that you've dared to complain, there will be no footnote glorifying your species."

"That's a shame, sir," I said, "but it has nothing to do with what I'm filing a grievance about. I'm filing on behalf of the Nairbs."

"What?" the Mogwa asked in confusion. "What for?"

"For their protection. They are citizens of the Empire as well, aren't they?"

"Why, of course they are. What exactly is the nature of your grievance?"

"*Their* grievance, sir," I said. "I wish to file an official grievance on behalf of the Nairbs. You're hereby formally notified of my intention to—"

"Stop! Stop this foul ejectus flying from your mouth-parts! I won't hear any more of this kind of—"

About then, a greenish blob popped up its head into view. I saw the grand admiral, who was lunging with multiple limbs, violently reach for the Nairb to shove him aside, but the Nairb ducked.

"I need council!" I shouted. "Official representation and adjudication!"

The Nairb burbled frantically into the translator. "Grand Admiral Sateekas—the situation has altered."

"Why haven't you been executed yet?" Sateekas complained.

"The situation has changed," the Nairb repeated. "By Galactic statute, we must hear out this primitive's grievance."

Sateekas looked ruffled and angry. His floppy side-gills were rising and falling rapidly.

"I must remind you, sir," the Nairb continued, "that every action you take is being recorded and relayed to the Core Worlds. Any violation of Galactic Law will likely result in harsh penalties."

"Harsh penalties? Are you daring to threaten a Mogwa commander?"

"Not at all, Grand Admiral. I'm merely informing you of the legal situation and your status within that framework."

"Double-talk!" Sateekas fumed. "This sort of thing is exactly why I wanted you out of the way."

"I'm sorry to disappoint, sir," the Nairb said primly. "But I'm quite certain that the human is within his rights to protest on our behalf."

"Oh, don't tell me… Now you're going to offer a protest to protect him, aren't you?"

The Nairb looked startled. His kind wasn't the corruptible type. They were naturally bureaucratic, more concerned with the rules than the results of their misapplication.

"I have no such intentions. I'm merely stating the obvious."

"Which is?"

"Grievances on the frontier must be handled by Nairb officials. If you delete all of us in this province, there will be no one to serve this function."

"Excellent!" Sateekas said, folding a medial limb and drawing out a weapon from his left side. "Then you've discovered the solution to my problems. I'll remove you first, then the humans, as they won't have anyone to appeal to."

The Nairb drew itself up and stood bravely in front of the weapon muzzle as the sighting frames fluttered and then locked in on the contours of his bulbous head.

"That would be unwise, Grand Admiral," he said and closed his eyes against the bright glare of the targeting mechanism.

"Why?" Sateekas asked. His optical organs slightly constricted into something like a squint.

"It would be construed as a manipulation of justice. A violation of Galactic Law. Even Mogwa are subject to it. Upon returning to the Core Worlds and making your report, you would likely face charges."

The Mogwa relaxed and wagged a gnarled digit at the Nairb. "I doubt that. My report, and the records that will exist at that point in time will show—"

"I must hereby inform you," the Nairb said in an official tone, "that the situation has already been relayed to the Admiralty via deep-link."

The grand admiral made a gargling noise of shock and rage which failed to be translated into our language.

"You've gone over my head? Already?"

"Not at all. I'm merely—"

But Sateekas took a swipe at him, forcing the Nairb to retreat.

"All right," the Mogwa said. "Never defeated in battle, but always losing to regulations. I'll allow your investigation to proceed."

Puffing up big and green again, the Nairb turned toward me through the camera pickup.

"All right then," he said. "Let's hear the details of your grievance. Possibly, it will be trivial and tossed out immediately."

Now, one has to understand that I've dealt with the Nairbs before. The right course with them was never to engage quickly, never to get to a hard conclusion. Investigations could easily take on a life of their own if you did it right.

"Sir," I said, "I must consult legal experts before making my formal complaint. My statements were only meant to serve as a notification of my intentions."

"Understood," the Nairb said. "Your comprehension of the process impresses us. How long will you need to organize your statement?"

"Uh… five months," I said.

"Five months!?" boomed Sateekas, unable to contain himself.

The Nairb adjusted his flippers. "The Grand Admiral is quite right," he said. "It's my educated opinion that a matter of this extreme import can't be formulated so quickly. I would suggest a period of two years at a minimum. We're talking about a situation spanning several star systems and a population of many thousands."

"Damned straight," I said.

The two then fell to arguing, the grand admiral aghast at the delay, the Nairb staunchly sticking to his regulations.

A light touch on my shoulder made me turn and face Natasha. She had a smile on her lips.

"That was masterful, James," she said in a whisper.

I smiled back. "That's how you handle two ornery swamp-snakes. Tie their tails together and let them fight it out."

She chuckled, shaking her head.

On the screen, the aliens were still going at it. I had the feeling they were going to be doing so for a long time, so I turned down the sound, leaned back in my chair and took a nap.

-64-

The next few days were a whirlwind. The battle fleet was stalemated in a legal battle, and I could almost feel their frustration as I stared out the windows of the highest offices in Central.

"That Sateekas fellow," I said, "he's really angry."

"That's right," Imperator Turov said. "And he's angry with *you*. I wonder if we could hand you over and get him to give up on burning Earth…"

That comment made me turn away from the window. The view through slanted, tinted glass had held my attention for a long time. They'd done a lot of reconstruction on old Central, and the gargantuan pyramid-shape structure was bigger than ever.

"You're not serious?" I asked her. "That kind of appeasement could only serve to whet his appetite. You don't feed a bear part of your sandwich and expect him to go away. He'll stick around, wanting it all."

Turov glowered at me, while Graves and Deech looked thoughtful.

"Don't give me any of your backwoods wisdom, McGill," Turov told me.

She seemed angrier every time I talked to her, so I shrugged and went back to staring up at the fleet overhead.

The Galactic ships really *were* blotting out the sky. There were so many—eight hundred or more—that people claimed portions of the Earth had dropped a few degrees in temperature over recent weeks due to less sunlight reaching the surface.

No one spoke much for the next several minutes. They did look uncomfortable and uncertain, however.

Finally, the man we were all waiting for arrived.

"Equestrian Drusus," Turov said. "So good to see you. Congratulations, again, on your promotion."

Something in her voice as she spoke these words tipped me off. That was it. She was angry because Drusus had gotten credit for our mission. He was in my chain of command, and he had therefore gotten the accolades for keeping Earth from certain destruction.

"Thank you, Imperator," Drusus said coldly.

"Can I ask on behalf of everyone here," she continued, "why you've called this meeting?"

"Certainly. First of all, I have an announcement to make: I've been awarded operational command of Earth's defenses."

Turov smiled, but her teeth were clenched. "That's wonderful," she managed to force out.

Drusus turned to me next. He stepped forward, and a tight smile appeared on his face.

"Centurion James McGill," he said. "A legend in his own time..."

"Thank you, Equestrian."

Drusus gave me a bemused headshake. "It's not entirely good—the legend you've created."

"I'll take it anyway. It's rare enough a man gets credit for anything around here."

Turov's eyes flashed when I said that. She took it as a barb—and it had been meant as one. She was infamous for stealing the thunder of everyone around her. The main reason she was pissed off today was she hadn't managed to convince anyone this solution had been her idea.

"McGill's right," Graves said suddenly.

Everyone looked at him in surprise. As a general rule, Graves never argued or spoke out of turn when in the presence of superior officers. He was as respectful of authority as he expected his own men to be.

"What do you mean, Primus?" Drusus asked.

"McGill deserves credit for this astounding scenario—all of it, I mean. The good, the bad—and the extremely bad."

"You're saying that without his influence, the Mogwa fleet wouldn't be hanging over our heads like the Sword of Damocles?"

Graves nodded. "Yes… that, and the deal with the Nairbs. He cut that on the spot without prompting or premeditation."

"A miraculous turn of events…" Drusus agreed. "On that point, I'm authorized to present Centurion McGill with a commendation."

He produced a small, black box. From this box he extracted a silver four-pointed star.

Turov's eyes flew wide. She stared as if mesmerized. "Is that the Dawn Star?" she asked in a hushed tone.

"Yes. The Ruling Council passed the resolution last night, in a closed session. For his part in this action, McGill is to be recognized as a planetary hero."

Turov seemed more stunned than I was.

"Here," Drusus said, offering her the sparkling medal. "You can do the honors, as he was below you in the direct chain of command."

This seemed to snap her out of it. She took the medal, and then she looked at Deech and Graves. It was sometimes customary to pass the duty of bestowing an honor down to the direct commanders.

But she passed on that idea. Instead, she took in a deep breath and stepped up to me.

I stood at attention, as stunned as anyone else in the room.

A medal? *I* was getting a medal? That just wasn't how things usually worked out for simple, old James McGill.

The medal was an old-fashioned thing, too. It didn't use nano-adhesives, probably having been manufactured a century ago. The legends said that there were only seven of these medals in existence, and those who held them had to surrender them at death.

Opening the clasp on the back, she smiled up at me, and I beamed back down at her.

384

"Centurion James McGill," she began in a formal voice. "I hereby honor you with the Dawn Star. Wear her with pride, honor, and distinction."

"Thank you, Impera—"

I stopped right there, because she jabbed the thing into my chest. The pin punched right through my dress uniform and stuck in my right pectoral muscle. Almost immediately, blood began to dribble down inside my tunic.

"You're welcome," she said, giving me a tiny, mean smile.

I'd managed not to yelp, or even gasp. To maintain the illusion that all was well, I kept smiling back at her, and I nodded my thanks.

Slightly put out that I'd done nothing to show pain, she turned around on her heel and presented me with a flourish to the group. They clapped with muted popping sounds as their hands beat together.

Right then, despite everything, I felt honored.

"All right," Drusus said. "Now that the festivities are over, we have some serious news to report. The Mogwa grand admiral has been on the deep-link to the Core Worlds for days."

We all sobered up in a hurry.

"Equestrian?" I asked.

"What is it, McGill?"

"That can't be a good thing. Sateekas is determined to do us harm. He must be appealing the legal actions of the Nairbs, or trying to speed them up, or something."

"That's what we assume," he agreed. "He'll be calling here shortly, and he's demanded that you be present for the call."

It was time for me to start sweating. I hadn't expected anything like this. I turned toward the back wall of Drusus' office, which was really a giant screen.

"Is there something special I should say, sir?" I asked.

"Yes," he said. "As little as possible, McGill—please."

"Right, got it."

The pin on the back of my new medal stung in my chest. I was glad we weren't wearing dress-whites, or everyone there would have seen the blood soaking into my uniform.

Sateekas didn't keep us waiting for long. Drusus connected up a holo-globe in the middle of the office and signaled that we were all assembled, as ordered.

"This is it?" Grand Admiral Sateekas asked. "The team of grunting humans that has so wrongly sought to evade justice?"

"We constitute the officers above McGill in the chain of command, sir," Drusus said. "I'm at the top of that chain, recently given the honor of coordinating all Earth's defenses."

Sateekas' numerous eyes swept over the group.

Suddenly, it occurred to me that this "honor" I'd been bestowed with, along with Drusus' sudden promotion, had been a setup. Perhaps the former commander hadn't felt like facing the music with the Mogwa today.

Wondering what fate might be offered to us, I looked at the Mogwa with a mix of curiosity and disgust. *Damn*, he was ugly. He reminded me of that time my cousin Shelby got poison oak on his balls and up his backside. I managed not to point that out, however, and felt proud of my self-control.

"Your species is to be offered a choice," Sateekas said. "Either your collection of star systems will be broken up on the grounds you now control an illegal number of worlds due to conquest, or you'll have to contribute to the Empire in a more meaningful fashion."

We eyed one another. What should we say? No one wanted to speak up and blow it.

Finally, when I'd been about to blurt the obvious question in everyone's mind, Drusus spoke up.

"May we ask what our contribution to the mighty Empire should be, sir?" he asked.

The Mogwa eyed him again. "There is another troublesome faction growing in a neighboring province," he said. "You would be tasked with quelling the growing threat. That would allow me to return to the Core Worlds sooner and with fewer losses."

We all frowned, not quite getting why we were being told all this.

"Grand Admiral," Drusus said, "we're honored you would include us in this conversation, but we aren't in charge of Earth. The Ruling Council—"

"No!" boomed the Mogwa. "I won't hear of such nonsense. Civil authorities never supervise military personnel. That's a perversion of order I won't accept in any species."

We were stunned. Was this alien actually asking *us* to make this fateful choice?

"Still... sir..." Drusus said, "we must consult others on a decision of such gravity."

"No," the Mogwa repeated. "You will choose *now*. This is an offer of settlement. Either way, all charges against Earth will be dropped. Your species will continue to infest this region of space—for now."

"We can't discuss this with anyone else?" Turov asked, daring to speak up.

"I said not. Are your auditory organs compromised in some fashion?"

She shook her head and stepped back.

Sateekas' eyes swept the group, and they landed on me.

"That one. The rebel. I want his opinion."

"Uh..." I said. "I'm not fit to judge, your excellency."

"No, you're not. But I want to hear your thoughts anyway. Will you cling to your little kingdom out here on the fringe of endless darkness, or will you go to war seeking the incomprehensible glory that awaits you even farther in the void?"

It was my turned to look scared. I admit, I'm sometimes a man who doesn't know his place, but I knew this was way above my pay grade. I pointed a finger at Drusus.

"He's the newly appointed Earth commander. I can't go against his wishes."

"Hmm," the Mogwa said, "it is as I thought. You're earlier actions *were* reflective of your superiors. Why else would you defer to them when asked for an opinion?"

"Um..." I said. "That's not what I meant."

"Your words reveal you, soldier. My respect grows. You have been honored today, I understand, with a trinket. Is this true?"

I looked down at the shining Dawn Star on my chest. I nodded slowly.

"What else would a soldier be rewarded for other than a job well done?" demanded the Mogwa. "Stop avoiding my query. What would be your choice? Would you keep your frail kingdom and fight for it, or would you give it all up for peace at any cost?"

My eyes slid from one face to another among the circle of officers. They looked scared. We all knew this was serious business.

"All right," I said, "as long as this is just an opinion—I'd take peace. Earth could stand alone again without her new possessions."

The Mogwa ruffled itself and looked around at the others.

"Which of you creatures signaled him to make this choice?" he demanded.

White-faced, they all denied it.

"Very well," he said coldly. "It doesn't matter anyway. You're a more clever lot than I'd imagined. I chose to ask this man's opinion because I'm sure there's no fear in his heart. Apparently, this isn't the case with all humans."

"Well, Grand Admiral," Drusus began. "Now that you've heard McGill's choice, for the sake of curiosity I'm sure, let's adjourn this meeting and—"

"No!" the Mogwa boomed again. "Stop squirming. I like food to wriggle, but you are just irritating me. I pose the same question to you, high commander of Earth—with a slight alteration."

"And... what would that alteration be, sir?"

"The removal of the peaceful option. McGill already took that one."

"Um... I don't understand, sir. There's only one other choice you presented—war. Is that right?"

"And they said you dark-worlders were all stupid. Yes, that's right. Choose."

"What's the point?" Drusus had the balls to say. "What kind of choice can be made from a list of a single option?"

"The point is that if you choose it, I will drop my legal actions against you and the Nairbs."

388

Drusus blinked, and then he stood tall. "In that case, sir, I would opt to keep our conquests and go to war on behalf of the Empire."

"Excellent!" the Mogwa said, suddenly happy. "I accept your offer. I hereby—"

At this point, a green bulbous head peeped up into view on the vid pickup.

"Excuse me," the Nairb said. "If I may be so bold as to request a clarification."

Sateekas looked annoyed, but he didn't say anything.

All of us were beginning to get it. This elaborate dance of offers, threats and declarations was part of some kind of arcane legal process. The Empire was old—countless millennia old—and like any old political entity it had the worst bureaucracy you could dream up.

"What is it?" Drusus asked.

"You're the chief defense coordinator of Earth?" the Nairb asked.

"Yes," Drusus admitted.

"You have chosen to accept the grand admiral's offer of settlement?"

"I have," Drusus said unhappily.

"Very well. Committed and confirmed. This case is now at a close. Court is dismissed. All charges are summarily dropped."

The orb suddenly went dark. All of us were left staring at it, dumbfounded.

"Uh..." I said. "You'd better relay that recording to the Ruling Council... I'm just saying..."

Turov stared at me. "That's why he went to you first," she said. "He wanted that answer all along. It was the only answer that would be acceptable to him."

"I guess so."

"I can't believe that happened," Drusus said. "I lost control of the conversation. The stakes were so high—I couldn't see a way out of it."

Drusus dismissed everyone, except for me. When they'd all left, he tapped my shoulder, and I stayed.

He looked me over with squinting eyes. "That's what it feels like to be you, isn't it?" he asked me.

"Pardon, sir?"

"I was faced with grim choices and put on the spot..." he explained. "Damned if you do or if you don't..."

"Oh, right—yes, that's exactly what it feels like to be me, sir."

Drusus nodded, his shoulders slumped. He waved me off, and I exited, dismissed.

-65-

We'd promised to wage war on an unknown alien menace in a neighboring province—but most of the people of Earth didn't know about that part. The Ruling Council had decided to swear us all to secrecy on penalty of perma-death. So far, we'd kept that promise.

Two months had passed since Battle Fleet 921 had left Earth's orbit for a second time. The people of our world were understandably relieved. Many were jubilant. There were parties, and rallies. Politicians promised the future would be brighter and different. Those they governed seemed to believe them even more than they usually did.

But I knew it was all a lie. War was again in our near future. War against an unknown enemy who lived on dirtballs like ours, circling distant stars. It was the same-old, same-old, for me.

When at last our legion mustered out, I returned home to Waycross. Etta hugged me—a shocker in itself—as did my parents. My mom wasn't in good shape, however.

"You're shaking, Momma," I told her, looking her over carefully.

"It's nothing, just a tremor," she said, forcing a smile on her face through her pain.

"That's good," I told her, giving her a smile back. "You look *good*."

I was lying, of course. She looked like she was on death's door. She was in a floating chair now, a machine equipped with padding, repellers and a touch-steering system.

"Come on in for supper," she told me, and the whole family circled around the table and ate.

My dad had done the cooking. I could tell this right off, because everything tasted like cardboard. Burnt cardboard. But I kept right on smiling and talking up everything all evening long.

Afterward, I snapped my fingers and stood up suddenly.

"What's wrong, James?" Momma asked.

"I forgot," I said. "I'm supposed to go pick up Della at the sky-train station."

"Della?" she asked, brightening. "She's coming here tonight?"

"That's right. You guys want to come along? One way or the other, I need to borrow the tram, Dad."

He gave me a funny look. He didn't seem to buy my sudden story. But that was okay, because Momma looked entranced. She still held out dreams that Della and I would form a normal relationship and raise a family in the traditional way.

"Well, son—" my dad began, but my mom interrupted.

"I want to go," she said. "I never go anywhere anymore. Can she stay for Christmas, James?"

"We can ask her."

"What about Etta?" she asked. "She's playing outside again."

I shrugged. "She's fine. She's got all the snakes, bones and mud she could ask for."

My mother made a face, but she didn't argue. Etta didn't like long tram rides. She'd rather run around outside.

"I'll have to go too," my dad said. "To help with her chair."

"Uh…" I said, trying to think of a way to get him to change his mind. I couldn't, so I gave up. "Okay. Let's go."

After we packed up her float-chair, a shawl, and a snack—Momma never let anyone go on a trip without a snack—I caught my dad's arm in the garage.

"Dad? Have you got those silver disks still, the ones we made back at the Mustering Hall?"

He frowned at me and nodded.

"I need those, please."

He stared at me, and again he slowly nodded. He went back into the house and presented them to me.

I took them and left them in my shack in a safe place. When I returned, my dad was more full of suspicion than ever, and Momma was going crazy with impatience.

"Come on, let's go!" she said. "The last train arrives at Albany in an hour. She must be on that one, right James?"

"You got it, Momma," I said automatically.

"The poor girl will be waiting for a long time. No wonder she ditched you."

"Aw now, that's a rude thing to say," I said, slipping behind the wheel and putting the tram into gear.

We rumbled out of the garage and into the night.

But we never made it to the sky-train station.

* * *

I was revived first, at about six a.m. the next morning. I snorted awake, bleary-eyed and itchy.

"What happened?" I asked the bio team at Central.

"We were hoping you might be able to tell us, Centurion," a bio said.

"I don't remember... I was driving my family down in Georgia... Hey, what happened to my folks?"

The bio people looked at one another. "I'm sorry, sir," said the woman in charge. "It's tragic, but there was a crash. There were no survivors."

"No survivors..." I said, doing my best to sound sad. Internally, I was relieved. My dad had been in the backseat, and I'd been worried he might survive in a coma or something.

"Centurion?" the bio asked. "Are you all right?"

"Yeah," I said. "I'm all right."

Sliding off the table, I dressed and walked out into the night.

A few people contacted me, giving me their condolences. The word was spreading. Della had already gone over to the house to check on Etta, and she reported back that the girl was fine.

But there was only one person I was interested in talking to: Anne Grant.

It took seven calls to get Anne to answer. When she did, she looked angry and wary.

"I can tell you're in town and the answer is 'no', James. Stop calling me."

"Hold on, hold on! Have you heard the news?"

"What news?"

I filled her in about the tram crash, and she was horrified. Then I told her I had disk copies of them—both of them.

She peered at me through slitted eyes.

"James…" she said. "This is either one of the worst ideas you've ever had, or an extreme attempt to get me back into bed with you on a sympathy plea. Either way, you're going to fail."

"No, no, no," I told her, "you've got it all wrong. Check the news, do a search. They really are dead. I died too."

She played with her tapper for a few minutes and gasped. "A forest fire? You ran into trees at high speed."

"Uh… I don't remember, exactly."

"Why would you—?"

"Listen, Anne," I told her, "I've got the disks down in Georgia. Will you at least come with me and check out my options?"

Eventually, a combination of intrigue and sympathy for my loss got her to see reason. She accompanied me back down to Georgia on a commercial flight.

As a centurion, I'd been given the keys to the local Chapter House for the legion. It was there, in the back of the equipment lockers, that I found what I was looking for. I showed it to Anne, and she yawned.

"What are we going to do with that?"

"It's a flesh-printer," I said.

"Yeah, so? You're not injured anymore."

The unit was one of the big, old-fashioned kind. Before we'd had revival machines, they'd been in vogue. In fact, they were capable of printing out a new limb or organ.

Producing the coin-like silver disk-copies of my parents, I jingled them in front of Anne.

"Could you do it?" I asked her. "You're the best bio I know—could you print out a new set of parents for me and imprint the mental engrams stored on this disk?"

She stopped mid-yawn, and she stared at me in horror. "That would be unethical, illegal, and maybe impossible!"

"Yeah," I agreed, "but will you do it?"

She picked up the disks in my hand, fascinated. "How'd you have these made?"

"It was a show-and-tell. My parents wanted to see where my career in the legion had all started."

Anne snorted. "What bullshit… but you've got me thinking. Could it be done?"

"Only one way to find out!"

The next several hours were long indeed. We'd arrived on Sunday after dinnertime, and we had to clear out of this place by morning whether we succeeded or not.

"James," she said, clasping my wrist. "This might get ugly. There might be mistakes. I—I don't know if you want to stay here."

Setting my jaw, I shook my head. "I'm in. I've helped bio people with difficult births on ten worlds, at least."

Shaking her head, she said, "don't tell me later that I didn't warn you."

Anne went to work after that, and I soon realized the girl was a certified genius. Rather than trying to print out limbs and organs and assemble them all into one, she just loaded the full file and began printing.

At first, the sprayed-on bone cells shaped up nicely. It wasn't until we got to the meaty parts, the sinews and muscle fiber, that things got messy.

"I don't think I can do it," she confessed at last. "The unit isn't big enough to put a whole body into—the chamber is only about a meter long."

395

"Yeah..." I said, seeing that all the pieces laid out weren't going together right. "Let's reroll, and this time—"

She pulled off a blue, snappy glove and put her hand on my cheek. It felt hot, and sweaty.

"James, I can't do it. You're going to have to face facts. You—you killed them and they're gone."

I stared at her for a minute, but I shook my head. Lifting up the two shining silver disks, I showed them to her.

"Their bodies are right here. Every cell. Their minds are stored in the data core at Central. We can download the files and install them through their tappers. Don't give up, all we have to do is get a bigger printing chamber."

"I don't know how to do that!" she said, throwing up her hands. "I'm a bio, not a tech!"

That gave me an idea. I contacted another girl from my past—Natasha.

She was too far off to help us in person, and she looked annoyed as soon as she learned Anne was with me. But the description of the tram accident and what we were trying to do changed her mind.

Natasha had always loved a technical challenge.

Using my tapper to show her a live vid feed, I panned it over the steaming mess we'd created.

"Your trouble is that chamber," she said. "It's only big enough for about half an adult."

"Right," I said, "what can we do?"

"Show me what else you've got in the vicinity."

I walked around the storage room, showing her cartons of old junk. She had me stop when I passed a suit of battle armor. It was an antique, earth-made using heavy steel and rubber.

"That's it," she said. "Your parents aren't fat, are they?"

"A little," I admitted. "But they should fit inside there if we squished them some."

"Send me the files. I'll edit down their BMIs."

I used my tapper to read the disks and transmit the massive data file. It was a good thing we'd recently upgraded our Wi-Fi at the Legion Chapter House.

"Okay…" Natasha said some time later. "I've got a new version. Get out an old tech's box and we'll store it there. I don't want to overwrite your original files."

"Got it."

We worked for another hour refitting the battlesuit. At last, the girls declared we were ready for another attempt.

"James," Anne said gently. "We're low on bone meal."

"Uh…" I said, looking at the time. "We've only got four hours left. Besides, I can't buy any more locally—"

She put up her hand to stop me. "I know all that. We're going to have to recycle what we already printed."

My eyes drifted to the skeletons we'd managed to assemble on our first try. They didn't look like my parents, although they were the right size.

That made me gulp hard, for some reason. I could recycle this. Hell, I'd recycled any number of soldiers on the field. But I realized that if we were short on materials on the next step, we might have to do this *again*. That meant I might have to take a full limb and run it through the system.

A little sickened, I took the stick-like bones and ground them up, forcing them into the input chute of the printer.

Natasha had helped us recalibrate the spray heads and position them correctly over the battlesuit. This old type of unit allowed you to lift away the front portion of the breastplate like two halves of a clamshell. That really helped us get it straightened out.

Sometime after three am, we got down to some serious printing. The machine hummed and stuttered. It produced a strange, hot, meaty smell that I didn't like, but I'd smelled it before.

"We've got a full skeleton again," Anne said breathing with excitement. "I'm going to engage the program for vascularity and musculature next. The organs go in last. Fill the suit with fluids, James."

It was soon a horrible stew. If you've ever looked inside the human body—I mean really, deep inside, it's not pretty.

Hours later, we were left slumped from exertion and stress. We had less than two hours left.

"It's my dad, isn't it?" I asked her.

"Yeah. Bigger skeleton."

The skin went on next, and the whole process sped up.

"What about their minds?" I asked Anne.

"Every tapper is organic," she said, "and it contains a base-line mental program. Enough for the body to breathe, pump blood, etc. We can load the full file afterward."

"Um… okay."

We kept working, and my dad became a person in that suit. He was thinner, and cleaner-looking than he had been. There was no body hair, other than a shock of gray on his scalp. We were always reborn without body hair—that had to grow in naturally over time.

Anne loaded him with a basic mind, and he began functioning. We watched in amazement. I'd participated in this process countless times, but more than ever before, I felt like we'd created a living person from scratch.

When he was shivering and wet, I took him out of the soupy suit and flushed it out. I almost dropped him on the concrete, and Anne yelled at me.

"Sorry," I said, "he's slippery, and I'm tired."

"This was your damned idea, James!"

"I know. I'm sorry."

I pressed him into a pile of spare, stale-smelling blankets from the emergency supplies and left him as comfortably positioned as I could.

Anne inserted the silver disk and started the mental upload, but I put my hand on her shoulder.

"What are we going to tell him when he wakes up?" I asked. "The last thing he's going to remember is that day we visited the Mustering Hall."

Anne made a piffing sound. "That's your problem. I'm just here to make them live again."

Resignedly, I helped her get the second body going in the printer. It was my mom this time, and the printing went faster due to her smaller size.

After another ten minutes or so, my dad opened his eyes and groaned. I knelt beside him, and I don't mind telling you, I teared up a little.

"Pop?" I called to him. "You okay?"

"James?" he asked. "What happened?"

"We had a little accident with the tram. We're taking care of it. You'll be fine."

"I don't understand. What—where are we?"

"Down in Waycross, Pop. Not far from home."

"I don't remember any of this," he said, looking lost. "We were at your Mustering Hall. It seems so much colder now—is it still summertime?"

He was befuddled, but I got him to lie quietly and rest. That was for the best. I didn't want to hit him with the truth yet. I wanted that to seep in slowly.

Dying your first time around was always hard. It was even worse when you remembered how you'd died. At least, in this case, that memory had been lost forever.

Anne worked with tireless professionalism. She did a great job, and I realized I now owed her a debt I could never fully repay.

My mom began to take form inside the old battlesuit, and to me that was ironic. For one thing, she'd birthed me once, and now it was my turn. In addition to that, I had to wonder how many times this suit had been used to kill in the distant past. I didn't know the answer to that, but I was fairly certain this was the first time it'd ever been used as a vessel to *create* life.

-66-

After I revived my parents into slightly younger, definitely healthier new bodies, you might think they'd have been grateful—but you would have thought wrong.

"What the hell were you thinking, James?" Mom demanded.

"Momma, I did what I had to. You'll live now. No more nanites, no more scarring—all that was edited out by the system automatically."

"That's great. I died in a fiery crash I can't even remember, and now I'm living in the wrong time. Everything's wrong. What happened at thanksgiving? Did Aunt Clara come over?"

"She sure did, and she loved the cooking."

She slapped me, hard.

"Stop lying all the time," she said. "Clara never appreciates anything."

My shoulders slumped, and I helped her out of the car. She could walk again, but not even that seemed to cheer her up.

"It's all wrong. It's not supposed to be so cold and dark out. I missed an entire fall season. I'll never get that back."

"Momma, come on," I pleaded. "You're alive and well again. You didn't lose anything, you'll have a healthier, longer lifespan now."

"What good is that?" she groused.

But then Etta came running out to greet us. Everyone got a desperate hug.

"I'm glad you're back," the little girl said. "I thought I would have to fend for myself."

"No," I told her, "I'd never leave you, doll. Not forever."

We went inside and were surprised to find the place was trashed. Etta had taken over the living room and the kitchen table with her bony exhibits.

Momma gritted her teeth and gave me an up-down motion of the eyebrows. I knew that meant she wanted me to act as the heavy and kick out the girl's nasty toys.

After some gentle effort, I managed to do so. It was clear to me that the girl had thought she owned the place, and she'd immediately taken over the main house.

Trying not to get angry, I helped her remove all the offending skulls and other things she'd gathered and moved them into the backyard where they belonged.

After a few days of settling into their new bodies, my parents began to cheer up. They were upset all over again by the following Monday, however.

"Our claim has been denied!" my father shouted. "I can't believe this—I paid for over thirty years, I have a legit death certificate—everything!"

"That's insurance for you," Mom said. "They always weasel."

"Are you talking about the tram, Dad?" I asked in concern. "Is the insurance going to replace it?"

"What? Well, sure. They will, despite the fact you were driving. But it's my term life I'm talking about. They reviewed my case, and they've denied the claim."

I blinked at him then laughed out loud. "You tried to make a claim against your life insurance?"

"Of course. I died, didn't I?"

"Yeah, Dad, but... you're alive again."

"Does that matter?" he said, smacking the policy with the back of his hand. "The contract says it pays in the case of unexpected death. If that's not what happened, I don't know what is. I'm looking into this. I'm getting a lawyer."

Shaking my head, I walked away. I could have told him the company would never pay. They'd known about legionnaires and our special ways to cheat death for a long time now. There were sure to be clauses to prevent shenanigans like what he was describing.

That night, I slept hard in my shack—but a tiny sound woke me up.

I sprang to my feet, fumbling out a combat knife. The lights went up, and the snarl on my face died.

"Etta? What are you doing lurking around here at this time of night? Get back in the house and go to bed."

She looked outside the cracked open door, then looked back at me. "Are you sure that's what you want?"

Frowning and scratching, I went to the fridge and dug out a beer.

"Yeah, I'm sure. What are you looking at? Another fox in the yard?"

"Possibly… but she could be much more dangerous than that."

I whirled around, spilling my beverage. Moving to the door in three strides, I pulled it open and flung it wide.

There, lying face down on the porch was a young woman.

"What'd you do, girl?" I demanded, giving Etta a shake.

She glared at me, trying to remove my grip, but I didn't let her squirm away. She wasn't good with authority figures, and she had a bad temper in her.

I checked the woman on the porch and saw with relief she was still alive.

"She was trying to sneak up to your house," Etta said. "I acted to save the family."

Snorting, I lifted the woman's hair to one side. It was about then that I recognized her.

"Sarah?"

"You know this person?" Etta asked.

"She's from my unit. What'd you do to her?"

"A strike from behind works wonders. I didn't hit her hard—her brains shouldn't leak out."

I glanced at Etta. "Sometimes, girl, you're too ornery for your own good. This lady was just shy, and she probably came to see me privately."

"Why?"

"Um… well, sometimes ladies and gentlemen—"

"Sex?" Etta asked. "You think she wanted sex? That's disgusting. I'm glad I hit her."

"Etta, you're going to stay here and apologize. She's coming around."

"I won't," she said, and then ran off into the darkness.

My teeth were clenched with anger. I'd brought home a monster, a barbarian that bashed people's brains out in the middle of the night.

Sarah groaned awake and sat up.

"What happened?" she asked. "Did you hit me, Centurion?"

"No. I have an overactive guardian living here with me. Come on, let me help you up."

She brushed away my hands and got up on her own. I appreciated that. After all, she was a Varus regular now. A knock on the head was no big deal to anyone from my legion.

"I heard you were in an accident," she said, massaging her neck. "That you were presumed dead, but you survived the crash."

Glancing down at my fresh body, which wasn't scarred, bruised or even abraded in any way, I felt embarrassed.

"I caught a revive, actually," I admitted.

"Well then…" she said stiffly. "I'm sorry to have disturbed you, Centurion. I'll be on my way."

"Hey," I said, calling her back.

She turned slowly, eyeing me over her shoulder. She had narrow shoulders, wide hips and a face like a pixie. It was a look I appreciated.

"Come on in and have a cold one," I suggested. "After all, you came all this way. We can talk about the campaign."

Sarah paused, despite the fact we both knew what her decision would be in the end. Still, she rubbed her head and pouted in the yard.

"I didn't hit you, girl," I said.

But she still didn't move.

"Ah well," I said. "Do what you want."

I went back inside, put a second beer on the table, and sat down on the couch. I'd left my door ajar.

Soon, a small attractive face poked its way inside. She reminded me of the foxes Etta kept locating somehow.

The night wore on, and Sarah kept me company. By morning, we'd both forgotten our troubles, our ranks, and the whorl of bright stars overhead that one day soon would call us back to fight among them.

Books by B. V. Larson:

UNDYING MERCENARIES
Steel World
Dust World
Tech World
Machine World
Death World
Home World
Rogue World

STAR FORCE SERIES
Swarm
Extinction
Rebellion
Conquest
Battle Station
Empire
Annihilation
Storm Assault
The Dead Sun
Outcast
Exile
Gauntlet

REBEL FLEET SERIES
Rebel Fleet
Orion Fleet

Visit BVLarson.com for more information.

Printed in Great Britain
by Amazon

64043699R00244